Samuel H. Kellogg

The Light of Asia, and the Light of the World

A comparison of the legend, the doctrine, and the ethics of the Buddha with the

story, the doctrine, and the ethics of Christ

Samuel H. Kellogg

The Light of Asia, and the Light of the World
A comparison of the legend, the doctrine, and the ethics of the Buddha with the story, the doctrine, and the ethics of Christ

ISBN/EAN: 9783744796781

Printed in Europe, USA, Canada, Australia, Japan

Cover: Foto ©Andreas Hilbeck / pixelio.de

More available books at **www.hansebooks.com**

THE LIGHT OF ASIA

AND

THE LIGHT OF THE WORLD

A COMPARISON OF

THE LEGEND, THE DOCTRINE, & THE ETHICS OF THE BUDDHA

WITH

THE STORY, THE DOCTRINE, & THE ETHICS OF CHRIST

BY

S. H. KELLOGG, D.D.

PROFESSOR IN THE WESTERN THEOLOGICAL SEMINARY, ALLEGHENY, PA., U.S.A.
ELEVEN YEARS MISSIONARY TO INDIA
CORRESPONDING MEMBER OF THE AMERICAN ORIENTAL SOCIETY
AUTHOR OF 'A GRAMMAR OF THE HINDI LANGUAGE, AND DIALECTS,' ETC.

' Woe unto them that put darkness for light, and light for darkness !'—*Isaiah.*
' If the light that is in you be darkness, how great is the darkness !'—*Jesus Christ.*

London
MACMILLAN AND CO.
1885

PREFACE.

THERE is reason to believe that a large class even of Christian people have a most exaggerated idea of the excellence of the great non-Christian religions, and the extent to which their teachings agree with those of the Gospel of Christ. This remark applies with special force at present to the case of Buddhism, in which, for various reasons, very many intelligent people, of every variety of religious opinion, have of late years come to feel a very special interest.

Such erroneous impressions in the case of many are doubtless due to a very pardonable ignorance or misapprehension of the real facts which bear upon the question. The data upon which one might base an intelligent judgment have not been as accessible to the general reading public as were to be desired. Even the valuable translations of the sacred books of the Buddhists, which have lately appeared from various sources, reach but a class of readers comparatively

small. The strangeness of the conceptions which they
express, the frequent obscurity to Western minds of
their mode of expression, and their often tedious repeti-
tions, combine to repel most readers from their careful
study.

And, again, even those who have surmounted these
difficulties, and have gained a certain familiarity with
the literature of the subject, are, in most cases, at a
great disadvantage in having no personal acquaintance
with the practical working of the non-Christian religions. Unfortunately, often in this case " distance
lends enchantment to the view," and impressions are
formed with regard to the merits of Buddhism and
other heathen religions, which a more intimate acquaintance with their actual working in human life
would in the case of most be sure to dispel. However
admirable many things in the Buddhist and other
ethnic religions may seem to some, the writer himself
has seen too much of the practical working of these
heathen systems to be deeply in love with them.

Again, erroneous impressions as to the relations
between Buddhism and Christianity are the more extended and deepened that, very naturally, many unconsciously import into the most pregnant and characteristic Buddhist words and phrases, conceptions purely
and exclusively Christian. How serious and influential

is this source of error will be abundantly manifest in the course of the following chapters. For the present it will suffice to call attention to the fact that, for example, such words and phrases as "lust," "sin," "salvation," "law," "new birth," etc. etc., as used by the Buddhist, denote conceptions totally different from the Christian sense of the same terms. From this illustration alone it will be easy to see that those who are not aware of the nature and extent of this Buddhist divergence from the Christian meaning of such terms are sure to derive, even from what they may imagine to be a careful study of Buddhism, an impression concerning the extent of agreement between the two religions which is not in the least justified by the actual facts of the case.

And there is reason to believe that sometimes another influence works in the same direction. Too many study this subject with certain preconceived and unsupported notions as to what the relations of the various religions of mankind to God, to man, and to each other *ought* to be, and, despite their intention to be fair and candid, their judgment, it is to be feared, is often warped in consequence. There can be no doubt that sometimes men who mean to be honest are thus unconsciously led to exaggerate and lay undue stress upon those points in Buddhism in which they

think that they discover agreement, while they fail to
direct equal attention to other points of greater consequence, wherein appears the most unqualified and
direct antagonism to the Gospel.

Howsoever, in any case, erroneous opinions on this
subject may be formed, it is plain that error in such a
matter cannot but be a very serious thing in its effect
on our belief and practice. It will inevitably affect
our views of the nature and extent of Divine revelation and inspiration, and the conditions of human
salvation; it will no less certainly determine our judgment as to the practical duty of Christians toward the
adherents of the Buddhist and other religions. That
such mistaken notions as to the relations between
Christianity and Buddhism widely prevail, is often
forced upon our attention, and that errors on this subject are at present doing no little mischief in unsettling
faith and misdirecting practice is scarcely less evident.

Observation of these facts, and frequent conversations with men in different parts of the world who
have had special opportunity to form a judgment in
the matter, have led the writer to feel that there might
be room for a book which should, in a more thorough
and systematic way than any which has been presented
to our notice, deal with the various questions which
have been raised with regard to the relations between

Buddhism and Christianity. He would, however, by this remark, on no account seem to ignore or depreciate the many valuable helps toward a correct understanding of the subject which have already been prepared by highly competent men on both sides of the Atlantic. To many of these he feels himself to be under deep obligation. Such books, however, have not commonly professed to deal with the subject in more than a partial way. Some have dealt with the legend, some with the doctrine or the ethics, but none that have come under our notice, in any formal and extended way, with all of these. Moreover, owing to the very small number of original Buddhist authorities which until recently has been accessible, the writers of such works have not been able to make such extensive reference to the Buddhist scriptures as, in such a comparison as this, is so important. We need to hear the apostles of Buddhism state their own case. Now, however, thanks to the invaluable labours of savants like Professors Max Müller, Oldenberg, Fausböll, Rhys Davids, and many others, the student of Buddhism is no longer hindered by such a scarcity of material as has embarrassed previous writers on the subject. From the original works which these eminent scholars have made accessible to the general public, as the following pages will show, the writer has drawn extensively.

Throughout the following pages he has endeavoured, as regards every point involved in the discussion, to let the Buddhist authorities speak for themselves, and state their belief in their own words. He believes that he will be found to have made no statement of any importance regarding Buddhist belief for which he has not given distinct Buddhist authority. As for the English form of such citations, he has uniformly followed the translations of well-known eminent Oriental scholars, such as Professors Max Müller, Oldenberg, Fausböll, Messrs. Rhys Davids, Hardy, Köppen, and others, whose names, to all who are acquainted with the literature of the subject, will be an abundant guarantee of the essential trustworthiness of their translations. Where diverse interpretations of the Buddhist teaching have obtained, the writer has endeavoured candidly to state the fact, with the reasons given *pro* and *con*, and indicate the bearing of each interpretation on the argument.

This book, it is frankly confessed, is not written from the standpoint of religious indifference. Those who, with some eminent scholars who have spoken on this subject, believe that only from such a position is it possible to treat the claims of another religion with fairness, will, we fear, find little satisfaction in these pages. The author made up his mind long ago, on what has seemed to him abundant evidence, that the records of the New Testament are deserving of credit, and that hence, by necessary consequence, the Gospel of Jesus Christ, the crucified and the risen Lord, is, in a sole and exclusive sense, the saving truth of God. He confesses himself unable to see that in order to be able to criticise error with impartiality, it is necessary that a man shall not have received the correspondent truth. He does not believe that even the most rigid claims of science require, for example, that a man shall ignore the ascertained facts concerning the system of the heavens, before he can be a competent and impartial judge of the truth or falsity of any astronomical theory, new or old. That *this* is so, indeed, no one believes. And if such a position of absolute intellectual neutrality is not a qualification essential to the critic in the field of physical science, he cannot see why it should be so in the field of research in religion. In point of fact, that absolute equipoise of mind on the subject of religion which some writers seem to make the *sine qua non* of candid and fair discussion of religious differences, is a practical impossibility. Suppose, for instance, that a man reject all religions alike as revelations from God, he yet must and does hold some view on the subject of religion. The belief of the positivist, the agnostic, or the atheist, just as truly as the most pronounced Christian faith, is a *religious* belief. And if Christian faith disqualify a man, as some will have it, for an unbiassed review of other religions, it is impossible to see why the belief of the positivist, the agnostic, or the atheist, should not be held equally to disqualify them also for a fair and unprejudiced judgment of the claims of any religion whatever.

It is proper to say that of the following chapters the first, in a form but slightly different from the present, has appeared in print before, in the *Catholic Presbyterian*, London and New York, July 1883. An article on the doctrines of the Buddha and the Christ which appeared in the *Presbyterian Review*, New York, July, 1883, has served as the basis for chapter v. The most of it has, however, been carefully rewritten, and extensive additions made, by which it is hoped that its value may have been materially enhanced.

For himself, the author has found the months of study which the preparation of this work has involved of much practical profit. By these studies his faith has been more than ever confirmed in the religion of Christ as the one and only divinely revealed system for the redemption of lost men. The impressions gained in many years of intercourse with the people of India, and study of their religious works, of the immeasurable disparity between the best that heathenism can offer, and the teachings of the Gospel of Christ, have been, by these literary labours in a related field, still further deepened and strengthened. He is more than ever convinced that by comparison with other religions, Christianity not only cannot lose to our mind its high pre-eminence, but, on the contrary, is sure—the more thoroughly that such comparisons are carried out—to appear in that pre-eminence the more solitary and sublime. It is only careless, hasty, and superficial study, and consequent gross misapprehension of facts, that can ever cause these comparisons to issue in unsettling the faith of Christians. For comparison with Christianity for apologetic purposes no religion can serve us a better purpose than Buddhism. For with all its admitted excellencies as compared with other ethnic religions, it is yet the fact that the contrast between Christianity and all other religions reaches in Buddhism its most extreme expression. The facts which are brought together in this book must, we feel, certainly convince every candid mind that it was with abundant reason that that eminent Buddhist scholar, Mr. Rhys Davids, assured those who listened to the Hibbert Lectures in 1881 that " the views of life set forth in the *Pàli Pitakas*"—the sacred scriptures of the Buddhists—are "fundamentally

opposed to those set forth in the New Testament."
With these prefatory words this book is now commended to the reader with the hope that it may be as
helpful and quickening to his faith in Christ and His
Gospel as the preparation of the book has been to the
author.

S. H. K.

WESTERN THEOLOGICAL SEMINARY,
ALLEGHENY, PA., U.S.A., 19th June 1885.

NOTES.

THE present work is based upon a study of the following Buddhist authorities :—

From the *First* or *Vinaya Pitaka*—the *Pâtimokkha*, translated by Professor Oldenberg and T. W. Rhys Davids, in *Sacred Books of the East*,[1] vol. xiii. ; the *Mahâvagga*, translated by the same, in *Sacred Books of the East*, vols. xiii., xvii. ; the *Cullavagga*, translated by the same, in *Sacred Books of the East*, vol. xvii.

From the *Second* or *Sutta Pitaka*—the *Dhammapada*, translated by Professor F. Max Müller, in *Sacred Books of the East*, vol. x. part 1 ; the *Sutta Nipâta*, translated by Professor V. Fausböll, in *Sacred Books of the East*, vol. x. part 2 ; the *Mahâparinibbâna Sutta*, translated by T. W. Rhys Davids, in *Sacred Books of the East*, vol. xi. ; the *Dhammacakkappavattanâ Sutta*, translated by T. W. Rhys Davids, in *Sacred Books of the East*, vol. xi. ; the *Tevijja Suttanta*, translated by T. W. Rhys Davids, in *Sacred Books of the East*, vol. xi. ; the *Âkankheyya Sutta*, translated by T. W. Rhys Davids, in *Sacred Books of the East*, vol. xi. ; the *Cetokhila Sutta*, translated by T. W. Rhys Davids, in *Sacred Books of the East*, vol. xi. ; the *Mahâsudassana Sutta*, translated by T. W. Rhys Davids, in *Sacred Books of the East*, vol. xi. ; the *Subbâsava Sutta*, translated by T. W. Rhys Davids, in *Sacred Books of the East*, vol. xi.

[1] Abbreviated in footnotes, *S.B.E.*

The following from the Northern Buddhist Canon:—
The *Saddharmapuṇḍarîka*, the sixth of the nine *Dhammas*,
translated by Professor Kern, in *Sacred Books of the East*,
vol. xxi.; the *Lalita Vistâra*, Text, and part of English
translation, published in the *Bibliotheca Indica*.

The following non-canonical authorities :—
Jâtakatthavaṇṇanâ, Text and Commentary, translated by
T. W. Rhys Davids, in *Buddhist Birth Stories*, Boston, 1880 ;
the *Fo-pen-hing*, a Chinese version of the *Abhinishkramana
Sûtra*, translated by Professor S. Beal, under the title of *The
Romantic Legend of Sâkya Buddha ; Buddhaghosha's Parables*,
translated from the Burmese by Captain T. Rogers, R.E.,
with Introduction by Professor Max Müller, London, 1870 ;
Mâlâlankâra Vatthu, and *The Seven Ways to Neibban*, translations from the Burmese by Bishop Bigandet, Vicar Apostolic
of Pegu and Burmah, published under the title, *The Legend
of Gaudama*, 3d ed., London, 1880.

Translations from the following works, comprised in
Hardy's *Manual of Buddhism*, namely,—*Pansiya panas jâtaku
pota ; Visuddhi mârggasanné ; Milinda prasnâ ; Pûjâwaliya ;
Saddharmâlankâré ; Saddharmaratnakâré ; Amûwatura ;
Th'upâwanse ; Râjawaliya ; Kayuwiratigâthâ sanné ; Kam-
mavâchan ; Sannés* belonging to various Suttas.

Pothiya Sambodhiyan, translated from the Siamese by
Henry Alabaster, in *The Wheel of the Law ;* the *Mahâvaṇsa*,
in Roman characters, with translation subjoined, and an
introductory Essay on Pâli Buddhistical Literature, by
Hon. George Turnour, Esq., Ceylon Civil Service.   Ceylon,
Cotta Church Mission Press, 1837.

Besides the valuable introductions to the above-named
texts, the following writers, among others, have also been
consulted upon topics connected with the discussions of
this book :—

Köppen, *Die Religion des Buddha und ihre Entstehung*, i. ii. Bd., Berlin, 1857, 1859 ; Wassillieff, *Der Buddhismus ;* Oldenberg, *Buddha, sein Leben, seine Lehre, seine Gemeinde,* Berlin, 1881 ; Seydel, *Das Evangelium von Jesu in seinen Verhältnissen zu Buddha-Sage und Buddha- Lehre,* u.s.w., Leipzig, 1882 ; Grätz, *Geschichte der Juden;* Lucius, *Der Essenismus in seinem Verhältniss zum Judenthum,* Strassburg, 1881 ; Kurtz, *Kirchengeschichte,* i. Bd., Mitau, 1874 ; Lorinser, *Die Bhâgavad Gîta,* übersetzt, u.s.w., Breslau, 1869 ; *Yahrbücher fur Protestantische Theologie,* Jahrgang, 1884, Leipzig, 1884 ; Burnouf, *Histoire du Buddhisme Indien,* Paris, 1844 ; St. Hilaire, *Le Bouddha, et sa Religion,* 3d ed., Paris, 1866 ; Childers, *A Dictionary of the Pâli Language,* London, 1875 ; Müller, *Lectures on the Science of Religion ; Chips from a German Workshop ;* Monier Williams, *Indian Wisdom,* London, 1876 ; Edkins, *The Religions of China,* 2d ed., Boston, 1878; *Chinese Buddhism,* London, 1880 ; Barth, *The Religions of India,* Authorised Translation, London, 1882 ; De Bunsen, *The Angel Messiah of Buddhists, Essenes, and Christians,* London, 1880 ; Rhys Davids, *Buddhism, a Sketch of the Life and Teachings of Gautama, the Buddha,* London ; *Lectures on the Origin and Growth of Religion, as illustrated by some points in the History of Indian Buddhism* (Hibbert Lectures, 1881), New York, 1882 ; Kuenen, *National Religions and Universal Religions* (Hibbert Lectures, 1882), New York, 1882 ; Arnold, *The Light of Asia ;* Alabaster, *The Wheel of the Law, Buddhism illustrated from Siamese Sources,* London, 1871 ; Wordsworth, *The One Religion* (Bampton Lectures, 1881), New York, 1882 ; Hardwick, *Christ and other Masters,* 4th ed., London, 1875; Clarke, *Ten Great Religions,* Boston, 1877 ; Eitel, *Three Lectures on Buddhism, its Theoretical, Historical, and Popular Aspects,* 2d ed., Hong Kong, 1873 ; Renan, *The Life of*

Jesus, London, 1864 ; Lightfoot, *St. Paul's Epistles to the Colossians and to Philemon*, a revised Text, with Introductions, Notes, and Dissertations, London, 1879 ; Meyer, *Critical and Exegetical Hand-book to the Gospel of John*, Am. ed., New York, 1884 ; Smith, *Mediæval Missions*, Edinburgh, 1880 ; Hardy, *Legends and Theories of the Buddhists*, London, 1866 ; *Manual of Buddhism*, 2d ed., London, 1880; *Folk Songs of Southern India*, London, 1872 ; *Proceedings of the General Conference of the Protestant Missionaries in Japan, held at Osaka, Japan, April* 1883, Yokohama, 1883 ; Dods, *Mohammed, Buddha, and Christ*, London, 1878 ; Martensen, *Christian Ethics*, Edinburgh, 1882 ; Abbott, *The Authorship of the Fourth Gospel*, Boston, 1880.

TRANSLITERATION OF PÀLI WORDS.

The system of transliteration which is followed in this work, is the same with that which is adopted in the *Sacred Books of the East*, with the exception that the usage of Professor Oldenberg and others has been preferred in the following cases :—The sound *ch*, as in " church," is represented by *c* instead of *k* ; *j*, as in " jay," is represented by *j* instead of *g*.

CONTENTS.

CHAPTER V.

CHAPTER VI.

CHAPTER VII.

CHAPTER I.

THE interest that has been taken of late in Buddhism by a large number of intelligent people in various Christian countries is one of the most peculiar and suggestive religious phenomena of our day. In the United States this interest had prevailed for a considerable time among a somewhat restricted number of persons who have known or thought that they knew something of Buddhism; but since 1879, through the publication of Mr. Edwin Arnold's *Light of Asia*, the popularity of the subject has in a very marked degree increased. Many who would have been repelled by any formal, drily philosophical treatise upon Buddhism, have been attracted to it by the undoubted charm of Mr. Arnold's verse. The issue of cheap editions of the poem, selling for only a few cents, has helped in the same direction, as this has brought the poem, and with it the subject, to the attention of a large number of persons not yet sufficiently interested in Buddhism to have cared to pay much more. And

B

so it has come to pass that everywhere among reading and intelligent people we find a very considerable
number who think that they now know something
about the Buddha and his religion, and have found
awakened in their minds—often quite unexpectedly to
themselves—a very surprising interest in this "venerable religion" which Mr. Arnold has presented to the
English-reading public in such an attractive guise.

Among these we find here and there some Christian
people, who seem to be somewhat disquieted by what
they have learned—or think that they have learned—
concerning Buddhism. They have met with so much
in the story of the Buddha and his teachings which
they had supposed to be peculiar to Christianity, that
a feeling of anxiety has arisen lest the evidence for
the supernatural origin and authority of the Christian
religion be thereby in some degree weakened.

On the unbelieving side, with many, a very different
feeling seems to prevail. Little they care that the
supreme authority of the Christian religion shall be
maintained. But they do feel a keenly sympathetic
interest in the religion of the Buddha, and in all that
relates to it,—much more in fact than they appear to
feel in the doctrine and story of Christ; and they are
ready to echo with unconcealed satisfaction the laudations which Mr. Arnold and others of his way of thinking have lavished on the religion which, in their judgment, was and is the Light of Asia.

As an outgrowth of this way of thinking, we have

seen within the last few years the rise and growth of
the so-called Theosophic Society, of which Colonel
Olcott and Madame Blavatsky have figured as the
chief apostles.   These have gone out to India to
realise in a practical way their fellowship with the
Buddhists of the East; and by the aid of the press
and the mysterious "adept," the "Brother," in Thibet,
to do what they can to conserve the venerable faith
which Mr. Arnold has glorified in his poem, and put
the people on their guard against the machinations of
designing Christian missionaries who would, if they
could, ruthlessly uproot the ancestral faiths of the East.
Not very numerous are the members of the Theosophic
Society; but it is a curious phenomenon, indeed, that
this century which began with sending missionaries
to convert the Buddhists should ere its close see a
generation arise in the midst of Christendom, which,
if one may judge by their own words, is itself almost
or quite converted to the faith of the Buddha.

To what causes may we attribute this special interest
in this most godless of all the heathen religions?

First among these causes may be named the extent
to which Buddhism, in some form or other, for more
than two thousand years, has been accepted by men as
the solution of the enigma of life.   It had indeed long
been known in a general way that the Siamese, Chinese,
Thibetans, and many other Asiatic peoples, held the
Buddhist faith, so that its adherents were very numerous.
But latterly, through the great increase of travel and

consequent personal acquaintance with the East and
with Eastern peoples, and the ever-increasing literature
devoted to these topics, the general public has come
to realise as never before the immense number of those
who believe in the Buddhist religion. What the real
number may be is indeed a matter of warm dispute. It has very commonly been estimated at about
400,000,000. Mr. Rhys Davids even makes the
number 500,000,000.[1] On the other hand, a veteran
missionary and Chinese scholar, the Rev. A. S. Happer,
D.D., of Canton, has lately published a brochure in
which he denies that the great mass of the Chinese
can rightly be reckoned the followers of Buddha. The
most should instead, he thinks, be counted as Con-
fucianists. If his argument be granted, then the
numbers of the Buddhists are brought down to the
comparatively moderate figure of about 73,000,000.
However this may be, we need not here attempt to
decide the question. The public generally has in any
case been taught, whether right or wrong, that a much
larger figure represented the real number of those
who followed the teachings of the Buddha. On this
estimate almost or quite one-third of the human
family have been regarded as professing to accept
Buddhism as the true religion and philosophy of
existence—a number which is considerably greater
than can be claimed for the followers of any other
creed.

[1] T. W. Rhys Davids, *Buddhism*, p. 6.

Now it cannot be doubted that with a considerable number of persons who have no faith in Christianity, and yet do not feel quite at ease without any religion at all, this assumed fact of the great numerical strength of Buddhism has had no little influence in inclining them to a sympathetic attention to its claims. That such a religion should have attracted so many followers, and so long maintained itself over a large part of the Eastern world, is indeed a remarkable fact, and well deserves attention, whatever be the explanation. But an increasing number in this democratic age are disposed to something like a deification of majorities. Having lost faith in God, or at least in His revelation, they have now no god left but man himself. And inasmuch as men differ very much among themselves, it is concluded that the likeliest way to arrive at the truth on religion, as on every other subject, must be to take a vote which shall express the preponderance of opinion.

Thus, assuming the essential goodness of human nature, it is argued, in politics, for example, that the voice of the majority expressed at the polls may be fairly presumed to be right. *Vox populi, vox dei.* Why should not the same principle apply also in the sphere of religion ? Why, it is reasoned, unconsciously perhaps, by many, is it not probable that the religion which, after centuries of trial, commands the largest suffrage of any, should be the religion which best deserves attention, as being presumably, in funda-

mental matters, the one which is nearest right? In
this way, if we mistake not, the great number of the
adherents of Buddhism is by not a few felt to be an
argument of no inconsiderable force in its favour—an
argument at least sufficient to throw a strong presumption in its favour as opposed to Christianity.

Again, as another element contributing to the sympathetic interest in Buddhism which is felt in the
anti-Christian camp, should probably be ·named the
wide acceptance of various theories of evolution. As
every one knows, there are many who think that if
once a theory of evolution be proved, then the hypothesis of a Creator of the world is thereby shown to
be a superfluity. As if the discovery of the *method* of

the formation of the universe, or of anything, relieved
us from the necessity of supposing an adequate efficient
cause! Such thinkers, of course, can have no patience
with a religion which teaches that "in the beginning
God created the heavens and the earth," and that the
soul of man was not developed from the soul of an
ape, but "breathed into him" from above by God.
Such a religion therefore as Christianity, with its
doctrine of a God and of supernatural interventions
from His hand, seems to thinkers of the class described
to stand in the way of all true scientific progress; and
so assuming, with a quiet assurance, an infallibility for
their science which they will not hear of in a religion,
they argue that no religion can stand which opposes
their theory of things.

Now, to men in such a state of mind, it is natural
that Buddhism should seem, as compared with Christianity, a far more reasonable religion. In the first
place, it has no God in it to interfere with the eternal
continuity of the evolution process. As Köppen has
well put it, "Buddhism recognises no eternal Being,
only an eternal Becoming."[1] Again, Buddhism, instead of having in itself no place for evolution, has
fully recognised a theory of evolution, and even raised
it to the dignity of a religion. For Buddhism teaches
that all that is, is simply the result of an evolution
from a previous state of things, as also that state of
things from one before, and so on, by an eternal process
of which a beginning is not even thinkable.

In full accord with the antitheistic type of evolution, Buddhism denies any impassable gulf between the /
irrational animals and man. A pig or a rat may
become a man, not indeed in the sense of the Western
evolutionist, but none the less truly. The Buddha
himself is declared at one time to have been a pig, and
at another a rat! The Buddhist, indeed, conceives of
the nature of the connection between the various forms
of life in a manner very different from the modern
European philosopher; but still the essential identity
and continuity between all different forms of life, on
which the modern theories of evolution so strongly insist, is fully recognised.[2] Herein certainly we may

[1] Köppen, *Die Religion des Buddhas*, p. 230.
[2] See some remarks on this relation of Buddhist speculations to

observe a bond of sympathy between modern anti-
Christian thought and the Buddhist philosophy which
goes far toward accounting for the interest which is
displayed in the sceptical camp.

Closely connected also with the fashionable enthusiasm over Buddhism is the disposition of the age
to glory in man, in his immeasurable possibilities of
development in power and knowledge. It is felt that
no one may venture to say what man may not do, or
may not become, all by his own unaided powers. The
Christian Scriptures do not indeed deny that there is
a glory in man, and possibilities of a greatness and
grandeur of attainment far transcending the wildest
dreams of science. But then they deny that man can
ever equal God. They also affirm an abasement as
well as a glory, weakness as well as strength, ignorance to be removed by none but God. These possibilities of glory which they set before man, are not for
man as he naturally is ; they are not to be attained
by the mere exercise and culture of his natural powers,
but only as through faith he shall come into a vital
union with the God-man, Christ Jesus. Let a man
presume to refuse that faith, in any way miss of that
union with the incarnate God, and he is doomed to an
ignominious and eternal disappointment of all his proud
aspirations. From this point of view the Scripture
cries, " Cease ye from man, whose breath is in his

modern thought, by Mr. Rhys Davids, Fausböll's *Buddhist Birth
Stories,* vol. i. p. lxxxv.

nostrils; for wherein is he to be accounted of?"[1] Nothing could well be conceived of more repellent to the boastful, self-confident spirit of our age than such a doctrine as this.

But men who, filled with the nineteenth century spirit of self-glorification, are for that reason repelled from Christianity, are for the same reason attracted to Buddhism. Even though they regard much that it teaches as mere superstition, yet none the less its spirit of proud self-assertion charms them. For where the Gospel tells of a God who became man to save him,—a doctrine in all ages foolishness to the wise of this world,—Buddhism tells of a man who became God, even the Buddha, who, under the Bo-tree, attained to all power and all knowledge! It tells us that this was not to save man, but to show men how they might save themselves. It ever insists that the Buddha, who attained all this, attained it by his own unaided strength and merit; and that any man who will take the same path may attain to the same heights. How completely the idea of man which Buddhism thus expresses falls in with the spirit of our modern materialists, agnostics, positivists! These all agree with Buddhism in that, in theory or fact, they make man his own god!

And when men of this age, impatient above all things of any assertion of the reality of the supernatural, who will hear nothing of a miracle, find that

[1] Isaiah ii. 22.

the most stupendous wonders are said to have been
performed by this Buddha, and to be within the power
of all who will follow him in the path of toilsome
labour and self-discipline, however incredulous they
may be of such stories, they feel themselves nevertheless to be in full and sympathetic accord with the
conception of humanity, the spirit of naturalism and
self-deification which these express; and, perhaps, in-
toxicated with the whirl of progress along the path of
physical science, half dream that very possibly some
such marvellous power over nature as is attributed to
the Buddha and the *aráhats* may yet be reached,—if
not by the transcendental methods of the Buddhist, as
the Theosophists boldly claim,—yet by the slower and
surer methods of modern science.

Not only the atheism of the Buddhist system, but
also the special form of its atheism, helps to gain for it
a kindly consideration from our modern sceptics. The
atheism which is in fashion in this generation is not
dogmatic and affirmative, but modest, negative, agnostic. It will not say, " There is no God "; but rather,
with Mr. Herbert Spencer, " The power which is manifested in the universe is utterly inscrutable." All
that is, is due to the Unknowable. This seems to be
the exact attitude of Buddhism also. There can be
produced, indeed, passages from Buddhist authorities
which positively deny and argue against the being of
a God ; but as to what the real cause of the eternal
succession of worlds may be, Buddhism holds a strictly

agnostic position. We read, "There is one thing which is not in the dominion of the intellect,—namely, to know whence come all the beings of the universe, and whither they go."[1] Not merely as atheistic, then, but more still as agnostic, does Buddhism find sympathising advocates or apologists among the agnostic atheists of Christendom.

But atheism and agnosticism both alike, if a man have in him the logic to see the inevitable conclusions from the premises of his system, lead straight on to pessimism. And so it has naturally come to pass, that under the influence of the agnostic speculation of the day, a considerable number have come sadly to doubt whether in life pain do not quite outweigh the pleasure ; and thus whether, in such a universe as this, not to be is not better than to be. As all know, this hopeless pessimism has of late years found earnest, often eloquent, expounders in such as Feuerbach, Schopenhauer, von Hartmann. These too have their many disciples, as the great increase in the ratio of suicide to population in the leading countries of Christendom sadly testifies.[2]

All who are affected with this sore malady of our time must, for this reason, again, listen to the words of the Buddha with a lively sympathy. For, as is known to all who have looked into the subject, the

[1] Quoted by A. Rémusat (*Mél. posth.* 121) from an ancient Buddhist *Sutta*. See Köppen, *Die Religion des Buddhas*, S. 231.
[2] See *Blackwood's Magazine*, June 1880, article "Suicide."

Buddha is represented as having made the absolute and necessary connection of sorrow with all individual existence to be the first of the " Four Noble Truths " which are the fundamental articles of the Buddhist creed. It is written, " This, O monks, is the holy truth concerning suffering. Death is suffering ; old age is suffering ; sickness is suffering ; to be united with what is not loved is suffering ; to be parted from what is loved is suffering ; not to attain one's desires is suffering." And to such words of the Buddha not a few, alas, in Christendom, having quite lost sight of Him who is the Light of the world, sigh their sad Amen, and not unnaturally think that the Buddha, who has so voiced their deepest feeling, must have been very wise !

To all this we must add that Buddhism doubtless attracts many by its remarkable system of ethics. This has often been said, and does not need to be argued. Every candid person will freely admit that in the Buddhist ethics, considered merely as an external system, there is much to admire. It is no less admirable that so great a religious importance should be ascribed to the performance of strictly moral duties. In these respects, among the various religions of the non-Christian world, it may be justly held to stand alone. It is not, therefore, strange that it should have won for itself a degree of admiration accorded to no other religion, excepting the Christian.

But, if we mistake not, it is not so much merely

the theoretic excellence of the Buddhist ethics of itself, which has so called forth the laudations of modern unbelievers in Christianity, but rather the fact that such a moral system — the only one which, in the opinion of many, can be fairly held worthy of comparison with that of the New Testament — should be found to belong to the one religion which is at the furthest possible remove from the religion of Christ, a religion which has in it no place for the being of a God or the existence of a Saviour !

To find such a system of morals in such a religion fills a certain class of minds with undisguised delight. For there are obvious indications of uneasy apprehensions arising of late among the advanced apostles of unbelief. More and more frequently, as the anti-theism of the day has spread among the masses, have been appearing in our time ugly symptoms, which seem to suggest that, very possibly, with the old faith in a God and a hereafter, even common morality may go down too. Hence the question has been raised and debated with warmth on both sides, whether, if the belief in God be denied or left out of life, there will any longer be left a sufficient basis for practical morals ? whether the purely *secular* type of society, which is the ideal and aim of so many, can possibly be a *moral* society ? Some unbelievers and rationalists have been frank enough to say—notwithstanding the publication of Mr. Spencer's *Data of Ethics*—that such an atheistic

rendition of the moral law as shall commend itself to
general acceptance as a satisfactory substitute for the
Christian, in the expected day when Christianity shall
have vanished from the earth, is yet to be elaborated;
and that just at present, when the modern scientific
view of the world is gaining adherents so fast, and the
old code of morals, based as it is on the idea of a God,
is thus losing its authority, the construction of a
system of morals upon a purely scientific basis, equally
effective for working purposes, is a desideratum of the
highest consequence. And while most profess a confidence that " evolution " will bring all out right in the
end, there is no little anxiety, heightened by every new
explosion of dynamite, as to what may happen first; and
some have suggested that we may not unreasonably
anticipate a moral interregnum in the world during an
approaching period in which, God having been dethroned
from His place in the minds of men, no sanction has
been discovered adequate to take the place of His
authority.[1]

To such anxious souls the ethics of Buddhism seem
to be full of consolation. It is not, indeed, that the
Buddhist system of morals is supposed to be adapted
altogether to the present " environment ;" but it is
thought by some to settle at least this, that a high
standard of morals, and its actual attainment in life,
is not inseparable from a belief in God, since here we

[1] See Renan, *Les Apôtres*, p. lxiii. ed. i. 1866; quoted in *The One
Religion*, p. 291.

have a moral code of a high order recognised where there is no belief in God at all.

In this light we can well understand the special enthusiasm of many of the unbelievers of Christendom over the moral system and especially the moral character of the Buddha. We may freely admit the singular beauty and attractiveness of the character of the Buddha without indulging in the unaccountable exaggeration of Mr. Arnold, who, in the Preface to the *Light of Asia*, ventures the astonishing assertion that the Buddhist books "agree in the one point of recording nothing—no single act or word—which mars the perfect purity . . . of this Indian teacher." While accessible facts should have prevented him from making any such statement as this, the best authorities certainly warrant us in ranking the Buddha as among the greatest and noblest of men,—one who seems to have lived, however mistaken we may deem him, in order that he might, if possible, lighten the miseries of his fellow-men. And yet he was a man who never by any recorded act or word showed any recognition of the being of God! and thus from the standpoint of unbelief in theism he affords a living argument to show that not only theoretical but practical morality of a high type may be realised without faith in the existence of God. No wonder, under the circumstances of the times, that men who have sagacity enough to see that the authority even of the second table of the decalogue must go with the loss of faith in God, find much com-

fort in the ethics of Buddhism and in the life of its
founder. Perhaps, however,—it may be suggested—if
such would study more carefully the practical operation
of the atheistic moral system of the Buddha in China,
Siam, and other lands, where it has had a fair and pro-
longed trial, their enthusiasm might be somewhat
diminished!

Again, modern unbelief in Christendom is distinguished by its utter contempt for all authority. Many
will have all things settled by the processes of exact
science,—commonly meaning by this, of course, physical
science; and what cannot thus be proven—what has
nothing but authority as of a professed revelation behind it—with that they have no patience. It is turned
over at once to the limbo of superstition, or consigned
to the abyss of the unknowable. No less naturally
than for the other reasons mentioned, Buddhism stands
commended to such by the whole history of its origin.
It began by rejecting *in toto* the whole Brahmanical
system of pretended revelations. As for the Buddha,
he had indeed knowledge to communicate to men, but
not a revelation. He did not therefore assume an
authoritative air, and denounce penalties against all
who would not receive his message. He spoke "as a
plain man," who had himself sought for "rest" and
found it,—found it without the help of Brahman
priest, or any so-called revelation whatsoever. Such a
religion as this, based in its very origin upon a revolt
against the conception of authority in religion, stands

by that fact in so far commended to the sympathy of all whose proud minds cannot endure those words of Christ, wherein upon all who will come unto Him for rest the condition is imposed, " Take my yoke upon you and learn of me."

But yet another circumstance which has of late had much influence is to be found in the number of supposed agreements in the story, the doctrines and the ethics of the Buddha, with the history, the doctrine, and the ethics of the Gospel. This has undoubtedly had more influence with the superficial than among the best informed in Oriental matters ; but among the former and naturally more numerous class, the supposed agreements between the Buddhist and the Christian religion have certainly excited great interest. At these unbelief has grasped eagerly, and with an exultation which already, as regards very many points, has been proved to be premature, has loudly welcomed Buddhism as an ally by whose help it might be shown that Jesus was not so original as has been supposed, and that Strauss and his school were essentially right after all ; that the Gospel story was in large part only a Palestinian version of old Buddhist or solar myths ; its doctrine largely a Judaised Buddhism ; its ethics scarcely inferior to those of Christianity ; its narrative, here and there, bearing sometimes even verbal traces of its Buddhist origin. What ground there may be for such opinions we propose to examine in the following chapters. And that such an examination, in view of

C

the apologetic interest which, for the various reasons
suggested in this chapter, has come to attach of late
to the comparison of Buddhism with Christianity,
is most desirable—will, we believe, be sufficiently
clear.

CHAPTER II.

BEFORE entering upon any such comparison between
the Buddhist and the Christian religions as was proposed at the close of the last chapter, it is important
as a preliminary to compare the historical data upon
which we depend for our knowledge of the facts in
either case. We shall at once see, as the result of such
inquiry, that the sources of our knowledge in each case,
as regards their comparative trustworthiness, present us
with a very striking contrast—a contrast of which we
must never lose sight in all the following discussion.

That such a person as Jesus of Nazareth lived,
scarcely any intelligent person longer doubts. The
attempt to account for Christianity apart from the
supposition of the actual historical existence of Jesus
the Christ, has been given up in despair by about
every unbelieving scholar. Not only is this true, but
all, even the most radical critics, are also substantially
agreed as to the time when this Jesus lived. The

utmost divergence of opinion on this matter does not
exceed six years. Not earlier than six years before
the Christian era, nor later than that date, Jesus of
Nazareth was born. It is also generally agreed that
Jesus lived not less than thirty-two nor more than
thirty-four years ;[1] so that His death must have occurred
not earlier than 26 A.D., nor later than 34 A.D.

The importance of this general agreement as to the
precise period of the life of Christ is most evident.
Let us suppose for a moment that the most competent authorities, instead of thus agreeing on this
matter, disagreed among themselves to the extent of
some two hundred years. What rational assurance
could any one have as to the evidential value of those
writings which make up the New Testament? As it
is, however, since it is held on all hands as an ascertained fact that Paul, for example, wrote the First
Epistle to the Corinthians about 58 A.D. ; and since,
again, the time of Christ's life is also definitely known,
it follows that Paul, as a contemporary and country-
man of Christ, may, at least, be a competent witness
as to what Jesus did and taught. Let us suppose,
however, that it were a question with scholars whether
perhaps Christ did not live some two hundred years
before the composition of that epistle or any other New

[1] It is perhaps scarcely necessary to refer, as exceptions, to the
opinion of E. de Bunsen, based upon John ii. 20, viii. 27, that Jesus
lived almost fifty years ; or to Keim, who thinks it possible that
Christ may have been forty. These exceptional opinions do not affect
in the slightest degree the argument of this chapter.

Testament document: what would then be the value
of the testimony therein given as to Christ and His
teachings? Under such conditions is it not quite
plain that what is to-day the doubt of comparatively
few well-informed persons, would extend and deepen
into a universal feeling of the most hopeless uncertainty
and practical ignorance as to the essential facts concerning what Jesus really taught and did?

But this supposition, which in the case of Jesus is
only a hypothesis, as applied to the case of the Buddha,
simply states the actual facts. We need to mark this
well. It suits the purpose of many to compare the
legend and the supposed teachings of the Buddha with
the story and the doctrine of Christ, as we have these
in the New Testament, as if both stood on the same
evidential ground, and therefore must both stand or
fall together. Nothing, however, could be further
from the truth than this most mischievous assumption,
which is so often tacitly and—let us hope—ignorantly
and unconsciously made. For while there is the most
emphatic and exact agreement among both believing
and unbelieving scholars as to the precise time when
Jesus lived, the most competent specialists in Buddhist
literature and archæology differ in their opinion as to
the date of the death of the Buddha to the extent of
almost two hundred years. Indeed, one might with
reason put the case more strongly still. For at least
twenty dates have been assigned for the death of the
Buddha, varying from 2420 B.C. to 368 B.C., a dis-

crepancy of more than two thousand years![1] It is
not strange that in view of this amazing disagreement
of authorities, the learned Professor H. H. Wilson
should have expressed a doubt whether any such person
as the Buddha ever existed at all.[2]

Most scholars to-day do not indeed go so far as
this, though Senart maintains that although Gautama
must have been a historical personage, yet the legend,
as we have it, is essentially a solar myth, wherein the
mythical and the historical are so interwrought that
no one can now determine with any certainty what is
history and what is not.[3] But Senart has not a large
following; it is commonly agreed that the Buddha lived,
and also that the dates earlier than the middle of the
sixth century B.C. are to be rejected. And yet, as remarked above, the ablest critics still differ as much as
nearly two hundred years in assigning the date of the
Buddha's death. Many writers take the date for this
event accepted by the southern (Ceylonese) school of
Buddhists, which fixes the end of the Buddha's life at
543 B.C.[4] The tendency, however, of critical judgment is at present to a later date. Professor Max

[1] Edkins, *Chinese Buddhism*, p. 12. Hardy has given a long list
of various dates which have been assigned to the death of the Buddha
in his *Legends and Theories of the Buddhists*, p. 78.

[2] Essay on "Buddha and Buddhism," *Journal of the Roy. Asiat. Soc.*,
vol. xvi. pp. 247, 248.

[3] *Essai sur la Legende du Buddha.* A summary of his views is
given by Rhys Davids, *Buddhism*, pp. 190-193.

[4] So, among others, H. H. Wilson, St. Hilaire, Burnouf, Dr. W.
W. Hunter, Childers.

Müller makes the Buddha to have died 477 B.C.; Barth, 482-472 B.C.; Mr. Rhys Davids, 410 B.C.; Kern, 388 B.C.; while Westergaard and Weber bring the time down to 370-368 B.C. Further investigation may, no doubt, somewhat reduce this discrepancy of opinion; but that when the critics shall have finished their work and done their best, we shall be able to fix the date of the life of the Buddha with anything like the precision with which we can that of Christ—this there is no good reason to expect. The reason for this lies very deep, and has been pithily and truly put by Professor Oldenberg, thus: "For the When of things men generally in India have never had a proper organ."[1] All this simply means that we are not *sure* within one hundred and seventy-five years as to when the Buddha really lived. As to the whole argument upon the subject, Professor Oldenberg and Mr. Rhys Davids tell us that "the details are intricate and the result uncertain;" and while they think that the uncertainty of a few decades which still remains in their mind is a matter of no great consequence, they yet express their regret that "our comfort is drawn from no better source than our want of knowledge."[2]

Now, when we contrast the facts in this case with the state of the case as regards the date of the life of Christ, it is plain that the significance of the contrast is most momentous. For while it is certain that

[1] *Buddha, sein Leben, seine Lehre, seine Gemeinde*, S. 82.
[2] Introduction to *Texts from the Vinaya, S. B. E.*, vol. xiii. p. xxiii.

whether the testimony, *e.g.*, of Paul or Matthew, be
true or false, since they lived in the first half of the
first Christian century, they *may* at least be competent
witnesses, it is equally certain that we cannot be thus
sure of the competency of any witness for the life and
the teachings of the Buddha. We are not *sure* as to any
witness that he lived nearer to the Buddha than almost
two hundred years. When, about forty years ago, the
critics of the Tübingen school flattered themselves that
they had succeeded in showing that none of our
Gospels could be traced up to the generation in which
Jesus lived, all felt that if that were indeed established,
the claim of those gospels to our faith would be very
seriously weakened. But the uncertainty as to the
distance of the testimony to the life and the teachings
of the Buddha from his lifetime, is even greater than
that which the Tübingen critics would have attached
to the date of our Gospels. One needs for this reason
to be very cautious in drawing conclusions as to what
the Buddha himself actually taught and did, as, indeed,
the best Buddhist scholars are. And whenever any
such conclusions may seem to any to conflict with
what has been regarded as essential Christian truth,
we are ever to remember that by no possibility can
this uncertain testimony concerning the teachings and
experiences of the Buddha be made to outweigh, or
even counterpoise, positive testimony such as we have
to the teaching and the works and experiences of Jesus
Christ; a testimony, which, whatever its value may be

in other respects, at least, by common admission, comes
from witnesses who lived in the same time and place
with Him of whom they wrote. And the truth of this
remark will appear abundantly evident in the sequel.

For even this is not the whole statement of the
case on this question of the comparative evidence of
Buddhism and Christianity. It must also be remembered that the life of Jesus falls in no obscure period
of history, nor was it lived in a region of the world at
that time little known. For Jesus lived and taught in
the Roman Empire, in one of its best known provinces,
and in the full sunlight of the Augustan age. The age
of Jesus was the age of Virgil, of Tacitus, of Suetonius.
It was not, as often carelessly asserted, an age of easy
going credulity, but the contrary;—it was an age in
which men, disgusted with the old superstitions, the
hollowness and absurdity of which they had discovered,
were rather ready in too many instances to reject the
supernatural altogether. The testimony, therefore,
which we have to the life of Jesus, be it true or false,
was at least given under conditions and circumstances
favourable to unprejudiced investigation. And when
we remember the amazingly rapid extension of the
new religion in that first century, formally attested to
us by a Roman official,[1] it seems impossible to avoid
admitting the *presumption* that that primitive testimony,
still preserved for us in the Gospels and Epistles, did

[1] Letter of Pliny the Younger to the Emperor Trajan. *Plinii*, lib.
x. *epist.* 96 [al. 97].

set forth facts which, however marvellous, were yet
found to be undeniable.

But let us now contrast these conditions under
which Christ did His work, with those which obtain in
the case of the Buddha.   As for the theatre on which
he lived and taught, instead of being one of the best
known parts of the world, India was a land of which
at that time we have scarcely any historical account
which we can trust.   Dr. Hunter, the learned historian
of India, who has written the article on India for the
Encyclopædia Britannica, makes the external history of
India to begin only with the Greek invasion under
Alexander the Great, in 327 B.C., almost half a
century after the latest date that has ever been
assigned for the death of the Buddha ; and in this he
is quite right.   A history of India in the age when
the Buddha lived we have not ; all is left to inference
and uncertain conjecture.

Again, the Romans and Greeks were peoples of a
historical spirit, so that writers like Herodotus, Thucy-
dides, and Tacitus deservedly rank still as witnesses
of the highest veracity.   Neither can the Jews themselves be rightly charged with a lack of this faculty
for history.   As contrasted with these, the Hindoos,
among whom the Buddha did his work, from the earliest
antiquity until this day have been noted beyond any
other cultivated people of the world for the total
absence of the historic spirit.   They have never concerned themselves to preserve an accurate record of

any historical events, even of those which have most vitally affected their own history. Quite characteristic therefore is the fact which, with good reason, Professor Oldenberg emphasises as a proposition fundamental to the whole discussion of the historical character of the tradition concerning the Buddha, namely : " A biography of the Buddha out of antiquity—out of the time of the sacred *Pàli* texts—has not reached us, and, as we may say with confidence, has never existed." [1] And the reason which he assigns for this fact,—a fact which, when we consider the remarkable character which the founder of such a religion as Buddhism must have had, seems so extraordinary,—he gives in these words :—" The conception of a biography was in itself foreign to the consciousness of that time." [2]

And so it comes to pass that, whether the Buddha lived in the fourth or the sixth century B.C., it matters not. In neither case have we any contemporaneous history in India, whether written by friend or foe, which might either directly or indirectly witness to so much as the existence of the Buddha or the manner of the early propagation of his doctrine. Indeed, even the Buddhists themselves do not claim that any record of the life and teaching of the Buddha was committed to writing in his lifetime, or for a long time afterwards. And this brings us to another marked contrast between

---

[1] *Buddha, sein Leben, seine Lehre, seine Gemeinde,* S. 80.
[2] *Ibid.*

the evidence which we have as regards the Buddhist scriptures, and that upon which we rest our faith as to the historical credibility of the Gospels and Epistles of the New Testament.

Constrained by the irresistible force of historical evidence, even the most radical of unbelieving critics have made the reluctant admission that the written testimony to the facts of the life and teaching of Christ comes from a period within a hundred years of His death ; and that many of the most important books of the New Testament, in particular the Gospels of Matthew, Mark, and Luke, existed in essentially their present form before the generation in which Jesus lived had passed away.   It suits a certain class of sceptics, imperfectly informed and hasty in judgment, to ignore this fact, and carelessly assert that no man knows when these Gospels were written.   Unbelievers, however, who are really at once learned and candid, know better than to make such statements.

As all who are familiar with the controversy know, the date of the Gospel of John has been more frequently called in question than that of either of the other Gospels. In any case it is agreed that it was the last written of the four.   But the stress of historical evidence has steadily driven those critics whose principles led them to maintain as late a date for this Gospel as possible year by year backward, nearer and nearer to the time of Christ's life, till now the most extreme critics admit that even this fourth Gospel was certainly written at least before the contemporaries of the apostle John, Christ's nearest friend, had all passed away. The facts stand as follows :—

About forty years ago Baur and Schwegler maintained that the Gospel of John was written not earlier than 160-170 A.D. The force of the testimony of writers of the second century, however, compelled Zeller and Scholten to set the date of the fourth Gospel back to 150 A.D.; still later, Hilgenfeld and Keim have fixed it at 120-140 A.D. ; while Schenkel thinks that it was written between 115 and 120 A.D.

Thus, even if we confine our attention to the latest of the canonical Gospels, and admit only the judgment of critics of the rationalistic school, still we may safely say that the very *latest* of the Gospel records was given to the world within a hundred years of the death of Jesus, and within thirty years of the death of the last of His apostles.

But the case for the Gospel testimony to the life and teachings of Jesus is much stronger than this. For even Baur, who assigned 160-170 as the date of the Gospel of John, placed the origin of the Gospel of Matthew at 130, and that of Luke between 130 and 110 A.D. But these extreme opinions are now abandoned even by the most radical critics. Volkmar, for example, fixes the date of Matthew's Gospel at 105-110 A.D.; while Schenkel says it was composed after 70 A.D.; and Keim, retreating still further, gives his judgment that it was written *before* the destruction of Jerusalem. And with this opinion sober criticism closely agrees. Thus the Gospel of Matthew, according to the most extreme opinion of the radical critics, was published, at the latest, within five or ten years after the death of John, but according to the present judgment of most of the ablest scholars, rationalistic as well as orthodox, within at most forty years after the crucifixion, and therefore during the lifetime of the contemporaries of Jesus.

Closely similar are the facts regarding the date of the Gospel according to Luke. While Baur and Zeller, a generation ago, fixed the date of this Gospel at 110-130 A.D., Hilgenfeld, Volkmar, and Keim make it not later than 100 A.D. Soberer criticism, however, assigns it to a date still earlier; as, *e.g.*, Weiss and Renan,[1] who place its publication between 70 and 80 A.D., while Godet extends these limits to 64-80 A.D.

The composition of the Gospel of Mark, as is now commonly agreed, must be placed earlier than either of the other three Gospels. Keim, indeed, unlike the most, assigns for the composition of this Gospel the date 115-120 A.D.; but Volkmar makes it 73 A.D.; Schenkel, before 60 A.D.; while Hitzig more precisely names 55-57 A.D. as the time of its composition. In any case it is evident, from these facts, that according to the general consensus of radical criticism, this Gospel of Mark, again, presents us with contemporary

---

[1] *Vid.* Renan, *Life of Jesus*, p. 9.

testimony to the facts concerning the life and teachings of Jesus.

Nor must we overlook here the additional fact that four of the most notable Pauline epistles—namely, those to the Galatians, the Romans, and the two to the Corinthians—are assigned by the practically unanimous consent of both believing and unbelieving critics to the same early period before the destruction of Jerusalem. Indeed, until within three years the consent of the critics has been quite unanimous, and has only now been interrupted by the extraordinary attempt of Professor Loman of Amsterdam to show that neither Paul nor Jesus ever existed, and that what we have in the Gospels and Epistles is in each case merely an incarnation, so to speak, of a popular conception.[1] But the utter untenableness of his position has already been fully shown, and he has been completely answered, not by theologians and critics of the evangelical school, but by extreme radicals like Scholten and Kuenen.

To sum up then, it is to be observed that the most extreme school of modern unbelieving criticism admits that of the books which are our chief authorities for the life and teaching of Jesus, the latest cannot possibly be placed later than about 130 A.D., while the earliest of them was probably written not later than 73 A.D., and very possibly as early as 55 A.D.—that is, within

[1] See *Yahrbücher für Protestantische Theologie*, 1883, *viertes Heft ;* article, "Zur Literaturgeschichte der Kritik und Exegese des Neuen Testaments," wherein Professor Loman's theory and the replies of his critics are fully discussed. Bruno, Bauer, and Pierson had no following.

twenty-two years of the death of Jesus, less time than has yet elapsed since the close of the civil war between the North and South.   This means, of course, that the most essential and fundamental of the records which form the basis of Christian faith can be traced up into the very generation in which the events narrated are said to have occurred.[1]   How stands the case with the records which profess to give us the life and the teachings of the Buddha ?   The question has been in part already answered, but deserves a full consideration.

In replying to this question, we have first to recall to mind the fact already remarked, that the most recent and competent critics differ in their judgment to the extent of full one hundred and seventy-five years as to the date of the death of the Buddha, and also bear in mind that this fact carries with it an equal degree of uncertainty as to whether we have any record dating nearer than this to that event.   Indeed, Mr. Rhys Davids tells us that it is even doubtful whether the art of writing was known in India so early as the date (410 B.C.) which he fixes as that of the Buddha's death.[2]   But passing by this additional element of uncertainty, it is plain that even if we could trace up the Buddhist records in the form in which we now have them to a point of time as near to the most recent date which has been assigned for the death of the Buddha, as the synoptic Gospels stand to the death of Christ, there would still remain the

---

[1] So Renan : see *Life of Jesus*, pp. 12, 13, 21.
[2] *Buddhism*, p. 9 ; *S. B. E.*, vol. xi. p. xxii.

uncertainty whether this supposed date of the Buddha's
death were nearly correct, and we should be still far
from having assurance that we possessed works dating
back to that generation which saw the work of the
Buddha.

But even if we ignore the great diversity of opinion
among Buddhist scholars as to the date of the Buddha's
death, and assume that the latest date which any have
assigned to that event is correct, still it is not yet
possible to prove that we have any *written* record of
the events of the Buddha's life which reaches back
nearly so far as this date of 368-370 B.C. The facts
which bear upon this question, so far as ascertained,
are as follows :—

The authorities for the life and teachings of the
Buddha are : (1) the *Tripiṭaka*, which is the canon of
the Southern Buddhists ; (2) the commentaries on the
same, called *Arthakathà ;* (3) the canon of the
Northern Buddhists, as accepted in Thibet and China.
Now, unfortunately, at the very beginning of our
inquiry as to the date and trustworthiness of these
writings, we are confronted by the fact that a large
part of these works has not yet been made accessible
to European scholars. What knowledge we have is
derived from comparatively few books. Of these,
again, many are not themselves originals, but translations of earlier works. Neither have we any assurance that these latter are in all cases, or even in any
case, *accurate* versions of the originals which they

D

profess to represent. If we may trust the testimony
of specialists in Buddhist literature, we look in vain in
these versions of various parts of the Buddhist scriptures for evidence of that conscientious care which
Christian scholars have given to the various translations of the Old and New Testaments. Professor Max
Müller remarks when speaking of these old Buddhist
translations, " The idea of a faithful, literal translation seems altogether foreign to Oriental minds." [1] Of
one of the most famous and reputable of these translators, Buddhaghosha (430 A.D.), he says, " In the broad
daylight of historical criticism the prestige of such a
witness as Buddhaghosha fades away, and his statements as to kings and councils eight hundred years
before his time are in truth worth no more than the
stories told of Arthur by Geoffrey of Monmouth, or the
accounts we read in *Livy* of the early history of Rome." [2]

The three collections which make up the *Tripiṭaka*
are severally entitled the *Vinaya Piṭaka*, which is a
collection of discourses addressed to the Order of monks;
the *Sutta Piṭaka*, or discourses intended specially for
the laity ; and lastly, the *Abhidhamma Piṭaka*, which
develops more specially the metaphysics of the system.[3]
Of the *Vinaya* texts a large part has been made
accessible to the English-reading student in the *Sacred
Books of the East*, by translations by Mr. Rhys Davids

---

[1] *Chips from a German Workshop*, vol. i. p. 95.

[2] *Ibid.*, pp. 195, 197.

[3] For a detailed list of their contents, see Rhys Davids' *Buddhism*,
pp. 18-21.

and Professor Oldenberg.[1]   Of these translated *Vinaya*
texts we are told that all those already published may
be regarded as dating back, in the opinion of the
translators, to a period thirty years earlier or later than
360 or 370 B.C.[2]   The *Pâtimokkha* especially is supposed by them to be "one of the oldest, if not the
oldest, of all Buddhist text-books."[3]   These contain
very little, however, but a collection of rules for the
daily life of the monkish Order.   Of historical matter
they give us little or nothing.   Many incidents are
indeed related of the Buddha which serve as a setting
for the rules, but the translators tell us that they
"have altogether the appearance of being mere inven-
tions," that "actual remembrance of the Buddha and
of his time could have sufficed only in the rarest
instances to give a correct historical basis for the rules
or ceremonies which had to be explained."[4]

According to Mr. Rhys Davids, "the oldest and
most reliable"[5] of all the Buddhist authorities for the
legend of the Buddha is the *Mahâparinibbâna Sutta*,
or *Book of the Great Decease*, which, according to his
judgment, may be assigned to the latter end of the
fourth or the beginning of the third century B.C.   He
is careful, however, to emphasise the caution that this
"should not be looked upon as anything more than a
good working hypothesis,"—"only probability, not

[1] Vols. xiii. and xvii.
[2] *Texts from the Vinaya*, p. xxiii. ; *S. B. E.*, vol. xiii.
[3] *Ibid.*, p. ix.   [4] *Ibid.*, p. xx.
[5] *Buddhism*, p. 14.

certainty."[1]   Whatever date may be assigned to this
Sutta, which forms a part of the second division of the
Tripiṭaka, to about the same period, in Mr. Davids'
judgment, must be assigned also the other six *Suttas*
which are translated in vol. xi. of the *Sacred Books of
the East*.[2]   But none of these *Suttas* give any account
of the life of the Buddha, excepting only that the
Mahâparinibbâna Sutta purports to give an, account of
the events immediately connected with his death.

Of the authors of these or of any of the books
which make up the Buddhist scriptures, nobody knows
anything.   More than that, Mr. Davids tells us as
regards the seven important *Suttas* of which we have
been speaking, that "they cannot unfortunately be
depended upon as entirely authentic; and it will
always be difficult, even when the whole of the *Suttas*
have been published, to attempt to discriminate between
the original doctrine of Gautama, and the later accre-
tions to or modifications of it."[3]

The *Sutta Nipàta*, another important authority,
from the second of the three *Piṭakas*, recently translated by Professor Fausböll in vol. x. of the *Sacred
Books of the East*, is regarded by him as "very old,"
and belonging to the period of primitive Buddhism,
for which opinion he gives cogent reasons.[4]   But who

---

[1] *Sacred Books of the East*, vol. xi. p. xi.
[2] *Dhammacakkappavattana, Tevijja, Âkankheyya, Cetokhila, Mahâsudassana*, and *Sabbâsava Suttas*.
[3] *Sacred Books of the East*, vol. xi. p. xx.
[4] *Op. cit.*, part 2, pp. xi. xii.

was the writer, how far it presents the actual teachings of the Buddha, to what extent it has been preserved uncorrupted, this no one is able to say with
precision. As to the life of the Buddha it tells us
scarcely anything.

One of the highest authorities for Buddha's doctrine,
though, like the foregoing, it tells us nothing of his life,
is the *Dhammapada*, another portion of the second part
of the *Tripiṭaka*. But of this, again, the authorship
and exact date of composition is involved in the same
haze of uncertainty as that of the others mentioned.

Professor Beal, who has published a translation of
a Chinese version of this work—not wholly identical,
however, with the text of the *Pàli* original—tells us
that according to the Chinese that text of the *Dhammapada* was compiled by one Dharmàtra.[1]   But as to
when this Dharmàtra lived there is extreme uncertainty. Professor Beal is inclined to place him at about
70 B.C. Professor Max Müller agrees with him in the
opinion that the first century before Christ was probably the time when the text of the *Dhammapada* was
formally settled[2] in writing. That these, in common with other portions of the Buddhist scriptures,
came down *orally* from an earlier period, there is no
reason to doubt, but how much earlier it is impossible
to say. Professor Müller gives his opinion as regards

---

[1] Or Dharmatràta.   See *Texts from the Dhammapada*, p. 8.
[2] Introduction to Captain T. Roger's translation from the Burmese
of *Buddhaghosha's Parables*, p. xxx.

the date of the *Dhammapada* in the following words :
" I cannot see any reason why we should not treat
the verses of the *Dhammapada*, if not as the utterances
of Buddha, at least as what were believed by the
members of the Council under Asoka in 242 B.C.
to have been the utterances of the founder of their
religion."[1]

But none of these scriptures give us more than a
few meagre hints as to the life and experiences of the
Buddha.   Where the Gospel histories and epistles are
full of allusions to the profane history of the time,
which enable us to test with satisfaction the question
of their date and authorship, these Buddhist authorities
contain not a trace of anything of this kind.   On this
whole matter we may again quote the decisive words
of that eminent *Pàli* scholar, Professor Oldenberg.   He
tells us that the original *Pàli* texts of the Buddhist
scriptures " contain neither a biography of the Buddha
nor even the slightest trace of the former existence of
such a work." [2]

As every one, however, who has read at all on this
subject knows, there is, if not a biography, at least a
legend of the Buddha.   The oldest form in which this
has been made accessible to the public is the *Jàtaka*
or *Book of Birth Stories*, translated into English from
the *Pàli* by Mr. Rhys Davids.[3]   This book consists of

---

[1] Introduction to Captain T. Roger's translation from the Burmese
of *Buddhaghosha's Parables*, p. xxiv.

[2] *Buddha, sein Leben, seine Lehre, seine Gemeinde*, S. 80, note 1.

[3] The *Pàli* title is *Jàtakatthavaṇṇanà.*   All the stories it contains

two elements—namely, the original texts of the *Birth Stories*, and a *Commentary* on those stories. As regards the *Birth Stories* themselves, the Buddhists declare that these were gathered immediately after the death of the Buddha, and give a very particular account of their transmission thereafter. But Mr. Davids assures us that this opinion of theirs " rests upon a foundation of quicksand ;" and that " the Buddhist belief that most of their sacred books were in existence immediately after the Buddha's death is not only not supported, but is contradicted, by the evidence of those books themselves." He continues : " With the present inadequate information at our command it is only possible to arrive at probabilities."[1] In this provisional manner he holds as the result of investigation thus far, that the *Birth Stories* were already popularly known in the third or fourth century B.C.[2] The *Commentary*, by an unknown author, which forms the larger part of the book as published by Mr. Davids, he assigns to a much later date, certainly not earlier than the beginning of the fifth century of our era, or almost a thousand years after the death of the Buddha.[3]

The most celebrated work, embodying the legend of

are also found in the *Cariyâ Piṭaka* of the *Second Piṭaka*. See *Buddhist Birth Stories*, vol. i. p. liii.

[1] *Buddhist Birth Stories*, vol. i. pp. ii. iii.

[2] *Ibid.*, p. lxxxii. But not until this time, in his opinion, were these stories applied to the Buddha.

[3] *Ibid.*, pp. lxiii-lxvi.

the Buddha in its fullest form, does not belong to the *Pâli* Canon, but is the Sanskrit *Lalita Vistâra*, a standard authority with the Northern Buddhists, the eighth of a series of nine works called the *Nine Dhammas*. Again, as regards this work also, we find the same utter lack of definite data which might form the basis for a confident opinion as to the date of its composition. A Thibetan version of this work[1] is attributed by Foucaux to a period not earlier than the sixth century of our era. How much older the original may be we do not know. The eminent Oriental scholar, Râjendralâl Mitra, says that as to the date of the composition of this work "we have nothing more positive than inference founded on insufficient conjecture."[2] Elsewhere, indeed, he apparently admits that a Chinese translation of the work was made about 69 or 70 A.D.[3] And so also, according to Seydel, Stanislaus Julien is authority for the statement that a Chinese catalogue of the writings contained in the first great compilation of the Thibetan Buddhist Canon, enumerates no less than four translations into Chinese of the *Lalita Vistâra*, and represents the oldest as having been made about this date of 70 B.C.[4] But whether the work known as the *Lalita Vistâra* at that time was the same as that which now bears the name,

---

[1] Under the title *Rgya t'cher rol pa.*

[2] *Lalita Vistâra*, Introduction, p. 48 (*Bibliotheca Indica*).

[3] *Ibid.*, p. 39.

[4] *Das Evangelium von Jesu in seinen Verhältnissen zu Buddha Sage und Buddha Lehre*, S. 77, 78.

or to what extent it corresponded with it, this no man
can say.   Mr. Rhys Davids says that Foucaux, who,
in the Introduction to his translation of the Thibetan
version, assigns the *Lalita Vistâra* to the first century
before Christ, does so "without any evidence whatever;"[1] and adds that it is "quite uncertain" how
much older than the Thibetan version "the present
form of the Sanskrit work may be."[2]   In a later
work he expresses the opinion that it was "probably
composed in Nepâl, and by some Buddhist poet who
lived between six hundred and a thousand years
after the death of the Buddha."[3]   As to the date of
this work, then, so much used by those who would ✗
insist on the agreements between the legend of the
Buddha and the story of Christ, it will be perceived
that there is an uncertainty among the most competent judges to the extent of several hundred years.
The real authority of this work is well compared by
Professor Oldenberg to that of the apocryphal Gospels,
or, better still, to that of the legends of the Middle
Ages with regard to Christ.[4]

Another work of some celebrity, the sixth of this
same series of the *Nine Dhammas* of the Northern
Buddhism, is the *Saddharmapundarîka*,[5] or *Lotus of*

[1] *Buddhism*, p. 11, note 1.   [2] *Ibid.*, p. 11.
[3] *Lectures on the Origin and Growth of Religion*, etc. (Hibbert
Lectures, 1881), p. 197.   See also pp. 198-204.
[4] *Buddha, sein Leben, seine Lehre, seine Gemeinde*, S. 75.
[5] Translated into French by Burnouf under the title, *La Lotus de
la Bonne Loi.*

the True Law.   The value of this work with regard to primitive Buddhism is nothing.   Like the *Lalita Vistàra*, in its present form, it is a late production. The Buddha, according to this book, is the Supreme Being, "the Father of the World, the Self-born." He has not become extinct and never will.[1]   Thus in many things the doctrine of this work is the exact reverse of the primitive *Pàli* canon.   Professor Kern has summed up the evidence as to its composition and date as follows.   He says, " It can hardly be questioned that these works (the *Nine Dhammas*) contain parts of very different dates, and derived from various sources ;"[2] and, with regard to the present work in particular, " we may feel that compositions from different times have been collected into a not very harmonious whole ; we may even be able to prove that some passages are as decidedly ancient as others are modern ; but any attempt to analyse the composition and lay bare its component parts would seem to be premature.   Under these circumstances, inquiry after the date of the work resolves itself into the question at what time the book received its present shape."[3] This question he answers by reference to the following facts.   The oldest of the Chinese versions of the work was made between 265 and 316 A.D.   In this version five of the present twenty-seven chapters are wanting ;

---

[1] *Saddharmapuṇḍarīka*, chap. xiv., *passim ; S. B. E.*, vol. xxi. pp. 302, 309, 310.

[2] *Ibid.*, Introduction, p. xi.   [3] *Ibid.*, p. xx.

these are reasonably to be ascribed to a later date. " The other and more ancient part came from a time some centuries earlier," how many, he does not say, but adds, " Greater precision is for the present impossible."[1] Another authority, also out of the Northern Buddhism, has been translated into English by the Rev. Samuel Beal, Professor of Chinese in Oxford, under the name of *The Romantic Legend*. This is a version of a Chinese translation of a Sanskrit work called the *Abhinishkramana Sútra*, itself, again, an enlarged and altered rendition of the *Lalita Vistàra*. This Chinese version Professor Beal attributes to about 70 A.D. Then from the fact that certain of the stories in the Chinese version are represented in carvings on the Buddhist topes in India, which he supposes to be somewhat older than the Christian era, he infers that the Sanskrit original of the version must have been composed somewhat earlier than this, probably between 300 B.C. and the Christian era. This is vague enough, but even this opinion is contradicted by Dr. Eitel, who asserts that " nearly all " the legends in this and other works " which claim to refer to events centuries before Christ, cannot be proved to have been in circulation earlier than the fifth or sixth centuries after Christ."[2] Another work, to which frequent reference is made in this discussion, is the *Manual of Buddhism*, by the Rev. Mr. Hardy of Ceylon, which consists chiefly of

[1] *Saddharmapuṇḍarîka*, Introduction ; *S. B. E.*, vol. xxi. p. xxii.
[2] *Three Lectures on Buddhism*, p. 15.

translations from the *Visuddhimaggo sanne*,[1] *Milinda Prasnà, Pansiyapanasjàtakapota*, and seven other works. Of these, the first is a translation into Singhalese of the very ancient *Pàli* work of Buddhaghosha (410- 432 A.D.) The *Milinda Prasnà* is a Singhalese trans- lation of an ancient *Pàli* work; its precise date is not fixed. The *Pansiyapanasjàtakapota* is a *Pàli* commentary on one of the books of the *Sutta Pitaka*, of high antiquity, and held of equal authority with the text. Of the remaining works from which transla- tions are given by Mr. Hardy, none seem to be older, and some are much later than the *Pùjàwaliya* (1267- 1301).[2] Bp. Bigandet, of Burmah, in *The Legend of Gaudama*, has given a translation of a Burmese Life of the Buddha, entitled *Màlàlankàra Vatthu*. But this was written only in the last century, though following closely older authorities.[3] Mr. Alabaster, of Siam, has translated a Siamese Life of the Buddha, called *Pothiya Sambodhiyan*, but of the author and date of the work nothing is told us.[4]

All this may have seemed tedious, but it has ap- peared not needless to give, even at the risk of apparent prolixity, some details of these hopeless uncertainties of opinion, in order to enable the reader to appreciate the almost immeasurable contrast which obtains, as regards our knowledge of the date and authorship,

[1] *Sanne* = "translation."
[2] Hardy, *Manual of Buddhism*, pp. 101, 529-540.
[3] *The Legend of Gaudama*, vol. ii. p. 149.
[4] Published in *The Wheel of the Law*.

between the Buddhist authorities and the books of the New Testament. On the one hand we have sharp historical precision, on the other the haze of uncertainty and conflicting conjectures.[1] But great as this contrast is, it becomes the stronger when we observe that in all this discussion of the date of the origin of the Buddhist scriptures we have not yet touched, except incidentally, the question of the origin of these authorities in their *written* form, but only that of the *oral tradition* which was at last embodied in the now existing books. For while a few of the extant Buddhist authorities are by the critics referred to a period so early as two or three hundred years before Christ, or perhaps from one to two hundred years after the death of the Buddha, it is commonly agreed that these were not committed to writing till about two hundred years later !

More than this is not claimed by the Buddhists themselves. The Buddhist historian, Mahànàma (459-457 A.D.), states that the Buddhist scriptures were first committed to writing in the reign of Vatta-gàmini, 86-76 B.C.[2] And while his authority cannot

---

[1] Professor Max Müller, reviewing the evidence, concludes that "we can hardly ever expect to get nearer to the Buddha himself and to his personal teaching" than "the Council under Asoka, in 246 B.C." —Introduction to *Buddhaghosha's Parables*, p. xxiv.

[2] *The Mahàvansa*, with the translation subjoined, by Hon. Geo. Turnour, Esq., Ceylon Civil Service, Ceylon, Catta Church Mission Press, 1837, chap. xxxii. p. 207. The words are: "The profoundly wise priests had heretofore orally perpetuated the *Pàli Piṭakatraya* and its *Attha Kathà* (Commentary). At this period the priests, fore-

be regarded as absolutely decisive, yet Professor Max
Müller, with other competent judges, is inclined
to accept this statement.[1] That the sacred words
were committed to writing at first is claimed by
no one.

Thus, even if we suppose what Professor Oldenberg
thinks *possible*, that the interval between the oldest
parts of the Buddhist *Pàli* texts and the death of the
Buddha was "not much longer, perhaps, in general,
not longer than the interval between the death of
Jesus and the composition of our Gospels,"[2] still the
case would not be parallel with that of the Gospels and
Epistles. For in the latter case it is not "parts," but
the whole; and not mere doctrines and rules, but
biographical matter also;[3] not merely their origination,
but their committal to writing that we are able to fix
in the first Christian century; while in the case of
the Buddhist scriptures, all that we have is derived
from a stream of oral tradition, which, although parts
of it may be traced almost to the time of the Buddha,
yet was not committed to writing, according to any
authority that we have, until from three to five hun-

seeing the perdition of the people (from the perversions of the true
doctrine) . . . in order that religion might endure for ages, recorded
the same in books."—See also *Ibid.*, p. ix.

[1] *Sacred Books of the East*, vol. x. part 1, pp. xiii. xiv.

[2] *Buddha, sein Leben, seine Lehre, seine Gemeinde*, S. 78.

[3] Professor Oldenberg is careful to state that these oldest *portions* of
the *Pàli* texts, which, in his opinion, *may* have come from a time so near
the Buddha, contain no biography of the Buddha. The whole legend
belongs to a later period. *Vid. sup.* p. 27.

dred years later.[1] In the West this fact would be
sufficient almost entirely to destroy the value of these
documents as evidence.[2] But although any one who
knows the remarkable powers of memory which the
Hindoos possess will easily believe that they might
transmit the substance of the voluminous documents
which make up the Buddhist Canon with a degree of
accuracy which would be impossible to western minds,
yet there are limits even to the powers of the Hindoos
in this respect. The Rev. Mr. Hardy, for more than
a quarter century in daily intercourse with the Buddhists of Ceylon, declares the alleged oral transmission
through so long a period to have been impossible even
in India. We may safely say that it was utterly impossible that, even with all the special safeguards
which we know to have been adopted, extensive corruptions should not in the course of centuries have
crept into the text.

[1] Mr. Rhys Davids has expressed a doubt whether the art of writing
was known in India so early as the time of the Buddha. In the Introduction to the *Texts from the Vinaya*, part 1, by Mr. Davids and
Professor Oldenberg, we are told that these texts show, as is plain on the
reading, that the art of writing was known at the time "when the
Vinaya texts were put into their present shape; but that they also
indisputably show that it was not used at that time for the recording
of a sacred literature."—*S. B. E.*, vol. xiii. pp. xxxii. xxxiii.

[2] It is with good reason that Professor Max Müller remarks with
regard to the probable date of the Buddhist canon, that "the evidence
on which we have to rely is such that we must not be surprised if those
who are accustomed to test historical and chronological evidence in
Greece and Rome decline to be convinced by it."—*S. B. E.*, vol. x.
part 1, pp. x. xi.

Professor Beal, for example, admits the probability of extensive additions to the legend of the Buddha as contained in the *Abhinishkramana Sûtra*, a translation of the Chinese version of which he has given us in the *Romantic Legend*.   His words are: "It would seem that originally the story of the *Abhinishkramana* was simply that of Buddha's flight from his palace to become an ascetic. . . . Afterwards, the same title was applied to the complete legend . . . which includes his previous and subsequent history." [1]   How much of this or of any existing version of the legend was in any case in the original of any given book, it would seem about impossible ever to determine with certainty.

And indeed, that the oral tradition on which these extant authorities are based was not transmitted with anything like perfect purity, is admitted by the Buddhists themselves.   They tell us in so many words that the reason of the committal of the Canon to writing at the late date named, was the fact that such a diversity of rendering had crept into the oral tradition that the reduction to writing was necessary in order to prevent final hopeless corruption.   The author of the Ceylonese chronicle, the *Dîpavansa*, charges that even the members of the Great Council which is said to have committed the Canon to writing, themselves corrupted it worse than before.   We read, according to Mr. Rhys Davids—

[1] *Romantic Legend*, p. v.

" The monks of the Great Council turned the religion up-
side down ;

.　.　.　.　.　.　.

They distorted the sense and the teaching of the five
Nikâyas.

In part they cast aside the *Sutta* and the *Vinaya* so deep,

And made an imitation *Sutta* and *Vinaya,* changing this
to that." [1]

While in these statements there may easily be exaggeration due to party spirit, yet both the presumption and
what testimony we have is more than sufficient to
prove that such solid assurance as we have of the
identity of the New Testament books with the original
documents, is utterly unattainable with respect to the
sacred books of the Buddhists.

The contrast in the two cases will be the more
evident when we remember that as regards the genuineness of the New Testament books and the purity of our
present text, we have *two* important lines of evidence,
both of which are absolutely and hopelessly wanting in
the case of the Buddhist scriptures. In the first place,
the present text of the New Testament authorities can be
compared with manuscripts which date back to within
three or four hundred years of the time of the apostles.
That these ancient manuscripts present a text essentially identical with the New Testament as we have it
to-day, is known to every intelligent person. To

---

[1] *Buddhist Birth Stories,* vol. i. p. lvii. To the same effect is the
statement in the *Mahâvansa,* chap. xxxii. p. 207. *Vid. sup.* p. 45,
note 2.

E

parallel this in the case of the Buddhist scriptures, it would be necessary to produce manuscripts which should date back to the time of Christ or earlier;—in other words, since the tradition was not committed to writing till the first century before Christ, the original documents, or at least first copies. But this is not possible. For because of the perishable nature of the material used for writing, and the ravages of climate and insects in India, it has come to pass that there is not a single Buddhist manuscript in existence older than a thousand years at the most; while it would be almost impossible to produce any manuscript so much as five hundred years old.[1] To compare, therefore, existing copies of the Buddhist sacred books with early authorities which might certify their general correctness and freedom from corruption, is not merely difficult but for ever impossible.

And then, again, the integrity of the Christian records is further certified to us by abundant citations in the writings of the early Christian fathers, and by the various versions made within the first two or three hundred years after Christ. But of analogous

[1] According to Dr. Eitel, "not a single ancient manuscript of the Buddhist authorities has survived the ravages of time." *Three Lectures on Buddhism*, p. 25. With this opinion Professor Max Müller fully agrees. He says, "All Indian MSS. are comparatively modern, and one who has handled probably more Indian MSS. than anybody else, Mr. A. Burnell, has lately expressed his conviction that no MS. written one thousand years ago is now existent in India, and that it is almost impossible to find one written five hundred years ago." *Sacred Books of the East*, vol. x. part 1 ; Introduction to the *Dhammapada*, p. xi.

writings dating from a similar period after the composition of the Buddhist scriptures, there is an utter
lack. Thus, not only were the Buddhist books not
committed to writing till two or three hundred years
after the death of the Buddha, but also, for the reasons
given, it is impossible for any one to prove, that many
of them, at least, have not been greatly corrupted since
first they were written.

Neither, again, do we know that the original Buddhist Canon was co-extensive with the Canon of to-day.
Primitive lists of the books comprised in the Canon,—
such as have come down to us of the books of the Old
and New Testaments,—there are none whatever with the
Buddhists. Whole books, for aught any one can prove
to the contrary, may have been added since the first
alleged settling of the Northern Buddhist Canon at the
Council of Kanishka in the first century of our era.
To use the words of Dr. Eitel,—" No reliable information
exists as to the extent and character of the Buddhist
scriptures said to have been finally revised by that
council. The very earliest compilation of the modern
Buddhist Canon that history can point out is that of
Ceylon. But the Canon of Ceylon was handed down
orally from generation to generation. Part of it was
reduced to writing about 93 B.C. . . . The whole
Canon, however, was first compiled and fixed in writing
between the years 412 and 432 of our era." [1]

---

[1] *Three Lectures on Buddhism*, pp. 16, 17. On p. 25 he also shows
that the Chinese Buddhist Canon was not completed until 1410 A.D.

We are now prepared to sum up briefly this part of our argument. In the case of Christ we are able to trace up the stream of doctrine which He is said to have taught, and the narratives of His life, to the very lips of His contemporaries and companions. Renan has told us, and no one will accuse him of partiality, that the three synoptical Gospels are "composed of the tender remembrances and simple narratives of the first and second Christian generations, and proceed from that branch of the Christian family nearest to Jesus;" and that Mark's Gospel, in particular, "is full of minute observations, coming doubtless from an eye-witness;"[1] and that, in a word, the Gospels of Matthew, Mark, and Luke were written "in substantially their present form" by the men whose names they bear. To the same effect, as regards both these Gospels and many of the Epistles, is the most recent testimony of many of the most radical of anti-Christian critics.

The fact also stands out clear and indisputable that this testimony of the apostolic preachers to the general facts recorded in the Gospels which form the basis of Christian faith, was received as true by multitudes in the very generation and even among the very people among whom Jesus had lived, taught, and died; while, on the other hand, not a solitary voice of contemporary unbelief is heard even attempting to disprove that testimony. Such, then, are the records ; and, according to the common consent of intelligent critics, these

[1] *Life of Jesus,* pp. 12, 13, 21.

records have come down to us from the time of their first publication without a single corruption which could possibly affect anything in the least essential to the faith.

In contrast with all this, the Buddhist authorities are variously estimated as dating, in their written form, from a period—varying for different books—of from four hundred to a thousand years after the death of the Buddha; and even the antecedent oral traditions, which these writings embody, while no doubt containing not a little matter which may reasonably be attributed to the Buddha or his immediate disciples, are yet confessed by the Buddhists themselves to have become corrupted and divergent at an early day. And at last these traditions themselves disappear in a mist of distance wherein nothing can be discerned with distinctness, at a time still from one to two hundred years before, ascending the stream of history, we reach the age of the Buddha himself. As to the life of the Buddha, not a single contemporary voice has come down to us, whether of friend or enemy, which should directly and incontrovertibly assure us of a single fact. What we probably do know on the subject is only by way of inference from authorities, none of which can be proved to have lived when he lived.

The apologetic bearing of these facts will be abundantly evident when in subsequent chapters we come to compare the legend of the Buddha with the life of Christ as recorded for us in the Gospels. Meantime

it may not be amiss to call attention to the bearing of
these facts upon an objection which is sometimes heard
from those who have not thought much or deeply on
these questions.   It is sometimes asked, what good
reason we can show, why, if we receive all the extraordinary stories which are recorded in the Gospels of
the doings of Jesus, we can justly object to the miraculous element which is found in some of the Buddhist
authorities, which tell us of the doings of the Buddha ?
Or it is asked again, why, if, on the other hand, we
reject, as we do without hesitation, the extravagant
stories which are told of the Buddha, we should not
treat the miraculous element in the history of Christ
in the same way ?

To this much might be said in reply; but the
facts which have been reviewed in this chapter supply
an answer which is itself quite sufficient.   Were there
no other reason whatever, we should still be obliged to
reject the stories of miracle recorded of the Buddha,
simply because not a single one of these stories can be
shown to rest upon the testimony of an eye-witness, or
even of a contemporary of the Buddha.   But when we
have, on the contrary, as Renan assures us, a record—
as, e.g., in the case of Matthew's Gospel—proven to have
come in substantially its present form from a personal
companion and intimate friend of Jesus, then it should
be clear as light to any ordinary mind that the case is
totally different.   And thus, to argue that because one
rejects the stories of the miracles of the Buddha, he

should in consistency reject also the testimony of the apostles to the miracles of Jesus, is only to display one's ignorance and folly.[1] To ignore, therefore, as too many anti-Christian apologists for Buddhism have done, the transcendent contrast between the Gospel records ✗ and the Buddhist scriptures as regards this matter of historic evidence, however necessary it may be in order to give force to an argument, will not be justified by any who really love the truth.

[1] It is, of course, still conceivable that these contemporary witnesses might have been mistaken in some things ; but, when their probity of character and clearness of mind is once fairly established, to reject their testimony to the occurrence of certain events which they claim to have witnessed, because these, if they really occurred, would have been miraculous, is not the part of wisdom.   However often this may have been done, and that by men whom the world thinks wise, it is the mark of a conceit and folly which, if we did not so often see it, would itself be as incredible as any one could think a miracle to be. ✗ For such treatment of the testimony could only be justified on the supposition that a miracle was impossible ; but to prove that, even if it were true, would require that we should know perfectly, not only the world in all time and space, but also the infinite God Himself.   In other words, to prove the miracle impossible, it would be necessary ✗ that the reasoner should himself be omniscient ; which is but to say that in order to get rid of admitting the possibility of a direct inter-position of God in nature, it were necessary that man should himself be God.

CHAPTER III.

1. *The Life.*

AFTER what has been shown as to the character and value of our authorities for the life and the teachings of the Buddha, it will be plain that he who will endeavour to eliminate the truth from the mass of legend in which it is enveloped, will have no easy task. Hence in attempting to indicate what appear to be the chief facts of his life, one can at most only profess to give probable not certain truth. Absolute certainty here is unattainable, and is likely so to continue. Still, where all the various accounts of conflicting schools agree, and no motive is apparent for falsification, we may reasonably infer with some confidence that we have before us what is substantially historic truth. Constructing thus the story of the life of the Buddha, as best we can, we are apparently led to something like the following, as an approximation to the facts.

About five or six hundred years before Christ, in

an Àryan tribe called the Sàkyas, in a village called Kapilavastu, about one hundred miles north of Benares, was probably born Siddhartha, or Gautama, or Sàkya Muni, as he is variously called, who afterwards became known to fame as the Buddha, "the Enlightened One." His father, the Ràjà Suddhodana, was the ruler of the Sàkyas; one, no doubt, of the many petty ràjàs who to this day are so numerous in India. His mother, the Ràni Màyà, had reached her forty-fifth year child-less, when at last to the great joy of the queen and the Ràjà, a son was born to them, who was afterward to be known as the Buddha. Seven days after the birth his mother died, when his maternal aunt, Prajà-patni, herself the Ràjà's other wife, took the place of a foster-mother to the orphaned child, and brought him up to manhood. Of the childhood and youth of the Buddha the accounts which are given are so full of discrepancies and enormous exaggerations, that from them we can gather nothing that can be safely re-garded as historical. It is to be noted, however, that the Buddhist authorities agree in that none of them attribute to the Buddha acquaintance with the systems of Vedic learning in which the Brahman youth were educated, and in this they are probably right.

When next after the days of his infancy the figure of the Buddha seems to appear in something like historic light, we find him at twenty-nine married to his cousin, the beautiful Yasodhara, of whom, according to the unvarying tradition, he had one son, Ràhula.

About this time it was, according to all the traditions, that Gautama, profoundly impressed with the greatness and universality of human misery, determined to renounce home, wife, child, kingdom, and all, and give himself up to the work of solving, if possible, this mystery of sorrow, and discovering, if it might be, some way for its mitigation or removal. This momentous crisis in his life is described with great fulness of detail in the later Buddhist authorities, and has given the name of " The Great Renunciation " to a Chinese version of the life of Buddha.[1] Whatever, more or less, there may be of truth in the details of the experience which led to Gautama's adoption of the ascetic life, it were nothing strange or surprising that in a country like India, a thoughtful and earnest man, surrounded on every side with the most abject poverty, and often compelled to face the added terrors of famine and pestilence, should find the burden of the world's great sorrow an oppressive weight upon his heart, and feel sometimes ready to give up all in order to solve, if possible, for himself if not for others, this awful mystery. Never has India, indeed, been without a generation of men who, often no doubt from motives similar to those which are said to have moved Gautama, have like him gone forth to " the homeless life," in the quest for that *Nirvâna* which should bring

---

[1] This has been translated into English by Rev. Samuel Beal, Professor of Chinese in Oxford University, England, under the title of *The Romantic Legend*.

an end of pain. In its essential features, then, we need not hesitate to accept this story of "the great renunciation," as a true account of what did really happen.

Passing by for the time many matters which are evidently of later and legendary origin, we may next note that he is said to have gone first to one and then to another of the many Brahman teachers—Gurus, as the modern Hindoo would call them—from each in succession seeking in vain to learn the way that should lead to the cessation of pain. Failing in this he next gave up all teachers, and took up a life of the most ✗ merciless and long-continued penance, in the hope thus he might become possessed of the secret after which he sought. To such an extreme did he carry these self-mortifications that, we are told, through his bodily exhaustion and mental distress, he one day fell fainting, unconscious, to the ground, and was supposed to be dead. However he revived, and now gave up his penances, found to be as useless as the "way of knowledge" in which he had travelled with the Brahmans. At this point, we are told, his few disciples forsook him. For, they said, "This man has not been able even by these years of penance to obtain omniscience; how can he do it now, when he goes begging from village to village and takes material food? And . . . they went away."

Some time, sooner or later after this, came the last decisive struggle, in which, as he conceived, he solved the enigma of life, made an end of pain, and therewith obtained the power to point out that way to others. This great struggle, according to the Buddhist writers, is the central and grand epoch in not only the life of the Buddha, but even in the history of the world.   It occupies in Buddhist thought a place analogous to that which the crucifixion of Christ has in the faith of Christendom.   On the description of that final struggle of Gautama with the Spirit of Evil, the Buddhist writers have exhausted their powers of description, and have lavished all the resources of Oriental imaginations.   More of this, however, when we come to speak of the legend.   That some such struggle or crisis in his personal experience took place, it is not hard to believe.   It was then that, according to all the Buddhist writers, he discovered " The Four Noble Truths," which, expanded, form the system of doctrinal Buddhism. These truths, to which we shall have repeated occasion to refer, and shall explain more fully hereafter, are as follows, viz.—

(1) The Fact of Sorrow, as inseparable from Existence ; (2) the Cause of Sorrow—namely, " thirst" or " desire" ; (3) the Destruction of Sorrow, to be effected by the destruction of this thirst ; (4) the Way to this end—namely, " the Eightfold Holy Path that leads to the quieting of pain."

Having found, as he conceived, the true solution of the problem of life, the way to the extinction of pain, the Buddha now began with genuine missionary zeal

to preach the way to others.   Five months, we are
told, after the struggle and the great victory, his disciples now numbering sixty persons, he sent them
forth to preach his new doctrine.   He himself with
certain disciples went to Ràjagriha, where long before
he had gone at the first beginning of his pilgrimage.
There he preached at first to great crowds for two
months.   But we are told of no converts during this
time except two ascetics.   It was charged, and that with
good reason, as the earliest teachings of the Buddhist
authorities distinctly show,[1] that the way to *Nirvàna*
which he preached, involving, as it did, the extinguish-
ing of all natural desire, either of what was reckoned
good or evil, and the adoption of a celibate and mendicant life, would break up families, and, practically,
carried out would put an end to society.

This charge the Buddha seems to have met by
simply replying that what they thought so evil was in
truth the very best thing that could be.   Still a social
community outside the society of the mendicant disciples was an absolute necessity to the very existence
of the latter.   Beggars must have people to beg from.
And thus it appears to have become practically necessary, from almost the very first, to devise some plan which
should at once permit of the propagation of the new
religion, while yet allowing the existence of families and
business communities.   This need was met by the pro-
mulgation of a *secondary* system of observances, which

[1] See, *e.g.*, the *Sutta Nipàta, passim; S. B. E.*, vol. x. part 2.

might be kept while yet the man need not leave the life of the householder. Not by these observances, indeed, could *Nirvâna* be attained, but their observance would at least render this present life more tolerable, and conduce in the next life to the attainment of conditions of existence more favourable than the present to the securing of that longed-for blessing.[1] Beyond this, of the details of his long life from the third year after his " enlightenment," we are told nothing upon which there is reason here to dwell. At the age of eighty, from a sickness brought on, it is said, by eating of unsuitable food, he died.

And so ends the story, so far as we are able to disentangle probable facts from the myths and legends with which they are interwoven. That we have in all particulars rightly separated the true from the false, we cannot dare to hope. But that something like this fairly represents with a reasonable degree of probability the chief features of the Buddha's life, will doubtless be admitted by most who have studied the subject. It will no less freely be admitted by all competent students that the multitude of marvellous incidents and astounding miracles which burden the narrative in many of the Buddhist authorities, are supported by no evidence worthy of the least consideration. In the oldest *Pâli* texts, indeed, very few of these are

---

[1] This is brought out very clearly in a text to which we shall have frequent occasion to refer, the *Dhammika Sutta*, in the *Sutta Nipâta*, translated in the *Sacred Books of the East*, vol. x. part 2.

found. And it is in these alleged supernatural incidents that a large part of the asserted agreements of the story with that of Christ in the Gospels are found.

It may indeed be well just here to pause and compare the life of the Buddha as thus outlined with that of the Christ, even as admitted, *e.g.*, by rationalistic critics, such as M. Renan. Not only is there no coincidence which would impress any one, but, on the contrary, for the most part, a striking contrast. Christ was born in poverty; the Buddha, in riches, in the palace of a king. The Buddha is represented, even in the legend, as born *in* marriage; the Christ as born supernaturally of a pure virgin, *before* marriage. The Buddha is represented as having himself been in need of salvation, and for a long time ignorant how to gain it; the Christ, never. The Buddha died, according to all the authorities, a peaceful, natural death, in a ripe old age, and surrounded by sympathising friends. The Christ, first forsaken by His friends, dies in opening manhood a violent death upon the Cross. Agreements are of comparatively little account in the presence of such contrasts.

2. *The Legend.*

The legend of the Buddha varies, as might be expected, considerably in different authorities. As we should anticipate, of the different forms, the earlier are the more brief and less extravagant, and the later, more and more extended and adorned with manifold wonders.

It may be well to add that the number of the supposed agreements of the legend with the Gospel narrative is greater in the later than in the earlier versions. In giving the legend we shall follow no single authority, but give the outline of the story, dwelling on the more essential features, and in particular incorporating all those elements from any quarter in which some have thought they could discern suggestive agreements with the Gospel narrative.[1]   The story runs as follows :—

As in the case of Christ the Scriptures teach us to recognise a threefold state—namely, the pre-existent state, the state of earthly humiliation, and the state of exaltation, so the Buddhist writers distinguish three "epochs" in the life of the Buddha. These are re-spectively called, by the author of the *Nidàna Kathà*, the "Distant Epoch," the "Intermediate Epoch," and the "Proximate Epoch." The first of these three, or the *Distant Epoch*, is reckoned from the time that the pre-existent Buddha formed a resolution to become a Buddha, to the time of his birth into the so-called Tusita heaven, from which he is supposed to have descended to the earth to become a Buddha. This corresponds in a general way, though not precisely, to the pre-existent life of the Christ.[2]   The second or

[1] In the following statement of the legend I have depended upon the *Nidàna Kathà*, as given in *Buddhist Birth Stories;* the *Fo-pen-hing*, or Chinese version of the *Abhinishkramana Sùtra*, translated by Professor Beal, under the title, *The Romantic Legend;* and, finally, the *Lalita Vistàra*. The first named represents a *Pàli* text, the other two are Sanskrit authorities.   [2] *Vid. infra.* chap. v.

Intermediate Epoch is said to comprehend the time from his leaving the Tusita heaven, to the attainment of omniscience on the throne of knowledge under the Bo -tree, near Gayà. The *Proximate Epoch* is said to cover the time from the attainment of the Buddha-ship on the throne of knowledge until his attainment of the supreme *Nirvàna* in his death.

It will be seen that the contrasts here with the Christian doctrine of the three states of Christ are much more striking than the agreements. The " State of Humiliation " of our Lord only terminated with His death ; the second state of the Buddha is supposed to have terminated long before his death, when he attained the exalted powers of a Buddha under the Bo-tree. The " Exaltation " of our Lord began only with His rising from the dead on the third day, and continues now and for ever in His heavenly resurrection *life ;* the exaltation—if we may use the word—of Sàkya Muni, began on earth and also ended on earth with his *death.*

While the Scriptures give little information as to the life of the pre-existent Christ, the legend of the Buddha is very full as to his wonderful doings in the Remote Epoch.

We are introduced to the Buddha first when he was living at an inconceivably remote period in the city Amaravati as a rich Brahman, by name Sumedha. This Brahman, reflecting on the vanity and sorrow in-separable from life, determined to renounce his wealth

F

and become an ascetic that he might so attain that
state in which there is no rebirth.   Thus he is represented as saying :—

> " I made an excellent hermitage and built with care a leafy
> hut.
>
> .   .   .   .
>
> Then I threw off the cloak possessed of the nine faults,
> And put on the raiment of bark possessed of the twelve
> advantages.
> I left the hut crowded with the eight drawbacks,
> And went to the tree-foot possessed of ten advantages.
> Wholly did I reject the grain that is sown and planted,
> And partook of the constant fruits of the earth, possessed
> of many advantages.
> Then I strenuously strove, in sitting, in standing, and in
> walking,
> And within seven days attained the might of the Faculties."

It was at that time, we are told, that the Dipankara Buddha[1] appeared in the world, and as on one
occasion he was coming where the ascetic Sumedha
was staying, the Bodhisat,[2] in the depth of his devotion,
cast himself in the mire that Dipankara might walk
over him, as on a carpet.   And then we read—

> As he lay in the mire, again beholding the Buddha-majesty
> of Dipankara Buddha with his unblenching gaze, he thought as
> follows :—
>
> " If I wished I might this day destroy within me all human
> passions.

---

[1] According to the Buddhists, Gautama Buddha was by no means
the first, nor will be the last Buddha.   The succession of the Buddhas
is believed to be without beginning or end.

[2] One who is to become a Buddha.

But why should I in disguise arrive at the knowledge of
the Truth ?
I will attain omniscience and become a Buddha, and (save)
men and angels.
Why should I cross the ocean, resolute but alone ?
I will attain omniscience and enable men and angels to cross.
By this resolution of mine, I, a man of resolution,

.   .   .   .

Embarking in the ship of the Truth, I will carry across
with me men and angels."

This is the famous resolution of the Buddha, this
his giving himself for the salvation of men which is
so greatly extolled.   This it is which has even been
regarded as a parallel with the self-sacrifice of the Son
of God who gave Himself for our redemption, as the
One sent of the Father.   The future Buddha having
it in his power then and there, as he lay in the mire,
by the might of his piety to attain *Nirvâna*, "in that
utter passing away which leaves nothing whatever to
remain behind," he yet determined to postpone that
day, that, becoming at last an omniscient Buddha, he
might be the means of delivering others also from the
evil of existing.   But it was not a giving of self, like
that of the Son of God, to shame and humiliation, but
a giving unto self-exaltation and self-deification.

Then the legend tells us how, in order to attain
this end, the Bodhisat resolved to give himself throughout countless ages to the practice of "the Ten Perfections,"[1] as the necessary conditions of at last attaining

---

[1] The Ten *Pàramîtàs*.   These are enumerated as Almsgiving,

Buddhahood. Five hundred and thirty times, according
to the legend, in various forms, as man and god, bird
and beast, was the Buddha, after the Buddhist manner
of conception, born and born again.   In each of these
he fulfilled "the Ten Perfections" in the highest
degree.   Thus, as regards the Perfection of *Almsgiving*,
it is written :—

> "In the birth as the Wise Hare. . . .
> When I saw one coming for food, I offered my own self !
> There is no one like me in giving, such is my Perfection of
> Almsgiving."

So again we are told how in another birth he fulfilled
the Perfection of *Equanimity* :—

> "I lay me down in the cemetery, making a pillow of dead
> bones :
> The village children mocked and praised : to all I was
> indifferent."

Such in outline is the description which the Buddhist
writers give of the pre-existent state of the Buddha in
the *Remote Epoch*.

Then begins the second or *Intermediate Epoch*.   At
this time we are told that the future Buddha, having
achieved in many births all the great Perfections, was
dwelling under the name *Santusita* in the so-called
Tusita heaven.   Then all the gods and other exalted
beings of that celestial abode, perceiving now that the

Morality, Self-Abnegation, Wisdom, Exertion, Patience, Truth,
Resolution, Good-Will, Equanimity.   See *Buddhist Birth Stories*,
vol. i. pp. 18-25 ; also Hardy, *Manual of Buddhism*, pp. 103, 104.

time was fully come for the appearance on earth of another Buddha, came to him and said, " O Blessed One, when thou wast fulfilling the Ten Perfections, thou didst not do so from a desire for the glorious state of an archangel, . . . or of a mighty king upon earth ; thou wast fulfilling them with the hope of reaching Omniscience for the sake of the salvation of mankind. Now has the moment arrived, O Blessed One, for thy Buddhahood ; now has the time, O Blessed One, arrived!"

Then after duly considering the time and place and manner in which he should again be born, he decided to be born of the Queen Màyà, the royal consort of the King Suddhodana in Kapilavastu, near Benares. And the conception took place on this wise :—

The queen had been married to Ràjà Suddhodana many years, but they had never had a child, although she was now more than forty years of age. But on this occasion she fell asleep and dreamed a dream. She dreamed that the four archangels, the guardians of the world, lifted her up in her couch, carried her to the Himàlaya mountains, and placed her under the shade of the great Sàla tree, seven leagues in height. Then their queens came and bathed, anointed, and perfumed her, and carried her to a silver hill into a golden palace, in which they placed her on a celestial couch. Then she saw the future Buddha, who in the form of a white elephant was wandering near by, approach her, and holding in his silvery trunk a white lotus flower, thrice doing obeisance, he seemed to enter her right

side. And thus, we are told, was the Buddha conceived.[1] She told her royal husband the dream, who
summoned the Brahmans to explain the mystery.
They said unto him, " Fear not, O king! your queen
has conceived, and the fruit of her womb will be a
man-child ; . . . if he adopts the religious life, he will
become a Buddha, who will remove from the world the
veils of ignorance and sin."

This marvellous conception was accompanied by
the most stupendous prodigies. We are told that
" the constituent elements of the ten-thousand world-
systems trembled and were shaken violently." In
them all " an immeasurable light appeared. The blind
received their sight; the deaf heard the noise; the
dumb spake one with another; the crooked became
straight; the lame walked; all prisoners were freed
from their bonds and chains; in each hell the fire
was extinguished; hungry ghosts received food and
drink, etc. etc."

Throughout the whole time until the birth the
queen and unborn child were guarded by four angels
with drawn swords. As the time of the birth drew
near she begged permission of the king to go to the
town of her own people.[2] He consented, but as she

---

[1] The *Lalita Vistàra*, not content with this, gravely states that
he actually entered her side in the form of a six-tusked white elephant !
The reader will find the story in chap. vi., Ràjendralàl Mitra's
translation, Fasc. 2. p. 94.

[2] So the *Nidàna Kathà*. The *Lalita Vistàra* only mentions a request
to go to the grove *Lumbini*. *Op. cit.*, chap. vii.

was on the road, in a grove called Lumbini, the future Buddha was born. The circumstances of the birth are described in the Buddhist authorities with a variety of astounding physiological details, which may as well here be omitted. Showers of water came down from heaven refreshing the Bodhisat and his mother. Four kings received him at the hands of gods, and when he was placed upon the earth he at once began to walk, and at the seventh step " sent forth his noble voice, and shouted the shout of victory, beginning with ' I am the chief of the world.' "[1] At every step a lotus sprung up. On that same day also celestial choirs in the Tavatinsa heaven waved their robes and rejoiced, saying, " In Kapilavastu, to Suddhodana the king, a son is born, who, seated under the Bo-tree, will become a Buddha, and found a kingdom of righteousness.[2] And a venerable ascetic, Asita,[3] who, having eaten his mid-day meal, had gone to heaven to rest through the heat of the day, saw the heavenly hosts rejoicing, and, learning the cause, immediately hastened down to earth to see the new-born child. When he came into the presence of the child the mother tried to make the infant salute the old saint, but the child persisted in

[1] The *Lalita Vistàra* puts much more in the speech of the new-born child, but all in the same strain. See *Lalita Vistàra*, Ràjendralàl Mitra's translation, chap. vii., Fasc. 2. p. 125.

[2] An inadequate rendering of *Dhammacakkam pavattesati*, but it is hard to find a better. See Rhys Davids' *Buddhism*, p. 45.

[3] In the *Nidàna Kathà* he is called *Kàla Devala*. *Buddhist Birth Stories*, vol. i. p. 69.

presenting his feet instead of his head to the sage.[1] The old man then took the child in his arms, and when the king urged that the child should worship him, this he opposed, saying, " Say not so, O king, for, on the contrary, both I and gods and men should rather worship him." Thereupon he carefully examined the body of the child that he might see whether the three hundred and twenty-eight marks of a Supreme Buddha were upon him. Having found them, and with his wisdom perceiving that he would not himself be permitted to live until the child should have attained to Buddhahood, and only when a hundred thousand Buddhas should have come, could gain any good from them, he

" Began to weep like a broken water-vessel, and cried—
By grief and regret I am completely overpowered !
Not to meet him when he shall have attained supreme
     wisdom !

.   .   .   .   .   .

Alas, I am old, and stricken in years ;
My time of departure is close at hand.

.   .   .   .

What happiness from the birth of this child shall ensue !
The misery, the wretchedness of men shall disappear !
And at his bidding peace and joy shall everywhere flourish."

On the fifth day was observed the ceremony of choosing a name for the child, and casting the augury

[1] We are told that if they had persisted in putting the child's head to the feet of the ascetic, the head of Asita "would have split in two."

for his future life. At that time it was announced by
the Brahmans that after seeing four omens—namely, a
man worn out by age, a sick man, a dead body, and a
monk, Gautama would forsake the world to become a
Buddha.

From that time all possible pains were taken by
his father to keep him from seeing any of these things.
He had magnificent palaces made for him ; no sign or
suggestion of pain or sorrow was allowed to come near
him, lest he should grow weary of the world. For his
enjoyment were provided three wives and six myriads
of concubines, with whom he lived for many years
after the usual manner of Oriental princes. Many are
the wonderful stories which are told of his life up to
this point. When he was taken to a temple, all the
images of the gods bowed down to him.[1] He was
charged by his clansmen with having neglected learning
for a life of pleasure. A most learned pundit was
therefore appointed to examine and instruct him, but
the Bodhisat confounded him with his own immeasurably superior wisdom, which knew all without the aid
of books.

While he was living after this manner in the royal
palace, we are told of a certain neighbouring king, one
Bimbasàra, who became possessed with the fear that
some king might arise who should despoil him of his
kingdom. He sent messengers who were charged to

---

[1] *Lalita Vistàra,* chap. viii. This story is not given in the
Nidàna Kathà.

make diligent search that they might learn whether there were any one who might be able to overcome him. After a while they returned, having heard of the Bodhisat, and " exhorted Bimbasâra at once to raise an army and destroy the child, lest he should overturn the empire of the king." But this the king steadfastly refused to do. " For," he answered them, " if this youth is to become a holy *chakravarti* râjâ, and to wield a righteous sceptre, then it becomes us to reverence and obey him. . . . If he becomes a Buddha, his love and compassion leading him to deliver and to save all flesh, then we ought to listen to him, and become his disciples. So it is quite unnecessary to excite in myself any desire to destroy such a being."

Time passed on, and despite the countless precautions which the king had taken, one after another he saw the fatal four omens,—a sick man, an old man, and a corpse, and a monk who had renounced the world. This brought home to his heart powerfully the fact that all pleasure must come to an end, and that the end of all life, even the happiest, was weakness, decay, and death. Learning that woe was thus absolutely universal, the thought from that time filled his heart. Henceforth the pleasures of the harem had no power to please him, but only became utterly repulsive. Soon the determination was formed to give his whole life up to the effort to discover, if possible, the secret of this mystery of sorrow, and a way in which men might be delivered from it. To do this he formed the resolution of what the Buddhist writers extol in most unmeasured terms as "The Great Renunciation,"— namely, to give up the palace and the kingdom, even also his favourite wife and child, that he might discover for himself and for the world the way of salvation from pain and woe.

He rose by night, and, taking a last look at his sleeping wife and child, departed. As he left the city Mâra, the mighty prince of evil, appeared in the air and cried to him, "Depart not, O my lord! in seven days from now the wheel of empire will appear, and will make you sovereign over the four continents, and the two thousand adjacent isles. Stop, O my lord!" He unwaveringly resisted the temptation, but Mâra from that time never left him, watching for some new chance to seduce him from his purpose, till the final victory under the Bo-tree. From that time began the "Great Struggle," which was to issue in the attainment of omniscience and *Nirvâna*. Six years he spent studying and learning from one and another holy Brahman sage whatever they had to teach him as to the way to attain the end of pain, but all in vain. He fasted until wasted to a skeleton, and at last fell as if dead upon the ground! When he recovered consciousness "he perceived that penance was not the way to wisdom," and from that time ceased his fasting. At this his few disciples concluded that he had now failed in resolution, and nothing was further to be gained by following him, so they forsook him and went to Benares.

At last the great day of inward victory came. He approached the sacred Bo-tree, and there sat down where the other Buddhas had attained supreme wisdom. And then he made the firm resolve, " My skin, indeed, and nerves, and bones, may become arid, and the very blood in my body may dry up; but till I attain to complete insight, this seat I will not leave!" Then began Màra's last and terrible attack. The account of this is given with the greatest fulness in the various Buddhist books. The following condensed account of the Great Temptation is taken from a previous essay of the writer upon the legend of the Buddha.[1]

" When Màra saw that the Bodhisat had taken this resolution, he came into his presence riding on an elephant two thousand four hundred miles high, appearing as a monster with five hundred heads, one thousand red eyes, and five hundred flaming tongues ; he had also one thousand arms, in each of which 'was a weapon, no two of these weapons alike. With him also came an army of hideous demons, of every conceivable frightful form ; an army so large that it extended on every side one hundred and sixty-four miles, and nine miles upward, while its weight was sufficient to overpoise the earth.

" First, Màra sent against the Bodhisat a terrific wind, which tore up the largest mountains ; then a rain-

[1] In the *Bibliotheca Sacra*, July 1882.

storm, every drop the size of a palm tree; then a
shower of burning rocks and mountains; then a shower
of swords and spears and all manner of sharp weapons;
then a shower of burning charcoal; then another of
burning ashes; and then another of burning sand, and
another of burning filth; and then a fourfold darkness. But the wind moved him not; the rain only
refreshed him; the burning mountains became garlands
of flowers; the weapons a shower of blossoms; the
burning coals rubies; the fiery ashes fragrant sandal-
powder; the burning sand a shower of pearls; and the
darkness a resplendent light.

"Then came the whole army of Màra, with the arch-
fiend at their head; but their combined assault did
not [move him. Then Màra himself, in a form of
frightful terror, cried with an awful voice, ' Begone
from my throne.' But the Bodhisat trembled not.
' For,' said he, ' to gain this throne have I practised
the ten virtues through more than four grand cycles
of ages. How canst thou possess it, who hast never
accomplished a single virtue?' Then he recounted
the alms that he had given even in a single birth, and
called upon the earth to bear him witness; and the
earth responded with an awful roar, ' I am witness to
thee of that!' And her voice was so terrible that
Màra and his army fled away discomfited. Then the
three daughters of Màra came to their father, and, to
comfort him, told him that in another way they could
overcome the prince. And they transformed them-

selves into several beautiful maidens, and, going to the tree where the Bodhisat remained sitting, sought in every way to seduce him from his resolution. But they were as unsuccessful as the demon army."

The last conflict was ended. And now as evening fell and night began, came the long sought-for gift of saving knowledge. And then we read—

" He acquired in the first watch of the night the Knowledge of the Past, in the middle watch the Knowledge of the Present, and in the third watch the Knowledge of the Chain of Causation which leads to the Origin of Evil. And then, having now attained the goal, he sung the hymn of triumph sung by all the Buddhas—

" Long have I wandered ! long !
    Bound by the chain of life,
        Through many births :
    Seeking thus long, in vain,
    Whence comes this life in man, his consciousness, his pain !
        And hard to bear is birth,
    When pain and death but lead to birth again.
        Found ! It is found !
    O Cause of Individuality !¹
    No longer shalt thou make a house for me :
    Broken are all thy beams,
        Thy ridge-pole shattered !

¹ This phrase must by no means be interpreted as referring to God. In the Buddha's belief as to the cause of individuality God had no place ; his view was very different. See Professor Max Müller's remarks on this famous passage as found in the *Dhammapada*, pp. 153, 154; *S. B. E.*, vol. x. part 1, pp. 42-44, footnote. For other translations see Hardy's *Manual of Buddhism*, pp. 184, 185. That in the text is given, with a valuable note, by Mr. Rhys Davids in *Buddhist Birth Stories*, vol. i. pp. 103, 104.

Into *Nirvâna* now my mind has past :
The end of cravings has been reached at last !"

From this time on the legend is less full. We are told that he immediately began to preach, that his preaching was accompanied by many wonderful miracles, and attended everywhere by great success.

His disciples increased in number more and more. Among them were soon counted his father and wife and child. For forty-five years his ministry continued, and then as he was eighty, the time of his departure drew near. With this the legend again grows more full. The *Mahâparinibbâna Sutta* is wholly occupied with the details of the closing events and the last instructions of his life. It was in these last days that, according to this authority, a transfiguration of the Buddha took place. The account is given in these words :—

" The venerable Ânanda placed a pair of robes of cloth of gold, burnished and ready for wear, on the body of the Blessed One, and when it was so placed on the body of the Blessed One, it appeared to have lost its splendour. And the venerable Ânanda said to the Blessed One : ' How wonderful a thing it is, lord, and how marvellous, that the colour of the skin of the Blessed One should be so clear, so exceeding bright ! For when I placed even this pair of robes of burnished cloth of gold on the body of the Blessed One, lo ! it seemed as if it had lost its splendour !'"

The Buddha explained :—

" On the night, Ânanda, on which a *Tathâgata*[1] attains to the

---

[1] A title of the Buddha. For its meaning see chap. iv., pp. 107, 108.

supreme and perfect insight, and on the night in which he passes finally away in that utter passing away which leaves nothing whatever to remain, on these two occasions the colour of the skin of the *Tathâgata* becomes clear and exceeding bright." [1]

When he died, his body was arranged and placed on the funeral pyre, which, however, for seven days refused to burn, but then at last took fire of itself. When it had consumed the body, then streams from heaven quenched the flames, and it appeared that only the bones were left; there was neither soot nor ash of any kind. To these particulars the Chinese version adds another of something like a resurrection. Dr. Eitel gives the story as follows:—

" After his remains had been put in a golden coffin, which then grew so heavy that no one could move it, . . . suddenly his long deceased mother, Mâyâ, appeared from above, bewailing her lost son, when the coffin lifted itself up, the lid sprang open, and Sâkya Muni appeared with folded hands, saluting his mother." [2] We hear in some accounts of the Buddha also ascending into heaven and descending into the hells to proclaim the way which he had discovered. But these ascensions and descents are represented as having taken place *before* and not after death.

Here certainly is variation enough from the story of the life and work of Christ as we have it in the

---

[1] *Mahâparinibbâna Sutta*, iv. 47-50 ; *S. B. E.*, vol. xi. pp. 80, 81.

[2] *Three Lectures on Buddhism*, p. 13. Dr. Edkins (*Chinese Buddhism*, p. 57) gives a slightly variant tradition to the same effect.

New Testament. And yet one cannot but be impressed with the frequent occurrence of coincidences with the Gospel narrative, which are at least sufficiently striking to demand an explanation. What the true explanation may probably be, we have to inquire in the next chapter.

CHAPTER IV.

No writer has summed up the various alleged coincidences of the Buddha legend in its various forms with the story of the Gospels, in a more impressive manner than the Rev. Dr. Eitel, who uses the following language :—

"Sàkya Muni, we are told, came from heaven, was born of a virgin, welcomed by angels, received by an old saint who was endowed with prophetic vision, presented in a temple, baptized with water and afterwards baptized with fire. He astonished the most learned doctors by his understanding and his answers. He was led by the Spirit into the wilderness, and having been tempted by the devil, he went about preaching and doing wonders. The friend of publicans and sinners, he is transfigured on a mount, descends to hell, ascends up to heaven ! In short, with the single exception of Christ's crucifixion, almost every characteristic incident in Christ's life is also to be found narrated in the Buddhistic traditions of the life of Sàkya Muni, Gautama Buddha."[1]

All will agree that, so far as such coincidences really exist, they certainly demand an explanation. And when unbelievers in Christianity urge against the credibility of the Gospel narrative facts of this kind, and ask how they can be reconciled with its trustworthiness, we must admit that the question is perfectly fair, and one to which the Christian apologist may well direct his attention.

The possible hypotheses upon this subject seem to be the following :—

1. The coincidences may be merely *imaginary*.

2. They may be real, but purely *accidental*.

3. They may be due to *the operation of similar causes* under *similar conditions*.

4. The *Buddhist legend* may have *derived* certain elements from *Christian* sources.

5. On the contrary, certain things in the *Gospel* records may have been derived either from the *Buddha legend*, or from some other ancient source, the common origin of both stories.

6. Or, finally, the complete explanation of the agreements in the two records may be found in the combination of some or all of these hypotheses.

Of these various suppositions the last but one has become specially popular of late with certain people. Renan, in his *Life of Jesus*, suggested some time ago

[1] *Three Lectures on Buddhism*, p. 14.

the possibility of Buddhist influences in Palestine in the first century.[1] Not very long ago Mr. E. de Bunsen published a work to show how the coincident features in the two stories pointed to a derivation of such elements in the Gospel narrative through Essenism from a solar myth in a Buddhistic form.[2] More recently Professor Seydel has published an elaborate work, of which the object is to prove that certain elements in the Gospel story must be attributed to a Buddhistic source.[3] And this theory has apparently found its poet in Mr. Edwin Arnold, whose poem, the *Light of Asia*, suggests, if it does not directly teach, the same relation of the two stories. The larger part of Professor Seydel's book is occupied with a "Buddhist-Christian Gospel harmony," wherein the harmony (?) between the two stories of the Buddha and the Christ is set forth under no less than fifty-one particulars. Of these, however, it should be said that Professor Seydel can scarcely have intended to call this a "harmony" in any other than the strictest *technical* sense of the word; for, according to his own showing,

[1] *Op. cit.*, chap. vi.

[2] *The Angel-Messiah of Buddhists, Essenes, and Christians*, London, 1880. Commenting on this title, Professor Kuenen with good reason exclaims, "The Angel-Messiah of the Buddhists, who know nothing either of angels or of a Messiah; and of the Essenes, who certainly were much occupied with angels, but of whose Messianic expectations we know nothing, absolutely nothing! *National Religions and Universal Religions*, p. 250 (Hibbert Lectures for 1882).

[3] *Das Evangelium von Jesu in seinen Verhältnissen zu Buddha Sage und Buddha Lehre*, Leipzig, 1880.

in very many instances we have absolutely no agreement at all, but often the most marked, and to our mind most significant, contrast.

Professor Seydel distributes the analogies between the Buddhist and the Christian tradition into three classes, as follows :—

1. Such as may be explained by the operation of like causes, or by like sources of origin on both the Buddhist and the Christian side.

2. Such as exhibit such a special and unexpected agreement that the hypothesis of a dependence of the one story upon the other affords the most natural explanation.

3. Such as also indicate one side rather than the other as the real origin of the features in question.

Of the analogies falling under this third class he asserts that the facts all point to Buddhism, rather than Christianity, as the more probable original source of such elements in every instance. It deserves to be noted, however, that out of his fifty-one analogies he assigns *only five* to this third class, though he remarks with some reason that if the dependence of the Christian upon the Buddhist legend be proved for these *five* cases, then thereby a more or less close dependence of the Gospel upon the Buddha legend is rendered probable as the true explanation of many agreements in the analogies of his first and second class also.[1]

---

[1] *Op. cit.*, S. 296 *et seq.*

The five incidents which, in his opinion, decisively point to a derivation from the Buddha legend to the Gospel are the following [1]:—

1. The presentation of Jesus in the temple. The introduction of this incident in the Gospel of Luke, in his critical judgment, is unnatural, and without any sufficient motive or occasion apparent; whereas the presentation of the Buddha in the temple in the *Lalita Vistâra* is so unconstrained as to indicate it as the original, and the incident in Luke as a clumsily inserted copy of the former.

2. The forty days fast of Jesus, which, he affirms, stands in contradiction to His teaching afterwards, wherein He emphatically discouraged fasting; whereas the fasting of the Buddha is in perfect keeping with the beliefs and habits of the Indian ascetics.

3. The pre-existence of Jesus " before Abraham." This, however, he thinks, " can be connected also with elements of the Hellenistic philosophy, and through that only indirectly with Oriental influences."

4. A sacred fig-tree is mentioned in the case of the Buddha as the place of the first conversions to his religion, and of his entrance on his ministry; so also John mentions a fig-tree in connection with the conversion of Nathanael and other early disciples at the beginning of Christ's ministry. In the Gospel, however, in Professor Seydel's judgment, this mention " appears as an incomprehensible remnant of a foreign context."

[1] *Op. cit.*, S. 296 *et seq.*

5. The question, "Who did sin, this man or his parents?" (John ix.) in the case of the man born blind. This Professor Seydel compares [1] with a parable of the healing of a blind man in the *Saddharmapuṇḍarìka*,[2] wherein the physician is made to say of him, "Because of the sinful conduct of this man (in a former birth) is this malady arisen." This, he rightly remarks, is a most natural thing to have been said in India, where the doctrine of transmigration has existed from the most remote times; but the question in John's Gospel is utterly out of place among a people like the Jews, holding a religion which knew nothing of a pre-existence of the human soul. The conception could only have originated in the East; and, in his opinion, the application of the moral of the case to spiritual blindness (vss. 39, 41) points distinctly to the parable in the work cited as the original of at least that part of the story.

To these five cases which, in Professor Seydel's judgment, are the only coincidences which *decisively* point to a dependence of the Gospel upon the Buddha story, he adds one more consideration which, in his opinion, still further supports the theory of such a dependence—namely, that the more striking agreements in the two stories cease from the point where the legend of the *Lalita Vistàra* ends. For, he argues, had the Buddhist story borrowed from the

---

[1] *Op. cit.*, 232, § 82 *et seq.*

[2] *Saddharmapuṇḍarìka*, chap. v. ; *S. B. E.*, vol. xxi. pp. 129-133.

Christian, then we should have found the agreements all the way through the two stories ; were the opposite the truth, then this were not to be expected. The borrowing would then end, as he says, where the Buddha story ends in the *Lalita Vistâra*, with the entrance on the ministry.[1]

Such then, in brief, is Professor Seydel's presentation of the argument on which he bases his " Buddhist-Christian Harmony." It is of interest to observe that even he makes the cases of what he considers demonstrable dependence of the Gospel on the Buddha legend very few. Whether such dependence can be proved even in these instances, we shall shortly see. First let us rather address ourselves to the general consideration of the whole question raised as to a possible dependence of the Gospel upon the Buddha legend.

1. In the first place, we affirm that a *presumption* of the strongest character lies *against* any such supposed transference of the incidents from the Buddha legend to the Gospel history of the life of our Lord.

This presumption rests upon two facts. In the first place, it cannot be proved that before the composition of our Gospels, Buddhist legends and doctrines had obtained any such currency in Palestine as should make an interpolation of these into the Gospel story possible.

---

[1] The force of this consideration clearly depends altogether upon the question, Whether the above coincidences can be shown to be of such a sort as to prove dependence of the one story on the other ?

It is true that Professor Seydel and others have
laboured much and with ability to show the contrary,
but assuredly their argument falls far short of demonstration. Professor Kuenen, who will not be suspected
of any anxiety to make out a good case for Christian
orthodoxy, has certainly said the utmost for Professor
Seydel's argument that can be said, when he expresses
his judgment thus : " The *possibility* of the influence
of the Buddha legend (on the formation of our Gospels)
must be admitted or denied on strictly objective
grounds, and, in my opinion, Seydel has established
it."[1] As to the *actuality* of any such influence, he
says, however, after referring in another place to Professor Seydel, " I think that we may safely affirm that
we must abstain from assigning to Buddhism the
smallest direct influence on the *origin* of Christianity."[2]

The whole question of the evidence of any currency
of Buddhist ideas in the West at the time required,
has been very ably and conclusively argued by Professor J. Estlin Carpenter,[3] as also by Bishop Lightfoot.[4] We cannot do better than briefly refer to the
arguments of these two eminent scholars, whose competency to form an opinion will readily be granted.

[1] *National Religions and Universal Religions*, p. 360 (Hibbert
Lectures, 1882).

[2] *Ibid.*, p. 251.

[3] In *The Nineteenth Century*, December 1880, article " Buddhism
and the New Testament."

[4] In his *Commentary on the Epistles of Paul to the Colossians and
to Philemon*, Dissertation II, " On the Origin and Affinity of the
Essenes," pp. 390-396.

In the first place, according to the best historical evidence, Buddhism was confined to India till as late as 250 B.C., when, under the reign of Asoka, the Buddhists began their foreign mission work. Not until the first century of the Christian era, however, had the religion of the Buddha reached eastward so far as China; while, as regards the west, the Buddhist authorities themselves do not pretend that any of their missionaries ever undertook to convert the peoples on the shores of the Mediterranean. It is indeed true, as Hilgenfeld says, on the authority of Köppen, that Buddhist authority represents the Buddhist religion as flourishing in the middle of the second century before Christ in the city of Alasadda, the chief city of the land of Yavana. By Alasadda, according to Hilgenfeld, must be intended nothing else than Alexandria, at that time the chief city of the kingdom of Greece (Yavana). Bishop Lightfoot, however, has effectually disposed of this inference. He reminds . us that the term Yavana " was the common Indian name for the Græco-Bactrian kingdom and its dependencies," and that the Alexandria referred to may therefore quite as easily be the city of Alexandria *ad* Caucasum. The story, moreover, in the Buddhist *Mahdvaṇsa*, to which Hilgenfeld refers, is accompanied by such extravagant and manifestly untrue statements as manifestly deprive the writer of all credit, even if, indeed, writing so late as he did,[1] he could in any case be a competent witness.

[1] See *Mahàvaṇsa*, Turnour's translation, p. 171. The date of the

In particular is his statement absurd that on the occasion of which he is speaking no less than 30,000 priests from this Alasadda went together to India to attend the founding of the great tope at Ruanwelli in India! Who can believe that Buddhism, about 150 B.C., was so strong in Alexandria, in Egypt, as to send such a delegation of monks to India, and that yet not a hint of the existence of this Buddhist community should have come down to us from any of the Greek and Latin historians!

As for Jewish intercourse with India, no proof is given that so early as the Christian era the Jewish dispersion had penetrated that country. If individual Jews were there, which is conceivable, they must at least have been very few in number and had little intercourse with their western brethren, for in an ancient list of synagogues for foreign Jews in Jerusalem there is no mention of an Indian synagogue.[1] As for intercourse, political and commercial, within the time required by this theory, there is nothing to show that it was other than of the most irregular and occasional kind. Bishop Lightfoot argues this conclusively from the ignorance of Buddhism which marks all references to India by writers of the period under discussion. Some suppose that Strabo speaks of Buddhist priests under the term Sarmanae; but then he does

oldest part of the *Mahâvansa* is fixed between 459 and 477 A.D. See *Sacred Books of the East*, vol. x. pp. xiii. xvi.

[1] Grätz, *Geschichte der Juden*, iii. Bd. S. 282.

not profess to have this information from any one
later than Megasthenes, the ambassador of Alexander;
and, in the second place, it is not even certain that
under this name he refers to Buddhists at all. Professor Max Müller [1] and Professor Lassen [2] both express
the decided judgment that not Buddhist monks but
Brahmans are here intended by Strabo. The other
references given by Bishop Lightfoot are from writers
later than the Christian era. Even these show very
little knowledge of Buddhism, and until Clement of
Alexandria there is not an ancient author who mentions the Buddha by name. All this is plainly incompatible with the supposition that there was so much
intercourse between the West and the East, that the
Buddha story could be so widespread in Palestine in
the first century as the theory before us demands.

To the same effect is the *negative* testimony of the
Jewish pre-Christian literature. If Buddhist ideas
were so widely diffused among the Jews as this theory
of the Gospels supposes, it were almost impossible but
that there should also be some trace of this familiarity
with Buddhist ideas in other Jewish literature of the
age immediately before Christ. But in point of fact
there is in this literature no trace of the kind.

As for the Essenes, whose ·doctrines and practices
have been imagined by some to be due to the influence

---

[1] *The Parables of Buddhaghosha,* translated from the Burmese by
Captain T. Rogers, R.E., preface, p. lii.
[2] *Indische Alterthums Kunde,* ii. Bd. S. 700.

of Buddhism, the best authorities refuse to admit such a connection. It is true that the Essenes, like the Buddhists, were monastics. But monasticism has been a very widely spread phenomenon, and is found among peoples where Buddhism cannot be supposed to have had any influence; and, again, the common engagement of the Essene monastics in manual labour is in direct contrast with the Buddhist monasticism, which system forbade it and enjoined mendicancy. As for celibacy, abstinence from flesh, and carefulness of animal life, these practices have been quite too often found in religious systems which have not had the slightest historical connection, to permit any argument to be based in the present case upon such coincidences.[1] As his conclusion upon this branch of the subject, Bishop Lightfoot declares that instead of there being a genetic connection between Buddhism and Essenism, which might afford the desired basis for a theory of Buddhist influence on the Gospels, on the contrary, " with one doubtful exception—an Indian fanatic attached to an embassy sent by King Porus to Augustus, who astonished the Greeks and Romans by burning himself alive at Athens—there is apparently no notice in either heathen or Christian writers which points to the presence of a Buddhist within the limits of the Roman Empire till long after the Essenes had ceased to exist."

---

[1] On the actual genesis of these peculiarities of the Essenes, see Lucius, *Der Essenismus in seinem Verhältniss züm Judenthum*, cap. v. S. 75-100.

As for Mr. de Bunsen's elaborate argument, *per contra*, Professor Kuenen has summarily disposed of its claims to our regard in the following sharp words concerning his *Angel Messiah of Buddhists, Essenes, and Christians:* —"It is one unbroken commentary on Scaliger's thesis that errors in theology . . . all rise from neglect of philology. A writer who can allow himself to bring the name of Pharisee into connection with Persia has once for all forfeited his right to a voice in the matter." [1] In the same connection he says again, speaking in general of such attempts at deriving various elements in Christianity from Buddhism, " A single glance is enough to teach us that inventive fancy plays the chief part in them ;" [2] and yet again, reviewing the line of argument above given, he concludes that there is " a total absence of historical witnesses " to any such intercourse between India and Palestine in pre-Christian times as the theory assumes.[3] The Buddhist scholar, Mr. Rhys Davids, expresses himself in like manner, thus : " I can find no evidence whatever of any actual and direct communication of any of these ideas common to Buddhism and Christianity from the East to the West." [4]

In a word, then, there is no proof that either by the help of Essenism or in any other way did Buddhist ideas and legends so gain admission to Palestine by

[1] *National Religions and Universal Religions*, p. 250 (Hibbert Lectures, 1882).   [2] *Ibid.*, p. 248.   [3] *Ibid.*, p. 249.
[4] *Lectures on the Origin and Growth of Religion*, p. 151 (Hibbert Lectures, 1881).

the Christian era, as to make it even possible that the writers of the Gospels should have borrowed Buddhist stories and beliefs and attached them to the person of our Lord. It is true that this is merely negative argument. It is not an absolute demonstration that Buddhist legends had not reached Palestine by the time of Christ. It is, we will grant, still abstractly conceivable that Buddhist ideas should have found their way into Palestine by that time to such an extent as to make it in so far possible to explain the alleged coincidences between the Gospel and the Buddha legend by their influence. But we insist that, with the facts before us, this abstract possibility is at the same time in the last degree improbable. All the facts in evidence furnish a most solid and weighty presumption against this theory of a use by the evangelists of Buddhist myths to adorn the simple narrative of their Gospels.

But, as already said, there is yet another basis for the presumption against this theory. We have already shown that the Gospels of Matthew, Mark, and Luke especially, according to the admissions even of the ablest rationalistic critics, are proved to have come from the generation which was contemporaneous with Jesus. And this fact gives a foundation for a presumption of immovable weight against the supposition of any such borrowing as Seydel and others would have us to believe took place. For if such a corruption of the tradition of the life and deeds of Christ occurred at all, it is plain that this could not have been until after the generation contemporary with Christ had quite passed away.   Indeed, we might even say that two or three generations would need to pass before the Buddha element could be incorporated into the Gospel story with any chance of securing its acceptance as part of the original history.   For such a personality as that of Christ could not have been readily forgotten.   It would thus have been exceedingly hard—or' rather, we should say, impossible—to persuade people who, if they had not themselves seen Jesus, had friends and relatives who had known Him, that any of these old Buddha stories really belonged to Him.   An attempt to introduce the Buddhist element into the Gospel story earlier than a hundred years or more after the death of Christ would, we may be certain, have met with utter failure.

But here we are confronted with the fact that the ablest critics of all schools agree in assigning the synoptic Gospels—the very Gospels, by the way, in which the most of the alleged Buddhist corruptions are to be found—to the first century of our era, a period throughout which those were yet living who had personally known Jesus of Nazareth.   For, as we have already seen, there is now general agreement among the critics in assigning the composition of the Gospels of Matthew, Mark, and Luke to dates variously taken between 57 and 100 A.D.[1]   If, then, ever the

---

[1] See chap. ii. pp. 29, 30.

Buddha legends became incorporated with the Gospel story, this must needs have taken place between the years 57 and 100. How was this possible? and that with the apostle John—not to speak of other less known contemporaries of Jesus—living throughout this whole period? And again, if possible, what conceivable *motive* can be named for such a corruption of the Gospel story? How does it come to pass that with so many living who must have been able to testify of personal knowledge to the falsity of these Buddha stories as applied to Christ, *not one* of all the millions of the bitter opponents of the Gospel ever seems to have charged the Christians with the telling fact—*if* a fact—of this gross corruption of their most fundamental authorities? How doubly strange thereby becomes, moreover, the admitted fact of the amazing progress which the Gospel made within that period, winning the hearty faith of millions!

Nor have we even yet stated the case at the strongest. For we have also to remember that the same criticism which has thus fixed the *date* of the Gospels, has also with like decisiveness declared that we must attribute their *composition* to the very men whose names they bear. We must then remember that not only were these Gospels produced in the generation in which Jesus lived, and in the land in which He did His work, but that two at least of their authors were men who were personally intimate

II

with Jesus. Luke describes himself as one who had
"traced the course of all things" which he narrates
"accurately from the first" to the ascension into
heaven.[1] Matthew, we know, was one of the twelve
apostles chosen to special intimacy with Jesus during
that three years' ministry of grace and wonder-working
power.

If we should yet conceive that such an interpolation of Buddhist elements into the Gospel story had
been possible to others of that day, yet how could
Matthew and Luke have done this? How is it conceivable that Matthew, for example, should have introduced these Buddha legends into his Gospel? If he
did this at all, he must have done it either consciously
and therefore dishonestly, or unconsciously and ignorantly. If we suppose the former alternative, then
what motive can be ascribed for such falsehood? Was
it to gain merit by exalting his Master to the utmost
by imputing to Him also many of the Buddha wonders?
But, according to his own statement, his Master ever
held up the terrors of eternal pain against all false
dealing. Could he have imagined that thus he could
glorify his Lord the more by thus making Him the
equal of the Buddha? That certainly is quite impossible, for, as Professor Kuenen has well pointed out, the
wonders ascribed in the *Lalita Vistàra* to the Buddha
far transcend the versions of those wonders as they are
supposed to have been transferred by the evangelists

[1] Luke i. 1-3 (R. V.)

into their story.[1]   This supposition of *conscious fraud*
is thus utterly untenable.

If, then, Matthew, for example, introduced Buddhist
elements into his gospel, he must have done it *ignorantly*
and *unconsciously*.   But is not this still more impossible ?   For how could any of the apostles ever have
succeeded in persuading themselves that these anti-
quated Buddha legends — which by the hypothesis
must have already been floating about Palestine for
some time before Christ—really represented incidents
in the life of one that they had known so well ?   And
even if *one* could be so absurdly deceived, how hard to
believe that *all* should have been victims of the same
extraordinary self-deception !

It will be said perhaps by some, however, that the
most of these alleged coincidences are found in the
period before the public ministry of Christ began, and
cluster around His birth and early years, before the
apostles had been taken into that personal fellowship
which was to qualify them as eye-witnesses to tell the
story of Christ.   But to this the answer is plain.   For,
in the first place, all the evangelists agree in representing the mother of Jesus as intimately associated with
her Son and His disciples throughout His public ministry.   Whether the apostles knew anything by *personal*
acquaintance of the early life of our Lord, they had
accessible the very best authority as to the actual facts,

---

[1] *National Religions and Universal Religions*, p. 361 (Hibbert
Lectures, 1882).

in the person of the mother of Jesus. Not only is this true, but *one* of the apostles, we are told, was "the brother of the Lord," and must therefore have had a personal knowledge of the facts as to the early life only less than His mother. That Buddhist legends should have been imagined to refer to Christ by members of a circle of which the mother and a brother of Jesus were members, is utterly incredible. We must therefore conclude that the supposition that the apostles should have either consciously or unconsciously interpolated the alleged incidents into the life of our Lord, is an utterly untenable hypothesis. We may add, moreover, that to have succeeded in persuading thousands of people equally well acquainted with the real facts to accept their story of Christ as true, as we know that they did, if it were not true, is if possible more incredible still.

The only resource left to those who argue for this so extraordinary theory, is to assume that in these supposed coincident elements we have the corruptions of a later day. But, as we have already remarked, for reasons already mentioned such corruption cannot be supposed possible before the latter half of the second century, and of such extensive interpolation in that period there is not the slightest proof. The evidence is all the other way. Had any one desired to improve upon the simplicity of the original story by the addition of the Buddha wonders, there were already by that time so many antagonistic parties calling themselves by the Christian name that such a corruption of all the numerous copies of the Gospels then existing, was utterly impossible. All the existing evidence, moreover, from quotations by the early fathers, and the most ancient versions, tells decisively against the supposition of a Buddhist corruption of the Gospels in this period.

We are then abundantly justified in affirming that the latest and most accurate results of the historical criticism of the Gospels are such as to establish a presumption against this new theory of the Buddhist origin of certain portions of them, which is nothing less than overwhelming. To *ignore* these ascertained facts concerning the date and authorship of the Gospels in considering the claim of this Buddhist theory or of any other, is the part, not of a truly scientific spirit, but the exact reverse. Even though, while denying a theory of borrowing of Buddhist elements, which is utterly irreconcilable with ascertained facts, we should have to confess that in our present state of knowledge we had no explanation to offer of the alleged coincidences between the two stories; yet with this frank confession, still to retain our faith in the trustworthiness of the Gospels, were far more scientific than in the presence of the above-mentioned facts to affirm the probable origin of much in the Gospel history from Buddhism. Every one knows that, in many instances, while we are not able to say what the explanation of a given fact really *is*, we are none the

less able to affirm with the most absolute confidence
what that explanation *cannot* be.

But the argument against the supposed borrowing
is yet stronger, that no man lives who is able to show
that the legend of the Buddha, in a form containing
any coincidence which could be held to argue such a
borrowing, was in existence before the Christian era.
It is clear that before this can be proved, the date of
all the Buddhist authorities which contain any part of
the legend must be finally settled by the application
of the same minute and exact criticism which has
settled the question with regard to the synoptic Gospels.
This work is not yet nearly done.   Meantime, however, Professor Oldenberg asserts that " no biography
of the Buddha out of the period of the ancient sacred
Pàli texts has come down to us, and," he adds, " we
can say with confidence that there has never been
any." [1]   He tells us, moreover, that not only do those
texts not contain any account of the " Four Omens "
and other particulars by which the later legend pre-
pares the way for the flight of the Buddha, but they
do not even mention Màra, the tempter, in their
account of the attainment of the Buddhahood. [2]

But, again, if it ever should be proved that any
authority containing the legend was of pre-Christian
origin, it would then be further necessary, by the same

[1] *Buddha, sein Leben, seine Lehre, seine Gemeinde,* S. 80 ; see also
foot-note 1.

[2] *Ibid.,* S. 105, 80.   For the oldest version of the departure of the
Buddha from his home, the "Great Renunciation," see *Ibid.,* S. 107, 108.

critical process, to show that the part of such version
of the legend which contained any given coincidence,
was as old as the rest of the text of which it formed a
part, and not perchance an interpolation of a later
time. Not only are such questions as these not all
settled, but the peculiar difficulties are such that—as
we shall see—it is doubtful if they ever will be. That
ever any such certainty will be attained with regard to
the Buddhist scriptures as we have respecting the
New Testament books, one cannot dare to hope. How
far we are from any such satisfactory results as regards
the Buddhist authorities for the legend will be plain
from the facts which have already been fully given in
Chapter II. It is certain that all the various versions
of the legend into Chinese, Thibetan, Siamese, and
Burmese, date from a time later than the Christian
era. Of the *Pàli* authorities the oldest texts do not
contain the legend of the incarnation, early life, and
struggle with Màra. The chief Sanskrit authority, the
Lalita Vistàra, as we have already shown, cannot be
proved, in the judgment of the most competent critics,
to have existed in its present form nearly as far back
as the Christian era.[1]

So then stands the case to-day; but more yet is to
be added. For if it should in any case be proved that
a given authority contained a coincidence of such a
kind as to compel us to believe that there had been a
borrowing on one side or the other, and also that this

[1] *Vid. sup.*, pp. 40, 41.

authority was certainly older than the Christian era; it would still remain to be proved, before a case could be made out against the Gospels, that the portion of the ancient authority which contained the supposed coincidence belonged to the original document, and was not perchance an interpolation of a much later date.   We may then affirm with the greatest confidence that there is no man living who knows enough to be able to affirm that between the Buddha legend and the Gospel story there is a single feature of agreement such as could possibly become a ground of charge against the integrity and strict historical character of the Gospels, which can be proved to have formed a part of the legend before the Gospels were written.

If asked then what explanation we are to give of the coincidences which cause some so much concern, we can best answer in the words of Professor Beal, who, in the preface to his translation of the Chinese version of the *Abhinishkramana Sutra*, before referred to, says that " in the present state of our knowledge there is no complete explanation to offer.   We must wait till dates are certainly and finally fixed." [1]   Still we believe that it is possible even now to give an explanation of many features of agreement between the two stories, which, if not complete, shall yet be quite sufficient and satisfactory; and also to indicate the elements which will doubtless enter into the final and complete explanation, should such an explanation ever be reached.

[1] *Romantic Legend*, preface, p. ix.

Before entering into a detailed examination of the alleged coincidences between the Buddha story and the Gospels, we may well pause to emphasise the sound principle laid down by Professor Kuenen in his brief critique of Professor Seydel's Buddhist-Christian Harmony. He says, "We must never forget that the derivation of this or that detail from a foreign *Sagen-kreis*—acquaintance with which is not proved already, but is the very thing to be proved—can only be allowed when it is clearly shown that the circle of ideas in which the writer unquestionably moved does not itself offer anything, or at least does not offer enough, to explain the details in question."[1] No remark could be more just than this. It is but to say that when a cause for a given phenomenon can be found immediately at hand, it is unphilosophical to postulate a cause more remote. The application of this principle at once disposes of one of the most plausible of Professor Seydel's five clear coincidences. It will be remembered that in John ix. the disciples asked Jesus concerning the man that was born blind, "Who did sin, this man or his parents, that he was born blind?" According to Seydel, as the doctrine of the pre-existence of souls was at that time unknown among the Jews, the thought here introduced into the Gospel must have come from a foreign, Oriental source. But, according to Meyer, one has no need to go outside the sphere of Jewish thought for an explanation of this

[1] *National Religions and Universal Religions*, p. 361.

part of the disciples' question. For, although the common people cannot be supposed to have been acquainted with the doctrine of the pre-existence of souls, yet it ✱ was a belief of the time that an unborn child could experience emotions, especially evil ones, and it is to this supposition of a possible sin of the unborn child in the womb that the question of the disciples alludes.[1] There is, therefore, no need to go to India for the explanation of the words.

1. Proceeding now to a more particular examination of the alleged agreements between the Buddha legend and the story of the Gospel, we have to remark, in the first place, that a considerable number of those which have been urged appear on a closer examination to be wholly *imaginary*. In many cases while there may be a nominal and apparent agreement, yet the contrasts so greatly outweigh coincidence in one or two features as to deprive the latter of all possible significance.

As one of these wholly imaginary agreements we may name the application of the title *Tathàgata* to the Buddha, which, according to Mr. de Bunsen, is to be regarded as the equivalent of the common appellation

[1] See Meyer, *Critical and Exegetical Handbook to the Gospel of John, loc. cit.* In illustration of this Jewish belief of the time he refers to Luke i. 41; and *Sanhedr.* f. 91. *Beresh. Rabba*, f. 38, 1, b. To this explanation Professor Kuenen seems to incline, though suggesting as another possible explanation (rejected by Meyer) "the Judæo-Alexandrine' doctrine of pre-existence" (*Sap. Sol.*, viii. 20), as also rendering the Buddhistic derivation of this thought "quite superfluous." See *National Religions and Universal Religions*, p. 362 (Hibbert Lectures, 1882).

by which the expected Messiah was designated by the
Jews *habbà*, or "the coming one."[1]   How Mr. de
Bunsen could have fallen into such a mistake as this
we are at a loss to conceive. The supposed agreement has no existence except in his imagination. The
word is compounded of the Sanskrit *tathà*, "so," and
either *gata*, past participle of the root *gam*, "to go," or
else the compound form *àgata*, "come." In the former
case *tathàgata* means, literally, "thus gone;" in the
latter, "thus come." In neither case is it possible to
get out of the word the sense of "the coming one."
For such an interpretation there is no authority. How
competent authorities do interpret *tathàgata*, will be
clear from the following definitions given by specialists
representing various departments of Buddhist scholarship. The Thibetan scholar Csoma, according to
Burnouf, tells us, "Tathàgata signifies the one who has
gone through his career in the same manner as his
predecessors." In the opinion of Burnouf, this is "the
original and most authentic definition." Another
definition—or rather interpretation—which he gives, is
as follows : "departed thus"—that is to say, "departed
in such a way that he will no more reappear in the
world." According to him the southern Buddhists
derive the word from *àgata* instead of *gata*, and therefore make *tathàgata* signify, "He who is come in the
same manner as the other Buddhas, his predecessors."[2]

---

[1] *The Angel Messiah of Buddhists, Essenes, and Christians*, p. 18.
[2] *Histoire du Buddhisme Indien*, pp. 75, 76.

According to the Chinese scholar, Dr. Edkins, the word means "thus come." He says, "It is explained, ' bringing human nature as it truly is, with perfect knowledge and high intelligence, he comes and mani- fests himself.'"[1] The Burmese scholar, Bishop Bigan- det, makes the word mean, "He who has come like all his predecessors. The Buddhas who appear . . . have all the same mission to accomplish; they are gifted with the same perfect science, and are filled with similar feelings of compassion for and benevolence toward all beings. Hence the denomination which is given to Gotama, the last of them."[2] The *Páli* scholar, Mr. Rhys Davids, translating the word "gone" or "come in like manner," says it means "subject to the fate of men;" that it was originally applied to all men, but was "afterwards used as a favourite epithet of Gautama."[3] In the more recent translation by Professor Oldenberg and Mr. Rhys Davids of the *Mahavagga*, the word is made to mean "he who has arrived there, *i.e.*, at emancipation."[4] Among all these various inter- pretations, whichever be correct, there is not one which warrants any one in connecting this word *tathâgata* with "the coming one" as the Jewish title of the Messiah.

---

[1] *Chinese Buddhism,* p. 6, note 2.

[2] *The Legend of Gaudama,* p. 15.

[3] Fausböll's *Buddhist Birth Stories,* vol. i. p. 71, note 2.

[4] *Sacred Books of the East,* vol. xiii. pp. 82, 83, note. We may also add the following explanation from the *Atthakathâ* (Commentary) to the *Dîgha Nikâya* which includes some of the explanations given in the text and adds others: "Bhagawâ (the Buddha) is *Tathâ-*

More plausible are the coincidence which have long
been urged between the legend of the incarnation of
the Buddha and the story of the incarnation of our
Saviour; but these also must be set down as agreements which are only superficial and apparent. The
points of agreement are that both in the case of the
Buddha and that of our Lord, we are taught that a
pre-existent being was born into this world as a man ;
that in both cases this birth was a voluntary act ; that
each came into the world out of love to man. Here
are indeed individual points of agreement which are of
great interest, and it is quite possible that for the
explanation of them we may have to seek further than
under the present head. And yet it must be maintained that the agreement is by no means so close
as, from the bare statement of these facts, might be
imagined ; and that, moreover, the contrasts are so
momentous that when we look at the two incarnations,

gata from eight circumstances. He who had come in the same
manner (as the other Buddhas) is *Tathâgata;* he who has gone in
like manner is *Tathâgata ;* he who appeared in the same glorious form
is *Tathâgata ;* he who in like manner acquired the perfect knowledge
of and revealed the *Dhammas* is *Tathâgata ;* he who in like manner
saw, or was inspired, is *Tathâgata ;* as he was similarly gifted in
works he is *Tathâgata ;* from his having converted the universe to
the recognition of his religion he is *Tathâgata."* Quoted by Turnour
in the Introduction to his *Mahâvansa,* p. lvi. I give the word "inspired" above, as Turnour ; but the original, *tathâ dassitâya,* suggests
no such idea as *inspiration* in *the Christian* understanding of that
word. Yet other interpretations of this notable word will be found
in Râjendralâl Mitra's *Translation of the Lalita Vistâra,* Fasc. 1,
chap. i., pp. 19, 20.

as a whole, in their real asserted character, and with
all their attendant circumstances, we can no longer
regard the two stories of incarnation as so coincident
that we must suppose either a common origin, or a
derivation of one from the other. The contrasts immeasurably outweigh the agreements.[1]

In the first place, there is a total contrast as to the
nature of the pre-existence taught in either case. While
in the case of Jesus His pre-existence is represented as
a fact unique and peculiar; the Buddha, in that he
pre-existed, only shared the common lot of all. Two
theories seem to prevail among the Buddhists as to
the nature of the existence of men before and after
this present life. According to the older and more
orthodox opinion, there is no such thing as soul in any
man separate from the body. That therefore which
exists after death or before birth, cannot be a soul. It
is conceived of as a pre-existence of a certain line of
karma or moral action, continuous through successive
existences. Deferring discussion of this perplexing
theory to another chapter,[2] it is plain that if the
Buddha be understood as pre-existing in no other
sense than this, then between his pre-existence and
that which Christ claimed for Himself there is absolutely
nothing in common.

---

[1] To feel the force of this, let any one read first Luke i., and then
any one of the accounts of the incarnation of the Buddha, as, *e.g.*,
Lalita Vistàra, chaps. vi. and vii., or in the *Nidàna Kathà*, as translated
in Fausböll's *Buddhist Birth Stories*, vol. i. pp. 58-68.

[2] See chap. v.

But this view of the case seems to have been too metaphysical for many of the Buddhists, especially in the North, where at least the common people, if we are correctly informed, believe that the soul of the Buddha pre-existed, as also, in their opinion has pre-existed the soul of every man and of every living thing. But even if this view be taken of the Buddha's pre-existence, there is still no analogy with the pre-existence of Christ. For Christ taught that He had pre-existed in a state of eternal and uninterrupted glory and communion with God the Father, with whom He declared Himself to be one.[1] That blessed fellowship with the Father He left for the first time, when He came into this world to be born as a man.

As contrasted with this, the Buddha is said to have taught that not only once, but again and again, he had come into the world, laboriously fulfilling in successive births those " Ten Perfections " of character which should at last fit him for the high rank of Buddha-hood.[2] Nor had his appearances been in this world only, but in the various heavens as well. Nor had he always existed in a condition of honour and glory. On the contrary, he had lived alike in forms of the highest honour and also of extreme degradation. Eighty-three times he had been an ascetic, fifty-eight times a king, twenty-four times a Brahman, twenty

---

[1] See John xvii., and New Testament, *passim.*
[2] *Nidâna Kathâ*, in Fausböll's *Buddhist Birth Stories*, vol. i. pp. 1-62.

times the god Sakka, forty-three times a tree-god, five
times a slave, once a devil-dancer, twice a rat, and
twice a pig![1] On this view of the nature of the
Buddha's pre-existence then, as truly as on the other,
there is absolutely no analogy with the existence of
our Lord before His incarnation, but the most complete
contrast. Surely learned men who think they can
discover an analogy between the doctrine of the pre-
existence of the Buddha and that of the Christ, must
have very hazy conceptions of Christian doctrine.[2]

But much is made by some of the virginal birth
which is claimed in either case. Mr. de Bunsen has
even been so bold as to head one of the sections of his
Angel Messiah, " Conceived of the Holy Ghost, born of
the Virgin Màyà ;" and Professor Seydel heads the third
section of his *Harmony*, " Conceived by the Holy
Ghost,"[3] though, as regards a Holy Spirit, we find
nothing in this section so far as relates to the birth of the
Buddha.[4] Is there really coincidence here ? We are by
no means concerned to deny it. Should it appear that
before the time of our Lord the Buddha legend repre-

---

[1] Hardy, *Manual of Buddhism,* 2d ed., p. 102 ; and, with some
variations in the numbers, in Fausböll's *Buddhist Birth Stories*, vol. i.
p. ci. It is indeed said that there are limits to the variety of the
births possible to a Bodhisat. He can never be born as a serpent, or
as any kind of vermin, or as a woman—in a word, in no form lower
than a snipe ! *Pùjawaliya Saddharmmaratnakàrc*, quoted by Hardy,
Manual of Buddhism, 2d ed., p. 108.

[2] See *Romantic Legend*, preface, p. viii.

[3] *Angel Messiah of Buddhists, Essenes, and Christians*, p. 33.

[4] *Das Evangelium von Jesu, u.s.w.*, S. 110.

sented him as having been born of a virgin, this could by no means, in the presence of facts above indicated, lead to the conclusion that in this the Christian story must be indebted to Buddhism any more than to any other similar myth concerning other ancient heroes, which represent them as the sons of virgins.

But those forms of the Buddha legend which have been made accessible do not as yet seem to give warrant for the assertion that the Buddha was made to be the son of a virgin. The earliest reference to the virginity of Màyà, his mother, that we have been able to find, is in the works of Jerome,[1] in which that father says that it was a belief of the gymnosophists that the Buddha was born of a virgin. In our own time, Bishop Bigandet of Burmah says, " The conception of Phra-laong (Buddha) in his mother's womb is wrapped up in a mysterious obscurity—appearing, as it does, to exclude the idea of conjugal intercourse. The Cochin Chinese in their religious legends pretend that Buddha was conceived and born from Màyà in a wonderful manner, not at all resembling what takes place in the order of nature." [2]   But the bishop gives no definite authority for this statement. The Thibetan scholar, Csoma, according to Mr. Hardy, speaks of the Mongolian accounts as laying much stress on the virginity of Màyà, but says that the Thibetan books make no mention of it.[3]   According to Mr. Davids, however,

---

[1] *Cont. Jovian*, lib. i.   [2] *Legend of Gaudama*, vol. i. p. 27, note 17.
[3] *Manual of Buddhism*, 2d ed. p. 145, note.

this reference of Csoma's to the Mongolian tradition of the virginal birth "has not been confirmed."[1]   Dr. Edkins, in his *Chinese Buddhism*, is silent as to any such belief among the Chinese.

On the other hand, in many forms of the tradition, statements are made which preclude a belief in the virginity of the mother of the Buddha.   It is said that she was not merely the betrothed, but the actual wife of King Suddhodana, and that she had lived with him childless till her forty-fifth year.[2]   The *Abhinishkramana Sùtra*, according to the Chinese version, states repeatedly, not only that Queen Màyà was married, but that she had lived with her husband after the ordinary manner.[3]   Thirty-two signs are enumerated which should distinguish the mother of a Buddha, among which it is mentioned that "she must be a woman obedient to her husband"—therefore a married woman —but that "she must not have borne a child before."[4] Under the heading, "Conceived by the Holy Ghost, born of the Virgin Màyà," Mr. de Bunsen says that,

[1] *Buddhism*, p. 183, note 1.

[2] So Mr. Rhys Davids, in *Buddhism*, p. 26.   He does not give the authority for this statement.   In the (late) *Lalita Vistàra* it is said that the mother of a Buddha must be "endowed with beauty and youth."   Ràjendralàl Mitra's Translation of *The Lalita Vistàra*, Fasc. 1, chap. iii. p. 43.

[3] *Romantic Legend*, pp. 36, 37, 41.   See also, to the same effect, the *Lalita Vistàrà*, as above, chap. v. p. 77.

[4] *Romantic Legend*, p. 32.   The *Lalita Vistàra* makes the ninth mark to be "childlessness"; the thirty-first, that she be "a woman faithful to her marriage vows;"   *Op. cit.*, chap. iii. p. 42.

according to the Chinese Buddhistic authorities, "it was the Holy Ghost, or Shing-shin, which descended upon the Virgin Mâyâ."[1] Unfortunately, however, he does not give his authority for this statement. But if such a doctrine be indeed found in any Chinese authority, two things are certain which make the fact—if a fact—of little concern to the Christian apologist. In the first place, the doctrine could not have come from the original Buddhism, for as that repudiates the existence of spirit, there is plainly no room in it for such an idea as a conception by a holy spirit. Such an idea, if it occur, must be of Chinese origin. And, in the second place, as Buddhism did not reach China till about 70 A.D., it is thus impossible that the Gospel should have borrowed the idea of the miraculous conception from Chinese Buddhism, though the reverse is by no means inconceivable.

In fine, so much as this seems clear with regard to this obscure and somewhat disputed subject. If any such doctrine as the birth of the future Buddha from a pure virgin be held anywhere in Buddhist countries, it is certain that it is far from being universal, and is in the highest degree contrasted with the teaching of the Christian Gospel as to the virginity of Mary, which holds no such subordinate and incidental place, but lies at the foundation of the whole conception of Christ's person and work as given in the New Testament. We may add that there is not a particle of proof in any

[1] *Angel Messiah of Buddhists, Essenes, and Christians,* p. 33.

case that any such belief in the virginity of Queen Màyà dates back to nearly the Christian era. That the Gospel should here have borrowed from the Buddha story is therefore not to be thought of, however it may be as to a possible borrowing on the other side.[1]

But not only may we safely say that the Buddhist accounts of the incarnation of the Buddha are contrasted with the Christian accounts of the incarnation of Christ in that they are silent as to the exclusion of human fatherhood, but they are no less contrasted in the manner in which they represent the event. What suggestion of similarity is there between the majestic annunciation of the miraculous conception to the Virgin Mary by the angel Gabriel, and the absurd and grotesque Buddhist story of the dream of the descent, or the actual descent, of the white elephant and his entrance into the side of the queen. One might, if disposed, enlarge also upon the gross and absurd character of the miracles which are said to have accompanied the birth of the Buddha, as contrasted with the simplicity and modest reticence of the Gospel story.[2] Or we might refer to the contrast in the circumstances into which the Christ and the Buddha were respectively

---

[1] There is, however, apparently no occasion to suppose a borrowing on either side. The conception that a saviour of men must be supernaturally born, is found with very many peoples, and is a very suggestive expression of man's deep consciousness of inability to save himself.

[2] See any of the authorities for the legend, as, e.g., in *Buddhist Birth Stories*, vol. i.; the *Nidàna Kathà*, pp. 66, 67 ; and authorities cited by Hardy, *Manual of Buddhism*, pp. 144, 146 ; also *Lalita Vistàra*, chaps. vii. and viii.

born ; but what has been said will suffice to make it
clear that while nominally we have a coincidence
between the fact of an asserted incarnation in either
case, yet the nature of that incarnation and the circumstances of it in the two cases are so diverse as fully
to justify us in reckoning this as a coincidence which
is much more in name than in reality, and of no force
whatever against the independence and originality of
either story.[1]   Contrast, not resemblance, is the rule
throughout the two accounts.

Professor Beal, in the *Romantic Legend*, has a chapter
entitled " The Fear of Bimbasâra."   Bimbasâra was a
king of a country in the East, who, when the Buddha
was now grown up to be a young man, was taken with
a fear lest there should be in some place or other an
enemy who might be able to destroy him and take his
kingdom.   Impelled by this anxiety, we are told that
he sent men to search and see whether in all the world
any so strong king existed.   Returning, they reported
that they had heard of this Gautama, son of Suddhodana, and urged the king that for his own safety he
should destroy him.   But instead of listening to this
advice the king, we are told, entirely refused to molest
the prince.   And this story Professor Beal calls "another
of the singular coincidences of the narrative of the
Buddha with the Gospel history !"[2]

[1] Unless possibly the above-mentioned story of the conception of
the Buddha by Shing-shin should prove to be an exception.
[2] *Romantic Legend*, pp. 103, 104.

The reader will no doubt agree with us that we may without hesitation set this down as a coincidence which is scarcely even apparent, but quite imaginary. Except that both Bimbasàra and Herod, who sought the young child Jesus to destroy Him, were possessed with a fear that some one might take away their kingdom, there is absolutely not one point of agreement between the two stories, but perfect contrast. At the time of Herod's fear, Jesus was but a babe; at the time of Bimbasàra's dread, the Buddha was grown up. The former sought to destroy Jesus; the latter, when exhorted to destroy the Buddha, refused to do so, and said that they ought rather, should he become a Buddha, to obey and follow his teachings. A "singular coincidence," truly! Reference has been made to a baptism in both cases. The only circumstance in the life of the Buddha which could possibly suggest such a parallel with the life of Christ is the bathing of Gautama in the river Nairanjana, shortly before his conflict with Màra and attainment of Buddhaship. Professor Seydel tells us that, according to the *Rgya tcher rol pa*,[1] while he was bathing, "thousands of the sons of the gods, wishing to render offerings to the Bodhisat, strewed divine aloes and sandal powder and celestial essences and flowers of all colours over the water, so that in this moment the great river Nairanjana flowed on full of divine perfumes and flowers."[2] Shall we call this

---

[1] The Thibetan version of the *Lalita Vistàra, vid. sup.*, p. 40.

[2] *Das Evangelium von Jesu*, u.s.w., S. 155, 156.

a coincidence with the story of the baptism of Christ by John before His temptation by Satan, or must we not class this also with the so-called "agreements" between the two stories which are purely *imaginary*?

Most extraordinary is the attempt of Professor Seydel to find also the analogue or prototype of the sending of the Holy Ghost, the Comforter, in the Buddhist stories. He tells us that, according to the *Mahápari-nibbána Sutta*, the Buddha promised the continuance of his work, and thus "in this sense his 'spirit,'[1] who should be to the disciples a teacher and master, when he himself should have gone away." But this does not appear to have fully satisfied him, and with good reason. For while it is true that in the Sutta quoted the Buddha is represented as predicting the continuance after his death of the religion which he had established, yet when Professor Seydel adds to this the words, "thus, in this sense, his *spirit*," he uses a word for which there is not in the *Mahápariníbbána Sutta* a syllable of warrant. No conception could well be further from the teaching of this and the other early Buddhist Suttas than this of the sending forth of a *spirit* of the Buddha after his departure. Hence it is, perhaps, that Seydel goes on to connect instead the doctrine of the sending of the spirit with the later Buddhist doctrine of the coming of the Maitreya Bodhisat.[2] According to the later Buddhism,

---

[1] *Das Evangelium von Jesu*, u.s.w., S. 263.
[2] *Ibid.*

Maitreya is a being now resident in the Tusita heaven, who is to appear in due time on the earth as the next Buddha. In the North, as especially in China, the worship of the Maitreya Bodhisat has taken a fore-most place.[1] In the *Lalita Vistâra*, which belongs to the Northern Canon, it is said that when the Buddha was about to leave the Tusita heaven he appointed the Maitreya Bodhisat to be his vicegerent after his departure. Seydel then runs a parallel in the follow-ing manner. " In the first place, the Maitreya Bod-hisat, before the Buddha came, was in heaven with the future Buddha, Gautama ; so was the Holy Ghost with Christ in heaven before He came to earth. When the Buddha came into the world the Maitreya Bodhisat remained behind in heaven as his representative ; so did the Holy Spirit remain in heaven when Christ came to earth as the representative of Christ in heaven. But after the death of the Buddha, Maitreya Bodhisat was to come into the world ; so, after the death of Christ, the Holy Spirit." Hence, argues Seydel, " we have in these features of the teaching of the legend touching the Maitreya Bodhisat the essential elements of the Christian doctrine of the Comforter." [2]

This supposed analogy, however, fails in the most essential features. In the first place, we have never found any place in the New Testament wherein the Holy Spirit is set forth as having been the repre-

---

[1] Rhys Davids, *Buddhism*, pp. 180, 120 *et seq.*
[2] *Das Evangelium von Jesu, u.s.w.*, S. 263, 264.

sentative of Christ in heaven during His humiliation. So this "parallel" fails on both sides. And as for the coming of the Maitreya Bodhisat, as compared with that of the Holy Spirit, the analogy breaks down as completely. For the Buddhists expect that the Maitreya Bodhisat, when he comes, will be a man similar to Gautama Buddha, going through similar experiences of incarnation, struggle, victory, and pro- pagation of the truth. But the Holy Spirit is not to come as a future incarnation; he is represented as having come already and dwelling in the hearts of all Christ's true people. Surely we must set this down also as a " correspondence " which has no real existence. This is by no means the only instance in the work of 人 Professor Seydel in which is evinced a degree of mis- apprehension as to the teachings of the New Testament which is truly marvellous.

To these imaginary parallels may be added an agreement which Mr. Rhys Davids thinks that he per- ceives between the development of belief concerning the glory of the Buddha and the development of Christian doctrine concerning the person of Christ. He remarks that the growth of the legends, with their ever new details adding to the glory of the Buddha, seems to him " to afford unmistakable evidence of a desire in the relaters of those legends to express—in the same spirit as has inspired many Christian writers —the greatness of Gautama's renunciation." And he thinks that if " we call to mind the process through which it has become possible for a Christian poet to sing of the carpenter's son—

> ' His Father's home of light,
> His rainbow-circled throne,
> He left for earthly night,
> For wanderings sad and lone,' "

it will be easy for us to understand and think even well of these glorifications of the Buddha so as " to recognise in them not merely empty falsehoods . . . but the only embodiment possible under those conditions of some of the noblest feelings which have ever moved the world."[1]

As to the similarity of the processes of development in the two cases which is herein commended to our attention, we entirely fail to see it, and have to add this to the long list of imaginary agreements. One often has occasion to notice that it is quite possible for a man to know very much about the " sacred books " of Buddhists and Brahmans and other non-Christian peoples, and comparatively little about the New Testament, its criticism, or the history of Christian doctrine. In this case had the lecturer been as well acquainted with the criticism of the New Testament as he is with that of the *Pâli* scriptures of the Buddhists, he would have recognised the fact that the imagery of the verse which he quotes represents no late development of doctrine, but a belief about " the carpenter's son "

---

[1] *Lectures on the Origin and Growth of Religion*, *etc.* (Hibbert Lectures, 1881), pp. 140, 141.

which dates back to the generation in which Jesus
lived. For the thought and imagery of this verse is
derived from the Apocalypse of John ; and it is the
somewhat singular fact that the critics who have been
and are so much in earnest to push the date of the
Gospel of John to the latest point possible, have in
the case of the Apocalypse only deviated from the
traditional date (about 98 A.D.) by making it some
thirty years earlier, in the reign of Nero—in other
words, about thirty years after the death of our Lord.
And this is the book in which we read of the throne
in the midst of which sits the Lamb ; a throne which is
at once "the throne of God and of the Lamb"; the throne
encircled " with a rainbow like unto an emerald ;"[1] a
book which, in its exalted adoration of the Lord Jesus
and attribution to Him of the glory of absolute Godhead, is second to none in the Christian Canon. There
is no analogy then here with the development of
doctrine regarding the glory of the Buddha, but the
exact opposite. At least, in order to make the cases
really similar, it will be necessary for Mr. Davids to show
that all the critics, the orthodox and the rationalists
alike, have been in error in assigning the Apocalypse
to a date within the lifetime of the generation that saw
and knew our Lord.

It may be remarked, finally, under this part of the
discussion, that a large part, if not all, of the *verbal* co-

[1] Compare with the lines cited Rev. iv. 3-5, v. 5, 6, xxii. 1 *et
passim.*

incidences of the Buddha story with the Scriptures, as
that story has been given by Mr. Arnold in the *Light
of Asia*, have nothing corresponding to them—so far
as we can find—in any of the original versions of the
legend.[1] Whether the poet has intended it or not, it
is certain that he has in that poem done much to
suggest to the general literary public, little acquainted
with the Buddhist texts, that between the stories of the
Buddha and of Christ is an agreement which extends
even to the very words of some of Christ's most
characteristic utterances.   Indeed, if the Germans
speak of a certain type of literature as " Tendency
Writings," we may with good reason speak of the
Light of Asia as a " Tendency Poem."   It is none the
less so, though we charitably assume that the poet was
unconscious of the tendency which his work would
have to undermine and weaken the faith of many in
the historical trustworthiness of the Gospel records.
How could it be otherwise, when it is suggested to the
reader that the likeness between the two stories extends to the very words, as in such passages as the
following.   Mr. Arnold tells us, for example, that
when the aged Asita blessed the infant Buddha, he
addressed the mother in words almost identical with
Luke ii. 35, saying—

". . . A sword must pierce
Thy bowels for this boy."

[1] The criticisms which follow under this head were given to the
public in nearly their present form in the *Catholic Presbyterian*, July
1883, article " Modern Unbelief and Buddhism."

Again, when Buddha declares his resolution to forsake home and kingdom that he may find out the way of deliverance from pain, we read—

> "I will depart, he spake ; the hour is come !
>
> .   .   .   . Unto this
> Came I, and unto this all nights and days
> Have led me.   .   .   .
>
> This will I do who have a realm to lose,
> Because I love my realm.   .   .   .
>
> .   .   .   Those that are mine, and those
> Which shall be mine, a thousand million more,
> Saved by this sacrifice I offer now."

And while he was wandering, seeking the knowledge which should free from pain, we are told—

> " . . . The Lord paced in meditation lost,
> Thinking, Alas ! for all my sheep which have
> No shepherd ; wandering in the night, with none
> To guide them. . . ."

In the Great Temptation by Màra, we are told in the poem, in accord with Luke iv. 3, that the tempter addressed Gautama with the words, "If thou be'st Buddh' ;" and afterward that, in the retrospect of his life, the Buddha saw where his path had often led—

> " . . . on dizzy ridges where his feet
> Had well-nigh slipped."

Did space permit, we might compare with the above poetical rendition of the story the phraseology of the corresponding passages in the legend as we have it in various native authorities.   It would form a most suggestive and remarkable illustration of the subject of poetic license.   We venture to doubt whether in any extant authority a warrant for these and other verbal coincidences can be shown.   It would at least be very desirable that Mr. Arnold should give to the public an edition of his poem embodying references to the Buddhist authorities which justify the language of these phrases.   Meantime, these unverified, and, if we mistake not, unverifiable and unwarrantable suggestions are doing their work in starting doubts in the minds of many as to the trustworthiness of the Gospel story—doubts which in no case have any reason in ascertained facts.   For even if, as we more than doubt, the equivalents of these phrases should be shown in some Buddhist authority or other, yet, as we have already seen, it would be utterly impossible to show good reason for believing that such verbal agreements as these above cited antedate the Gospel story, and were not instead Buddhist imitations of New Testament language.   The few slight resemblances in language, other than such as those above quoted, which really do occur in the Buddhist scriptures, readily admit, as we shall see, of an explanation perfectly consistent with the entire independence of both the Buddhist authorities and the Gospels.

   2. Another class of coincidences present us with an agreement which is indeed real, but purely *accidental.*

Such can of course have no apologetic significance. In
this category we may certainly place the circumstance
that in both the case of the Buddha and that of Christ
a *fast* is represented as having preceded the entrance
on the ministry of preaching. Professor Seydel, it will
be remembered, thinks that in this we have one of the
five cases in which it is clear that the Gospel story
must have borrowed from the Buddha legend.[1] His
reason for this opinion is found in the asserted inconsistency of such a fast in the case of Jesus with his own
teachings as contrasted with those of John the Baptist.
On the other hand, the fast attributed to the Buddha
is in full keeping with the general teachings of all the
Indian religions, and with those of Buddhism in particular. Hence, he argues, the Buddhist story must in
this case be regarded as the original, and the mention
of the fast of Jesus in the Gospels must be due to the
influence of the Buddhist legend !²

In reply to this, it is to be said that it is not true
that fasting was wholly foreign to the conception which
Jesus held of a religious life. Instead of this, the fact
is that He approved of fasting, and in the sermon on
the mount gave directions for the proper performance
of the duty.[3] And when, on a later occasion, He was
asked why it was that while the disciples of John and
the Pharisees fasted, His disciples fasted not, He did

---

[1] *Vid. sup.*, p. 86, 2.
[2] *Das Evangelium von Jesu*, u.s.w., § 154, 155, 296, 297.
[3] Matt. vi. 16-18.

not answer by declaring that fasting was in itself foreign to His religion, but that its obligation was determined by circumstances; that, for example, for them, " the children of the bride-chamber," to fast while He, " the bridegroom, was with them," was out of place; but that when He, the bridegroom, should be taken away, then for them to fast would be right and proper.[1] It may be further added that Jesus, in thus maintaining that fasting had a place in the religious life, was not only at one with the practice of the Jews of His own time, but was also sustained by the example of Moses, as given in the Pentateuch, of whom it is written that, in like manner, he fasted in Mount Sinai forty days and forty nights.[2]   It is then an utter mistake to assert that, for the reasons given by Seydel, it is incredible that Jesus should have begun His ministry by a long fast, as we are told.   There is not the slightest necessity of postulating a Buddhist origin for the story as we have it.   There is without doubt a real coincidence here, but it is due to the accidental circumstance that the Jewish religion agreed with the Indian cults in making fasting a religious duty, although indeed on very different grounds.

No more, nor indeed as much, can be said of the correspondence which Professor Seydel sees in the incident concerning Nathanael and the fig-tree.[3]   For, in the first place, in the Buddhist story it is the

---

[1] Matt. ix. 14-17.   [2] Exod. xxxiv. 28.
[3] John i. 47-50; *vid. sup.*, p. 86.

Buddha who gains his first disciple under the fig-tree; in the Gospel it is not Christ, the Master, but Nathanael, the disciple, who, before his conversion to Christ, was seen by Christ under a fig-tree. In the Gospel we are not told that Nathanael or any one else was converted under a fig-tree, but instead of that, on a subsequent occasion,—how long after or how far away we are not told. It is true that the presence of the Buddha under the sacred fig-tree was a necessary "sign of his Buddhahood," but it is astonishing that Professor Seydel should suppose, as he seems to, that Nathanael recognised the mere mention of a *fig-tree* as a wonderful sign of Christ's Messiahship,—a fig-tree too under which he, and not the Lord, had been. Surely any well-instructed Christian child could have told the Professor that what gave Nathanael the assurance of the Messiahship of Jesus was not the mention of a fig-tree merely as a *fig-tree*, but the revelation of the *omniscience* of Jesus, who showed by His remark that He had seen him even in the solitude of his retirement. Absolutely the only correspondence in the two stories is this, that in the narrative of the first conversions, in both the case of the Buddha and that of Christ, a fig-tree is mentioned. Apart from this, in every particular there is the widest possible difference between the two stories. And it is such a coincidence as this that the Professor thinks of so great significance that he counts it one of his five instances of an agreement of such a kind as only to

K

be accounted for upon the supposition that the apostle knew and used the Buddha legend in working up his Gospel !

Under this same head may be properly classified the presentation of both the Buddha and the Christ in a temple. As to this, Seydel himself, indeed, suggests that if the presentation of Jesus could in any way be shown to be according to Jewish law, then serious doubt would be thrown upon the originality of the temple scene in the Buddha legend. There being, however, according to him, no adequate reason shown why Jesus should have been presented in the temple, he concludes that the story must have been borrowed from the Buddha story. It is true there are notable differences. For example, we are told that when the Buddha was taken to the temple 100,000 gods drew the carriage which contained him, and showers of flowers were rained down by heavenly nymphs; the earth quaked as he entered the temple; music sounded from invisible performers in heaven; the images of the gods in the temple came down from their places, and advanced and humbly fell at the feet of the Buddha child, when the gods concluded the scene with a hymn of praise to the wonderful child. But these slight discrepancies in the story of the Buddha from Luke's account of the presentation of the infant Jesus, Professor Seydel omits to notice, further than quietly to remark—as if it were the most self-evident thing conceivable—that " the adorations of the gods are repre-

sented in the Christian Gospel by the hymns of praise
which were sung by Simeon and Hannah!"[1]

Most readers, however, we are persuaded, will agree
rather with Professor Kuenen, who says, "the difference
appears to me far to overbalance the resemblance, and
to throw it into the shade. The simple scene in the
temple at Jerusalem is really no parallel at all to the
homage rendered to the Buddha child."[2]

As for Professor Seydel's assertion that there is
nothing in the Jewish law which could be conceived of
as requiring the presence of the child Jesus in the temple, and that it only speaks of offering for the purifica-
tion of the mother,—more careful reading would have
caused him to modify that assertion. For as to the
offering it was required that the mother should *herself*
appear with the offering at the door of the tabernacle[3]
(or of the temple); and—to say no more—when we
remember that the offering was to be presented at the
temple at the expiration of forty days from the birth,
it is easy to see that for a mother who had any distance
to go, it would be necessary for her to take a babe of
that age with her. Besides this, we know that, apart
from this necessity, with the Jews it was the custom
often, instead of redeeming a first-born son, formally
to dedicate him to the Lord,[4] and that this was
naturally and most fitly done in the temple, as is

[1] *Das Evangelium von Jesu*, S. 147.
[2] *National Religions and Universal Religions*, p. 362 (Hibbert
Lectures, 1882).   [3] Lev. xii. 8.
[4] See Meyer, *Handbook to the Gospel of Luke, sub loc. cit.*

illustrated in the case of Hannah.[1]   In this case
certainly, assuming the circumstances which are narrated concerning his birth, there was enough special
reason why the child Jesus should not only be
brought to the temple with His mother from necessity,
but also there formally presented to the Lord as the
predicted "Servant of Jehovah."   There is therefore not the slightest reason for the affirmation of
Seydel that the reference to the Jewish-law is "an
irrelevant and artificially contrived device to give the
story support for the ideas of his Jewish readers."[2]

The presentation of the child Jesus, if not according
to the very letter, was according to the spirit of the
commandments to which Luke refers in that connection.   It remains, therefore, that the only point of
correspondence between the two stories is that in both
cases the young child was presented in a temple; a
circumstance this, both in Jewish and in Indian custom, so usual as, in our judgment, to justify us in
regarding the agreement in this one particular—notwithstanding Professor Seydel's fears for the originality
of the Buddha legend—as purely accidental.

In the same class we would include the *royal birth*
which is attributed to either child.   There is nothing,
surely, in the mere circumstance of royal descent, so
strange or peculiar that we cannot suppose it should
really have been the fact in both cases, and that the

---

[1] 1 Sam. ii. 24 ; Ex. xiii. 13.
[2] *Das Evangelium von Jesu*, S. 147, 296.

coincidence should be purely accidental. As in former cases, so here again the differences outweigh the agreements. Both were, indeed, according to the two stories, of royal descent, but only the Buddha was of royal parents. He was surrounded, according to the legend, with wealth unbounded; but Jesus was born of a mother so poor that the largest sacrifice she could command was the smallest permitted by the law, " a pair of turtle doves, or two young pigeons." [1]

Much has been made by some of the blessing of the infant Jesus by Simeon, which such have sought to identify with the blessing of the infant Gautama by Asita. To the verbal coincidence between the two stories which Mr. Arnold has ventured to suggest in the *Light of Asia*, reference has been made already. We can well pass that by here without further remark, as wholly without foundation in fact. As regards the two stories in general we have to remark, as again and again before, that the contrasts utterly overbalance the resemblances. In fact, omitting the one circumstance of a blessing of a child in each case by an old man,— no extremely unusual circumstance, one would say,— the two stories of Simeon and Asita present *not* agreement, but *contrast* throughout. In the case of the Buddha child, the blessing of Asita takes place at the palace of the king, and directly after the birth; in the case of Christ, the blessing of Simeon is given in the temple, and at some time after the birth. Simeon

[1] Luke ii. 23, 24 ; Lev. xii. 6.

is found in the temple, where he was wont to remain,
worshipping God; Asita, we are gravely told, to see
the child, came down from heaven, whither he had
gone for refreshment in the heat of the day! Simeon
recognises by the inspiration of the Holy Ghost the
true character of the infant Jesus; Asita is told of the
birth of the future Buddha by the gods in heaven, and
even then does not seem to be satisfied; for, coming
where the child was, we are told that he ·at once proceeded to look on his body for certain thirty-two marks
which should betoken the person of a Buddha. Simeon,
having recognised the Christ, rejoiced, saying, " Lord,
now lettest thou thy servant depart in peace, for mine
eyes have seen thy salvation." Asita, on the contrary,
congratulates the king, but breaks into violent weep-
ing as he mourns—

> " Alas, what loss, what damage is mine !
> Alas, I am old and stricken in years !
> My time of departure is close at hand."

Absolutely the *only* coincidence, we repeat, is found
in the solitary circumstance of a benediction or con-
gratulation . by an old man in both cases. Is this a
coincidence of such a sort,—a circumstance so singular
and exceptional, as not to be accounted for except upon
the supposition that one of the two stories must have
copied it from the other? Surely common sense will
affirm that such an agreement must be set down as
purely *accidental.*

Doubtless many other points of agreement of minor

consequence might be discovered in the two stories, which, according to the judgment of unbiassed common sense, must in like manner be set down as due alone to accident, and as having therefore not the slightest importance in any question as to the origin or integrity of the two stories. But these already mentioned will suffice for illustration.

3. Another cause which has without doubt occasioned frequent agreements between the two stories, will be found in *the operation*, in both cases alike, *of identical or similar causes.*

Under this head, for example, may be classified a large number of close agreements of thought and even of phraseology with the Gospels, in passages not only in the legend, but also in the *Dhammapada* and other Buddhist works professing to contain the teachings of the Buddha. Many illustrations might be given, of which the following may be taken as examples :—

" What is the use of platted hair, O fool ! what of the raiment of goat-skins ? Within thee there is ravening, but the outside thou makest clean." [1] So also Christ said, when the Pharisee marvelled that he had not washed before dinner, " Now do ye Pharisees make clean the outside of the cup and the platter ; but your inward part is full of ravening and wickedness." [2] So again, as our Lord to the woman of Samaria represented His salvation as a " living water," [3] in like

[1] *Dhammapada*, 394 ; *S. B. E.*, vol. x. part 1, p. 90.
[2] Luke vii. 39.   [3] John iv. 10-14.

manner the Buddhist " salvation " in the *Saddharma-pundarìka* is likened to " water for all." [1]   Again we read, " The world is dark, few only can see here ; a few only go to heaven, like birds escaped from a net ;" [2] with which may be compared the frequent description in the Christian Scriptures of the world and of those who are living in sin, as being and walking in darkness ; [3] and also our Saviour's words, " Narrow is the way that leadeth to life, and few there be that find it ;" and those of the Psalmist, " Our soul is escaped like a bird out of the snare of the fowler." [4]

In the *Tevijja Sutta* the Buddha is represented as describing the false Brahmanical teachers in the following words :—

> As when a string of blind men are clinging one to the other, neither can the foremost see, nor can the middle one see, nor can the hindmost see, just so, methinks, Vàsettha, is the talk of the Brahmans versed in the three *Vedas*.[5]

With which, naturally, may be compared the words of Christ with regard to the Pharisees and scribes, " Let them alone ; they be blind leaders of the blind. And if the blind lead the blind, both shall fall into the ditch." [6]

In all these and many other like examples which might be given did space permit, the similarity of

---

[1] *Op. cit.*, chap. v. ; *S. B. E.*, vol. xxi.
[2] *Dhammapada*, 174 ; *S. B. E.*, vol. x. part 1, p. 47.
[3] John xii. 35, 36, *et passim* in N.T.
[4] Matt. vii. 14 ; Ps. cxxiv. 7.
[5] *Tevijja Sutta*, i. 15 ; *S. B. E.* vol. xi.   [6] Matt. xv. 14.

thought is easily to be explained by reference to
the similarity of the circumstances under which both
the Buddha and Christ taught, and the condition
of men which they both perceived and faithfully
described. That, under such circumstances, when the
same world lay before each, replete with vivid illustrations of these spiritual facts, both should have
selected similar illustrations, when these were at once
so manifest and so intrinsically fit, were surely nothing
strange! Even agreements of phraseology, as well as
of thought, under such conditions, may not have the
slightest apologetic significance.

But we return for illustrations of the point before
us to the legend itself. To this principle of similar
cause we must certainly refer the fact that both to the
Buddha and to Christ men are represented as having
brought gifts on the occasion of their birth. But in
this case again, as before, the differences between the
two stories are so great as to preclude, one would
think, from the beginning, all thought of any copying
on either side. In the case of Christ it was, as all
know, three Magi from the East who said, " We saw
his star in the east, and are come to worship him."
And then we read that when they had found Him,
" opening their treasures, they offered unto him gifts,
gold, and frankincense, and myrrh." [1]   In the case of
the Buddha the gifts begin *before* his birth, with the
present of certain drops of mysterious dew from the

[1] Matt. ii. 2, 11.

great god Brahmâ, which contained in themselves "the power of all the forces of the world." After the birth multitudes of gods, nymphs, kings, and Brahmans, come to present him with various gifts, baby-linen, etc., among which are mentioned "incense and nard." Of a star in the East or anywhere else, which moves all these to go to make their presents to the infant Bodhisat, we read nothing.

All then is contrast, except the single circumstance that in both cases birth-presents are made. But all through the East, as indeed also in the West, it has been a common custom to make presents to new-born children, especially to those of royal birth. This solitary "coincidence" is explained by the prevalence of this custom.

Mr. Arnold, in the preface to the *Light of Asia*, speaks in tones of impressive reverence of "the miracles which consecrate the record" of the Buddha's work. It is true that miracles are attributed to the Buddha, even as they are to Christ, though how far, when the inner nature and character of the most of them is considered, they can be said to "consecrate" the record in which they find a place, will be a matter of doubt to many. As to the significance of this agreement, it is plain that stories of miracle are quite too common in history for the occurrence of a miraculous element in any two stories to raise of itself the slightest presumption for a borrowing on the one side or the other. Such a supposition can only find place if in certain given instances the character of the miracle in both cases is unusual and closely similar.

Now when we compare the miracles which are found in the legend of the Buddha with those which we have in the New Testament, we find that as a general rule they are marked by the most striking dissimilarity, both as to their external form and their internal ethical character. It is a very peculiar fact that those of the wonders related in the Buddha story which most resemble those in the Gospels, as a general thing are not represented as the result of the direct efficiency of the Buddha, but merely as spontaneous concomitants of certain critical events in his life. Thus at the time of the conception we are told that "the blind saw, the deaf heard, the lame walked," as also, indeed, many other things, as that "hungry ghosts received food and drink," etc.[1] So also with reference to the "transfiguration" described in the *Mahâparinibbâna Sutta,* as occurring not very long before his death, the Buddha is made to say :—

There are two occasions on which the colour of the skin of a Tathâgata becomes clear and exceeding bright. . . . On the night on which a Tathâgata attains to the supreme and perfect insight, and on the night in which he passes finally away in that utter passing away which leaves nothing whatever to remain, —on these two occasions the skin of the Tathâgata becomes clear and exceeding bright.

Not much likeness here, all will agree, to the narrative in Matthew xvii. !

[1] *Nidâna Kathâ:* Fausböll's *Buddhist Birth Stories,* vol. i. p. 64.

(handwritten) 2.3.22

When we compare with the Gospel miracles those
which are attributed to the Buddha himself, one cannot but be impressed with the crude and often grotesque
character of the latter, and especially their total dis-
connection in about every case with any conceivable
ethical aim.   For example, the Buddha is said often to
have sat without support in the air.   In an athletic
contest he astonished all by throwing an elephant
sixteen miles.   Just before his attainment of Buddhahood, having eaten the rice given him by the girl
Punnâ, we are told that he took the golden vessel
which she had given him and said, "If I shall be
able this day to become a Buddha, let this pot go up
the stream."   Thereupon he threw it into the water,
and it went eighty cubits, swiftly as a race-horse, up
the stream, and there, diving into a whirlpool, it went
to the palace of the Black Snake King!   On another
occasion it is said of the light that emanated from his
body that it had the power of making the sick well,
the crippled whole, of removing hunger and poverty,
anger and hate, etc.[1]

In some cases, where the miracles of the Buddha
legend have at the first glance a certain similarity to
those which are told of Christ, the resemblance upon
examination proves to be only superficial and apparent,
and, as in so many instances already mentioned, to

[1] In the *Mahâvagga*, i. 15-20, we have a description of a succession of miracles of a similar wild and bizarre character, wrought to
convince a certain ascetic who thought of the Buddha : "He is not so
holy as I am!" *S. B. E.*, vol. xiii. pp. 119-134.

be quite overbalanced by the differences. Thus we are told of an appearance of the Buddha after his death, which some have ventured to regard as a parallel to the resurrection of our Lord; but, unlike our Lord's resurrection, this appearance of the Buddha is represented as a temporary phenomenon, followed by no abiding continuance in life. Moreover, while the resurrection of our Lord is made the foundation of Christian faith, this *post-mortem* apparition of the Buddha not only has no essential connection with the rest of the legend or with the doctrine of his religion, but is directly inconsistent with the repeated statement of the Buddhist scriptures that when the Buddha died it was "with that utter passing away in which nothing whatever remains behind."[1]   With the resurrection narratives of the Gospels may be compared the Buddha story as given by Dr. Edkins in the following words:—

After the body of the Buddha had been consumed upon the funeral pile, Anuruddha went up to the Tusita heaven to announce these events to Màyà, the mother of Buddha. Màyà at once came down, and the coffin opened of itself. The honoured one of the world rose up, joined his hands, and said, "You have condescended to come down here from your abode far away." Then he said to Ànanda, "You should know that it is for an example to the unfilial of after ages that I have risen from my coffin to address inquiries to my mother."[2]

---

[1] *Mahâparinibbâna Sutta,* iv. 57 ; so also iii. 20, v. 20, *et passim;* *S. B. E.,* vol. xi.

[2] *Chinese Buddhism,* p. 57.   Both in this case and in the Chinese version of the ascension story which follows, the Chinese origin of the legend is clearly suggested by the so characteristic emphasis put upon

We read also of a miraculous ascension into heaven. But this is represented as having taken place, not after his death and resurrection, but during his lifetime, and was, according to one account, in order to preach his doctrine to the gods; according to another, a Chinese version of the story, it was "to instruct his mother Màyà in the new law."[1] In no case then is there any analogy with the ascension of Christ. Ascensions to heaven for various purposes are among the most common miracles attributed to Indian saints.[2]

Whether there may be possibly one or two of the miracles imputed to the Buddha in the legend, which are so closely similar to certain miracles recorded in the Gospels, as to suggest a derivation from one story to the other, it may not be possible to answer with absolute certainty; but it is certain that there is no proof of the existence of any such professedly miraculous element in the legend, which can be shown to antedate the Christian era.

In general, then, we may safely say that, as a rule to which there is probably no exception, agreement between the two stories in the matter under discussion extends only to the mere circumstance that miracles

the filial relation. The Buddha is the pattern son. Professor Childers says, "There is no trace in the *Pàli* scriptures or commentaries (or, so far as I know, in any *Pàli* book) of Sàkya Muni having existed after his death or appeared to his disciples.—*Dictionary of the Pàli Language*, p. 472, note 1.

[1] Edkins, *Chinese Buddhism*, p. 39.
[2] See, *e.g.*, the case of Asita; *sup.*, p. 71.

are attributed both to the Buddha and to Christ. As much might be said, however, not of Buddhism only, but also of all the great historical religions. The records of all these contain accounts of supposed miracles by the prophets and founders of each religion. The reason for a fact like this, common to all religions, is assuredly not to be sought in any supposed borrowing by one from the other, but in the depths of man's moral nature.

Man everywhere and always feels that all is not well with him. He is consciously the victim of powers and forces of evil within and without, which are far too much for his strength. Yet the most of men, despite appearances, believe in the possibility of help for this great need. But believing this, man is constrained by his experience of his own personal insufficiency for self-redemption, to impute to the being, whether god or man, in whom he supposes the redemptive power to be embodied, a might which is superhuman—in other words, a power of working miracles. Hence the Buddhist, believing that the Buddha had conquered the power of evil, naturally believed that he must have shown supernatural power. Without that he could not have sustained his claim to faith.

But it does not follow from this, by any means, that because of this tendency in the human mind to impute the power of working miracles to those whom they have believed to be redeemers of the race, therefore *all* accounts of miracle-working are of necessity

to be discredited.   On the contrary, if that universal
sense of need of salvation by a power which is more
than human, express a fact, then it is certain, that if
God in His mercy should send a deliverer adequate to
the need and spiritual helplessness of man, that deliverer would, without doubt, be manifested as a person
having superhuman power.   And thus, when we notice
that the miracles attributed to Christ, unlike those
which are attributed to the Buddha, are miracles, not
of caprice—not mere grotesque and objectless exhibi-
tions of power—but are all distinctly redemptive in
their character, distinguished by a lofty dignity, both
in conception and in execution ; and when we add to
this, again, the exalted and unique nature of the teachings of which they were professedly the seal ; and also,
above all, the proven redemptive power of Christ in
human history ; then assuredly the contemporaneous
testimony to the miracles of the Christ seems by no
means incredible.   Nor is it one whit the less credible
because men, under the influence of that deep sense of
need which brought Christ into the world, mistakenly
imputed to the Buddha powers which no one believes
that he possessed.   And so the only coincidence which
here concerns us—the coincidence as to the fact of
asserted miracles—is fully explained, in both cases
alike, by the fact of man's conscious need of a superhuman power of salvation.   This it was which gave
birth to the miracle-stories of the Buddha legend ; this
need also it was, which, according to the contempor-

aneous testimony of the four evangelists, in the fulness of time brought into the world the Christ of God, working wonders for the salvation of men from sin and death.

In this same connection may well be considered the two stories of the temptation. The Buddha, we are told in the later accounts,[1] suffered a terrible temptation from the evil one, Màra, the destroyer. In the struggle he conquered, and his conquest, according to Buddhist representations, brought light and hope to man. Then began his ministry. So also Christ is represented as having, in like manner, just before His entrance on His public ministry, had a solitary struggle with the evil one. He also conquered, and His victory was ours. Is there not possibly a borrowing here, on the one side or the other ? That there is in this instance a very remarkable agreement between the two stories will not be denied. Especially striking is it to find that—not indeed on the occasion of the Great Temptation—but at an earlier time, Màra is made to promise the future Buddha a universal kingdom if he will but renounce his intention of going out to seek a way of salvation for the world.

Still it has to be remarked that the extent of the coincidence has sometimes been much over-stated and exaggerated. Professor Seydel, for example, calls atten-

---

[1] The older *Pàli* texts refer to Màra as the adversary of the Buddha, but are silent as to the Great Temptation under the Bo-tree, of which the (later) legend as we have it, has so much to say.

tion to the fact that, according to the *Nidâna Kathâ* of the *Birth Stories*, the Buddha, when assailed by the wiles of Mâra's daughters, after Mâra's own assault had failed, " answered them with verses out of the *Dhammapada*, thus with passages of the Holy Scriptures."[1] A special analogy is thus suggested with a striking circumstance of our Lord's temptation, where, in fact, is no analogy at all. According to the Buddhist belief, the *Dhammapada* is a collection of the sayings of the Buddha himself.[2] For this reason it is reckoned among their scriptures. In putting words, therefore, which are found in the *Dhammapada*, in the mouth of the Buddha on the occasion of the temptation, the legend does not represent him as referring to a sacred scripture anterior to himself in the world, nor indeed to scripture at all. But the " Scripture " to which Jesus appealed was an authority in the world before His advent; and to it Jesus appealed as a word not His own, but the word of the living God, His Father. We have here then, not similarity, but direct contrast. The words cited from Seydel are utterly and inexcusably misleading.

More serious than this, however, because more elaborate and in a more popular form, is the misrepre-

---

[1] *Das Evangelium von Jesu*, u.s.w., S. 157, 158.

[2] Professor Max Müller tells us that the verses of the *Dhammapada*, "if not the utterances of the Buddha," were "what were believed by the members of the Council under Asoka in 246 B.C. to have been the utterances of the founder of their religion," *Buddhaghosha's Parables*, p. xxiv.

sentation of the Great Temptation which is contained
in Mr. Edwin Arnold's *Light of Asia.* According to
the version of the temptation of the Bodhisat which is
given in that poem, the first temptation by Màra was
to the sin called *attavàd.* This sin is explained by
Mr. Arnold in the following language as being

> " The sin of self, who in the universe
> As in a mirror sees her fond face shown,
> And crying ' I ' would have the world say, ' I,'
> And all things perish so if she endure.
> ' If thou be'st Buddh,' she said, ' let others grope
> Lightless ; it is enough that thou art thou
> Changelessly. Rise, and take the bliss of gods
> Who change not, heed not, strive not.' " [1]

It is undoubtedly true that the Buddha legend does
represent the Bodhisat as having been tempted to the
sin called *attavàd.* But the nature of this sin Mr.
Arnold seems to have utterly misunderstood ; and as
the result he has given to the conflict an ethical
similarity to the temptation of Christ for which there
is not the slightest warrant in the original story.
Evidently the poet takes *attavàd* to mean " selfishness ;" and, as plainly, selfishness was distinctly suggested as an element of sin in at least two of the
temptations with which the devil is said to have
assailed Christ. If it were really true that there was
coincidence here in the ethical nature of the temptation, it were no doubt a very interesting fact. In
reality, however, instead of similarity, we have here

[1] *The Light of Asia*, book vi.

one of the strongest contrasts of the Buddha legend with
the Gospel story. For *attavâd*—literally, " self-saying,"—does not mean " selfishness," or anything like
it. It is a Buddhist technical term which designates
the first of the Ten Sins (also called *sakkâyadiṭṭhi*) ; its
meaning is "the affirmation of the existence of an
abiding soul or self.[1] According to the legend, therefore, the first temptation of the future Buddha was to
believe that he had a soul! Not much likeness here
to the Gospel account of Christ's temptation ! Happy
had it been for the world, if in this temptation Mâra
had conquered !

Nor does the misrepresentation end with this ; for
Mr. Arnold, it will be observed, puts in the mouth of
Mâra the words, "If thou be'st Buddh'," thereby
recalling to our minds that Satan is said to have
addressed Christ in similar language, " If thou be the
Son of God, cast thyself down." So far, however, is
the poet from having any warrant for placing these
words in the mouth of the tempter in the Buddha
legend, that not only do they not occur in any version
of the legend, but, from a Buddhist point of view, it
were absurd to have supposed the tempter to have
addressed to Gautama such words at that time. For
not until *after* that temptation did Gautama become

---

[1] Rhys Davids' *Buddhism,* pp. 95, 109. Professor Childers defines
it as "the assertion of self or individuality ;" and illustrates by Mr.
Alabaster's explanation of the term as "the belief that I and mine
exist," see Childers' *Pàli Dictionary, sub. voc. ;* also Alabaster's
Wheel of the Law, p. 239.

Buddha, "the enlightened one." At that time he laid no claim to be as yet the Buddha. It looks in this case as if desire to assimilate the legend as closely as possible to the Gospel had led the poet into a serious anachronism. Against such use of Gospel phraseology every right-minded man will protest in the interest of common truth and fairness.

But the assimilation of the legend to the Gospel story in this poem does not end here; for a little further on we are told that the Bodhisat was also tempted to the sin *arùparàga*, which the poet renders, "lust of fame." That the Bodhisat was tempted to *arùparàga*, according to the legend, is quite true; but again, as before, there is no warrant for the meaning given this *Pàli* term. The real meaning may be best understood by the aid of the term used in Mr. Arnold's poem to describe the previous temptation—namely, that to the sin called *rùparàga*. This word he renders, more correctly, "lust of days." Precisely so, these two words, *rùparàga* and *arùparàga*, both mean "desire for existence;" the former desire for existence in the Buddhist *rùpaloka*, "the worlds of *form*," the latter, desire for existence in the *arùpaloka*, or "the *formless* worlds." Hence Mr. Rhys Davids has happily rendered them into Christian terms of thought by translating the former "desire of life on earth," and the latter "desire for life in heaven."[1] These are given in the Buddhist lists as respectively the sixth

[1] *Buddhism*, p. 110.

and the seventh of the Ten Sins. Thus, with this explanation of the real meaning of the term used by the poet, it appears that instead of having here a temptation to ambition—which would naturally remind one of the suggestion of Satan to Christ to get to Himself all the kingdoms of the world at once by worshipping him—we have, as in the former case, a thought as far removed as possible from anything that a Christian conscience regards as sin. Happy, again we might say, if in this case also, the tempter had conquered! The Buddha when tempted to *arûparâga* was tempted to desire to live in some one of the formless heavens !

We must also much regret that in this poetic version of the Buddha legend of the temptation the resemblance to the Gospel story is not only made to seem far closer than it is by this misinterpretation of Buddhist terms, but also by selecting those parts of the story which suit that purpose, and keeping other and more numerous contrasted features almost out of sight. The horribleness, the grotesqueness, the wild exaggeration, the indecencies of the original legend,[1] in the *Light of Asia* are all carefully suppressed. Let them but have the place that they have in the original story, and it is certain that no one would call the two stories alike. And yet the fact that, in both cases a great assault of the evil one is made immediately to precede

---

[1] *Vid. sup.*, pp. 76, 77, and compare *The Romantic Legend*, pp. 204-224; Fausböll's *Buddhist Birth Stories*, vol. i. pp. 96-101; Hardy, *Manual of Buddhism*, 2d ed., p. 183.

the active entrance upon saving work, remains as one
of the most striking and conspicuous features of each
narrative.   What is the significance of this coincidence?
To the mind of the writer there is, in the first place,
nothing here which could lead one to suppose that
either the legend or the Gospel had in this borrowed
from the other.[1]   Rather in both alike we are to see,
as in the case of the miracles, the operation of a deep
moral cause, to which, in different ways, each story
stands related.   For whether the existence of a
spiritual power of evil, a devil, be admitted or not, it
is certain that men, casting about for the source of that
mysterious power and providence of evil which they
have perceived in the history of the world,[2] have very
extensively been constrained to believe in the existence of such an evil personality to whom they were
subject, and from whom they needed a deliverance
beyond their own power to attain.   Thus, as in the
case of the miracles, it has been felt that whoever
should be a saviour of men, he must, in the nature of
the case, be supposed to have met, grappled with, and
overcome this evil power in his own person.   For how
otherwise could he be supposed to have the power
to deliver or to point the way of deliverance to others?

[1] On this point Professor Oldenberg is very emphatic.   He says, with
regard to the Buddhist and Christian stories of the great temptation,
"Influences of the Buddhist tradition on the Christian are not to be
thought of." *Buddha, sein Leben, seine Lehre, seine Gemeinde*, S. 118.
[2] For suggestive remarks on a providence of evil, see Martensen,
Christliche Dogmatik, § 99 *ff.*

And, again, if we assume that the narrative in Genesis of the temptation and the fall, and the promise of a future redemption from the power of the serpent through the seed of the woman, represents essentially historical facts, then the widely-spread belief in such conflicts and victories of supposed saviours is yet the more readily explained. For, if there really was such a temptation from a spirit of evil, which proved the beginning of human sin ; and, again, such a promise of a deliverance from the power of the tempter by one who should bruise the head of the serpent ; then nothing were more likely than that even for centuries the memory of that promise, however faded, should still remain, and give colour and form to the beliefs and anticipations of the race regarding salvation. Men would then be sure to hold it necessary that whoever the expected deliverer of men might be supposed to be, he should bruise the serpent's head as was predicted. Both the sense of need then, certainly, and possibly also the unconscious influence of such a redemptive tradition, would account for the genesis of the story of the conflict of the Buddha with Mâra. Among all those who regarded him as in any sense a saviour, such a conflict would appear a necessity.

And again, arguing as before with regard to the miracles, both these considerations would also require the *actual* occurrence of such an experience, a personal conflict and victory over the prince of evil, in the person of one who should in fact be the promised

deliverer, whenever he should come.   It could not but
take place in some form or other.

This view of the matter is the more likely to be
correct, that—unlike any theory of a borrowing upon
either side, Buddhist or Christian—it accounts not only
for the two stories which we have been specially considering, but also equally for all the numerous similar
stories of supposed deliverers of men, who have been
believed each to have had their conflict, under some
name and form or other, with the power of darkness.
That explanation is the most likely to be correct
which accounts for all the phenomena of the same
class.

4. But has there been, then, no transference of
elements from one story to the other, either way?
Can we claim that the suggestions thus far made are
quite sufficient to account for every coincidence which
can be pointed out between the Buddha legend and
the Gospels?   This we cannot say.   We believe that
no one as yet knows enough to be able to give to this
question a positive and final answer.   Now and then,
as the exception, one does meet with what not unnaturally suggests a borrowing on one side or the
other.   It is even possible that some points of agreement which have been dealt with under one or other
of the above heads, should be explained in this way.
Such possibly might be, for example,—among the
miracles—the resurrection of the Buddha, of such sort
as it is.   More striking and suggestive, again, is the

resemblance, not indeed to anything in the life of Christ, but to the story of the day of Pentecost, in the following legend. We are told that on the occasion of the Buddha's first sermon, " The various beings of the world all assembled, that they might receive the ambrosia and nectar of *Nirvâna.* All the various worlds, except the formless heavens, were left empty, as all the gods and heavenly beings came to hear the Buddha preach. So crowded were they that a hundred thousand gods had no more space than the point of a needle." And when the Buddha spoke, " *though he spoke in the language of Magadha, each one thought that he spoke in his own language ;* and all the different sorts of animals listened to him under the same supposition." [1] One certainly cannot help thinking how, on the occasion of that first preaching by the apostles, it was said, " How hear we each every man in his own language wherein he was born ?"[2]

Without pretending to decide the question, however, in any particular case, it may safely be added that it is at least quite possible that a transference of certain particulars from one story to the other, may prove at last to be an element in the final explication of the

[1] Hardy, *Manual of Buddhism,* pp. 191, 192. The Buddhist authority he cites—the *Pujàwaliya*—it should be remembered, is very late, not earlier than 1267 A.D.

[2] Acts ii. 1-8. But assuming the truth of the tradition that the Apostle Thomas,—who, according to this passage, shared with the twelve the gift of tongues,—preached the Gospel in India, the question arises, whether possibly this narrative may not embody a reminiscence of this Apostolic work in India in the first century ?

relation of the Buddha legend to the Gospel. But if the conclusions of the best critics as to the date and authorship of our Gospels be granted, then, as argued above, it is clearly incredible that their authors, men who personally knew Jesus, should, either consciously or unconsciously, have worked legends concerning the Buddha into a narrative given out by them as a true account of the doings and teachings of Christ. It is perfectly certain, therefore, even on this ground alone, that if it should be necessary at last to assume a borrowing on one side or the other to account for any particular in the two stories, then it must have been of the legend from the Gospel, and cannot have been the opposite.

Now that such a transference from the Gospel to the legend was possible, can be very clearly shown.

In the first place, it is to be remembered that, as we have already shown, there is no existing authority for the Buddha legend, which can be traced back, *in its present form*, so far as the first Christian century. It is no doubt true that, according to good authority, the Buddhist Canon was committed to writing a century or so before Christ. But no one pretends to be able to prove that in the legend, as contained in that first written pre-Christian Canon, was a single element having such a likeness to the Gospel as to compel us to suppose a transfer of that element from the legend to the Gospel. Of books supposed to have been in that Canon, it is not possible to prove that a single one has

come down to us without serious corruption and interpolation. Ancient MSS., as we have seen, there are
none ; neither have we in the absence of these, contemporary testimony from other ancient writers which
might assure us of the integrity of the text of the
authorities for the legend as we have it. We have
only been able to discover among the ancients, the
testimony of Clemens Alexandrinus, and of Jerome.
Of these the former only says that some of the Indians
"worshipped Buddha as a god," while the latter makes
a mere allusion to the belief of some of the people of
India, that the Buddha was born of a virgin. Further
than this they give us no information about the legend.

It is still further against the existence in the first
centuries of Christianity of the Buddha legend, in any
form which could be imagined to give the Christian
apologist trouble, that none of the early opponents of
Christianity, such as Celsus and Porphyry, ever made
use of these alleged coincidences, in their arguments
against the Gospel story. Can any one doubt that
they would have done so, had the legend been known
in the West in their day, in the form in which some
present it to us now ?—unless, indeed, they were
aware that it was of so recent importation or of so
uncertain origin as to be of no use for their purpose ?

In reply to this, however, it has been argued—or
rather suggested—by Professor Beal, that the sculptures
upon the famous Buddhist topes in India at Sanchi
and Bharhut contain evidence of the existence of a

Buddha legend containing features coincident with the
Gospel story, some time before the Christian era.   In
the preface to his translation, *The Romantic Legend*,
he says, " Many of the stories related in the following
pages are found sculptured at Sanchi, and some, I
believe, . . . at Bharhut. . . . If the date of these
topes is to be placed between Asoka, about 300 B.C.,
and the first century of the Christian era, it will be
seen that the records of the books and of the stone
sculptures are in agreement."

But when we look into the facts with care, it
appears that there is nothing at all in any of the
stories which are said by Professor Beal to be represented on the Buddhist topes, which could possibly
warrant the supposition that anything in the Gospel
had been borrowed from any story represented on these
topes.   The exact facts are as follows.   On careful count
we find that of the stories which are translated in *The
Romantic Legend*, twenty-four, according to Professor
Beal, are found illustrated on the sculptures in question.
But of these twenty-four only two prove to have even
a nominal connection with anything in the Gospel !
These two are, first, the incarnation, and second, the
blessing of the infant Bodhisat by Asita.   As regards
the former, we are told that the sculpture represents
the Bodhisat as entering the side of his mother in the
form of a white elephant.   Surely Professor Beal cannot mean to suggest that this—even though we date
the sculpture three hundred years before Christ—can

cast the slightest doubt upon the originality of the
first chapters of Matthew's and Luke's Gospels! or
suggests in the faintest degree the story of the incarnation of our Lord as there given! To base an argument against the integrity of the Gospel on such a
foundation as this, were truly absurd.

And the second of Professor Beal's two instances is
no more decisive than this. For truly it is too much
to be asked to believe that a sculpture upon a Buddhist tope in India, 300 B.C., of an old man holding a
little child in his arms, tends to show that Luke, when
he wrote of Simeon blessing the infant Jesus, must
have heard of the legend represented on that tope!
It will take, we are persuaded, more than suggestions of
this kind to convince most men of an original identity
of anything in the Gospel with anything in the Buddha
legend. With none the less confidence, then, for anything that Professor Beal has suggested, may we maintain our position on this subject. We reaffirm again
that up to the present time, no one has yet proved
that a single feature in the Buddha legend which could
possibly suggest a dependence of the Gospel on that
legend, or *vice versâ*, dates from a period earlier than
several centuries after Christ.

The conclusion from these facts is evident. If the
legend of the Buddha, in any form that in the least
concerns us in the present argument, disappears in an
indefinite haze long before, following it up through the
centuries, we reach the time of Christ, then it is idle

to talk of a transference of elements from that legend to the Gospel; and if any one will still insist with regard to any feature, that there must have been a borrowing on the one side or the other, then the facts compel the inference that such transfer can only have been from the Gospel to the legend, and not the opposite.

Now it is most pertinent to observe that within the limits of time and place imposed by the facts, an opportunity for the introduction of Christian elements into the legend of the Buddha did actually occur. The first fact to be called to mind in this connection is the existence of a Syrian Church in India from a period earlier than any certainly ascertained date for the Buddha legend in its now existing form. Whether we accept the unanimous tradition of that still existing Syrian Church, that it was established in India by Thomas the apostle, or whether, with some modern critics, we assume that the Thomas of whom they speak was a Syrian Thomas of the third century,— this does not affect our argument; for no coincidence of the Buddha story with the Gospel, of present concern to us, can be traced back even as far as the later of these dates.

The second fact bearing on this question is the great revival of missionary activity in the Nestorian Church in the sixth and seventh centuries of our era.' This missionary enterprise of the Nestorians of that time extended eastward into China, and was represented, according to good authority, by " multitudes of missionaries." [1] Direct testimony to this fact is given by an inscription in China, which states that the Gospel was preached there in 636 A.D. by a missionary named Olopen. [2] Indirect but no less decisive testimony to the extent and efficiency of this work is afforded by the fact that in the next century we are told that the Nestorian patriarch, Salibazach, appointed metropolitans of Samarkand and China,—an act which, of course, presupposes the existence at that time of a very considerable number of Christian communities in those parts of Asia.

And now be it noted that it is at *just about this period of history* that we have found ourselves arrested in the attempt to trace up with certainty the existence of the Buddha legend in its present form. No one can prove, for example, that the *Lalita Vistâra*, upon which most stress has been laid in this question, dates *in its present form*, with any certainty, earlier than this Nestorian revival. [3] It is certain that no one can show in any case that it is as old as the Syrian Church in Malabar.

This, of course, is not a demonstration that there

---

[1] Mosheim, *Ecclesiastical History*, vol. i. p. 421 ; Kurtz, *Kirchen Geschichte*, S. 190, 191 ; Smith, *Mediæval Missions*, pp. 203, 204.

[2] Mosheim, *Ecclesiastical History*, vol. i. p. 421, note 1 ; Smith, *Mediæval Missions*, pp. 205-209. The genuineness of this inscription is vouched for by Huc, Abel Rémusat, and other high authorities.

[3] The Thibetan translation, it will be remembered, is said by competent authority to have been made in the sixth century A.D.

actually was a borrowing from the Gospel by the
Buddhists, and that it took place at the time and in
the way suggested; but it does prove that such a
borrowing, if we are forced in any case to assume it as
fact, *could* have taken place; while the appearance of
the legend in its modern form, at about the time of
these aggressive movements of the Church in High Asia
and China, as also in India, at an earlier day, is a
circumstance of much significance.[1]   In a word, that
an opportunity for a transference from the Gospel to
the Buddha story did exist in that age, is an indubitable
fact.

The significance of this is the greater that we have
good reason to believe that Christian elements were
introduced into one or two of the Hindoo sacred books
in these same post-Christian centuries.   Professor
Lorinser has called attention to the numerous points
of contact between the *Bhàgavad Gìta* and the New
Testament.   In the *Bhàgavat Puràna* there is good
reason to suspect similar corruption from similar
sources.   In the Krishna legend, as therein given, the
story of the wrath of Ràjà Kans at Krishna's birth,
his effort to destroy him, the massacre of the innocents,

---

[1] The modification, or rather total transformation, of certain
Buddhist doctrines as represented in the "Lotus of True Law"
(*Saddharmapundarìka*), it is quite possible that one may ascribe in
part to Christian influences.   The date of the work, it will be remembered, is uncertain,—before 250 A.D., but how much no one can say.
Professor Seydel's numerous agreements (?) with the Gospels drawn
from this book have therefore little apologetic importance.

M

the flight of Krishna's supposed father with the child,
the healing of the woman bowed with a spirit of
infirmity—not to speak of other stories—have long been
perceived to point distinctly toward an adornment and
amplification of the Krishna legend by the help of
incidents borrowed from the Gospel story as preached
in early days in India.

We may sum up then our argument as regards the
probable relation between the Buddha legend and the
Gospel narrative as follows.   In the first place, there is
a twofold presumption against the supposed introduction of certain Buddhist elements into the Gospels.
This presumption rests, first, upon the total absence of
proof that by the time required by the hypothesis
Buddhist ideas had gained any such currency in
Palestine as to make the assumed transference possible.
In the second place, this presumption rests upon the
facts which have been critically established regarding
the date and authorship of, at least, the three synoptic
Gospels.   They are critically proven to have come out
of the circle of Christ's immediate disciples.   That
these men should either consciously or unconsciously
have introduced Buddhist myths into their story, and
succeeded in palming it off as veritable history upon a
contemporary generation, is impossible.   Some other
explanation of the coincidences must be sought which
shall recognise and be consistent with these *critically
ascertained facts* with regard to the composition of the
Gospels.

Again, the derivation of anything in the Gospel from a foreign source is only justifiable on scientific principles, when once it is shown that the circle in which the Jewish writers moved and thought, did not furnish anything which could account for the element in question. This has not been shown, and cannot be. In the last place, as regards the agreements which have been urged upon our attention, there is reason to believe that whenever the full explanation shall be possible—which as yet it is not—it will be found to comprehend several elements, as follows. In the first place some of the alleged coincidences are merely *superficial* and *imaginary*, and disappear entirely upon careful examination. In the second place, others are clearly *accidental*. Others again may with reason be ascribed to the influence of *similar causes*, of different kinds in different cases. Finally, it is possible—though by no means certain—that in a *few* instances the correspondence may prove to be of such a nature that it can only be reasonably explained by a transference of certain elements from the Gospel to the Buddha story during the early centuries of the Christian era. That abundant opportunity occurred for such a commingling of the two stories, has been made abundantly clear. That such a transfer from the Gospel to the story of Krishna did take place within those centuries, seems to be quite well established. If this happened in that case, it might quite as easily have taken place in the case of the Buddha story also.

And yet, whether as regards the legend of the Buddha, it will be found necessary to resort to this last explanation in any case, we confess that we greatly doubt. Others, most competent to judge, have spoken to the same effect, and still more decidedly. We may well close this chapter by giving the opinions of two such men, neither of whom will be suspected of any bias of judgment in consequence of any prejudice toward Christian orthodoxy.

In criticising the above-cited work of Professor Seydel with reference to the five coincidences upon which he lays the most stress as indicating a derivation, in at least those cases, of the Gospel story from the Buddha legend, Professor Kuenen says: " In my opinion, these parallels completely fail to give us that firm basis which we should require to enable us confidently to go on further. And when it appears, as it actually does, that the details of the second group find their origin explained, so far as any explanation is needed, in the Old Testament, then, to me at least, the alleged Buddhistic influence becomes in the highest degree questionable." [1]   To the same effect that eminent Buddhist scholar, Mr. Rhys Davids, has expressed himself repeatedly in still more positive language. Thus —to refer to one place out of many which might be noted from his writings—in the introduction to the *Tevijja Sutta*, he says: " Very little reliance can be

[1] *National Religions and Universal Religions*, pp. 362, 363 (Hibbert Lectures for 1882).

placed, without careful investigation, on a resemblance,
however close at first sight, between a passage in the
Pàli Pitakas and a passage in the New Testament.   It
is true that many passages in these two literatures can
be easily shown to have a similar tendency.   But when
some writers on the basis of such similarities proceed
to argue that there must have been some historical
connection between the two, and that the New Testament, as the later, must be the borrower, I venture
to think that they are wrong.   There does not seem
to me to be the slightest evidence of any historical
connection between them; and whenever the resemblance is a real one—and it often turns out to be
really least when it first seems to be greatest, and
really greatest when it first seems least—it is due, not
to any borrowing on the one side or the other, but
solely to the similarity of the conditions under which
the two movements grew."   And, if possible, still more
explicitly, with regard to a reviewer who has drawn
the conclusion that the parallels adduced by Mr. Davids
between the New Testament and the Buddhist scriptures, are "an unanswerable indication of the obligations of the New Testament to Buddhism," he adds :
" I must ask to be allowed to enter a protest against
an inference which seems to me to be against the rules
of sound historical criticism." [1]

[1] *Sacred Books of the East*, vol. xi. pp. 165, 166.

CHAPTER V.

1. *Introductory.*

IT is a familiar fact of our times that a large and increasing class of writers on religious topics deny, ignore, or seek to minify to the utmost, the differences between the doctrine of Christ and that of other religious teachers. Of this the necessary and already manifest effect has been to weaken, and, for many, to break, the force of those high and exclusive claims which the Gospel undoubtedly makes upon the faith and obedience of all who hear it. Hence the recognised importance in modern Christian apologetics of the careful comparison of the doctrines of the various religions of men. It is of great consequence for every intelligent Christian, and especially for every Christian minister in our day, that he gain correct ideas as to the relations of the different religious systems of the world to that system of doctrine which was delivered by Christ.

In such a comparison of doctrine, that of the Buddhist and the Christian systems has in our day assumed, for the reasons indicated in our first chapter, perhaps the highest importance of all. For in our time, if one may judge from much that we hear and read, there are many who seem to have persuaded themselves, and would fain persuade others, that the differences between the Buddhist and the Christian religions concern, not fundamental doctrines, but merely matters of unimportant detail, so that they can scarcely fail each to conduct him who will faithfully walk in the path they respectively point out, to the goal of a happy future, in the life after death—if there is one.

This is argued or assumed by different parties upon different grounds. In the first place, there are those who—whether upon atheistic, pantheistic, or deistic assumptions—deny the possibility of any supernatural revelation from God to man. This being taken for granted, a theory of a purely natural evolution is called in to explain and account for the origin and the relations of all religions. All alike are supposed to be merely products of the human mind, working under the influence of various " environments." Christianity and Buddhism, like all other religions, are thus made to be systems exclusively human. Of these, indeed, one may be more perfect than the other; one may have more, the other less of error; one may be better, the other worse adapted to the " environment ;" but in neither have we absolute, divine truth. Both alike are made up of reasonings and speculations which are only human, wherein there is much, no doubt, that is true, but much also in both, no less certainly, that is false and is to be rejected.

Others profess to occupy a different position. They adopt the language of orthodox Christianity and speak of the Christian religion as a revelation from God. But they insist that for us to regard Christianity as the only religion which may be truly so described, is altogether wrong, and can only serve to evince a narrow and unscientific spirit. Christianity, we are told, is no doubt from God, and—more than that—the clearest and fullest revelation of His will that has yet been given. But so also, and none the less, are the other religions of the world, each in their measure, revelations from Him. We are forbidden to contrast non-Christian religions with the Christian as the false with the true, or the natural and human with the superhuman and divine. That may have done for a former and less enlightened age, but not for these days of education and progressive thought. Rather are we to think of Buddhism, for example, as standing to Christianity in a relation analogous to that of Judaism. Both are from God ; both are, or have been, in their time and place, as lights to the world. Only, in both and in all cases, the truth which other religions set forth imperfectly and incompletely, Christianity reveals in its fulness, or

at least in greater fulness than any religion yet made
known to man. Thus, Professor Max Müller com-
plains that " we have ignored or wilfully narrowed the
sundry times and divers manners in which God spake
in time past unto our fathers by the prophets ;" [1] and
again tells us that " if we believe that there is a God,
and that He created heaven and earth, and that He
ruleth the world by His unceasing providence, we cannot believe that millions of human beings, all created
like ourselves in the image of God, were in their time
of ignorance so abandoned by God that their religion
was a falsehood, their whole worship a farce, their
whole life a mockery. An honest and impartial study
of the religions of the world will teach us that it was
not so, . . . that there is no religion which does not
contain some grains of truth. . . . It will teach us to
see in the study of the ancient religions more clearly
than anywhere else, the divine education of the human
race." [2]

In this we shall all admit that there is much that
is true. No Christian apologist will feel called upon
to dispute the assertion that " there is no religion which
does not contain *some grains* of truth." No less true
is it that we are to regard all the religions of the
nations, according to the very teaching of the Christian
Scriptures themselves, as serving a divinely ordained
purpose in the education of the race. But surely it is
not involved in either of these facts that all religions

---

[1] *Science of Religion*, p. 103.   [2] *Ibid.*, pp. 105, 106.

alike must be revelations from God, so that no one of them can be called false. That individual truths are wrought into a system either of scientific or religious doctrine, surely does not prove that such a system is therefore true as a whole. We may admit, what is quite true, that Buddhism recognises and insists upon many indubitable truths and unquestionable duties, in full accord with the religion of Christ, and yet it may be none the less just, none the less *scientifically correct*, when we speak of it as a *system*, to call it—as contrasted with Christianity—a *false* religion, even as we call the Ptolemaic—as contrasted with the Copernican—a *false* system of astronomy.

Nor does the inculcation of undoubted truths and of manifest duties, in the Buddhist or in any other religion, prove that in those cases, at least, there must have been a supernatural revelation. It is not by supernatural revelation only that men may come to know moral and spiritual truth. Nature also is a revelation from God. "The heavens declare the glory of God, and the firmament showeth forth his handiwork."[1] Conscience also reveals truth. This is emphasised in the New Testament, where we are told that those "who have not the law, are a law unto themselves, which show the work of the law written on their hearts, their conscience also bearing witness."[2] And so it were passing strange if in Buddhism or in any other religion of the non-Christian world there

[1] Psalm xix. 1.   [2] Rom. ii. 14, 15.

should be no "grains of truth." But, clearly, the
presence there of truths ascertainable by the light of
nature and of conscience, argues no revelation in any
supernatural way from God.

No more does the admitted fact that God uses all
religions alike in one way or another for the education
of the race warrant the conclusion that therefore they
must all of them have God in some true sense for
their author.   A parent may, and often does, teach
a child no less truly by withholding direct instruction
than by imparting it.   In this way the child will often
learn—better than in any other—from the conse-
quences of his own errors—the extent of his ignorance,
and his great need of that instruction which perhaps
before he had despised.

We admit then that truth may be found recognised
in Buddhism as in all the religions of men; we admit,
what history has made so clear, that all religions must
be regarded as subserving each a more or less important purpose in the divine education of the race.
But we deny that this involves the affirmation of
supernatural revelation in each case.   We deny that
these facts give us the slightest right to speak of
all as if they were, in the same sense as Christianity,
all alike revelations from God!   We insist that the
distinction between religions as *false* and *true*, against
which high authority in the scientific world has of
late so warmly protested, is a *valid* distinction, and
one of the *highest* and most *vital* consequence.   And

yet, while all this should be quite clear—as one would think—to any ordinary mind, it is evident that very different, false, and anti-Christian conceptions of the relations of the non-Christian religions to that of Christ, dominate the thinking of many—often men of the highest ability and undoubted sincerity—who write in our days on the subject of comparative religion. Influenced—often unconsciously, no doubt—by their erroneous postulates, they are led to magnify the agreements, and at the same time minify the contrasts of the ethnic religions with the religion of Christ to the very utmost.

The general confusion of thought on this subject is the more increased, as remarked in the preface, by the constant use of English terms, expressing various Christian conceptions, to express very different ideas peculiar to one or another false religion.[1] In this way it comes to pass that the doctrines most characteristic of these erroneous systems are made to appear to the ordinary reader, uninstructed in the technicalities of Oriental theology and philosophy, as only slightly variant renditions of the most fundamental and essential truths of the Gospel of Christ. Especially is this the case with regard to the religion of the Buddha. English words, which in the Christian religion have come to have a very precise and definite meaning, are employed by many writers to translate Buddhist terms, with the actual historical sense of which they

---

[1] For illustrations, *vid. infra.*, pp. 201-203, 216, 217, 280 *et seq.*

have little or nothing in common, while often not a hint is given of the foreign meaning which has been attached to the words. Hence arise in the minds of very many the most woful and mischievous misapprehensions as to what the Buddhist religion really is.[1]

From such misconceptions, again, such persons commonly draw one of two equally erroneous and anti-Christian conclusions. Either, holding on to the old faith in the Gospel as a divinely given revelation, men conclude that it is not, after all, as once had been supposed, the only supernatural revelation of the will of God to man; or, on the other hand, assuming that Buddhism is not a revelation from God, it is inferred that if so many of the distinctive truths of the Gospel are to be found also in the Buddhist scriptures, where undeniably they must be regarded as a product of mere human thought, then there is no reason any more to attribute a supernatural origin to anything that we find in the New Testament. Practically Christianity, in either case, is taken to be simply a Jewish form—as Buddhism is an Indian form—of the one universal religion.

---

[1] Many illustrations might be given. Thus when the *Sangha* (Order of Buddhist Monks) is rendered "church," or *ariya* (as in *Dhammapada*, 208, 236 *et passim*, by Professor Max Müller) "elect," surely to most Christians the words suggest ideas wholly foreign to Buddhism. Surely there can be no "elect" without an "election," and no election without an electing God! But Professor Max Müller assures us emphatically that of a God Buddhism knows nothing. Why not then render *ariya* "noble," "honourable"?

It needs no argument to make clear the immense importance of the comparison of doctrine to which we are thus challenged.   Is there then, between Christianity and Buddhism, such a degree of doctrinal agreement as to compel us to infer that they must have had a similar origin?   Is it such as to force upon us—as some insist—the alternative either of a supernatural origin for both, or a supernatural origin for neither?   This is the question before us.   Buddhism has been lately held forth to the admiration of the English reading public as "The Light of Asia."   If Christianity is the light of the West, in Buddhism we are asked to behold the light of the East!   But if Christianity is the light of the West, it is so only because it is a revelation of the truth of God.   Falsehood is not light, but darkness.   In like manner if Buddhism be the light of Asia, it must be so because it also is a revelation of the truth of God.   Furthermore, since truth is one, whether in the East or in the West, it follows that if Christianity be the light of the West and Buddhism be justly called the light of the East, then the fundamental teachings of the two religions must be identical.   It is indeed true that the same doctrines might quite conceivably be expressed in the two religions in widely different forms; it is also true that it is quite possible, on this assumption, that of two religions, both true, like ancient Judaism and Christianity, the one may be a much fuller revelation of the truth than the other.   But, for all this, they cannot in any matter contradict each other. If contradiction be proven, then it is utterly irrational to speak of both of them as being revelations, in any sense, from God.

Should this prove to be the case as regards the religion of the Buddha and that of Christ, then if any one will still hold Buddhism to be " the Light of Asia," he must make up his mind to let Christ go. While, on the other hand, if we admit that the Gospel of Christ is the light, because it is the truth, then in such case of proven contradiction it will follow that Buddhism, so far from being the *Light* of Asia, is instead very *darkness* and death.

Now we affirm and expect to prove that precisely this is the real state of the case. We affirm that the fundamental doctrines of Buddhism, when rightly understood, are not in agreement with those of Christ, but in direct opposition to them. We affirm that the difference between the two religions does not lie in a more or less full and clear enunciation of truth, but in the difference of affirmation and denial—of point-blank contradiction. We affirm, moreover, that these contradictions have to do, not with unessential details, but with the most fundamental matters conceivable— matters which must be considered in any and every religion, if it is to be called a religion at all. These are strong affirmations, but it will not be hard to make them good. Indeed, so clear and unmistakable are the facts, that it is matter for ever-growing astonishment that any who have had any opportunity to acquaint themselves with the facts, should have ever been able to persuade themselves that Buddhism, like Christianity, might be rightly set forth as a " light " for erring men, divinely given for human salvation.

2. *The Doctrine concerning God.*

First of all, we have to do with the question whether there be a God or not? Assuredly no question can be of more fundamental consequence. If there be a God and I fail of knowing this, I must therefore fail of serving Him. If there be a God and He has revealed Himself, even in ways of nature, so that I might know Him, then not to recognise Him and my relation to Him must be nothing less than fatal. Failure to know and recognise God, if there be a God, must inevitably vitiate all doctrine and all practical ethics as well. For if there be a God then all truth must exist in relation to Him; and, since His will must be law, all right action must be to Him and for Him. What Jesus taught on this question we all know. He said, " God is a Spirit, and they that worship him must worship him in spirit and in truth."[1] And so had taught the Old Testament prophets before Him. They spoke of a God who formed the earth and made it; who " measured the waters in the hollow of his hand, and meted out heaven with the span, and comprehended the dust of the earth in a measure, and

[1] John iv. 24.

weighed the mountains in scales, and the hills in a
balance."[1] So also, according to the apostles of the
New Testament, it is God who created all things and
upholds all things, and will at last judge the secrets
of all men, and reward every man according to his
works.[2]

Now Buddha, we are told, was "the Light of Asia."
What then does he teach on this vital question ? The
answer does not seem to be even a matter of dispute
with competent authorities. "There is no God," is
the initial assumption of Buddhism. To this effect is
the testimony of all the Buddhist books, and in this
respect it is generally agreed that the authorities,
however late, do not materially misrepresent the
opinions of the Buddha himself. The Light of Asia has
thus no light at all to give on this most momentous of
all questions ! It is true that some have questioned
whether the Buddha himself went so far as to deny in
so many words the existence of a God, and have
thought that his actual position might better be
described by the term " agnostic " than " atheist "
Some representations that we find in the Buddhist
books seem to favour this, as some also the other
opinion. Thus, on the one hand, we are told of a
conversation between the Buddha and a Brahman,
wherein the Buddha is represented as saying, " I do
not see any one in the heavenly worlds, nor in that of
Mâra, nor among the inhabitants of the Brahmâ-worlds,

---

[1] Isaiah xl. 12.   [2] New Testament, *passim.*

N

nor among gods or men, whom it would be proper for
me to honour." [1]   These words certainly mean a denial
of the existence of a God.   So also, elsewhere we read,
—" Without a cause, and unknown, is the life of mortals
in this world." [2]   This also is certainly a dogmatic
denial of God.   But frequently the Buddhist authorities either decline to consider the question whether
there be a first cause or not, or assert that it is unknown or unknowable.   Thus the Rev. Mr. Hardy,
quoting from a Buddhist authority, tells us that " when
Mâlunka asked the Buddha whether the existence of
the world is eternal or not eternal, he made him no
reply ; but the reason of this was that it was considered by the teacher as an inquiry that tended to no
profit." [3]   Again, the Buddha is represented as using
to his disciples the following language : " Ye disciples,
think not thoughts as the world thinks them : ' The
world is eternal, or the world is not eternal.   The
world is finite or the world is infinite.' . . .   If ye
(so) think, ye disciples, ye might thus think : ' This is
the sorrow ;' ye might think : ' This is the origin of
sorrow ;' ye might think : ' This is the removal of
sorrow ;' ye might think : ' This is the way to the
removal of sorrow.'" [4]   Again, in an authority translated by Mr. Hardy, we read, " All being exists from
some cause, but the cause of being cannot be dis-

[1] *Texts from the Vinaya ; Pârâjika ; S. B. E.*, vol. xiii.
[2] *Sutta Nipâta ; Salla Sutta*, 1 ; *S. B. E.*, vol. x. part 2, p. 106.
[3] *Manual of Buddhism*, 2d ed., p. 389.
[4] *Buddha, sein Leben, seine Lehre, seine Gemeinde*, S. 258.

covered."[1]   Other Buddhist authorities go further, and formally deny and argue against the being of a God.

But whether we call the doctrine of Buddhism atheism or agnosticism, it makes little difference. Agnosticism—whether it be that imputed by some to the Buddha, or that of Mr. Herbert Spencer—from a moral point of view, is virtual atheism.

All agree, moreover, that, in any case, the Buddha constructed his whole system without once introducing in any way the idea of God.   We read, indeed, much of the " law " which he preached, but he did not regard this as the law of God.   What he called sin, as we shall see, was not conceived or represented as having anything to do with a God or our relation to Him. We read, no doubt, in the Buddhist books, much about the " gods," but never once of God.   As for these imaginary beings which Buddhism calls gods, they are, for the most part, the old deities of the Hindoos, brought over into the Buddhist system, but lowered from the position that they held in the Hindoo system, to be the inferiors of the Buddha.   None of them are held in Buddhism to be, either singly or jointly, the creators or the rulers of the world.   They are only finite beings of a higher order than man, but all of them, like man, subject to impermanence and death, as also to sin and moral infirmity.   Of any being, corresponding even in the most general way to the ordinary theistic conception of God, Buddhism, we repeat, knows nothing.

[1] *Manual of Buddhism*, 2d ed., p. 414.

To the correctness of this assertion, the most
abundant and unimpeachable testimony can be adduced.
Professor Monier Williams tells us, "The Buddha recognised no Supreme Deity. The only God is what
man himself may become."[1] Barth declares that
Buddhism is "absolutely atheistic."[2] Professor Max
Müller assures us, "Difficult as it seems to us to conceive it, Buddha admits of no real cause of this unreal
world. He denies the existence, not only of a creator,
but of any absolute being."[3] And again, he says, that
as to "the idea of a personal Creator, . . . Buddha
seems merciless."[4] Archdeacon Hardwick says, "Of
Buddhism, . . . we need not hesitate to affirm that
no single trace survives in it of a supreme being."[5]
Köppen is no less decided. He assures us that Buddhism recognises "no God, no spirit, no eternal matter
as to be supposed antecedent to the world. Only . . .
the act of movement and change is without beginning,
—is eternal; but matter . . . is not eternal,—has a
beginning. In other words, there is only an eternal
Becoming, no eternal *Being. . . .*"[6] Among the very
latest investigators of Buddhism is Professor Oldenberg.
Scholars will generally agree that no one can be held
higher authority as to the real teaching of Buddha
than he. He has expressed himself in terms of the

[1] *Indian Wisdom,* p. 57.   [2] *The Religions of India,* p. 110.
[3] *Chips from a German Workshop,* vol. i. p. 227.
[4] Introduction to *Buddhaghosha's Parables,* p. xxxi.
[5] *Christ and other Masters,* p. 163.
[6] *Die Religion des Buddha;* i. Bd. S. 230.

same purport as the foregoing.   Contrasting Buddhism
with Brahmanism, he says, " The speculation of the
Brahmans laid hold of the Being in all Becoming;
that of the Buddhists, the Becoming in all apparent
Being.   *There* we have substance without causality;
here, causality without substance.   Where the sources
lie from which this causality derives its law and its
power, this Buddhism does not inquire. . . . Where
there is no being, but all is a coming to pass, there
can be recognised as the First and the Last,—not a
substance, but only a law."[1]

To the same effect as this testimony of eminent
scholars in Europe is that of missionaries in Buddhist
lands.   Thus the Rev. Mr. Hardy, long a missionary
to the Buddhists of Ceylon, tells us that, " by Buddha
all thought of dependence on any other power outward
to man . . . was discarded."   He writes, that although
there are some among the Buddhists of Ceylon, " more
especially among those who are conversant with the
truth of the Bible, who believe in the existence of one
Almighty God, while others confer upon the *devas* the
attributes of God;" yet " the missionaries are frequently
told that our religion would be an excellent one, if we
could leave out of it all that is said about a Creator."[2]
To the same effect is the testimony of Dr. Edkins,
missionary to China.   He says, " Atheism is one
point in the faith of the Southern Buddhists.   By the

---

[1] *Buddha, sein Leben, seine Lehre, seine Gemeinde*, S. 257, 258.
[2] *Legends and Theories of the Buddhists*, p. 221.

Chinese Buddhists each world is held to be presided over by an individual Buddha; but they do not hold that one supreme Spirit rules over the whole collection of worlds."[1]   A Siamese nobleman of our day, in a work in part translated by Mr. Alabaster, formally argues against the existence of a God, from the existence of evil, and from the unequal distribution of the blessings of life, quite in the manner with which we are familiar in the West.   Mr. Alabaster tells us that this man in his beliefs is a fair representative of the best educated and least superstitious among the Siamese.[2]   So also is the Buddhist doctrine understood by the Hindoos in India to-day.   The writer, when resident in India, has often heard the Brahmans speak of the Buddhist religion as *nàstik mat, i.e.*, the religion which is characterised by affirming, " *Nàsti* "— that is, " He (God) is not."   But it is needless to multiply witnesses.   Nothing is more certainly established with regard to the teachings of the Buddha than that he in no way whatever acknowledged the being of God. In the light of well ascertained facts it passes understanding how any can assert, as Mr. de Bunsen does, that " the doctrine of Gautama Buddha centred in the belief in a personal God."[3]   The fact is the exact

---

[1] *Chinese Buddhism*, p. 191.   [2] *The Wheel of the Law*, pp. 7-10.
[3] *The Angel Messiah of Buddhists, Essenes, and Christians*, p. 48. So Mr. James Freeman Clarke tells his readers, " Sàkya Muni did not ignore God.   The object of his life was to attain *Nirvàna*, a union with God, the Infinite Being !"   Of this astonishing statement no proof is offered.— *Ten Great Religions*, p. 168.

reverse of this.[1] While Christianity assumes the existence of an Almighty, most holy and most merciful
personal God, the Creator of the world, and the Father
of spirits; Buddhism, on the authority of its founder,
refuses to admit that there is any such Being. It
tells us that this belief is a delusion. And we are
asked to recognise the Buddha as the *Light* of Asia,
and are even called upon by some to admire the
marvellous agreement between the teachings of this
Buddha and those of Jesus Christ! Truly, in the
presence of this momentous contradiction, all agreements upon other points, whatever they may be, sink
into insignificance!

In the light of this one fact of the Buddhist denial
of a God, one can see of how little account are the

---

[1] Only a single passage in the Buddhist scriptures can be cited, which,
taken by itself, could be even imagined to refer to a personal God.
That passage is in the famous hymn of triumph, said to have been
sung by the Buddha, when he gained his great victory over Mâra:
" Without ceasing shall I run through a course of many births, looking for the maker of this tabernacle. . . . But now, maker of the
tabernacle, thou hast been seen; thou shalt not make up this tabernacle again." On this passage Professor Max Müller comments as follows: " Here in the maker of the tabernacle, *i.e.* the body, one might
be tempted to see a creator. But he who is acquainted with the general run of thought in Buddhism, soon finds that this architect of the
house is only a poetical expression, and that whatsoever meaning may
underlie it, it evidently signifies a force subordinate to the Buddha, the
Enlightened." Thus he does not hesitate to affirm, " As regards the
denial of a Creator . . . I do not think that any one passage from
the books of the Canon known to us, can be quoted which contravenes
it, or which in any way presupposes the belief in a personal God or
Creator. . . ."—*Buddhaghosha's Parables*, Introduction, pp. xxxviii.
xxxix. Also see above, p. 180.

attempts which have been made by some to show an
analogy between the Christian doctrine of the Trinity
in Unity, and the threefold " refuge " of the Buddhist,
Buddha, Dharmma, Sangha, " the Buddha, the Law, and
the Order." Indeed, even if it were true that Buddha
admitted the being of a God above himself, still
there would be no analogy here. The three of the
" refuge " are not one ; they are not even of the same
order of being. The first and the third denote persons,—the Buddha, and the Order of Monks, his disciples ; the second denotes an abstraction. Neither is
any one of the three supposed to be divine, in the Christian sense of that word. There could therefore be no
likeness to Christian doctrine, even if Buddhism admitted the existence of God ; but as it denies this, it
is plain that to imagine here an analogy between what
is often miscalled " the Buddhist trinity," and the
Trinity of Christian faith, is the part of the wildest fancy.

But the contradictions between the two religions by
no means end here, as it were indeed impossible that
they should. Since, according to Buddhism, there is
no God, it follows by necessary consequence that there
can be according to the Buddhist doctrine no such
thing as revelation or inspiration. Thus, to speak, as
many do, of the inspiration of the Buddhist scriptures,
were according to those authorities themselves to use
words without meaning. Without a God inspiration
and revelation are alike impossible and inconceivable. Hence all Buddhist authorities with strict con-

sistency represent the doctrine they contain, not as
having been revealed to the Buddha by any superior
power, but as having been thought out by the Buddha
himself.

Thus, to illustrate, we are told in the *Nidàna
Kathà* that the Buddha spent a week seated in a house
of gems, " thinking out the *Abhidhamma Piṭaka* . . .
in respect of the origin of all things as therein
explained.[1]   So also in the *Abhinishkramana Sùtra*,
the Buddha is declared to be " the supreme teacher of
gods and men. . . . In him alone can be found the
source of the true faith."[2]   So again, in the same work,
we are told that the Buddha, after his victory over the
evil one under the Bo-tree, remained there seven days
and nights.   " On the first night he considered in their
right order the twelve *Nidànas*,[3] and then in a reverse
order.   He identified these as one and the same; he
traced them from the first cause and followed them
through every concurrent circumstance."[4]   All this he
did, we are expressly told again and again, not as a

1 Fausböll's *Buddhist Birth Stories*, vol. i. p. 106.

2 *The Romantic Legend of Sàkya Buddha*, from the Chinese-Sans-
krit.—Professor S. Beal, p. 246.

3 *Nidàna* means " origin," "cause ;" technically, in Buddhism, the
chain of causes which ends in suffering.   They are said to be " Ignorance " or "Error" (*avijjà*), "Action (*karma*), Consciousness, the Individual, the Six Organs of Sense, Contact, Sensation, Desire, Attachment, Existence, Birth, Suffering."—Childers, *Dictionary of the Pàli
Language, sub. voc.*, p. 278.

4 *The Romantic Legend of Sàkya Buddha*, from the Chinese-Sans-
krit.—Professor S. Beal, p. 236.

god or as a superhuman being, or as a man under some special influence unattainable by other men. On the contrary, what the Buddha became, all may become ; what he attained is attainable by all, and that through the mere persevering exercise of our native powers. Thus we are told that when the Râjâ *Bimbasâra* asked Gautama who he was, he "answered plainly and truthfully, 'Maharâjâ ! I am no god or spirit, but a plain man, seeking for rest.' "[1] To the same effect, in the same work, the Buddha is represented as saying, in reference to his own attainment of supreme wisdom :

" Let a man but persevere with unflinching resolution,
And seek supreme wisdom, it will not be hard to attain it."[2]

Such words, it is clear, entirely exclude everything like revelation or inspiration from any superhuman source whatever.

How marked the contrast here, again, with the Lord Jesus, with the apostles and prophets, scarcely needs to be illustrated. Whatever any may think as to the *fact* of a revelation in the Christian Scriptures, there can be no doubt that they *profess* to contain a revelation from God to man ; that the writers profess to be speaking, *not* by their own unaided powers, but by the Holy Ghost. We read of Scripture which is "given by inspiration of God," *lit.* " God-breathed."[3] Buddha expressly professed to come in his own name ;

---

[1] *The Romantic Legend*, p. 182.
[2] *Ibid.* p. 225.   [3] 2 Tim. iii. 16.

Jesus as expressly claimed to have come in the name
of God the Father.[1] The former is said to have proudly
claimed that his doctrine was his own ; the latter as
explicitly claimed that He spoke not of Himself, and
that His doctrine was not His own, but the Father's
which had sent Him.[2] Here, then, again is a full
and explicit contradiction between the word of the
Buddha and the word of Christ. The one declares,
not only that there is a God, but that He has spoken
to man. The other, as it denies the former, denies of
necessity the latter also. No wisdom higher than the
wisdom of man has ever found a voice in this world.

3. *The Doctrine concerning Man.*

It is agreed by the highest authorities on the subject, almost without exception, that Buddhism, according to the teaching of the Buddha himself, so far as we
can ascertain it from the *Pitakas*, does not admit the
existence of the soul. A few, indeed, doubt or deny
this. Thus, *e.g.*, Professor Beal refers in a disparag-
ing way to "numerous writers on Buddhism, who in
their lectures and articles, tell us that it teaches . . .
atheism, annihilation, and the non-existence of the soul."
He remarks that "such statements are more easily
made than proved," and that it were "better if they
were not so frequently repeated in the face of contrary
statements made by those well able to judge." [3] Proof

---

[1] John v. 43.   [2] John viii. 28.
[3] *Romantic Legend*, Introduction, p. x.

of the opinion thus suggested he does not, however,
give.

Professor Max Müller admits that certain of the
Buddhist scriptures do undoubtedly teach the non-
existence of the soul, but does not think that this could
have been the teaching of the Buddha himself, but a
later corruption.   His argument is, briefly, as follows.
He admits that the orthodox metaphysics, as contained
in the third *Piṭaka*,[1] denies any substantial reality of
the soul.   He urges, however, that passages occur in
the other two *Piṭakas*, which are not to be reconciled
with this utter nihilism, and also refers to the asserted
fact that the doctrine in question does not appear in
its crude form in the first and second *Piṭakas*, and
refers to the opinion of some ancient authorities that
the third *Piṭaka* was "not pronounced by the Buddha."
He also urges that not only is this true, but that certain
passages occur in the first and second *Piṭakas* which
are in open contradiction to this metaphysical nihilism.
According to him, therefore, the Buddhist scriptures
contradict themselves on this most weighty question of
the existence of the soul.   The Buddha himself, he
thinks, could not have taught the doctrine of the non-
existence of the soul; he argues, that if the sayings
which teach the other doctrine have maintained themselves, in spite of their contradiction to orthodox

---

[1] The Buddhist canonical writings are known as the three *Piṭakas*,
called respectively *Vinaya*, *Sutta*, and *Abhidhamma*. For an account
of their contents, see Rhys Davids' *Buddhism*, pp. 18-21.

metaphysics, the only explanation, in his opinion, is, " that they were too firmly rooted in the tradition which went back to Buddha and his disciples." [1]

To our mind the Professor, however, does not prove his point. As to the alleged absence of the doctrine in question, from the first and second *Piṭakas*, he appears to have been mistaken ; for Mr. Davids has given two lengthy extracts from two different portions of the second *Piṭaka* which *formally* teach that man has no soul.[2] And even if we admit that the Buddhist scriptures in this matter contradict themselves, instead of arguing—for the reason given by the Professor— that the doctrine of the existence of the soul must needs be the original teaching of the Buddha, we should rather argue that such a preposterous doctrine as the contrary, flatly denying—as it does—the testimony of our own consciousness, was not likely to have gained currency at so early a date, *except* it were under the influence and personal authority of the Buddha ; and that the intimations of the being of the soul, which are supposed by a few to be scattered through the Buddhist books, are most naturally to be explained as simply the protest of the human consciousness against

---

[1] *Science of Religion; Buddhist Nihilism*, pp. 140-143.

[2] *Buddhism*, pp. 94 *et seq.* To the same effect Professor Childers, criticising Professor Müller, says, " that it is a fatal objection to his theory, that the doctrine of the *Abhidhamma* is identical with that of the other two *Piṭakas*, and that the expressions relating to *Nirvāna* used in the *Abhidhamma* are in reality taken from or authorised by the *Vinaya* and *Sùtra (Sutta) Piṭaka.*"—*Dictionary of the Pāli Language*, *sub. voc.*, *Nibbānam*, p. 265.

the nihilism with which the religion began. The unanswerable testimony of consciousness was too much even for the authority of the Buddha himself.

The direct and positive testimony to the fact, however, that Buddhism, according to its own highest authorities, does deny that there is a soul, seems unanswerable.

Thus in the *Sutta Nipàta* we read: "Only the name remains undecayed of the person who has passed away."[1] This certainly denies the survival of a soul after death in so many words; while in the *Nidàna Kathà*, of the *Birth Stories*, the statement is made without any limitation that the Buddha, after his attainment of Buddhahood, called five of his disciples together, and "preached to them the discourse *On the Non-Existence of the Soul.*"[2]

Mr. Rhys Davids has summed up the evidence that this is the teaching of orthodox Buddhism in a very clear and conclusive manner. His argument, in brief, is as follows. "In the first place, the *Pitakas* teach the doctrine directly and categorically. Thus we are told in the *Sutta Pitaka*: From sensation . . . the sensual, unlearned man derives the notions, 'I am,' 'this I exists,' 'I shall be,' etc. But the learned disciple of the converted . . . has got rid of ignorance and acquired wisdom ; and therefore the ideas, 'I am,' etc., do not occur to him." So also he refers to another

---

[1] *Sutta Nipàta; Jarà Sutta,* 5 ; *S. B. E.,* vol. x. part 2, pp. 154, 155.
[2] Fausböll's *Buddhist Birth Stories,* vol. i. p. 113.

passage in this first *Piṭaka*, wherein the Buddha is said
to have enumerated sixteen heresies teaching a conscious existence of the soul after death; then eight
heresies teaching that it has an unconscious existence
after death; and, finally, eight more which teach that
the soul exists after death in a state neither conscious nor unconscious. It is difficult indeed to see
how the doctrine of the non-existence of the soul
could be more explicitly set forth than by these two
passages.

But, in the second place, Mr. Davids argues that
this understanding of the doctrine of the Buddhist
scriptures is confirmed by what they indirectly teach
as bearing on the same subject. In particular he calls
attention to the fact that the Buddhists have two words
in their religious vocabulary expressly denoting as a
heresy the doctrine that man has a soul. These words
are *sakkáyadiṭṭhi*, "the heresy of individuality," and
attaváda, *lit.* "self-saying," "the assertion of self or
individuality." [1] Another proof that Buddhism denies
the existence of soul is found in the fact that the
Brahmans, their opponents, understood them so to
teach. Finally, the parables and illustrations used by
the Buddhists themselves to set forth and explain their
meaning, show that they themselves so understood the
doctrine of their sacred books. For example, it is
argued that just as a chariot is made up of various
parts, no one of which is the chariot, but which yet

[1] See Childers' *Páli Dictionary*, *sub. voc.*

by their union form the chariot, while yet there is no
existence separate and distinct from these, which con-
stitutes them jointly a chariot; so also is man made
up of various parts, and when these are united we say,
"This is a man;" while yet it does not follow that
there is in this case, any more than in that of the
chariot, any essence separate from these, which we
should call the soul.[1]

With this conclusion agree other eminent scholars
in Buddhism. Thus M. Barth affirms that the doctrine
of the non-existence of the soul is "the doctrine of
the entire orthodox literature of Southern Buddhism;"
and that while the books of the North appear to
concede . . . an ego passing from one to another
(in transmigration), yet this is but "a vaguely appre-
hended, feebly postulated ego."[2] Professor Oldenberg
maintains the same view. He says that, "while we are
wont to regard our interior life as only comprehensible,
if we are allowed to regard its changing content, every
individual feeling, every individual act of will, as in
relation to one and the same abiding ego, to think in
this manner is in total opposition to Buddhism. . . .
A seeing, a hearing, a becoming self-conscious, above
all, a suffering takes place; but an *essence*, which is that
which sees, hears, suffers,—this the Buddhistic doctrine

---

[1] One is reminded here of Professor Huxley's famous argument from
the non-existence of "aquosity" to the non-existence of vitality.

For Mr. Rhys Davids' argument in full, see his *Buddhism*, pp.
94-100.

[2] *The Religions of India*, pp. 111, 112.

does not recognise." He gives several illustrations out of the Buddhist texts, of which we may instance the following :—

> Màra, the tempter, who strives to confuse men with error and heresy, appeared to a nun and said to her, "Thou art the one by whom personality is created, the creator of the person : the person which comes into being, thou art that : thou art the person which ceases to be." She replies, "How thinkest thou, that there is a person, Màra? False is thy doctrine. This (which thou callest a person) is only a mass of changing forms :[1] there is no person here. As where the parts of a waggon are combined, the word 'waggon' is used, so where the five groups[2] are, there (we apply the word) 'person.' That is the catholic doctrine. Suffering alone it is, that comes into being : suffering, that which exists and ceases to be : nothing else than suffering comes into being : nothing else disappears again."[3]

To this testimony might be added yet others, but this should abundantly suffice to show how baseless, in the judgment of the highest authorities, is the opinion of some, as Mr. James Freeman Clarke,[4] Mr.

---

[1] Pàli, *sankhàrà*, is a term very difficult to translate ; Mr. Rhys Davids renders it "tendencies," "potentialities"; Oldenberg, "Gestaltungen."

[2] Pàli, *Skandha*, including *Rùpa*, *Vedanà*, *Saññá*, *Sankhàrà*, *Viññàna*, rendered by Rhys Davids, "*material* qualities," "*sensations*," "abstract *ideas*," "*tendencies* of mind," and "*mental powers*." Man is regarded as the sum total of these. See Rhys Davids' *Buddhism*, pp. 90 *et seq.*

[3] *Buddha, sein Leben, seine Lehre, seine Gemeinde*, S. 264 *ff.*

[4] *Ten Great Religions*, p. 167. Mr. J. F. Clarke—if we understand him—seems to regard St. Hilaire as admitting the existence of the soul as a doctrine of Buddhism, because he emphasises the doctrine of transmigration as one of the *principia* of Buddhism. For, he says, if

O

de Bunsen,[1] and a few others, that Buddhism teaches the existence of the soul.   If any still doubt such testimony as the above, surely special reliance is to be placed upon the statements of missionaries who have lived their whole life in intimate association with Buddhists, in daily conversation with them on these very matters.   And while they tell us that many Buddhists, constrained by the witness of their own consciousness, believe in the existence of the soul, they also agree that those who thus believe, believe—not according to their scriptures—but in opposition to them.   Just in the same way is it also true that while, as all admit, Buddhism, as such, knows nothing of a God, yet men, urged on by the inextinguishable instincts of the soul, have made Buddha himself into a god, and have even—as in Thibet—imagined a Supreme Buddha out of which, as they fancy, all the human Buddhas, by a kind of emanation process, have proceeded. But this no one would take to prove that the doctrine of a God properly belonged to Buddhism as a system.

Of missionary testimonies may be instanced the

there be no soul, there can be no transmigration. But Mr. Clarke omits to note the fact that St. Hilaire, while emphasising the place of transmigration in the Buddhist system, was nevertheless convinced that Buddhism did *not* teach the existence of soul, and asserts this in the most explicit terms. St. Hilaire's words are : '' Le textes à la main, je soutiens que le Bouddha n' admet pas plus l'âme de l'homme qu'il n' admet Dieu. Je ne crois pas qu'il soit possible de citer un seul texte bouddhique où la distinction la plus simple et la plus vulgaire de l'âme et du corps soit établie, ni paraisse même soupçonne.''—*Le Bouddha et sa Religion*, Paris, 1866, p. vi.

[1] *The Angel Messiah of Buddhists, Essenes, and Christians*, p. 48.

following. The Rev. Mr. Hardy tells us that "the belief in a soul is perhaps general among the Singhalese, *though so contrary to the teaching of Buddha.*[1]" What Buddhism, by its highest authorities, *teaches* its votaries on this subject, he very clearly tells us. He says, "To prove the impossibility of the existence of a soul, many a long and weary conversation is recorded in the *Abhidhamma.* All thought is regarded as a material result. The operation of the mind is no different in mode to that of the eye or ear."[2] The teaching of the Chinese Buddhists Dr. Edkins gives us in the following citation from the *Leng-yen-king*, one of their chief authorities. Buddha, we are therein told, taught as follows: "The mind . . . is without substance and cannot be at any place; . . . that the mind is unsubstantial can easily be shown, etc."[3] And Bishop Bigandet, of Burmah, tells us that the same is the doctrine of the Burmese Buddhists. In the end of his volumes on the *Legend of Gaudama,* he gives us an abridged translation of a Burmese work, entitled *The Seven Ways to Neibban,* which he tells us may be looked upon as a faithful exposition of the tenets of Buddhism as they are held both in Siam and in Burmah. Therein we read that "in the five aggregates constituting man . . . there is nothing else to be found but form and name. We are thus brought to the materialist

[1] *Legends and Theories of the Buddhists,* p. 220 (italics ours).
[2] *Legends and Theories of the Buddhists,* p. 211 ; see also Appendix, note Z.
[3] *Chinese Buddhism,* p. 299.

conclusion, that in man we can discover no other element but that of form and name."[1]   Here, then, we have
explicit testimony, not from scholars at a distance and
acquainted with Buddhism only at second hand, but from
missionaries, who have had everywhere the advantage of
ascertaining from the Buddhists themselves what they
understand their scriptures really to teach.   The testimony cited comes from each of the three great Buddhist countries—China, Farther India, and Ceylon, and
from men whose names are of high authority.   They
all agree that the teaching of Buddhism is understood
by the people, alike in China, Siam, Burmah, and Ceylon,
to deny the existence of a soul.

It is true indeed that, as Professor Max Müller
asserts, much may be produced from the Buddhist
authorities which—if understood as we in the West
naturally understand it—appears to teach, or at least
imply, the existence of the soul.   This is especially
true as regards what is written in the *Jàtakas* and
elsewhere touching the transmigrations and previous
existences of the Buddha and others.   Professor Frankfurter refers to this and remarks upon the matter as
follows : " It has often been asked how . . . the
denial of the existence of a soul, can be brought into
agreement with the fact that Gautama knew in what
particular characters he had previously appeared among
living beings, and how he could preserve consciousness,
such as is related of him in the *Jàtakatthavaṇṇana*

---

[1] *The Legend of Gaudama,* vol. ii. p. 213.

(the *Birth Stories*)." He then shows first that the original book of the *Jàtakas* did not contain these references to the previous lives of the Buddha, which were afterwards added by the commentator on the stories, and then adds, " It is, therefore, the commentator who is responsible for the perversion of the original doctrine. All vague assertions about the non-agreement of the denial of the soul with the fact of Gautama's knowledge of his previous existences are worthless. It is to be inferred, therefore, that through taking the *Jàtaka* with the commentary as the original, the opinion arose that what the Buddha knew of his previous existences was due to the knowledge he had of the future, present, and past, which was one of the attributes of Buddhahood."[1]

The Rev. Mr. Hardy, in the appendix to his *Legends and Theories of the Buddhists*, notices this same difficulty, and explains the real belief of orthodox Buddhists by an extract from the writings of another learned missionary; his predecessor, the Rev. M. R. Gogerly, with the remark that among the Buddhist priests of Ceylon " there are none of authority who now dispute his conclusions." Not to give the whole of his argument, we are told that the King Milinda inquired " if a living soul is received upon transmigration ; and the priest replied, ' In the higher or proper sense of the word, there is not.' . . . The king inquired further, ' Is there anybody or being—*satto*—which goes from this body to

---

[1] *The One Religion* (Bampton Lectures, 1881) ; Appendix i. pp. 350, 352.

another body ?'   'No, great king, . . . by this *náma-rùpa*[1] actions are performed, good or bad, and by these actions another *námarùpa* commences existence.'"[2] From these and other like explicit statements of the Buddhist authorities, Mr. Hardy concludes, in full accord with the eminent European savants above cited, that "Buddhism denies the existence of a soul,—of anything of which a man may rightly say, 'This is I myself.'" The unanimity of the testimonies upon this subject surely ought to be decisive. What, in fact, is to be understood by the Buddhist doctrine of transmigration, if the existence of an abiding soul be denied, Mr. Rhys Davids,—in the preface to his translation of the *Buddhist Birth Stories*, or tales of the experiences of the Buddha in what we should call his previous births,—has clearly explained. He says :—

> The reader must of course avoid the mistake of importing Christian ideas into the conclusions (of these several birth stories), by supposing that the identity of the persons in the two stories is owing to the passage of a "soul" from the one to the other. Buddhism does *not* teach the transmigration of *souls*. Its doctrine . . . would be better summarised as the *transmigration* of *character*, for it is entirely independent of the early and widely-prevalent notion of the existence with each human body of a distinct soul, or ghost, or spirit. The *Bodisat*, for example, is not supposed to have a soul which, on the death of one body, is transferred to another, but to be the inheritor of the characters acquired by the previous *Bodisats*. . . . The only thing which

---

[1] Literally, "*name* (*and*) *form*"—that which, according to the Buddhist conception, forms the sum total of the man.

[2] *Legends and Theories of the Buddhists*, p. 238.

continues to exist when a man dies is his *karma*, the result of his words and thoughts and deeds, literally, "his doing ;" and the curious theory that this result is concentrated in some new individual is due to the older theory of soul."[1]

And in the preface to his translation of the *Sabbà-sava Sutta* he sums up the case as regards the Buddhist position on this question as follows :—

Buddhism is not only independent of the theory of soul, but regards the consideration of that theory as worse than profitless, as the source of manifold delusions and superstitions. Practically this comes, however, to much the same thing as the denial of the existence of the soul ; just as agnosticism is, at best, but an earnest and modest sort of atheism. And we have seen above that *anattam*—the absence of a soul or self as abiding principle—is one of the three parts of Buddhist wisdom and of Buddhist perception.[2]

We have been thus full in the discussion of this subject, because in nothing, as it seems to us, is the teaching of Buddhism more often misapprehended than on this point. To sum up the case, so far is it from being true that "the soul's immortality is a radical doctrine in Buddhism," and this doctrine "one of its points of contact with Christianity," as has been asserted,[3] that even the existence of the soul is not

[1] *Buddhist Birth Stories*, introduction, pp. lxxv. lxxvi. Mr. Childers quotes from the learned Mr. Gogerly of Ceylon words of the same purport ; see his *Dictionary of the Pàli Language*, p. 525.

[2] *Sacred Books of the East*, vol. xi. p. 294.

[3] *Ten Great Religions*, p. 167. This could at most only be true of the type of Northern Buddhism represented in the *Lotus of the True Law*. It is declared there of the Buddha that he lives for ever, and others seem to share his immortality. But this is not the doctrine of orthodox Buddhism as represented in the *Piṭakas*, and we

admitted, and the affirmation of its being is specially stigmatised as a *heresy*. There is nothing but "name and form,"—that is all. No God! No revelation! No soul! And we are told that Buddhism is the *Light* of Asia! Truly, the words, to one who has learned from Him who is the Light of the world, seem to have a ring of irony!

4. *The Doctrine concerning Sin.*

But, obviously, having gone so far, the Buddhist cannot stop here. We have next to compare the teaching of Buddhism concerning *sin*. We hear much of the high morality of Buddhism, and, by consequence, it seems to be commonly imagined that however the Buddhist and the Christian religions may differ in other respects, they must at least be very much at one in their teachings as to sin. What, for example, could sound more like Christian teaching than the following words from the *Dhammapada*:—

> "Rise up! and loiter not!
> Follow after a holy life!
> Who follows virtue rests in bliss,
> Both in this world and the next!
> Follow after a holy life!
> Follow not after sin!"[1]

---

cannot credit the Buddha with it. It is the protest of man's ineradicable instinct of immortality against the dreary negation of the older and still *orthodox* Buddhism. See *Saddharmapuṇḍarīka*, chap. xiv. *passim*; *S. B. E.*, vol. xxi.

[1] *Dhammapada*, 168, 169. We follow Mr. Davids' translation in his *Buddhism*, p. 65.

Such words as these, however, greatly mislead those who will read into the essential terms their Christian sense. The Buddhist idea of sin is as far as possible from the conception which Christianity holds forth. What the Bible teaches on this subject is sufficiently clear. We may define sin, with the Divines of the Westminster Assembly, as "any want of conformity to, or transgression of, the law of God;" or, with others, as "the voluntary transgression of known law;" or in any other way that any Christian theologian has adopted : as regards the present point, it will make no difference. For all these various definitions agree in this, that they affirm sin to be a disorder in the normal relation of the soul to God. As John the Apostle puts it, all "sin is the transgression of law," and that law is the law of God. Even where the sin, in its external form, is a sin against one's neighbour, it is none the less, in its innermost essence, sin against God. Thus, while as to its outer form, the sin of David, which he laments in the 51st Psalm, was adultery and murder, yet in his confession the thought which above all others burdens him is this, "Against thee, thee only have I sinned, and done this evil in thy sight."[1] Although this conception of the nature of sin finds its fullest expression in the Christian Scriptures, it is by no means peculiar to them. On the contrary, it is found among all those who—whatever of error they may hold on other subjects—have at least held fast their

[1] Psalm li. 4.

faith in a personal God. Granted the existence of such a
Being as the Creator and moral Ruler of the world must
be, this idea of sin follows by necessary consequence.

But it is no less plain that, in the very nature of
the case, such a view of the nature of sin can have no
place in Buddhism. Such a conception presupposes a
personal God, who is at once the giver and the executor
of law; whereas Buddhism knows nothing of any such
being. It follows from this, of necessity, that if there
be no Being above man whose will, imposed as law, is
the standard of action for man, then law, *i.e.*, the ultimate
standard of moral action, must be found in the will
of man himself, and sin can only be defined as an evil
having a certain relation to the will of man.

Now, in fact, this is the highest conception of sin
which is to be found in any Buddhist book. Nowhere
do we meet with the slightest intimation that sin has
to do with any but man. That which Christianity
regards as the essence of all sin is the revolt of the
will against the authority of God. That which Buddhism regards as the essence of all sin is something as
different as possible from this. The one characteristic
element in all sin is always represented as *trishnà* or
tanhà. This word, in English translations of Buddhist
works, is often rendered " lust," and thus, again, is the
teaching of Buddhism made to seem very like that of
the New Testament; for has not the Apostle James
said, "When lust hath conceived, it bringeth forth sin "?[1]

[1] James i. 15.

But *trishnà* or *tanhà*—"lust," if any one will use the word—in the mouth of a Buddhist has no such meaning as *epithumia* in the mouth of a New Testament writer. In the New Testament, it is hardly necessary to say, it is desire—not merely as desire—but as the desire of something which God has forbidden, which is declared to be the root and the essence of sin.

Whatever *tanhà* with the Buddhists mean, it is agreed on all hands, that it means nothing like this. What it does really comprehend seems to be to some extent a matter of debate. Some understand it to denote desire *universally*, for anything whatsoever. Certainly, if this be the content of the term, this leads to a conception of sin totally different from that which we find in Christianity. For then, to be rid of desire, of all desire for anything good or evil, is to be rid of sin. There are certainly many passages in the Buddhist scriptures, taken by themselves, would seem to favour this meaning. Thus we read :—

For him who wishes for something, there are always desires and trembling in the midst of his plans ; he for whom there is no death and no rebirth, how can he desire anything ?[1]

As in the middle (*i.e.* depth) of the sea no wave is born, (but as it) remains still, so let the *Bhikkhu* be still, without desire ; let him not desire anything whatever.

[1] *Sutta Nipàta ; Mahàviyùha Sutta*, 8 ; *S. B. E.*, vol. x. part 2, p. 172. See also vers. 5-7, wherein "virtue" and "purity" are named as among the objects of the disapproved desires. *Vid. infr.*, p. 310.

In the same Sutta the inquirer after the "state of peace" is directed :—

All the desires that arise inwardly, let him learn to subdue them. [1]

And in the *Dhammapada*, again, it is written :—

He who fosters no desires for this world or for the next, has no inclinations and is unshackled, him I call a Brahman.

He who, having no desires, travels about without a home, in whom all concupiscence is extinct, him I call a Brahman. [2]

Such passages as these, which might be cited in great number, would certainly seem to stigmatise all desire, without exception, as evil.

On the other hand, there are here and there passages which might seem to restrict somewhat the comprehension of this fatal "thirst" or desire. Thus we read :—

Thirst is threefold—namely, thirst for pleasure, thirst for existence, thirst for prosperity. [3]

From such passages Mr. Davids infers that the unrestricted meaning which is sometimes assigned to *tanhâ* is erroneous. He tells us that we are to understand by it, not mere desire as such, but only "evil desires, grasping selfish aims." [4]   Now at first sight

---

[1] *Sutta Nipata; Tuvataka Sutta*, vi. 1, 2 ; *S. B. E.*, vol. x. part 2, pp. 174, 175.

[2] *Dhammapada*, 410, 416.

[3] *Mahâvagga*, i. 6, 20 ; *S. B. E.*, vol. xiii. p. 95.

[4] *Lectures on the Origin and Growth of Religion*, etc. (Hibbert Lectures, 1881), p. 207.

this might seem to be essentially the same as the conception of "lust" in the New Testament, and yet it is
as wide asunder from it as the other explanation of
the term.   For Mr. Davids himself elsewhere tells us
that these selfish aims include, not only much (though
not all) that the Christian would call sin, but also
"sensuality, desire of future life, or love of the present
life." [1]   To the same effect also Professor Frankfurter
says that all the varieties of *tanhà* described by Buddhist authorities may be distributed under three classes,
—"craving for sensual pleasure, for continued existence,
and for non-existence." [2]   Professor Childers shows
that the Buddhist authorities classify the various *tanhàs*
in different ways.   Thus, we read not only of *tanhà*
as a "thirst for the pleasures of sense, for existence,
and for non-existence," but also of *kàmatanhà, rùpatanhà,*
arùpatanhà, or desire for existence in either one of
the three forms of existence; also again, "for existence
either in the worlds of form, or in the formless worlds,
or for annihilation." [3]   To our own mind there seems to
be an inconsistency on this subject in the Buddhist
authorities.   While undoubtedly we do find *tanhà*
defined and its varieties classified as above indicated,
yet it is certainly the natural understanding of various
passages that *all* desire is evil, not only that which
might plainly fall under the above categories, but also

---

[1] *Buddhism*, p. 107.
[2] *The One Religion* (Bampton Lectures, 1881), Appendix i. p. 346.
[3] *A Dictionary of the Pàli Language ; sub. voc., tanhà.*

desire even for virtue itself. Those are condemned who "wail for what is pure," and those are approved who do not pray for either purity or impurity ;[1] and he who has no desires, absolutely—as we have seen above—is held forth as the perfect man.

But whichever view of the inclusion of this term be correct, it is clear that the conception of sin thus indicated is in either case alike as wide asunder as the poles from the New Testament conception of sin. Hence the man who, when he meets in Buddhist writings with this word "sin," or any of its equivalents, by such words understands by it what in Christendom is meant by sin, reads into the text an idea which has no place there whatever.[2] What the Buddhist really does understand in such cases is well put by the Rev. Mr. Hardy, from whom again we quote :—

The proper idea of sin cannot enter into the mind of the Buddhist. His system knows nothing of a Supreme Ruler of the universe. . . . There is no law because there is no law-giver,—no authority from which law can proceed. Buddha is superior in honour and wisdom to all other beings ; but he claims no right to impose restrictions on other beings. He points out the course to be taken if merit is to be gained ; but he who refuses to heed his words does the *Tathàgato* no wrong. Religion is a mere code of proprieties, a mental opiate, a plan for being free from discomfort, a system of personal profit. . . .

[1] *Sutta Nipàta ; Mahàviyùha Sutta*, 4-7 ; *S. B. E.*, vol. x. part 2, pp. 171, 172.

[2] So Mr. Rhys Davids rightly says that "the Christian idea of sin is inconsistent with Buddhist ethics."—Introduction to the *Sabbàsava Sutta ; S. B. E.*, vol. xi. p. 295.

As there is no infinite and all-worthy being to whose glory we are called upon to live, when we commit evil the wrong is done to ourselves and not to another.[1] . . . Hence the impossibility of making the Buddhist feel that he is a sinner, when the commandment is brought home upon his conscience. A native has been heard to say that he never committed sin since he was born, unless it were in catching fish ! [2]

And Dr. Edkins gives a similar account of the notions the Chinese Buddhists have of sin. He says, " They hold that sin is the cause of suffering. Yet they do not mean by this wilful sin, but some improper act done unconsciously, or in childhood, as treading on an insect, wasting rice-crumbs, or misusing paper that has the native characters upon it. . . . Hence they regard themselves as more to be pitied than blamed for the *tsui* or ' sin ' of which their ill-fortune gives evidence."[3] And *this* is what the *Light* of Asia has taught men concerning sin !

5. *The Doctrine concerning Salvation.*

It follows, both logically and actually, from all the above, that the Buddhist doctrine of *salvation* stands in no less open contradiction with that which was taught by Christ. This is true as regards every point involved in the Scriptural doctrine of salvation—as to

[1] One is reminded of Feuerbach's definition of religion, as "the relation of a man to himself."

[2] *Legends and Theories of the Buddhists*, pp. 213, 214.

[3] *Chinese Buddhism*, p. 193.

its *nature*, its *ground*, the *means* thereto, and the *author* of the salvation.   On each and every one of these points the teaching of the Buddha stands in the most unqualified antagonism to that of the Christ.   The teaching of the Scripture is so clear as scarcely to need a statement here.

As to the *nature* of the salvation, all agree that the salvation which is offered by Christ is a salvation, *not*, primarily, from *suffering*, but from *sin*, and from suffering only in that it is the penal consequence of sin. In other words, Christ in His salvation proposes to deliver man from sin and death, and give him everlasting life in holiness.   The formation of an eternally holy character is the objective point of Christ's work as regards the individual man.[1]   As regards the *ground* on which any man receives this immeasurable blessing, Christ uniformly taught that His *death* was the ground.   He gave His life " a ransom for many."[2] His blood, He declared, was " shed for many for the remission of sins."[3]   So also His apostles taught that this salvation, being wholly on the ground—not of what the sinner had done, or could do, or become,— but wholly and exclusively on the ground of what Christ had done for us, was all of grace and not of works.[4]   As regards the *means* of salvation, we are everywhere told that it is received by faith, and maintained by the believing use of all the ordinances

---

[1] Rom. v. 9 ; Eph. v. 25-27.   [2] Matt. xx. 28.
[3] Matt. xxvi. 28.   [4] Rom. xi. 6 ; Eph. ii. 8.

appointed by the Lord for this end.[1] As regards the
author, it is everywhere taught in the Christian Scriptures that—whether we regard salvation as *objectively*
wrought out for us on the Cross, or as originated and
carried on for us *subjectively* in regeneration and sanctification—in every point of view, the author of our salvation is Christ.[2] Salvation is not of man in any way;
he neither saves himself, nor helps to save himself;
" salvation "—wholly and absolutely—" is of the Lord."
    Now this doctrine of salvation taught by Christ, so
far from having any similarity or analogy with that
set forth by the Buddha, as some would persuade us,
stands contrasted with it in every particular. As to
the *nature* of salvation, whereas Christ makes it to
consist essentially in salvation from *sin*, Buddhism
makes it to consist,—*not* in deliverance from sin—not
even from that which the Buddha calls sin,—but in
salvation from *sorrow*, and that, ultimately, as we shall
see, through salvation from *existence.* It is quite true
that the Buddhist books are full of exhortations against
sin, and many of these, according to the letter, are, as
all will agree, most excellent. But none the less is
even the highest and purest morality represented, *not*
as an end in itself, but only as a means to an end,
which end is, to bring to a final termination that line
of personal existence of which the life I now live is
the present manifestation. Thus, even if the Buddhist
conception of sin were identical with that of the

---

[1] Rom. iii. 28 ; John xv. 1-10.   [2] Tit. iii. 4-6.

P

Christian—as it is not—still there would be a *vital* difference as regards the nature of salvation, in that *character* is made, *not* the *end* of salvation, but merely a *means* to an end.

For, according to the Lord Jesus, the supreme evil is sin ; according to the Buddha, the supreme evil is not sin, but *suffering*, and *existence*, as necessarily involving pain. Hence their respective teachings as to the nature of salvation differ totally. The whole doctrine of the Buddha as to salvation is summed up in what are called the four words of truth, namely : *Duḥkha,* "pain ;" *Samudaya,* "origin ;" *Nirodha,* "destruction ;" and *Márga*, " road." The signification of these four words which, expanded, form what are known as " the Four Noble Truths," is set forth in the following verses from the *Dhammapada :*—

" He who with clear understanding sees the four holy truths :
    Pain ; the origin of pain ; the destruction of pain ; and the
    eightfold holy way that leads to the quieting of pain ;
    That is the safe refuge, that is the best refuge.
    Having gone to that refuge, a man is delivered from all pain."[1]

Professor Max Müller correctly expounds these verses as follows : " The four holy truths are the four statements that there is pain in this world, that the source of pain is desire, that desire can be annihilated, that there is a way shown by Buddha by which the annihilation of all desires can be achieved, and freedom be obtained."[2]

[1] *Dhammapada,* 190-192.
[2] *Buddhaghosha's Parables,* p. cxiii.

Thus we have the highest authority for affirming that—not the removal of *sin*—but the removal of *pain* is the objective point of the whole Buddhist system of salvation. And it is also of the greatest importance to observe that even pain is misunderstood. For pain is not in Buddhism regarded as merely the necessary effect of sin, but as the necessary condition of *all individual existence*, alike in earth, and hell, and heaven, in bird, beast, worm, or man or god. For pain, argues the Buddhist, is because of *tanhá, trishná*, " desire." By this, as already noted, is intended not merely desire after that which is morally evil, but desire after much that is lawful, and especially after existence, here or hereafter. It denotes that state of mind which is usually enkindled by the contact of the mind or the senses with the external world. Wherever this state of mind exists, continued existence is made necessary. For desire, *tanhá*, is the cause of "action," or, in Buddhist phraseology, *karma*. I die and pass away, but my *karma* lives on, and renders necessary the production of another being after me to reap the fruit of my action. And so long as this chain of existence is continued, so long is there with existence the continued liability to new craving, and therefore to new pain. I see, I hear, I feel, I taste, I remember, and because of this arises desire; and because so much that I perceive seems good, I desire to live and I love the world. And this desire—whether it be of that which is evil or, in many cases, of that which is good

—even desire to live in heaven, as well as the desire
to live on earth—is the root and source of pain and
sorrow. It is so because desire implies the non-pos-
session of that which is desired; and not to have what
we desire, of necessity means pain and sorrow. The
desire may be of that which is good, but except it be
at once completely satisfied, it must become a cause of
pain. This is by no means saying that all desires are
equally reprehensible. Gautama clearly. saw that
certain things were evil in a sense in which other
things were not. Conscience, despite the power of a
false philosophy, never becomes extinct. Hence the
Buddha freely admitted that certain desires, having an
intrinsic evil character, brought more pain than others,
and therefore were to be the more carefully avoided.
Hence lying, hatred, and anger are denounced as being
in an especial sense occasions of pain and sorrow.
Thus we read :—

" The fields are damaged by weeds, mankind is damaged by
   hatred.
   The fields are damaged by weeds, mankind is damaged by
   vanity."

All this is true, but then we also read in the next
verse :—

" The fields are damaged by weeds, mankind is damaged by
   wishing.
   Therefore a gift bestowed on those who are free from wishes,
   brings great reward."[1]

---

[1] *Dhammapada*, 357-359.

"*Wishing*" or "*craving*" is the root of all evil, and hence is inferred the third of the Noble Truths, namely: that since desire is the cause of all pain, the extinction of all pain will follow the extinction of desire. And thus we are brought to the fourth and last of the Four Noble Truths, that this end—the extinction of desire—can only be attained by walking in what is called "the Noble Eightfold Path." What that way is we need not consider just here.[1] At present we are to note the contrast between the Christian and the Buddhist doctrine as to the nature of salvation. Salvation, as regards the individual man, consists in the extinction of sorrow by means of the extinction of desire. Its relation to what *we* call sin is merely casual and incidental.

Here it is important to observe that the Buddhist salvation, in *this* sense, does not consist in the cessation of existence. This is plain, to go no further, from the Buddhist doctrine as to the nature of man. For, according to the Buddhist authorities, when a man dies, his body having perished, there remains no other part of him which can continue to exist. This is as true of the worldly as of the religious man. It is plain from this alone that when the Buddhists speak of *Nirvàna*, the personal salvation, they cannot mean thereby the extinction of the individuality. For this befalls every one at death, whereas *Nirvàna* is the

---

[1] See chap. vi., "The Ethics of Buddhism and the Ethics of the Gospel," where the "Path" is fully expounded. *Infra*, p. 301 *et seq.*

attainment of comparatively few.   This is the plainer
from the use of the term in the Buddhist scriptures.
We find it constantly used to describe something
which is attained and enjoyed before death, and in this
world.   Thus we read :—

If thou keepest thyself silent as a broken gong, thou hast
attained *Nirvâna*.[1]

Desire is the worst ailment, the body the greatest of evils.
Where this is properly known, there is *Nirvâna*, the highest
bliss.[2]

The destruction of passion, and of wish for the dear objects
which have been perceived, O Hemaka, is the imperishable state
of *Nirvâna*.[3]

Such passages as these, however, do not represent
the whole truth.   The Buddhist authorities set forth
the great salvation, to the attainment of which the
Buddha professed to direct men, under a twofold
aspect.   In the first place, as Professor Max Müller
has clearly shown from the collation of a large number
of passages like the above, *Nirvâna* sometimes denotes
a mental and spiritual state attainable in this present
life.   It denotes the state of the man who has entered
the Fourth Path, has succeeded in overcoming Desire,
and is victor over the Ten Sins.   In this sense of the
word, *Nirvâna* or " salvation " designates a certain state
of mind, which being reached, the man is in this life
freed from pain.   To use the term " holiness," however,

---

[1] *Dhammapada*, 134.   [2] *Ibid.* 203.

[3] *Sutta Nipâta; Pârâyanavagga*, ix. 3 ; *S. B. E.*, vol. x. part 2,
p. 202.

as some have done, to denote this state of mind, is utterly misleading. Such a use of the word "holiness" cannot be too severely condemned. It produces an impression of agreement between Christianity and Buddhism, where, in reality, no agreement whatever exists. For the Biblical idea of holiness, like that of sin, never loses sight of a person. It is not mere morality, which is rightness toward men; it is rightness toward God, which, indeed, implies morality, but is yet much more.

Shall we then say that the Buddhist idea of salvation is the attainment of an ideal morality? This neither can we do, though he who has attained *Nirvána* will be what the world calls a moral man. Shall we say with Mr. Davids that the Buddhist salvation to be found here in this life, consists " in an inward change of heart"?[1] Certainly the parallel which such language suggests between the Buddhist doctrine of salvation and that of Christ—a doctrine of a salvation consisting fundamentally in a regeneration—has absolutely no foundation in fact. This phrase, "a change of heart," which in the Christian religion has a very definite and precise meaning, ought not to be used in this connection. Christ represents this regeneration, or change of heart, as consisting essentially in the impartation of a new spiritual life, by the power of the Holy Ghost. We have already seen enough to make

[1] Introduction to the *Dhammacakkappavattana Sutta*; *S. B. E.*, vol. xi. p. 143.

it clear that for such a conception there is no room in Buddhism.

To reach the Buddhist idea of salvation, considered as a good attainable in this life, we must recur to the Buddhist doctrine concerning sin. Not only does the Buddhist conception of sin have nothing to do with a man's relation to God, but, besides, along with many acts which are sins, either against ourselves or against our fellow-men, it also includes many other acts and states, which have nothing sinful in them; and again, in many cases, stigmatises that as evil which is good. A sufficient proof of this we have in the common enumeration of the Ten Sins. While among these are enumerated "hatred," "pride," and "selfishness," we also find reckoned with these "belief in the existence of the soul," "desire of life on earth," and "desire of life in heaven." Since the *Nibutta*, the saved man, is a man "who has overcome the ten sins," he will therefore, without doubt, be conceived of as a man who has been freed from hatred, pride, and selfishness and all unlawful lusts, and thus will be, according to the theory, what we call a moral man; and yet that is not a full account of him. To be kind, humble, chaste, this alone is not *Nirvâna*. Not until a man has also extinguished the delusion of the existence of a self, the desire of life on earth, and even the desire of life in heaven, has he attained *Nirvâna*. The truth is, that, even taken in the best sense possible,—that of deliverance from what the Buddhist holds as sin,—

Nirvâna, the Buddhist "salvation," is something utterly diverse from the Christian idea of deliverance from sin. To use, therefore, such Christian terms as "salvation," "holiness," "saved," and "holy," in describing the nature and result of the Buddhist salvation—except the reader be put on his guard—is only to lead the common reader, unfamiliar with the technicalities of Buddhist theology, utterly astray.[1] Buddhism, indeed, makes salvation to involve deliverance from what *it* calls sin, though *always as a means to an end;* but as its idea of *sin* differs *in toto* from that of the Christian Scriptures, its *salvation*, in the best construction, is a very different thing from that which is offered us by Christ.

But is this all that Buddhism presents as involved in salvation? We think not. While this is a true account of the Buddhist salvation as far as it goes, and explains all those passages which speak of *Nirvâna* as a present possible attainment of the living man, it is not all that the word involves. It does not bring before us the absolute ultimatum of the Buddhist system. For while it is true that, according to the Buddhist scriptures, there is after death no surviving soul of *any* man, yet though my soul does not survive me, my *karma* or my works do survive me. And if I die, with the craving after life still unextinguished, then the power of this, my *karma*, will necessitate the birth, in heaven, earth, or hell, of a being,—*another* being,

[1] See *S. B. E.*, vol. xi. p. 243.

according to Western metaphysics, the *same,* according
to the Buddhist,—in which this unextinguished *trishnà*
or "desire" will burn on, and so continue all its possibility of woe.   But it is the blessed issue of the state
of mind described as *Nirvâna,* that—desire being now
at an end—nothing now remains in the man, which
could entail any moral necessity for the production at
his death of a being who should reap the fruit of his
karma.   In other words, that particular continuous
chain of personal existence in which I, for example, as
now existing, am a single link, is thereby brought to
an end.   And this, according to Mr. Davids, is what
the Buddhists call, by way of distinction, *Parinibbâna,*
the supreme *Nirvâna.*

This doctrine, that the most absolute and everlasting cessation of being is the consummation of the life
of the *Nibutta*—him that has attained *Nibbâna* [1]—finds
repeated expression in the Buddhist scriptures.   As
the fact that Buddhism teaches such an annihilation as
the final issue of its so-called salvation, has been so
stoutly disputed, we give the following citations :—

From the cessation of all the *sankhâras,* and from the destruction of consciousness, will arise the destruction of pain. [2]

Who except the noble deserve the well-understood state of
Nibbâna?   Having perfectly conceived this state, those free from
passion are completely extinguished. [3]

---

[1] *Nibbâna-nirvâna.*

[2] *Sutta Nipâta; Dvayatânupassana Sutta,* 9 ; *S. B. E.,* vol. x. part 2
p. 135.

[3] *Ibid.,* 42 ; *S. B. E.,* vol. x. part 2, p. 145.

Again, in a conversation between the Buddha and one *Upasîva*, the latter formally raises the question we are discussing, and the Buddha answers it in the most emphatic manner, as will appear in the following extract :—

UPASÎVA : He whose passion for all sensual pleasures has departed, having resorted to nothingness, after leaving everything else, and being delivered in the highest deliverance by knowledge, . . . (and if) he becomes there tranquil and delivered, will there be consciousness for such a one ?

BUDDHA : As a flame blown about by the violence of the wind, O Upasîva, goes out, cannot be reckoned (as existing), even so a Muni, delivered from name and body, disappears, and cannot be reckoned as existing.

UPASÎVA : Has he (only) disappeared, or does he not exist (any longer), or is he for ever free from sickness ? Explain that thoroughly to me. . . .

BUDDHA : For him who has disappeared there is no form, O Upasîva; . . . that by which they say "He is," exists for him no longer.[1]

Again, of one *Subhadda*, it is said that having attained "to that supreme goal of the higher life, he became conscious that birth was at an end, that the higher life had been fulfilled, that all that should be done had been accomplished, and that after the present life there would be no beyond."[2]

And the doctrine is again declared in the most categorical manner in the following passage from the

[1] *Sutta Nipâta ; Pârâyanavagga*, vii. 4-8 ; *S. B. E.*, vol. x. part 2, p. 199.

[2] *Mahâparinibbâna Sutta*, v. 68 ; *S. B. E.*, vol. xi. p. 110.

Vinaya Piṭaka : " By the destruction of Thirst Attachment is destroyed, by the destruction of Attachment Existence is destroyed, by the destruction of
Existence Birth is destroyed, by the destruction of
Birth old age, grief, lamentation, suffering, dejection,
and despair are destroyed."[1]

So also, again and again, the attainment of *parinibbàna* by the Buddha in his death is described as " that
utter passing away in which nothing whatever is left
behind."[2] To statements such as these it would be
easy to add others, no less clear and unambiguous;
but these will, we think, suffice to make it clear that
if the extinction of the individual as such is not the
essence of salvation, seeing that the individual, in any
case, perishes at death, yet Buddhism does hold up as
the ultimatum of salvation an annihilation of existence
far more sweeping and comprehensive — namely, the
eternal destruction of that particular line of sentient
being which I represent! And this is brought about
by the annihilation of the generating power of my
works, through the extinction in me of desire ![3]

---

[1] *Mahàvagga*, i. 1, 2 ; *S. B. E.*, vol. xiii. p. 77.

[2] *Mahaparinibbàna Sutta*, iii. 20, iv. 57, v. 20 ; *S. B. E.*, vol. xi.
pp. 48, 84, 90.

[3] Professor Childers, in a long article on the word *Nibbàna* in his
Pàli Dictionary, has argued with great force to this same conclusion
that the ultimatum of the Buddhist salvation is absolute annihilation.
He says, " A creed which begins by saying that existence is suffering,
must end by saying that release from suffering is the highest good, and
accordingly we find that annihilation is the goal of Buddhism, the
supreme reward held out to the faithful observer of its precepts."

And this is the ultimate consummation of the highest salvation which Buddhism has to offer. This was the salvation which we are told the Buddha found, for himself first of all, under the Bo-tree. This was the " Gospel," the discovery of which, according to Mr. Edwin Arnold, made that morning after the great temptation "break gloriously," "radiant with rising hopes for man." This is the final issue of that great salvation, over the Buddha's supposed discovery of which the poet apologist for heathenism waxes so

The disagreement among European scholars as to whether *Nirvàna* mean annihilation or not, he ascribes to the fact we have above illustrated, that two sets of expressions are used with regard to *Nirvàna*, the one implying blissful existence, and the other annihilation. Arhatship, or the state of him who has entered the Fourth Path—in other words, who has here attained *Nirvàna*—he describes as "final and perfect sanctification, a state in which merit and demerit, original sin, desire, attachment, are rooted out, in which all that binds man to existence, all that leads to rebirth or transmigration, is rooted out." Again he asserts, "Not only is there no trace in the Buddhist scriptures of the Arhat continuing to exist after death, but it is deliberately stated in innumerable passages, with all the clearness and emphasis of which language is capable, that the Arhat does *not* live again after death, but ceases to exist. There is probably no doctrine more distinctive of Sàkya Muni's original doctrine than that of the annihilation of being." Again he remarks, with regard to the term *amata*, which has been rendered by Professor Max Müller (*Dhammapada*, 21) as "immortality," that the word "is an adjective, and whatever it means, cannot well mean immortality." In a word, then, his conclusion is that the word *Nibbàna* (*Nirvàna*) sometimes denotes a mental state such as is above described, attainable in this life,—a state which, however, infallibly issues in total and everlasting extinction of being, which extinction is again also termed *Nibbàna* (*Nirvàna*). The Buddhists use two phrases to describe *Nibbàna* in these two aspects— namely, for the *subjective* state called *Nibbàna*, *savupàdisesa-nibbàna*, *i.e.*, "*Nirvàna with* a remnant of the elements of existence;" and, enthusiastic, when he tells us, in language far different from the descriptions of the Buddhist books themselves, that even in nature

" . . . the Spirit of our Lord
Lay potent upon man and beast."[1]

This is what he calls—

" . . . that life which knows no age,
That blessed last of deaths when death itself is dead."[2]

Blessedness no doubt some may choose to call it, but it is the bliss of utter extinction and absolute unconsciousness, better described by Mr. Arnold himself elsewhere as "lifeless, timeless bliss"[3]—a bliss which finds its final and uttermost expression in eternal lifelessness, absolute and everlasting cessation of existence. Death itself, indeed, under the supposed conditions, is dead ; but not because *life* has triumphed, as in the Christian salvation, but dead, because life having

secondly, *anupàdiscsa-nibbàna*, "*Nirvàna without* a remnant of the elements of existence," which, of course, denotes an absolute extinction of being. This, in his judgment, was the *original* sense of the word. —*Dictionary of the Pàli Language, sub. voc., Nibbànam*, pp. 265-274.

This interpretation of the Buddhist doctrine has been so warmly controverted that it may be well to add the judgment of yet another eminent *Pàli* scholar and Buddhist specialist. Mr. Rhys Davids says, "When a Buddhist has become an Aràhat, when he has reached *Nirvana*, . . . he is still alive ; . . . his body with all its powers— that is to say, the fruit of his former sin—remains. These, however, will soon pass away ; there will then be nothing left to bring about the rise . . . . . of a new individual, and the Aràhat will no longer be alive in any sense at all ; he will have reached *parinibbàna*, complete extinction.—*Buddhism*, p. 113.

[1] The *Light of Asia*, book vi.   [2] *Ibid.* book viii.   [3] *Ibid.*

ceased to be, there is nothing left upon which death may feed.

And even this most beggarly salvation, we are told, can be attained by very few, and in general by none except those who forsake home-life, put on the yellow robe, take up the begging dish, and enter a Buddhist monastery. Only two laymen are said ever to have attained this salvation, and even among the monks, only one or two since the time of the Buddha.[1] And all the boasted morality, the conquest over the ten sins, and the renunciation of all the best of what men naturally hold dear, comes to this in the end ! And yet Mr. Arnold has the assurance to tell us—not in the enthusiasm of the poet, but in the plain language of the prose of the Preface to his *Light of Asia*— that Buddhism has in it " the eternity of a boundless hope," and " an indestructible element of faith in final good ! " Could words be chosen which should be further from describing the actual fact of the case ? Could there well be a contrast more profound than between the salvation which the Buddha proclaims and that which is offered to us in the Gospel of Jesus Christ ?

We must not indeed omit to observe that while this is the ideal salvation which orthodox Buddhism holds forth as the *summum bonum*, yet for the fancy of the many who do not feel prepared to enter on the path that leads to *Nirvâna*, Buddhism proposes what

[1] Rhys Davids, *Buddhism*, p. 125.

we might call minor salvations, consisting in rebirth, in the Buddhist sense, in some one or other of the Buddhist heavens. The distinction appears already in the *Dhammapada*, where we read :—

> Some people are born again; evil-doers go to hell; righteous people go to heaven ; those who are free from all worldly desires attain *Nirvâna*.[1]

And to the same effect also in the *Sutta Nipâta* the Buddha is made to say that the pious householder, though he enter not on the Noble Path, yet if he obey the eight commandments appointed for such, strenuously, he "goes to the gods by name *Sayampabhas*."[2] It is easy to believe what we are told, that in Buddhist countries a large part of the common people, having no desire to give up the world, even to attain *Nirvâna*, are well content if they can be religious enough while holding on to the world, to go to heaven. Thus Mr. Alabaster tells us: "The ordinary Siamese never troubles himself about *Nirvâna;* he does not even mention it. He believes virtue will be rewarded by going to heaven (Sawan); and he talks of heaven and not of *Nirvâna*. Buddha, he will tell you, has entered *Nirvâna*, but, for his part, he does not look beyond *Sawan*. The man of erudition would consider . . . that heaven is not eternal. The ordinary Siamese does not consider whether or not it is eternal."[3] Similar

---

[1] *Dhammapada*, 126.
[2] *Sutta Nipâta; Dhammika Sutta*, 29 ; *S. B. E.*, vol. x. part 2, p. 66.
[3] *Wheel of the Law*, p. xxxviii.

notions seem to prevail with many in China; for while some, according to Dr. Edkins, adhere to a contemplative school, which seeks to attain *Nirvâna* in this present life, in a profound meditation wherein the ideas of virtue and vice alike disappear, the people generally look forward to going to the heaven of the gods, others, to the western heaven, where Amitabha Buddha is supposed to live.[1] So, again, M. Barth tells us that even *Nirvâna*, to the larger part of the Buddhists of to-day, is "a sort of eternal repose or negative blessedness."[2] But howsoever the minds of many in Buddhist countries may have revolted against a system that failed to satisfy man's natural craving for immortality, yet, if we are to be guided by the authorities of the Buddhist religion, it must none the less be admitted that the facts fully justify the strong language of M. Barth, who says again, "If there is a conclusion which asserts itself as having been that of Buddhism in all ages, which follows from all that it insists on, and from all that it ignores, it is that 'the way' conducts to total extinction, and that perfection consists in ceasing to exist."[3]

It is indeed true that there are a few who refuse to admit that this is the doctrine of Buddhism. Thus we must do Mr. Arnold the justice to say that he will not admit that nothingness is the final goal set before

---

[1] *Chinese Buddhism*, pp. 197-199.
[2] *The Religions of India*, p. 114.
[3] *Ibid.* p. 113.

Q

the Buddhist.[1]   While claiming in the Preface to the
Light of Asia that the views of Buddhism, set forth
in his poem, " are at least the fruits of considerable
study," he adds, frankly enough, that they are not
derived from the study of the authorities *alone*, but
" also of a firm conviction that a third of mankind
would never have been brought to believe . . . in
nothingness as the issue and crown of being." We
venture, however, to suggest that a correct judgment
as to the actual teachings of a religion cannot be easily
attained by either the exclusive or the partial use of
the *a priori* method.   Whether or not nothingness
seem to Mr. Arnold a desirable issue of life, it is
absolutely certain that to a very considerable proportion of our fellow-men the case appears quite otherwise.
The proven increase of suicide in modern Christendom,
concurrently with the growth of atheism and disbelief
in a hereafter, is an ascertained fact which must not
be lost sight of, and which may be set over against
Mr. Arnold's *a priori* assumption.

But even if we should grant what some urge, even

[1] Mr. James Freeman Clarke also must apparently be counted in
this same class.   He tells us, "*Nirvàna*, to the Buddhist, means the
absolute eternal world, beyond time and space ; that which is nothing
to us now, but will be everything hereafter."   Of this statement he
gives no proof.   In the light of the facts we have reviewed he appears,
in this definition, to have missed both the meanings of the word
illustrated above.   Still farther from the truth is he when, on the
same page a little farther on, he makes *Nirvàna* to be equivalent to
"a union with God, the Infinite Being !"   Yet he admits that "the
weight of authority is in favour of the meaning 'annihilation !'"—*Ten
Great Religions*, pp. 162, 168.

against the highest authorities, that Buddhism *does* teach the existence of a soul, and its survival after death, therein agreeing with the Brahmanical doctrine which preceded and in India has outlived it, yet, practically, the case is not altered. *Practically*, it is still true that death ends all. For no one, either among the Brahmans or Buddhists, maintains that in the transmigration of the soul *memory* and the *consciousness of personal identity* go over into the life after death. For, as in the present life I have no memory of the life before the present, so it is freely admitted that there is no reason to believe that in the life after this I will have any memory of the present, or any recognition of myself as the same person. Instead of teaching, like Christianity, that memory and the sense of personal identity survive death, the Buddhist scriptures clearly teach the contrary. They teach that the power of thus looking backward through the series of bygone lives—whatever the phrase may mean—was one of the *special* attainments of the Buddha. In this respect it was, among others, that he, as " the enlightened one," was distinguished from other men.[1] But if it is believed that personal consciousness ends with death, then it is plain that this must have the same practical effect as a belief in the most absolute annihilation. To me, *as a self-conscious person*, existence will come to an end when I die. This is the clear teaching of Buddhism.

---

[1] See the *Nidâna Kathâ* in Fausböll's *Buddhist Birth Stories*, vol. i. p. 102.

That this cessation of *personal* existence seems to multitudes of our fellow-men a blessing to be supremely desired, of this—Mr. Arnold and others to the contrary notwithstanding—we have no doubt. It may indeed be hard for us, under so different and more tolerable conditions of existence, to understand how the principle that existence is *per se* an evil, can be assumed as fundamental in so many Oriental religions and philosophies. But under conditions such as prevail in India and China, the case is very different. Through the overcrowding of population, the phrase "struggle for existence" comes to have an intensity of meaning which it has not in America, or even in Europe. Moreover, the various public philanthropies which do so much to mitigate the evils of poverty in Christian lands are, with very rare exceptions, wanting there. Finally, the conception of a kind and good God, a Saviour, and a hope of a blessed immortality beyond death, which lightens for millions among us the burden of life, is absent from the mind of the Hindoo and the Buddhist. And if even in Christian lands, at this late day, the question has been soberly raised, and has been earnestly discussed in our reviews, whether, even at the best, life be worth living, how is it inconceivable that to millions living as the great mass of the population have lived for ages in India, the assurance that "nothingness is the crown of being," should come as a kind of gospel ? If it bring nothing better, it at least brings the faith that suffering is not—or, at least, *may*

not be—everlasting; and to millions there is a sad
comfort even in that.

Thus, howsoever Western *littérateurs* and professors,
writing in their comfortable studies,—surrounded from
their earliest recollection with all the external blessings that Christianity brings with it, even to those who
reject it—may think it inconceivable that life should
not seem sweet to all, yet it is the stubborn fact that
annihilation—if not of the essence of the soul, yet at
least of self-consciousness and personality—has been
the *summum bonum* offered in all the great Indian
religions and philosophies.[1]   The form in which it is
taught may vary; it may be pantheistic, as among the
modern populations of India; or, materialistic; or
atheistic or agnostic, as in other Indian philosophies,
and especially in the religion of the Buddha; but the
essential idea is ever the same.   The eternal extinction of personal self-consciousness is the best that any
of them has to offer as the end of life, and to attain
this is the supreme object of religion.   In this, the
Gospel according to the Vedantist and the Gospel
according to the Buddha are at one, and thus in the
very nature of the salvation which they promise, they

---

[1] Professor Oldenberg's remarks (referring to Professor Max Müller's
opinions on this same subject) are quite to the point.   He says, "We
do not follow the renowned investigator when he seeks for the limit
between the possible and the impossible in the development of
religion.   In the sultry, dreamy stillness of India thoughts arise and
grow,—every anticipation and speculation grows—in another way than
in the cool air of the West."—*Buddha, sein Leben, seine Lehre, seine
Gemeinde,* S. 274.

alike stand in direct contradiction to the Gospel of Christ. Where Christ promises " eternal life," they agree in promising eternal extinction of individual conscious life as the highest end of being and of all religion. Call it what they will, *parinibbàna, mukti, nistàra,* it all comes to this. The long, long chain of births and deaths shall end, and in one way or another man may help to speed that issue. And that is the gospel alike of Buddhism and of Brahmanism. Existence is *per se* an evil ; for so long as there is existence, there is no security from pain. Hence salvation *must* have cessation of personal existence as its ultimatum. To be is to suffer. This thought finds an expression singularly sad and touching in the following words of a Canarese song :—

> " A weary and broken-down man,
>   With sorrow I come to thy feet:
> Subdued by the fate and the ban
>   That hides the long future I meet.
> I suffer, without ceasing, the pain
> Of sorrowful, infinite life." [1]

Does it appear as if the extinction of existence, which Mr. Arnold finds so inconceivable as an object of desire, seemed wholly undesirable to the man who wrote those words ?

But higher authorities than Mr. Arnold have sought to convince their readers that the Buddhist ultimatum of salvation could not be imagined to lie in this final

---

[1] *Folk Songs of Southern India,* p. 39.

extinction of existence. Thus, while Professor Max Müller admits that "no person who reads with attention the metaphysical speculations on the *Nirvàna* contained in the Buddhist Canon can arrive at any other conviction than that expressed by Burnouf—namely, that *Nirvàna*, the *summum bonum* of Buddhism, is absolute nothing,"[1] he yet pleads, in part on grounds which have been already reviewed, that this could not have been the teaching of the Buddha himself. To the arguments previously criticised, however, he adds another consideration which shows us that his judgment also was determined in part by considerations purely *a priori*. For he says, "If the soul becomes quite extinct, then religion is not any more what it ought to be—a bridge from the finite to the infinite, but a trap-bridge hurling man into the abyss, at the very moment when he thought he had arrived at the stronghold of the eternal."[2] But this argument rests on a manifest assumption—namely, that every religion *must* be "what it *ought* to be," a means of salvation to those who hold it, or, in the language of the Oxford professor's theology, "a bridge from the finite to the infinite."[3] But what warrant has any one for this assumption? It will certainly not be accepted by any who hold the teachings of Christ to be the unerring standard of faith. But we will not further discuss this matter.

---

[1] Lecture on "Buddhist Nihilism" in *Science of Religion*, p. 140.

[2] *Ibid.*

[3] See Professor Oldenberg's criticism on this argument of Professor Müller, quoted in foot-note, p. 229.

For the present argument would not be weakened even if we should assume the views of the Buddhist salvation which are held by Mr. Arnold and Professor Müller to be correct. For, in that case also, it would still be true that the salvation which was preached by the Buddha was not, as to its nature, the salvation which Christ preached, but something totally different. There is no evidence that the Buddha ever so much as had an idea of such a salvation as that which the Lord Jesus proclaimed, and which He claimed to have secured for men.

But certainly—as so often remarked before—the conclusions of missionaries who, through years, have had daily converse with the votaries of Buddha—whose object it must be, in order to success in their work, to find out if possible what the people for whom they labour really believe—are above all others deserving of consideration. And their testimony is unanimous and unmistakable. Thus, the missionary, Bishop Bigandet, of the Romish mission to Burmah, says :—

The *role* of Buddha from beginning to end is that of a deliverer, who preaches a law designed to secure to man deliverance from all the miseries under which he is labouring. But by an inexplicable and deplorable eccentricity the pretended saviour, after having taught man the way to deliver himself from the tyranny of his passions, only leads him, after all, into the bottomless gulf of total annihilation.[1] . . . My information has been derived from the perusal of the religious books of the Burmans, and from frequent conversations on religion during

----

[1] *The Legend of Gaudama,* preface, p. x.

several years, with the best-informed among the laity and the
religious whom I have had the chance of meeting.[1]

Who in this matter is more likely to be right—
the missionary bishop, or the Oxford professor who
quotes this testimony and goes on to show that the
bishop must be mistaken ? If we turn to Ceylon
we have the same testimony as to the belief of the
Ceylonese Buddhists, from the late venerable missionary
Hardy, of the English Wesleyans, already quoted, one
for more than a quarter century in daily converse with
that people. He quotes from the *Suttanta*, called
Sámanya Phala, the paragraphs which end with these
words : " He knows I have overcome the repetition of
existence, all that I have to do is done." He thereupon makes the following pertinent comment :—

Here I pause ; and I ask myself, in bitterness of soul, is
this all ? With all his reputed wisdom can Buddha lead his
followers to nothing higher, nothing superior ? . . . For what
is the next stage in the supposed uprising of this privileged
priest ? He has done all that he has to do. . . . The goal,
the long anticipated reward, the final consummation of the
whole series of births and deaths is now attained. But what is
it ? *Nothingness.* In the whole story of humanity, . . . in all
the conclusions to which disappointed man has come in his far
wanderings from God, there is nothing more cheerless, more
depressing, or more afflictive, than the revelations of the
Suttanta, in which Buddha tries to set forth the highest privi-
lege of the highest order of sentient beings.[2]

---

[1] *The Legend of Gaudama*, preface, p. xiii.
[2] *Legends and Theories of the Buddhists*, pp. 183, 185.

To the same effect Dr. Edkins, of China, enumerating some of the most prominent doctrines of Buddhism, names the happiness of the *Nirvâna* as a state of "unconsciousness" which frees him who attains it from the miseries of existence.[1] We repeat, then, the conclusion which is inevitable, that as in the former particulars, so again, as regards the nature of the salvation which man needs, Buddhism not only differs from the doctrine of the New Testament, but differs from it in the way of direct contradiction. If the one is true, the other must be false. Christianity affirms that salvation consists in eternal salvation from *sin ;* Buddhism, that it consists first in salvation from pain through extinction of desire, then, in its *final issue*, in eternal salvation from *existence.* While the former offers us eternal *life*, the latter holds forth, as its *summum bonum*, everlasting *death*.[2] And we are asked to recognise in " this venerable religion " " the eternity of a universal hope," " and an indestructible element of faith in final good ;" and because of "this Gospel of the Buddha" to revere the Buddha as " the Light of Asia "!!

But the contrasts between the two religions as regards this vital matter of salvation do not end with

---

[1] See *Chinese Buddhism* and *Religions of China, passim.*

[2] "It may even appear incredible to some that, having imagined a state of blissful purity to result from such a life, he (the Buddha) should have made it end in annihilation. That he did so, however, is certain."—Professor Childers, *Dictionary of the Pâli Language*, *sub. voc.*, *Nibbânam*, p. 268.

this, though this were indeed enough. For even if all the above argument be set aside, and the fatal difference as to the nature of salvation be ignored, yet no less momentous contradictions still remain, as regards the *ground* and the *means* of salvation. As to the *ground* of our salvation the Gospel declares first, negatively, that "by the deeds of the law shall no flesh be justified."[1] "Not by works of righteousness which we have done, but according to his mercy he saved us."[2] Positively, the Gospel everywhere asserts that we are saved by the works of another, even Jesus Christ, the righteous, who has by His death made atonement and "propitiation for our sins."[3] "Christ hath once suffered for sins, the just for the unjust."[4] "Christ hath redeemed us from the curse of the law, being made a curse for us."[5] Nor is this the teaching of Paul or the other apostles only, as it is the fashion of some to assert. For, according to the Gospel of Matthew, the Lord Jesus himself said expressly that He came "to give his life a ransom for many,"[6] and all the synoptists testify that when He instituted the Holy Supper, He declared that His blood was shed for us sinners, "for the remission of sins."[7] This, then, according to the Gospel, is the sole meritorious ground of our salvation. All reliance on any works of our own, however excellent they may seem, is everywhere

---

[1] Rom. iii. 22.   [2] Tit. iii. 5.   [3] 1 John ii. 2.
[4] 1 Peter iii. 18.   [5] Gal. iii. 13.   [6] Matt. xx. 28.
[7] Matt. xxvi. 28.

denounced in the most unsparing terms, as sure to end in utter ruin. " As many as are of the works of the law are under the curse." [1]   But what does the Buddha say ?   All who have given the least attention to the subject know that the Buddhist scriptures as constantly insist on the exact reverse of all this.   The idea of salvation by the merits of another does not more emphatically distinguish Christianity, than salvation by one's own merits distinguishes Buddhism.[2] The following passages will illustrate Buddhist teaching on this question :—

> By one's self the evil is done ; by one's self one suffers ; by one's self evil is left undone ; by one's self one is purified.   Lo, no one can purify another. [3]
>
> O Bhikshu! empty this boat! if emptied, it will go quickly ; having cut off passion and hatred, thou wilt go to *Nirvâna*. [4]

The *Parables of Buddhaghosha* were composed in exposition of the meaning of the *Dhammapada*.   In them the doctrine is expounded, for example, as follows : " Whoever shall do nothing but good works, will receive nothing but future excellent rewards." [5]   Again, we read of twenty-one kinds of evil actions, concerning which it is said that among those who commit them " there are nineteen who, if they see to their ways, perform good works, steadfastly observe *Saranâgamana*,[6]

---

[1] Gal. iii. 10.   [2] Cf. *The One Religion*, p. 90.
[3] *Dhammapada*, 165.   [4] *Ibid.*, 369.
[5] *Buddhaghosha's Parables*, p. 123.
[6] The repetition of the formula, "I take refuge in the law, the Buddha, and the brotherhood."

listen to the law and the five commandments, and
keep good watch over their bodies, shall be released
from their sins."[1] Personal merit is then, according
to the Buddhist teaching, the sole and exclusive ground
of our salvation. But this merit is not made to consist
merely in the practice of moral duties. Great emphasis
is laid on the performance or non-performance of
actions which are wrong or have no moral quality whatever. Thus he who seeks the destruction of all desire,
and thereby salvation, is exhorted to practise "the duty
of eating alone and sleeping alone."[2] He is told that
"if a man has ceased to think of good or evil, then
there is no fear for him while watching,"[3] and that
he will be saved who is "without thirst or desire;"[4]
that meditation on the formula called *Saranâgamana*
"has the power of preventing all evil emotions."[5] Of
atonement for sin by any manner of vicarious suffering
or sacrifice, Buddhism knows absolutely nothing. Yet
Mr. Arnold could write as follows of the Buddha,
making him to say on his renunciation of his home,—

> "This will I do who have a realm to lose,
> ' Because I love . . .
>
>   . . . these that are mine and those
> Which shall be mine, a thousand million more,
> Saved by this sacrifice I offer now."[6]

---

[1] *Buddhaghosha's Parables*, pp. 183, 184.
[2] *Dhammapada*, v. 305.
[3] *Ibid.*, 39.   [4] *Ibid.*, 351.
[5] *Buddhaghosha's Parables*, p. 54.   [6] The *Light of Asia*, book iv.

The parallel with the work and even the words of Christ which these words can scarcely fail to suggest, has absolutely no existence. Such writing is fatally misleading. Even Mr. Arnold himself elsewhere puts in the mouth of the Buddha words which contradict the Christian sense of the above citation. No language could more explicitly deny the possibility of a vicarious atonement than the following :—

> "Nor, spake he, shall one wash his spirit clean
> By blood ; nor gladden gods, being good, with blood ;
> Nor bribe them, being evil.
> .   .   . Answer all must give
> For all things done amiss or wrongfully,
> Alone, each for himself, reckoning with that
> The fixed arithmic of the universe
> Which meteth good for good, and ill for ill,
> Measure for measure, unto deeds, words, thoughts."[1]

Language such as this, however inconsistent with what we find elsewhere in the poem, is in full accord with what we find in the *Abhinishkramana Sùtra*, wherein the Buddha is made to argue with the sacrificing sages of Vaisali, thus: " I will ask you, then, if a man in worshipping the gods sacrifices a sheep, and so does well, why should he not kill his child, his relative or dear friend, in worshipping the gods, and so do better ? Surely, then, there can be no merit in killing a sheep ! It is but a confused and illogical system this."[2] On this point of the impossibility of

---

[1] The *Light of Asia*, book v.   [2] *Romantic Legend*, p. 159.

atonement by another, Buddhism is so explicit that
there is no dispute among authorities upon this subject.   Even Mr. de Bunsen, who has so boldly endeavoured to connect the doctrines of the Gospel with
Buddhism through Jewish Essenism, is constrained to
admit, with regard to this most essential and characteristic feature of the teaching of Christ, that "Buddhism knows absolutely nothing of the idea of an
offended God who requires reconciliation by vicarious
suffering," and that the doctrine of atonement by
vicarious suffering is "absolutely excluded by Buddhism." [1]   As to the ground, then, of our salvation—
no less than as to its nature—the doctrine of the
Buddha directly contradicts that of the Gospel.   The
latter affirms vicarious atonement as that ground ; the
former declares that vicarious atonement is impossible.

As to the *means* of salvation, according to each of
the two religions, there is, of necessity, no less total
contrast.   For, according to the Gospel, in order to be
saved, we must believe upon the Lord Jesus Christ.
It is, then, faith—this act of personal trust and self-
committal to an almighty Saviour—that is the means
of procuring our salvation.   The Bible statements to
this effect are so familiar as not to require citation.
But, according to the Buddhist system, the means
of salvation is the walking in the Eightfold Noble
Path.   This is formally declared as the fourth of the

[1] *The Angel Messiah of Buddhists, Essenes, and Christians*, pp. 49,
50.

Four Noble Truths. Primary and fundamental to all else in the Eightfold Path, however, is *knowledge*. It is not by faith that we are saved, for there is no one to trust in; the Buddha is dead and gone; and even when he was alive, professed to be able to save no one. The means of salvation is primarily *knowledge*, expressed, as the first step in the Eightfold Path, by the phrase "Right Views." Reserving a full discussion of the Eightfold Path for a subsequent part of this work,[1] it is sufficient to note here the continued opposition on this point, as on all before, to the teachings of Christ.

From all that has been said, it follows that there must be no less total contradiction between the two religions as to the author of salvation. According to the Gospel, the author and efficient cause of our salvation is the Lord Jesus Christ; according to Buddhism, the author and efficient cause of salvation is the man himself. Buddha, therefore, stands in no such relation to his followers as Christ to His. To speak of him as a saviour, a deliverer—if one is left to understand that these terms mean what they do when applied to Christ—is wholly to misrepresent the case. As for Christ—however a certain class of thinkers may ignore the fact—He certainly claimed to be Himself a Saviour in the fullest sense of that word. He said that He was "come to seek and to save that which was lost."[2] He did not propose to save them merely through moral influence—by preaching to them, for instance, or

---

[1] *Vid. infra*, pp. 302 *et seq.*   [2] Luke xix. 10.

by setting them a perfect example—but by dying for them. He said in so many words that He, the Son of man, came " to give his life a *ransom* for many." [1] He promised further to send the Holy Spirit, even Him who proceedeth from the Father, to renew the inner nature of man with a divine life.[2] He did not therefore come, as many seem to imagine, to show men how to save themselves, but by His mighty power to save them Himself alone. And this, and nothing less, is what Christ meant when He called Himself a Saviour and a Redeemer. But we open translations of Buddhist books, and often find these terms applied, without note or explanation, to the Buddha. Naturally, those who are uninstructed as to the facts of the case hastily infer that the claims of the Buddha were identical with those of Christ, whereas in reality they have nothing in common.

Instead of teaching that the Buddha had the power to save others, the Buddhist scriptures represent the Buddha as having been a sinner like the rest of men, and in the first instance as seeking salvation for himself as well as others. It is true that the Buddha is described as one " whom no desire with its snares and poisons can lead astray ;" [3] and so even Màra is made to say, " For seven years I followed Bhagavat (the Buddha) step by step ; I found no fault in the per-

---

[1] Matt. xx. 28, λύτρον ἀντὶ πολλῶν, "a ransom in the stead of many."
[2] John iii. 5 ; xiv. 16, 17 *et passim*.
[3] *Dhammapada*, 180.

fectly enlightened, thoughtful (Buddha)."[1] But such
claims as these are made *after* the Great Renunciation,
and especially after Gautama's attainment of Buddhahood. Again, we are to remember that even in these
cases we cannot understand by "sin" what the Christian understands by sin.[2] And, yet again, we are told
in so many words that instead of living a sinless life,
up to the time that he forsook home to take up the
ascetic life, he lived a life of carnal indulgence.[3] In
full consistency with such representations it is that the
Buddha is represented as seeking salvation not for
others only, but, no less, for himself. Thus, for
example, we read in the *Abhinishkramana Sùtra* that
the Ràjà Bimbasàra asked the Buddha, while he was yet
living as an ascetic seeking for enlightenment, "'Who
or what are you? Are you a god, or a Nàga, or
Brahmà, or Sakrà, or a man, or a spirit?'" Then

---

[1] *Sutta Nipàta; Padhàna Sutta*, 22 ; *S. B. E.*, vol. x. part 2, p.
71. After this same model the (much later) *Lalita Vistàra* describes
the Buddha as "perfect in morality, tranquil in his actions, un-
fathomable in his understanding," *Lalita Vistàra*, translated from
the original Sanskrit by Ràjendralàl Mitra, LL.D. ; Fasc. i. p. 3 ;
(*Bibl. Ind.*, new series, p. 455).

[2] *Vid. sup.*, pp. 200 *et seq.*

[3] The exact words are such as these : "He indulged himself in all
carnal pleasures ;" "he remained in the indulgence of his animal
passions," etc. etc. See, *e.g.*, Professor Beal's translation of the *Fo-
pen-hing* (*Abhinishkramana Sùtra*), *The Romantic Legend*, pp. 101,
102, 111, 115 *et passim*. In the face of such statements, how Mr.
Edwin Arnold, in the preface to the *Light of Asia* could venture the
assertion that "the Buddhist books agree in recording no single word
or thought, act or deed, which mars the perfect purity of this Indian
teacher," we are quite unable to understand.

Bodhisatwa, having entirely got rid of all crooked ways, answered plainly and truthfully, " ' Mahàràjà ! I am no god or spirit, but a plain man seeking for rest, and so am practising the rules of an ascetic life.' " [1]

Nor does Buddhism teach that the Buddha, after he had attained enlightenment, then gained the power to save others, or ever claimed such a power. Indeed, nothing is more plainly taught than the contrary. In no works do we probably come nearer to the actual teaching of the Buddha himself than in the *Dhammapada* and the *Mahàparinibbàna Sutta*. Their testimony on this subject is given in such language as the following :—

By one's self the evil is done, by one's self one suffers ; by one's self evil is left undone, by one's self one is purified. Purity and impurity belong to one's self, no one can purify another.[2]

You yourself must make an effort. The *Tathàgatas* (Buddhas) are only preachers.[3]

We are told again that, shortly before the death of the Buddha, he said to Ànanda, one of his disciples—

O Ànanda, be ye lamps unto yourselves. Be ye a refuge to yourselves. Betake yourselves to no external refuge. Hold fast to the truth as a lamp. Hold fast as a refuge to the truth. Look not for refuge to any one besides yourselves.[4]

The *Parables of Buddhaghosha*, as already remarked, .give us by the help of parable an exposition of the meaning of the *Dhammapada*. They as clearly teach

---

[1] *Romantic Legend*, p. 182.   [2] *Dhammapada*, 165.   [3] *Ibid.*, 276.
[4] *Mahàparinibbàna Sutta*, ii. 33. ; *S. B. E.*, vol. xi. p. 38.

the same doctrine. We are told by Buddhaghosha, for example, of certain disciples of the Buddha, who, although they had reached the state of holy men, yet, on account of a sin formerly committed, fought among themselves, and all killed each other, and the Buddha had no power to prevent their suffering the punishment of this sin. Other illustrations are given by the writer to show the absolute powerlessness of the Buddha to save men who have committed sin from suffering its punishment.[1]

This naturally leads to a consideration of the doctrine of orthodox Buddhism as to the person of the Buddha. Professor Beal has referred to the Buddhist doctrine of the pre-existence of the Buddha as having an analogy with the Christian doctrine of the pre-existence of Christ.[2] In reality, however, there is no analogy whatever between the two doctrines of pre-existence. It is probable that the Buddha, in accordance with the notions concerning transmigration, so early prevailing in the East, believed in some sort of transmigration, and therefore in his own existence, in some sense, in a previous state. It is quite certain that the Buddhists themselves, on the authority of their sacred books, believe that the Buddha existed before he appeared in this world. But as to how the Buddha pre-existed, or any other man pre-existed, there are, as we have seen, two

[1] *Buddhaghosha's Parables*, p. 154.
[2] *Romantic Legend*, p. viii.

opinions. Whichever view of the Buddhists we regard, in neither case is there any real analogy between the alleged pre-existence of the Buddha and the pre-existence of our Lord as taught in the Holy Scriptures.

For, in the first place, if we assume the Buddhist doctrine to be that which the oldest Suttas seem to teach, and which is accepted as their teaching by a large part of the most eminent specialists in Buddhist studies, namely that Buddhism does not admit the existence of the soul as distinct from the body, then there was no pre-existence of the soul of the Buddha in the Christian sense of the word, for there was no soul to pre-exist.[1] As thus understood, the many stories ascribed to the Buddha in which he tells what he was and what he did in former lives, cannot refer to a pre-existence of his personality, but to the various manifestations of that pre-existent *karma*, or line of moral activity, which in due time necessitated the existence of Gautama Muni. But it needs very little knowledge of the Bible to see that *this* theory has nothing in common with the Scripture doctrine of the pre-existence of Christ.

Neither, if we reject this interpretation and understand the Buddhist scriptures to teach what no doubt multitudes of Buddhists, unskilled in metaphysics, believe,—that the *soul* of the Buddha existed before his appearance in this world,—is this a doctrine such

---

[1] See the citation from Mr. Rhys Davids' translation of Fausböll's *Buddhist Birth Stories*, given above, pp. 198, 199.

as the Scriptures teach concerning Christ. What
Christ taught is, according to the Gospel, plain enough.
He taught, without doubt, that He had existed before
He came into this world. He said, for example, that
He had come from the Father and come into the world,
even as again He left the world and went unto the
Father.[1]   He declared of Himself, " Before Abraham
was, I am." [2]   In the second place, He no less clearly
taught that in this respect His case was among men
alone and peculiar. For He said again 'in so many
words : " No man hath ascended to heaven but he that
came down from heaven, even the Son of Man which is
in heaven." [3]   In contrast with this, the Buddhist books
teach us that whatever was the nature of the pre-existence of the Buddha, in this he had no peculiar pre-eminence above others, but simply shared the common lot of
all men, and indeed of all organic beings. Moreover,
Christ taught that until the time of His incarnation He
had lived a life of changeless glory in the fellowship of
the eternal Godhead. The Buddha, on the contrary, is
represented as teaching that, previous to the last occasion, he had existed, not only in heaven, but also on
earth, and that again and again, and often in a degraded
and bestial form. And Professor Beal and others with
him think that they can discover an analogy between
the doctrine of the pre-existence of the Buddha and the
pre-existence of the Christ ! [4]

---

[1] John viii. 42 ; xiv. 28 *et passim.*   [2] John viii. 58.
[3] John iii. 13.   [4] *Romantic Legend*, Introduction, p. viii.

It is indeed true that the Thibetan Buddhists have a doctrine of the pre-existence of the Buddha which in its external form at first sight seems much more like the Christian doctrine. They tell us of an *Ādi-Buddha*, or Primal Buddha, infinite, self-existent, and omniscient. From this Primal Buddha all things that are, have in order come forth. Hence it is true that in him, in the Ādi-Buddha, Gautama Muni pre-existed, and from him came forth.[1] And yet even this corrupt form of the Buddhist teaching has only the most superficial resemblance to the doctrine of the pre-existence of our Lord. The true analogy of this theory is not with anything that the Church has ever understood the Gospels to teach, but with the ancient gnostic doctrine of the " emanations," of which Christ was supposed to be one. And it is of significance to note that this doctrine,—with whatever of superficial likeness it may have or seem to have to the Christian doctrine,—does not appear in any of the old Buddhist authorities, but was invented, at least in its full modern form,[2] about the tenth century of our era—some fifteen hundred years after the days of the Buddha !

[1] For a full exposition of this Thibetan theory, see Rhys Davids, *Buddhism*, p. 206 ; Hodgson's *Illustrations of the Literature and the Religion of the Buddhists*, p. 31.

[2] We find the doctrine in an *incipient* form in the *Saddharmapund-arīka*, a late work of the Northern Canon, cir. 250 A.D., wherein the Buddha is made not only omniscient, but self-existent and everlasting. —*Op. cit.*, chap. xiv. *et passim ; S. B. E.*, vol. xxi.

6. *The Doctrine concerning the Last Things.*

Last of all, we have to note the Buddhist eschatology. We shall find that in its doctrine as to the future the teachings of Buddhism are no less in direct antagonism to Christianity than in all the foregoing. Two fundamental questions come up in eschatology. First, What is to be the future of the individual ? and second, What is to be the future history of the world ?

As regards the first of these questions, the Holy Scriptures, as understood by the great body of Christians in all ages, answer that men after death are consciously happy or miserable, according to their works. It is further agreed that they will continue after death in a disembodied state until Christ shall come the second time : and that when Christ comes, He will come to judge all who have ever lived ; that He will raise the dead, and change the living into bodily forms, adapted to an unending state of being. Finally, it has been the general understanding of Christ's teaching, that from that time the ultimate destiny of all individuals thus raised or changed, and judged, shall be eternally fixed ; that the wicked "shall go into everlasting punishment, and the righteous into life eternal."

But what is the teaching of Buddhism on this subject ? The answer has been already anticipated, and we need to add but little. That answer is twofold, according as we take one or the other interpretation of the Buddhist scriptures. If we take the view which is maintained by Burnouf, St. Hilaire, Rhys Davids, and others, then we must answer that Buddhism teaches that death is the end of man. Since there is nothing to man but *nâmarûpa*, "name and form," there is nothing substantial remaining when we die which could continue after death. Nothing survives us but our works.[1] My works indeed will necessitate the immediate production of another being —god, man, or beast—to reap the fruit of my doings in reward or retribution; but that new being is not, according to *our* common use of language, I myself, but another and distinct being. Its connection with me is not essential—not by identity of substance—but is only moral and ideal. There is, therefore, if we rightly understand the Buddhist scriptures, no existence of the human personality after death. *Death ends all.*

But the instinct of immortality and the consciousness of a spiritual and invisible personality are very strong in all men. And so we can easily believe what we are told, that whatsoever may be the teachings of Buddhist metaphysics, very many Buddhists of to-day look forward to a continuance of life after death. Yet even thus they are still in hopeless contradiction with the teaching of Christ. In the first place, the Christian doctrine as to the future life of every man in heaven or hell is not the doctrine of Buddha, even as thus repre-

---

[1] The analogy of this conception with the Positivist doctrine of the immortality of deeds will occur to every one. The two systems are more fully compared by Wordsworth. *Vid. The One Religion* (Bampton Lectures, 1881), pp. 268, 269.

sented.   Buddhism has indeed its heavens many, and
also its hells many.   And it is also true that after death,
according to the view we have at present before us, I
may find myself in one or the other of these diverse
places.   But this is very far from certain.   The Buddhist teaching is thus given :—

> Some people are born again; evil people go to hell; right-
> eous people go to heaven; those who are free from all worldly
> desires enter *Nirvâna*.[1]

"Some people are born again."   That is, instead of
going either to heaven or to hell, I may be born again
on earth, and go through no one knows how many
stages of existence before I arrive at the final rest of
Nirvâna.   And even if I go to hell or heaven when I
die, what then ?   If I go to hell, I may indeed come
out again, after that, incalculable ages hence, I shall
have exhausted the retribution due my sin ; there is
some consolation in that.   But, unfortunately, the
same is true as to life in heaven also.   There I may
remain ages, but it is nevertheless certain that, sooner
or later, I must leave heaven either to sink into the
annihilation of *parinibbâna,* or, more probably, to
return to the world and begin again the weary round
of birth and death.

Of a deathless life, then, a life of eternal incorrup-
tion, Buddhism knows nothing.   It tells us, indeed, as
Mr. Arnold puts it, of "means to live and die no
more." [2]   But these words mean, in Buddhist parlance,

---

[1] *Dhammapada,* 126.   [2] The *Light of Asia,* book vii.

an end of *living* as well as of *dying*, to be attained at last, if ever, through the *parinibbâna*. Of immortal and unending life anywhere, we repeat, that Buddhism knows absolutely nothing. The idea is utterly foreign to Buddhist thinking. On nothing do the Buddhist books insist more than on their doctrine that there is nowhere, in heaven, or earth, or hell, any permanence in anything. And inasmuch as, according to Buddha, existence anywhere or in any place involves pain sooner or later, existence, therefore, is *per se* an evil, and eternal existence would be eternal evil. So far, therefore, from existence in heaven being regarded as desirable, desire of life even in the highest and most pure and spiritual of the Buddhist heavens is named, as we have already seen,[1]—under the name of *arû-parâga*,—as the seventh of " the ten sins," which must be overcome before a man can attain *Nirvâna*. Herein, again, we have reason to complain that Mr. Arnold uses language utterly misleading. He tells us that the Buddha anticipated that, as the result of all his self-sacrifice,

> " That should be won for which he lost the world,
> And death should find him conqueror of death." [2]

The analogy with the teaching of Christ which is suggested in this phraseology is without the least foundation. Death, according to Buddhism, is indeed destroyed ; but only because that existence is eternally

---

[1] *Vide supra*, pp. 149, 150.   [2] The *Light of Asia*, book iv.

destroyed which is the condition of death. Plainly, when nothing is left to die, then death is impossible; but is, then, to conquer death, the same thing as to be conquered by death? No less misleading—if we have rightly understood the teaching of the Buddha—is the translation which Professor Max Müller gives of the *Dhammapada*, 21: "Reflection is the path of immortality." Surely not even the Professor will claim that the Christian doctrine of immortality is taught in the Buddhist scriptures! In fact—if we may trust so eminent a Pàli scholar as Mr. Rhys Davids—Professor Müller has been misled by an etymology. Commenting on the same Pàli word *amata*, which is used here, as translated by Professor Beal in his *Romantic Legend*, Mr. Davids uses the following language: "The expression, 'to open the gate of immortality to men,' being quite unbuddhistic, has probably arisen from a misunderstanding of the word *amata*, 'ambrosia,' or 'nectar.' This (word)," derived from the Sanskrit *amrita* (from *a+mri*), "is a name applied to *Nirvàna* as being the heavenly drink of the wise, who are above the gods; it never means 'immortality,' and could not grammatically have that sense. So that the striking parallel between the Chinese verses (in the *Romantic Legend*) and 2 Tim. i. 10 falls to the ground." Of an unending life after death, then, Buddhism knows nothing.[1] And if it does not admit the

---

[1] Professor Oldenberg maintains that the position of the Buddhist authorities as regards a hereafter is simply non-committal. He cites

immortality of the soul, much less has it any place for the Christian doctrine of a resurrection.

All this being so, it follows that the Buddhist doctrine of future rewards and retributions has little in common with the doctrine of Christ except the indissoluble nexus between sin and suffering and virtue and happiness. That Buddhism should hold fast to this doctrine and so daringly attempt to reconcile it with its nihilistic metaphysics, is a most impressive and suggestive illustration of the hold which " the fearful looking for of judgment" has upon a sinful man. But even if any insist—as it seems to us, in the face of the clearest evidence—that Buddhism does admit the continuance of the individual after death to suffer in hell or enjoy in heaven the reward of his works on earth, yet were this not the Christian doctrine. It were not even equivalent to the teachings of Christian restorationists. For if the retributions of the Buddhist hells might seem to be at least less dreadful, that sooner or later the unhappy victim, having exhausted

many passages wherein the Buddha is said to have been asked this precise question, whether there were a life after death or not, and to have declined to answer. Granting this, the Buddhist position should more justly be described as agnostic regarding this matter. But even in that point of view, it is still true that Buddhism has no doctrine of a life after death. And when we recall the undisputed statements already noted as to the non-existence of the soul, and remember that, according to Professor Oldenberg, the Buddha, when pressed with the obvious conclusion as regards a future state, declined to disavow the inference, the above representations do not appear to be too strong. See Oldenberg, *Buddha, sein Leben, seine Lehre, seine Gemeinde,* S. 273 *ff.*

the demerit of his works, will be released from his torments : yet even this is not, as restorationists teach, in order that the man may enter then upon unending blessedness in heaven.   Again he must begin the almost interminable round of birth, and life, and death, with all their possibilities of woe.   Or if, perchance, from hell the sinner mount to one of the Buddhist heavens, neither is there permanency there.   For the doctrine of future reward with the Buddhist is not a doctrine of *eternal* reward.   No one in the highest of "the formless heavens" shall stay there for ever. Nowhere is there anything that abides, is the continual and most sad refrain of all Buddhist teaching.   The only hope in this life the Buddhist can have, if he do believe in existence for himself hereafter, is that, if he *must* be born again, it may be in a condition more tolerable than this ; one in which he may possibly be able by high resolution and endeavour to break the chain which binds him to the wheel of life and death, and end all conscious being.   We may well sum up the case as regards this part of the Buddhist eschatology in the eloquent words of the Rev. Mr. Hardy :—

The system of Buddha is humiliating, cheerless, man-marring, soul-crushing.   It tells me that I am not a reality ; I have no soul.   It tells me that there is no unalloyed happiness, no plenitude of enjoyment, no perfect, unbroken peace, in the possession of any being whatever, from the highest to the lowest, in any world.   It tells me that I may live myriads of millions of ages, and that not in any of these ages, nor in any portion of an age, can I be free from apprehension as to the future until I attain to a state of unconsciousness; and that in order to arrive at this consummation I must turn away from all that is pleasant or lovely, or instructive, or elevating, or sublime. It tells me by voices ever repeated, like the ceaseless sound of the sea-wave on the shore, that I shall be subject to sorrow, impermanence, and unreality, so long as I exist, and yet that I cannot now cease to exist, nor for countless ages to come, as I can only attain *Nirvâna* in the time of a supreme Buddha. In my distress I ask for the sympathy of an all-wise and all-powerful friend. . . . But I am mocked instead by the semblance of relief; and am told to look to Buddha, who has ceased to exist; to the Dharmma,[1] that never was an existence; and to the Sangha,[2] the members of which are real existences, but, like myself, partakers of sorrow and sin.[3]

When the Christian dies, or when we lay a Christian friend in the grave, we sorrow indeed, but *not* as without hope. When the Christian mother lays her beloved child in the grave, we comfort her with the reminder that the child is not lost, but only gone before, and that though the child shall not return to her, she shall go to the child. But what does Buddhism tell such a stricken parent? We have it in a discourse which is said to have been spoken by the Buddha himself—the parable of *Kisâgotamî :—*

Kisâgotamî was a young mother who had given birth to her first-born, but " when the boy was able to walk by himself he died," and the story goes on thus: " The young girl in her love for it carried the dead child clasped to her bosom, and went about from house to house asking if any one would give her

---

[1] Law (of the Buddha).   [2] The Brotherhood of Buddhist Monks.
[3] *Legends and Theories of the Buddhists*, pp. 217, 218.

medicine for it. When the neighbours saw this they said, 'Is the young girl mad that she carries about on her breast the dead body of her son?' But a wise man—thinking to himself, 'Alas! this *Kisâgotamî* does not understand the law of death; I must comfort her'—said to her, 'My good girl, I cannot myself give medicine for it, but I know of a doctor who can attend to it.' The young girl said, 'If so, tell me who it is.' The wise man continued, 'Buddha can give medicine; you must go to him.' *Kisâgotamî* went to Buddha, and doing homage to him, said, 'Lord and master, do you know any medicine that will be good for my boy?' Buddha answered, 'I know of some.' She asked, 'What medicine do you require?' He said, 'I want a handful of mustard seed.' The girl promised to procure it for him. But Buddha continued, 'I require some mustard seed taken from a house where no son, husband, parent, or slave has ever died.' The girl said, 'Very good,' and went to ask for some at the different houses, carrying the dead body of her son. . . The people said, 'Here is some mustard seed, take it.' Then she asked, 'In my friend's house has there died a son, a husband, a parent, or a slave?' They replied, 'Lady! what is this that you say? *The living are few, but the dead are many.*' Then she went to other houses, but one said, 'I have lost a son;' another, 'I have lost my parents;' another, 'I have lost my slave.' At last, not being able to find a single house where no one had died, from which to procure the mustard seed, she began to think, 'This is a heavy task that I am engaged in. I am not the only one whose son is dead. In the whole of the *Sâvatthi* country, everywhere, children are dying, parents are dying.' Thinking thus, she acquired the law of fear, and putting away affection for her child, she summoned up resolution, and left the dead body in a forest; then she went to Buddha and paid him homage. He said to her, 'Have you procured the handful of mustard seed?' 'I have not,' she replied; 'the people of the village told me, *The living are few, the dead are many.*' Buddha said to her, 'You thought that you alone had lost a son. The law of death is that among all living creatures there is no permanence.' " [1]

And that was all the comfort that he had to give. Could anything be more sad ? Could anything more touchingly illustrate the utter helplessness of Buddhism to comfort in the presence of death ? How impressive the contrast with the words of Him who once stood near an open grave, and said unto the mourners, " I am the resurrection and the life ; he that believeth in me, though he were dead, yet shall he live." And yet Mr. Arnold, in the sober prose of the preface to the *Light of Asia*, extols Buddhism as having in it " the eternity of a universal hope " ! ! And Professor Max Müller thinks that he sees in this inexpressibly sad story, with its gospel of helplessness and universal doom, " a specimen of the true Buddhism,"—wherein, no doubt, he is right,—" language, intelligible to the poor and the suffering, which has endeared Buddhism to the hearts of millions . . . the beautiful, the tender, the humanly true, which, like pure gold, lies buried in all religions, even in the sand of the Buddhist Canon !" [2]

It may be well to place here, for the benefit of any who may have been unable to see any material difference between the hope of the Buddhist and the hope of the Christian believer, the inspired words of the Apostle Paul to the Thessalonians :—

[1] *Lectures on the Science of Religion*, by Professor Max Müller, pp. 145, 146.   [2] *Ibid.* p. 147.

We would not have you ignorant, brethren, concerning them that fall asleep ; that ye sorrow not, even as the rest, which have no hope. For if we believe that Jesus died and rose again, even so them also that are fallen asleep in Jesus will God bring with him. For this we say unto you by the word of the Lord, that we that are alive, that are left unto the coming of the Lord, shall in no wise precede them that are fallen asleep. For the Lord himself shall descend from heaven with a shout, with the voice of the archangel, and with the trump of God : and the dead in Christ shall rise first ; then we that are alive, that are left, shall together with them be caught up in the clouds, to meet the Lord in the air ; and so shall we ever be with the Lord. Wherefore comfort one another with *these words*.[1]

No brighter prospect does Buddhism hold forth to the world and to the race than to the individual man.[2] What the Bible promises in this matter we all know. Not only does it hold forth to the individual man the promise of salvation from the guilt and power of sin, and everlasting life in resurrection glory, but also what we might call a social and governmental redemption of the human race on earth. Christ bade us to pray, that the will of God might be done on earth even as it is done in heaven ; and so no doubt it will be. All nations, we are assured, shall serve and obey the Christ of God, and over all the earth " there shall be one Lord and his name one."[3] Holiness shall so univer-

---

[1] 1 Thess. iv. 13-18 (R. V.)

[2] The statement of Buddhist teachings in the following paragraphs concerning the future of the world, we have drawn from the translations given by Mr. Hardy in his *Manual of Buddhism*. The early *Pàli* scriptures, so far as published, have next to nothing to say on the subject.   [3] Zech. xiv. 9.

sally prevail that it is said, in the glowing language of the prophet, that even "upon the bells of the horses shall be holiness unto the Lord."[1] The law of love shall be the law of the world. And although it is true that the Scriptures do point us forward to a coming judgment and visitation of the world that now is, by fire, yet those final judgments are said to be only that the Son of Man may purge out of His kingdom "all them that do iniquity."[2] And the consuming fires, which, according to the Word of God, shall yet enwrap the world, shall not be for the annihilation of the earth, but that as after the flood, so again life may bloom on earth anew, but not as now in sin, but in redemption. For "we look, according to his promise, for a new heaven and a new earth wherein dwelleth righteousness."[3] Thus, in the closing chapters of the Apocalypse, dark though they be with excess of brightness, yet so much as this is clear. As in the far distance we lose sight of the history of this planet, it disappears in the full glory of a finished and complete redemption, wherein even the very earth itself has been made to share. And among the last words which are borne to our ears are these, "There shall be no more death, neither sorrow nor crying; neither shall there be any more pain."[4] Truly these are wondrous words, and full of hope for those whose hearts are heavy now with the burdens and woes of humanity. The Gospel

---

[1] Zech. xiv. 20.   [2] Matt. xiii. 41.   [3] 2 Pet. iii. 13.
[4] Rev. xxi. 4.

is as full of hope for the world as for the individual man.

But what says the Buddha? No such prospect opened to him. He who guessed at so much, did not once guess this. He came, we are told, to preach deliverance to the world. At the best, as we have seen, it was but a sorry deliverance. And yet, worse still, such as it was, it was not to last. On the contrary, we are everywhere assured that however general the moral reform which may be effected by a Buddha, sooner or later the tide of evil will roll back as before, and the whole human race will sink back into the mire of sensuality, from which the Buddha came to free them. Not only morals, but, we are told, at last even civilisation and intelligence will also disappear. This will by and by necessitate the appearing of another Buddha to do the work of his predecessor over again. Yet he will achieve no more permanent success than Gautama Muni. Again will ensue the inevitable moral retrogression, till another Buddha shall appear. And so the dreary history is to go on and on repeating itself, for ever and for ever, till one cannot but feel that if this were indeed the truth, then Buddha *was* right after all; *not* to be were better than to be, and to exist is verily the sum and source of all evil. All this can be abundantly proved, did space permit, from the Buddhist authorities themselves. The Rev. Mr. Hardy quotes from Mr. Turnour's translation of the Buddhist *Mahávansa*, the statement that in the interval between one Buddha and another "not only does the religion of the preceding Buddhas become extinct, but the re-collection and record of all preceding events are also lost."[1]

With reference to the future of the earth itself the Christian Scriptures plainly teach—as already re-marked—that when the Lord Jesus shall return, the earth shall be visited with a general conflagration, issuing in the final destruction of the wicked from off the face of the earth. But this fiery visitation is not to result in the destruction of the planet as such, but is to be followed by the appearance of a new earth which shall be the abode of righteousness.[2] Nothing could be plainer than these words of the Apostle Peter :—

"The heavens that now are and the earth, by the same word"—which brought about the former destruction of the world by the waters of the deluge—"have been stored up for

---

[1] Professor Seydel (*Das Evangelium von Jesu*, u.s.w., S. 265-267) gives a different view of Buddhist eschatology, drawn from *Le Lotus de la Bonne Loi (Saddharmapundarîka)*. He represents, on this authority, the course of moral degradation as ending with the destruction of Mâra in the last five hundred years of this *kalpa* (world-period). After this comes a destruction of the world by fire, and the appearance after-wards of a world of purity and happiness. As to whether that shall abide nothing is said ; and as Buddhism fundamentally insists on the im-permanency of all that "becomes," we must presume the contrary. It is to be remembered that this authority is of very late date ; Seydel places it before 200 A.D.—the earliest possible date. Remembering this, the possibility of Christian influence on the earlier doctrine is naturally suggested.

[2] *Legends and Theories of the Buddhists*, p. 199.

fire, being reserved against the day of judgment and destruction of ungodly men. . . . The day of the Lord will come as a thief ; in the which the heavens shall pass away with a great noise, and the elements shall be dissolved with fervent heat, and the earth and the works that are therein shall be burned up. . . . But, according to his promise, we look for a new heaven and a new earth wherein dwelleth righteousness."[1]

And so also Buddhism teaches a future destruction of the world by fire, and the appearance of a new earth after this present earth shall thus have passed away, wherein many have imagined that they have seen another point of coincidence, if not a genetic connection with the Christian doctrine. But like about all the fancied coincidences between the doctrines of the Christian Scriptures and the teachings of Buddhism, the supposed agreement disappears upon examination.

In the first place, while the Scriptures reveal only one such catastrophe in the future, the Buddhist scriptures predict an innumerable series of catastrophes of world-destruction, followed by world-renovations. Of these it so happens that the Buddhists say that the next will be by fire; but others will be by water; others, again, by wind. The Rev. Mr. Hardy sums up the Buddhist teaching on this subject as follows :—

The earth inhabited by men, with the various continents, *Lokas* and *Sakwâlas* connected with it, is subject alternately to

---

[1] 2 Pet. iii. 7, 10, 13 (R.V.) ; *cf.* Rev. xxi. 1 *et seq.*

destruction and renovation, in a series of revolutions to which no beginning, no end, can be discovered. Thus it ever was; thus it will be ever. There are three modes of destruction. The *Sakwálas* are destroyed seven times by water, and the eighth time by water. Every sixty-fourth destruction is by wind.[1]

Thus, while the Scriptures teach a single destruction of the earth in the future, to be followed by a new earth which shall abide for ever, Buddhism teaches the very different doctrine of an unending series of destructions and renovations.[2] Moreover, the Scriptures hold forth the prophecy of the new earth as full of hope and glory. As contrasted with the present earth, the new earth will be one "wherein dwelleth righteousness." In it "there shall be no more curse."[3] "The creation itself, also," as well as redeemed humanity, "shall be delivered from the bondage of corruption into the liberty of the glory of the children of God."[4] As opposed to all this, Buddhism teaches that, both morally and physically, each of the new earths which after each great catastrophe shall succeed to the foregoing will be like unto the earth which now is. As the next destruction of the world shall be produced by the wickedness of men as a moral cause, so shall it always be. In the next earth men will again be produced, and again go through a process of physical and moral degradation, only checked for a season, but not permanently arrested, by the appearance of another Buddha,

---

[1] *Manual of Buddhism*, 2d ed., p. 5.

[2] See note 1, p. 261.   [3] Rev. xxii. 3.   [4] Rom. viii. 21.

till again the world shall be destroyed by reason of the wickedness of the men who inhabit it. " As the world is at first produced by the power of the united merit of all the various orders of beings in existence, so its destruction is caused by the power of their demerit." [1] " Previous to the destruction by water, cruelty or violence prevails in the world; previous to that by fire, licentiousness ; and previous to that by wind, ignorance." [2]

So far from any agreement here, we thus find, as in everything previously noted, the most complete and total contrast. The Bible teaches us to look for a social regeneration of man upon the earth, and finally the redemption of the earth itself from sin and the curse. The Buddha saw no such bright prospect. As regards the race, his mission of redemption, so extolled by Buddhists and the apologists of Buddhism in Christian lands, according to the uniform teaching of the Buddhist authorities, was, from the first, certain to end in failure. The decay of morals would only be at the best checked for a little, but not stopped. And when at last, because of the wickedness of men, the world and all upon it would be destroyed by fire, then, indeed, we are told that a new earth will appear, but *not* a new earth " wherein dwelleth righteousness." It will be another earth just like this present, an earth

---

[1] Hardy, *Manual of Buddhism*, 2d ed., p. 36.
[2] *Manual of Buddhism*, p. 34. See also *Pallegoix*, vol. i. pp. 430, 475 ; cited by Köppen, *Die Religion des Buddha*, i. Bd. S. 287.

wherein shall dwell sin, violence, and uncleanness. Again a new race of men shall go through the same long course of dreary and inevitable decline, which no Buddha ever to appear shall be able to prevent; and again shall come the awful world catastrophe, wherein all shall perish. So shall it be, not once or twice, but in unending cycles of sin and retribution, for ever and for ever. Where, in all this, is any analogy with the teaching of the Scriptures ?

And this is all the light which the Buddha had to shed upon the future, either for the individual or the race. The facts are indisputable, and may be verified by any one who will take the trouble to look up the authorities. The truth is, that so far from having in it, as Mr. Arnold ventures to assure us, " the eternity of a universal hope . . . and an indestructible element of faith in final good," these words express the most complete contradiction possible of the actual facts of the case. So far is this from being true that, to us, it quite passes comprehension, how Mr. Arnold, or any man professing the familiarity that he does with ac- credited sources of knowledge on the subject, could have so amazingly overlooked or misunderstood the plainest and most matter-of-fact statements. The truth is, that Buddhism, judged—not by the words of foreign expositors, intent, at all hazards, on making out an agreement in essentials between Buddhism and Christianity—but by the repeated and most explicit statements of its own recognised authorities, is one of the most uncompromising and unmitigated systems of pessimism that human intellect, in the deep gloom of its ignorance of Him who is the Light and the Life of men, has ever elaborated.

Thus we have finished our comparison of the doctrinal systems of Buddhism and Christianity. As the result we have found them sharply contrasted in the following points. Christianity teaches that there is a God, who is our Father in heaven; Buddhism denies that there is any such Being. Christianity teaches that God has spoken to man, and that for his salvation; Buddhism denies that ever has been heard in the world a voice which was Divine. Christianity teaches that man has a soul; Buddhism denies it. As to sin, Christianity teaches that it has to do with man's relation to God; Buddhism, that it has to do only with man himself. Christianity teaches that salvation consists in the eternal deliverance of man from sin, and from all the effects of sin in soul and in body; that this deliverance is only on the *ground* of the meritorious work of the Lord Jesus, the incarnate Son of God, who is also Himself alone the *author* of man's salvation. Buddhism teaches that salvation consists essentially in deliverance from suffering, and finally from individual existence, which ever makes suffering possible; that the ground of this salvation is the man's own merit; and that the author of salvation is also the man himself. Finally, Christianity teaches that man survives death, that he will be raised from the dead to eternal happiness and holiness, or in sin and misery; orthodox Buddhism teaches that death ends all, other sects, that man, indeed, survives death; but all agree that there is *no permanence anywhere*, in earth, or heaven, or hell. Christianity teaches the everlasting triumph of righteousness in the kingdom of God, in the new heavens, and the new earth; Buddhism knows only of unending cycles of evolution ever followed by physical and moral degeneration and final dissolution.

Such are the doctrines of the two religions. Is it hard to judge between them? Can both have come from God? Can both conduct him who trusts them to the same final goal? What shall we say, then, of the many who in our day are calling upon us to recognise Buddhism as the Light of Asia, and thereby challenge a comparison of the doctrine of the Buddha with that of the Christ of God, of Him who is, in truth, the Light, not of Asia only, but of the whole world? To what have we come, that in the full blaze of our boasted nineteenth-century enlightenment, learned professors in Christian universities, poets and editors, men supposed to represent the intelligence of the age, can find it in them to extol and glorify a heathenism which is stamped with the confession of its own impotence, and condemned still more by an unvarying record of two thousand years of spiritual failure to regenerate a single tribe or people, and subdue the inborn evil of the human heart! Buddhism, "the Light of Asia!"

Can the Christian help recalling to mind those ancient words of the Holy Spirit of God by the prophet: " Woe unto them that call evil good, and good evil : that put darkness for light, and light for darkness " ?

CHAPTER VI.

1. *Excellences of Buddhist Ethics.*

IT is for its ethical system that Buddhism has been chiefly extolled. Such, we are told, is its moral code, and so high is the place which morality is made to hold in this system of religion, that it may even claim, in the opinion of some, to be no unworthy rival of Christianity! Professor Max Müller tells us that the moral code of the Buddha, " taken by itself, is one of the most perfect which the world has ever seen." He quotes with approval the words of M. Laboulaye, of the French Academy, who says, " It is difficult to comprehend how men not assisted by revelation could have soared so high and approached so near to the truth."[1] Köppen, in his enthusiastic admiration of the Buddhist moral system, expresses himself in still stronger terms. Comparing the Buddhist decalogue with the Mosaic, and—rightly—expressing the opinion

[1] *Chips from a German Workshop,* vol. i. p. 217.

that, there is no historical connection between them, he remarks that " in that case it follows that the creaturely, heathen, unenlightened reason, illuminated only by its own intelligence, has here attained to results quite similar to those of the inspired reason."[1]

How far such strong commendations of the Buddhist ethics are justified by the facts, we shall see in the sequel. Meantime, we may at once freely admit that in regard to its moral system Buddhism does stand pre-eminent among the non-Christian religions. Many of its moral injunctions are in the letter, at least, identical with some of the noblest precepts of the religion of Christ. In the five commandments which form the basis of the Buddhist moral code are included duties which should be observed by all men everywhere who will lead a right life. These five commandments are as follows :—Not to kill (anything that has life) : not to steal : not to lie : not to drink what can intoxicate : not to commit adultery.

We may say even more than this. For as our Lord expounded the commandments of the Mosaic decalogue as reaching far beyond the mere letter of the law and the outward act, to the temper and disposition of the heart, forbidding the hatred which may issue in murder, and the unchaste thought which may prove the beginning of adultery, and is indeed adultery in the heart; in the same manner are the Buddhist

[1] *Die Religion des Buddha*, i. Bd. S. 446.

commandments expounded also. Thus we read, concerning the duties of the Buddhist layman :—

Let him not kill, nor cause to be killed, any living being, nor let him approve of others killing, after having refrained from hurting all creatures.

Let him abstain from (taking) anything in any place that has not been given (to him), knowing (it to belong to another) ; let him not cause any one to take, nor approve of those who take ; let him avoid all sorts of theft.

Let the wise man avoid an unchaste[1] life as a burning heap of coals : not being able to live a life of chastity, let him not transgress with another man's wife.

Let no one speak falsely to another in the hall of justice or in the hall of the assembly, let him not cause (any one) to speak (falsely), nor approve of those that speak (falsely), let him avoid all (sort of) untruth.

Let the householder who approves of the Dhamma not give himself to intoxicating drinks ; let him not cause others to drink, nor approve of those that drink, knowing it to end in madness.[2]

To these specific and fundamental precepts may be added many others, which, at least if taken according to the letter, will be admitted by all to be most beautiful, and as true as beautiful. Thus we read that the Buddha, on one occasion, being asked to declare " the highest blessing," answered in words such as the following :—

[1] Mr. Rhys Davids (*Buddhism*, p. 138) renders this "married," but as this is said to be the law for the household, it would seem that Professor Fausböll's rendering is to be preferred, as in the translation given.

[2] *Sutta Nipâta ; Dhammika Sutta*, 19-23 ; *S. B. E.*, vol. x. pp. 65, 66.

Waiting on father and mother, protecting child and wife, and a quiet calling, this is the highest blessing.

Giving alms, living religiously, protecting relatives, blameless deeds, this is the highest blessing.

Ceasing and abstaining from sin, refraining from intoxicating drink, perseverance in the Dhammas, this is the highest blessing.

Reverence and humility, contentment and gratitude, the hearing of the Dhamma at due seasons, this is the highest blessing.[1]

To these we might add many such beautiful sayings from the *Dhammapada*, as for example :—

He who holds back rising anger like a rolling chariot, him I call a real driver ; other people are but holding the reins.

Let a man overcome anger by love, let him overcome evil by good ; let him overcome the greedy by liberality, the liar by truth.

Beware of the anger of the tongue, and control thy tongue ! Leave the sins of the tongue, and practise virtue with thy tongue.

Beware of the anger of the mind, and control thy mind. Leave the sins of the mind, and practise virtue with thy mind.[2]

In this same connection we must notice with commendation the clear recognition in Buddhism of the truth so emphasised by our Lord, that it is not outward and ceremonial derelictions that can make a man truly unclean, but sin only. Thus we read :—

Anger, intoxication, obstinacy, bigotry, deceit, envy, grandiloquence, pride, and conceit, intimacy with the unjust; this is uncleanness, but not the eating of flesh.[3]

---

[1] *Sutta Nipâta ; Mahâmangala Sutta*, 5-8 ; *S. B. E.*, vol. x. p. 44.

[2] *Dhammapada*, 222, 223, 232, 233.

[3] *Sutta Nipâta ; Âmagandha Sutta*, 7 ; *S. B. E.*, vol. x. p. 41.

Of high moral value also is the emphatic recognition in Buddhism of the inevitable connection between sin and pain, even though the evil be but in thought. Thus we are told :—

If a man speaks or acts with an evil thought, pain follows him, as the wheel follows the foot of the ox that draws the carriage.[1]

Illustrations of these points might be indefinitely multiplied, but these will suffice to show that it is not without reason that the Christian is called upon to admire many things in the ethical code of Buddhism.

And yet our investigation thus far of the actual relation of the Buddhist and Christian religions, the profound contrasts which we have found to exist in the doctrinal sphere, only thinly veiled by superficial or merely apparent resemblances, should lead us to look more carefully before we join with many in the *unstinted* praise which would raise the moral system of Buddhism to a level equal to or closely approaching that of Christianity.

In comparing Buddhist with Christian ethics we need, for practical purposes, to attend to four things. These are, first, the fundamental postulates of the two systems ; secondly, the moral codes themselves ; thirdly, the motives by which the precepts of the two systems are severally enforced ; and, lastly, the practical working of the two systems as applied to human life.

[1] *Dhammapada*, 1.

T

2. The Postulates of the Two Systems.

Christian ethics assumes as its fundamental postulate that there is such a being as a free, self-existent, eternal, and unchangeable God, of whom, and through whom, and to whom are all things, who is in His very nature infinite in wisdom, power, holiness, goodness, justice, and truth. It assumes, in the second place, that man is a living soul, made in the image of God, so that like Him he is a free, self-determining moral agent, whose perfection is to be found in representing in his life as man, according to the measure of the creature, the infinite perfections of God.

It follows from this that the Christian ethics must assume, as it does, that the moral intuitions of man are always to be trusted, and that universal instincts and aspirations were not placed in him to be disappointed.

For to suppose it were otherwise were to assume that the God who created man—who is by the foregoing postulate a being of infinite truth and goodness—had so made man as that his nature should compel him to believe a lie, a supposition which, if there be such a God as Christian ethics assumes, cannot for a moment stand.

It follows further, that by logical necessity the Christian ethics must and does assume that personal existence is not in itself evil, but good. To deny this would involve us, first, in the absurdity of supposing that the personal existence of infinite goodness and blessedness in the case of the Supreme Being was not good, but evil, which were a contradiction in terms. In the second place, to deny this would compel us to suppose that a Being, by the original postulate infinite in goodness, should, by creating man and giving him personal existence, have dowered him with evil instead of good. But this, also, were a self-contradictory supposition, contrary to the first principles, not only of Christian, but even of theistic ethics.

The importance of these assumptions needs not to be argued. To raise on the contradictory of these postulates a moral system, which should be identical with any which should be based upon them, were not merely difficult, but impossible. The contrast between any system which affirms these postulates, and one which refuses to affirm them, however it may be disguised by superficial agreements, must be most profound and ineffaceable. Now it is the undeniable fact that these fundamental postulates of Christian ethics, which determine the innermost character of the system, Buddhism either refuses to admit or categorically denies. As the proof of this has been already fully given,[1] we need only here briefly to recapitulate and emphasise the fact of this fundamental contrast in the two systems of ethics, the Buddhist and the Christian. As for the first postulate, we have already seen that, if the Buddha did not categorically deny the existence of a God, he at least utterly refused to re-

[1] See chap. v. p. 176 et seq.

cognise His existence in his dogmatic or ethical system. As for the second postulate, it has also been already shown that not only did the Buddha not regard man as made in the image of God,—as, indeed, denying the existence of God, he could not,—but also he denied that he even possessed a soul. In the third place, Buddhism also, in its moral system, unlike Christianity, assumes that the moral intuitions as to personality and the existence of a soul are not to be trusted. That man has also everywhere and always an instinct which leads him to desire life both here and after death, Buddhism recognises, but only to brand this as sin.[1] For, as we have already noted, Buddhism makes both the desire of life on earth and the desire of life in another spiritual world, to be two of its Ten Sins, which absolutely *must* be rooted out before the salvation which it sets before its votaries can be possibly attained. Thus we read :—

Whatsoever brother . . . has not got rid of the desire after a body . . . whatsoever brother may have adopted the religious life in the aspiration of belonging to some one or other of the angel hosts, . . . that such a one should reach up to the full advantage of, should attain to the full growth in this doctrine and discipline—that can in nowise be.[2]

And again—

Him I call indeed a Brahman who fosters no desires for this world or the next.[3]

---

[1] See chap. v. p. 211 *et passim*.
[2] *Cetokhila Sutta*, 9, 12 ; *S. B. E.*, vol. xi. pp. 226, 227.
[3] *Dhammapada*, 410.

Such passages might be quoted in great number.
What they mean has been clearly expressed by Mr.
Davids, who tells us that Buddhism teaches that " of
sentient being, nothing will survive save the result of
their actions; and he who believes, who hopes in anything else, will be blinded, hindered, hampered, in his
religious growth, by the most fatal of delusions."[1]

It is another universal instinct that leads all men
everywhere naturally to seek the married state, to
desire and take delight in the life of the family and
the raising of children. This instinct also Buddhism
stamps as sinful, and teaches that so long as the least
trace of this natural feeling remains, so long it is impossible that a man should attain salvation. The
proof of this is abundant. It is given in the story
of the life of the Buddha himself, as in the *Jâtakas*,
the *Lalita Vistâra*, and in the *Abhinishkramana Sûtra*,
or *The Great Renunciation*, wherein the Buddha, as the
ideal man whom every good Buddhist is supposed to
make the ideal of his life, is ever extolled for having
deliberately forsaken his loving wife and child in order
to take up the religious life. Yet further proof is
furnished by the declarations of the sacred books of
the Buddhists. In the *Dhammapada*, for example, we
read :—

So long as the love of man toward women, even the smallest,
is not destroyed, so long is his mind in bondage.[2]

---

[1] *Lectures on the Origin and Growth of Religion*, etc. (Hibbert
Lectures, 1881), p. 214.   [2] *Dhammapada*, 284.

Other illustrations will be found in another place, but these will be enough to show that whereas Christian ethics assumes that the intuitions of man can always be trusted, and that universal instincts and desires are presumably right and intended to have their satisfaction, Buddhist ethics teaches the contrary. The noblest and purest of all the natural desires of man, that after immortality, is a delusion, and if a man will attain *Nirvàna*, it must be rooted out. It is plain that these assumptions of Buddhist ethics can only be justified either on the supposition that there is no God, or that He is an evil and untruthful Being who has made man with a nature which is a lie, and cheats him with false hopes, which are rooted in his very nature, but for which, nevertheless, there is no possibility of satisfaction.

Finally, whereas Christian ethics assumes that personal existence is not evil, but good, and contains in it a possibility of infinite blessedness and perfection, the hope of attaining which becomes one of the highest motives to patience in suffering and faithfulness in duty, Buddhist ethics not only assumes but explicitly teaches, in its most fundamental dictum, that existence is evil—everywhere, and always evil—whether it be on earth or in heaven.

All created things are grief and pain,—he who knows and sees this becomes passive in pain ; this is the way that leads to purity. [1]

---

[1] *Dhammapada*, 278. See also the passage quoted p. 12, *sup.*

> How transient are all component things !
> Growth is their nature and decay :
> And then is best when they have sunk to rest.[1]

This is the continual refrain of all Buddhist teaching. It is the one assumption which is never lost sight of in their whole system of doctrine and morals. Not to be is better than to be. If there be no God, then indeed this assumption may be justified, and if so, must give form to any ethical system which shall be adjusted to the reality of life. But if there is a God, then, plainly, this assumption is a bold traducing of His goodness, and the Buddhist in laying down this postulate as fundamental to His whole system of doctrine and ethics, thereby makes the slander of God, if there be one, fundamental to his system of morals ! The contrast between this and the counter assumption of the Christian system of morals surely needs no emphasis.

Such, then, are the contrasts between the two ethical systems in their fundamental postulates. One might almost be content to stop here. For it is plain that though, so far as consistent with ignoring or denying the being of God, all the precepts given for the regulation of our life should be identical, yet the contrast between the two ethical systems, which is already involved in these opposing postulates, would

---

[1] *Mahâsudassana Sutta*, ii. 42 ; *S. B. E.*, vol. xi. p. 289. See also the comment on this famous passage in the Introduction to the above Sutta ; *S. B. E.*, vol. xi. pp. 239-243.

immeasurably outweigh all outward and formal resemblances.   That, however, with such irreconcilable
contrasts in their fundamental assumptions, the pre-
ceptive system of the two religions should be identical,
were not to be expected.   And how widely, in fact,
despite the superficial agreements which have been so
emphasised by many, they really differ from each other,
we shall shortly see.

3. Law in the Two Systems.

We have next to compare the law which the
Buddhist and the Christian religions respectively lay
down for the regulation of life.   It is of importance,
however, before entering into a detailed discussion of
this matter, to observe that the word "law," of which
we hear so much in Buddhism, connotes a very
different set of ideas from that which the word calls
up in the mind of one educated in a Christian land.
The "law" of the Buddhist, in which he is directed
to meditate, by which he regulates his life, is, fundamentally an observed and unchangeable order of things,
according to which we must regulate our lives if we
will escape pain.   It is *not* the law which is written
on the conscience, which we are to understand by this
word as we meet it in Buddhist translations, but
that law or order which is formulated briefly in the
Four Noble Truths—namely, that all existence involves pain ; that pain is because of desire ; that the

removal of pain can only come from the extinction of desire; and that this may be attained by walking in the Eightfold Noble Path. This is the boasted law of the Buddha!

Very beautiful are the following words, and as true as beautiful, if applied to that moral law which is revealed in the conscience, and set forth in the Sermon on the Mount :—

The gift of the law exceeds all gifts, the sweetness of the law exceeds all sweetness, the delight in the law exceeds all delights.[1]

But when once we understand what in the mind of the writer, and as understood by the Buddhist, was intended by the " law " in these words, we shall only be able to call them true and beautiful, if the atheistic pessimism of the Four Noble Truths, be the truth, and even then the beauty is gone; for in such a creed and such a conception of an iron law of doom which sternly condemns even the desire to live in earth or heaven, and drives all creatures to final extinction, there is neither truth nor beauty, only falsehood and a rayless gloom.

As for the specific precepts which in the Buddhist theory are based upon this fundamental " law," it is plain, from what has already been shown, that they neither have nor can have behind them any commanding power. We hear indeed of the " Ten Commandments " of Buddhism, but while it may be

[1] *Dhammapada*, 354.

difficult to find a better translation of the Buddhist
phrase so rendered, we must not introduce into the
phrase the idea of moral law, *as a commanding authority*,
derived from our theistic and Christian modes of
thought.   In fact, the word *sila*, rendered "commandment" in the above phrase, has no such idea as command in it.   Indeed, it is plain enough, from what
has been already shown of Buddhist teaching, that the
idea of a moral *obligation*—in our sense of that phrase
—to do or not do anything, an obligation quite independent of its effect upon my happiness one way or
the other,—such an idea not only is not in the Buddhist system of ethics, but absolutely could not find a
place there; for this conception of obligation implies an
authority, and thus assumes the existence of a Being
superior to myself, who has the right and the power
to exact obedience.   If, as in Buddhism, no such
power be recognised, then the ideas of authority and
obligation have no logical basis.   Could they rest, as
some say, upon an imagined claim of collective
humanity upon the individual ?   So some tell us.
But as respects Buddhism, even were this true, it could
avail nothing in defence of the ethical system ; for the
simple reason that the Buddha never rests the argument for the fulfilment of the Dhamma, the "law,"
upon any such relation of the individual to the whole.[1]

[1] "To Buddhist thinking, the will of a Supreme Lawgiver and
Ruler in the kingdom of the moral world, even as little as a bare
claim of the Universal . . . that the Individual should yield to. it,

And even were this not so, still how could any such claim come with authority, except it could be made to appear that in wisdom and in righteousness, as well as in power, collective humanity can justify a right to command? Has this collective humanity, the idol of the positivist, thus far shown any such eminent wisdom and righteousness above the individuals in the social body, as to justify its imposing a law upon the conscience of the individual, and exacting obedience if perchance a Socrates choose to disobey?

But whatever any among ourselves may have argued, in the vain attempt to show how the sense of *obligation* and the *authority* of moral law may be maintained where the belief in a personal God has been really given up, or left out of the system of thought; the Buddha, it must be said to his praise, was too wise a man to assert, when he had banished from his religious system the idea of a Supreme God, that men were or could be under obligation to obey all or any of his so-called "commandments." Never once have we found a passage in any of the Buddhist books thus far made accessible, which, read in the light of the context, reveals a trace of such an idea. With the Buddha, the whole moral system is not mandatory, but merely advisory. The idea of authority, supreme, absolute, and uncompromising, which is omnipresent

can appear to be the ground on which rests the nature and power of the moral command."—Oldenberg, "*Buddha, sein Leben, seine Lehre, seine Gemeinde,*" S. 295.

in the ethics of the Bible, is wholly absent from Buddhist ethics. The Buddha constantly, with the utmost frankness, rests the whole argument for the observance of his so-called precepts upon mere expediency. If you do so and so, you may escape suffering ; if you do not, it will be worse for you. This is the one argument which is everywhere in endlessly varying form iterated and reiterated in the Buddhist sacred books. " You will of course be a very foolish man, if once instructed as to the Noble Path by entering which you may put an end to sorrow, you still refuse to enter. You hold on to the world only to ensure the continuance or increase of sorrow. But, nevertheless, if you choose to do so, the Buddha claims no authority to condemn any one, nor does he know of any higher power who will." Citations in almost any number might be given in proof of this point. For example, we read :—

" If a man acts or speaks with an evil thought, pain follows him as the wheel follows the foot of the ox that draws the carriage." [1] To the same effect is the argument of the whole chapter. Again we are told in the same work that " the Buddhas are," not lawgivers vested with authority, but " only preachers." [2] Indeed, on this vital point the authorities seem to be quite at one. Not to multiply testimonies, we may cite the words of the Rev. Mr. Hardy :—" There is properly no law. The Buddhist can take upon himself

[1] *Dhammapada*, 1.   [2] *Ibid.*, 276.

certain obligations . . . as many or as few as he
please, and for any length of time he pleases.   It is
his own act that makes them binding, and not any
objective authority." [1]

A sorry and impotent law, then, this much praised
" law " of the Buddha proves to be, a law with no
lawgiver, and with no authority behind to enforce it.
We are told that the Buddha came to establish a kingdom of righteousness, and perhaps it would be hard to
find a better translation of the title of one of the most
ancient and famous of the Buddhist Suttas than that
which Mr. Davids has given it—namely, " *The Foundation of the Kingdom of Righteousness.*" [2]   And here, again,
some have asked with eagerness and anxiety, have we
not another striking coincidence with a Christian conception ?   But the imagined agreement becomes of
very small consequence when once we thus discover
this " kingdom " of the Buddha is a kingdom without a king !   In the Christian system of moral law
the king, even the Lord God Almighty, is everything ;
every precept, the most momentous and the most
minute alike, derives its sole authority from this,
that it is the will of that peerless King, that blessed
and only Potentate, who is infinite at once in power,
wisdom, love, and righteousness.   But in the Buddhist " kingdom of righteousness " there is no king,—
only an empty throne !

[1] *Manual of Buddhism*, p. 525.

[2] *Páli, Dhammacakkappavattana Sutta.*   See Mr. Davids' remarks
on this rendering in his *Buddhism*, p. 45.

But it is time that we should now compare the
precepts of the law of this kingless "kingdom" with
these of the law of the kingdom of Christ. That
there are in the precepts of the two religions points
of agreement we have already seen. But the subject demands a more particular comparison of the
precepts of the Buddha with those of the Holy
Scriptures.

As to the former, the Christian moral law in its
general outline is so familiar to all that we do not
need to go into a detailed exhibition of its contents.
It is briefly summed up, as every one knows, in the
ten commandments, which Moses claimed to have
received from God. In the Sermon of Christ upon
the Mount we have a full spiritual exposition of the
scope and meaning of its precepts, and the principles
which are to rule in its interpretation and application
to the individual life. The duties enjoined may be
briefly summed up as duties to God the Lawgiver, and
duties to our fellow-creatures. The first table of the
decalogue gives us the former, the second table gives
us the latter. In the later books of the Scriptures,
especially in the New Testament, we find the full
expansion of these various commands, and abundant
illustrations of their application to the various relations
and circumstances of life. All the law is comprehended, however,—duties to God, to our fellow-men,
and to ourselves,—in the words of the Lord Jesus
Christ, "Thou shalt love the Lord thy God with all

thy heart, and with all thy mind, and with all thy strength," and "Thou shalt love thy neighbour as thyself."[1] And the apostle expresses the same thought when he tells us that "love is the fulfilling of the law."[2]

In this moral law, let it never be forgotten, there is nothing merely permissive or advisory. Everywhere and always we hear the accent of the most absolute command. We are told concerning the effect of the Sermon on the Mount, when first delivered by our Lord, that the people were specially impressed by this tone of absolute authority with which He spake; "the multitudes were astonished at his teaching, for he taught them as one having authority."[3] It must also be noted and remembered, as of great significance in the present comparison, that this moral law is everywhere represented as *one* and *unalterable*. Not only are its words words of command, but they are commands for *every* one, for the worst as well as the best, for the weakest as well as the strongest. Of different codes of varying strictness for different people, or for different circumstances, Christian ethics knows nothing. Herein the moral law which we have in the New Testament, we may well remark in passing, shows itself to be in perfect analogy with the system of physical law as the Creator has ordained it in material nature. The law in both cases alike is one and unalterable in its demands. In both cases alike, if we

---

[1] Mark xii. 30, 31.   [2] Rom. xiii. 10.
[3] Matt. vii. 28, 29.

obey, it is well with us; if we fail, even through ignorance or weakness, we suffer.

Such, then, is the moral law of the Christian Scriptures. What is the "law" which the Buddha proclaimed? How far do these two agree? To hear the words of some, one would think that the Buddha was very much at one with Christ, the apostles, and prophets, as regards the moral law. How much truth there is in this opinion, we shall shortly see.

In the first place, let it be observed that it follows at once from the rejection by the Buddha of the primal Christian postulate of the being of a God, that Buddhist ethics knows nothing of any duty owed by man to Him. To the commands of the first table of the decalogue there is therefore, and could be, nothing analogous in Buddhism. Whatever be the belief of any one as to the existence of God, it is plain that this single point of contrast, though there were no other, is of incalculable moment. For if there is a personal God, to whom man owes supreme love and allegiance, then, clearly, the omission of any recognition of these duties from the moral code must be *fatal*; while on the other hand, if there is no such being, then the system of Christian ethics is chargeable with a large element of superstition. In no case can this omission be of trifling moment in a just comparison of the two ethical systems.

But the contrast does not end with this; on the contrary, this is but the beginning. For, in the second

place, while the Christian law is *one* and *unalterable*
for all circumstances and conditions of men, the
Buddhist code of morals is threefold. There is *one*
code for the *layman ;* there is a *second* for the *Bhikkhu*,
who has entered on the Noble Fourfold Path, which is
supposed to conduct to salvation ; there is a *third* for
the *Arâhat*, which must be observed by him who will
here attain *Nirvâna*. All is based in the Four Noble
Truths.

First of all, then, is the *"pachasìla*," or " five commandments " of Buddha, obedience to which, indeed, is
not represented as *obligatory* on all, or on any one,—
though of the highest expediency,—but is required, in
theory at least, of all who will enter the ranks of the
Buddhist *laity*. For the Buddhist monks who enter on
the Noble Path, there is added to this first code, somewhat modified, another code of five commandments !
All who have entered the sacred order, the *Sangha*, must
vow observance of this second code. Lastly, to this
again, is added yet another set of precepts, much more
numerous and complicated, which must be observed and
practised by all who would attain to Arâhatship, or that
state of mind which is called *Nirvâna*, and which, attained, breaks and ends the chain of birth and death.

The first, and—be it carefully marked—in the Buddhist system, *the lowest code* is briefly comprised in
the following five commandments as given above—*viz.*
(1) Not to take life (from any living thing); (2) Not
to lie ; (3) Not to steal ; (4) Not to commit adultery ;

U

(5) Not to drink what can intoxicate. Here, indeed, is similarity to the second table of the Mosaic decalogue, but by no means perfect agreement. For example, we read in both a prohibition of killing. But in the Mosaic code the prohibition refers only to the taking of *human* life *unjustly ;* in the Buddhist, the taking of any life is forbidden, even that of noxious beasts and insects. The full text of the command reads, " Let him not kill nor cause to be killed any living creature, . . . both those that are strong, and those that tremble in the world." [1] The Buddha is represented as having said that " this law is broken by the killing of so much as a louse, a bug, or a tick." [2] In illustration of the great sin involved in even such a trifling breach of the commandment, he is said to have added that " the Rishi Pandukabra, as a consequence of his having, when he was a carpenter, pierced a fly with a splinter of wood, had, while engaged . . . in the performance of good works, to suffer the torture of being impaled." [3] We have not found any passage in accessible authorities in which this precept is expressly applied to the prohibition of executions, but that it was historically interpreted by the peoples of India who accepted the Buddhist doctrine, as prohibiting the punishment of death for any crime, witness the Chinese pilgrims Fa Hian and Hiuen Thsang.[4] It is therefore correct to

---

[1] *Sutta Nipàta ; Dhammika Sutta*, 19 ; *S. B. E.*, vol. x. p. 65.

[2] *Buddhaghosha's Parables*, translated from the Burmese by Captain T. Rogers, R.E., chap. xiii. p. 153.   [3] *Ibid.* p. 154.

[4] According to Köppen, *Die Religion des Buddha*, i. Bd. S. 457.

say, that while the Biblical ethics even enjoins that murder shall be punished with death,[1] the Buddhists have understood this command not to kill as forbidding capital punishment.

As in the Christian system, however, so also in the Buddhist, it is insisted not only that man should not kill, but that he should not cherish hatred toward any one, even toward his enemies. Thus we read:—

> He abused me, he beat me, he defeated me, he robbed me, —in those who harbour such thoughts hatred will never cease.
> For hatred does not cease by hatred at any time : hatred ceases by love ; this is an old rule.[2]

The command not to lie is expanded as follows : "Let no one speak falsely to another in the hall of justice or in the hall of the assembly, let him not cause (any one) to speak (falsely), nor approve of those that speak (falsely), let him avoid all (sort of) untruth."[3] Buddhaghosha tells us that the Buddha said of this precept, " This law is broken by even jestingly uttering a falsehood which will affect the advantage and prosperity of another."[4] The command, " Not to commit adultery," in the letter is the same as the seventh of the Mosaic code, and is also expounded somewhat as our Lord expounded it in the Gospel. We are told that the Buddha said, " This law is broken by so much as looking at the wife of another with a

---

[1] Gen. ix. 6 et passim.   [2] Dhammapada, 3, 5.
[3] Sutta Nipáta ; Dhammika Sutta, 22.
[4] Buddhaghosha's Parables, chap. xxiii. p. 153.

lustful mind." [1]   This indeed does not go so far as the
words of our Lord, "whosoever looketh upon"—not
merely the wife of another—" a *woman* to lust after her
hath committed adultery with her already in his heart;"[2]
but it at least recognises, as in previous cases, the truth
that even the thought or wish of sin is sin.

The fifth command of these five has nothing corresponding in Christian ethics.   For while drunken-
ness and excess is everywhere condemned without
sparing in the New Testament as in the Old, still the
Bible as constantly assumes the lawfulness, under
some conditions, of the moderate use of wine.[3]   The
command of the Biblical decalogue to honour our
parents, and to abstain from all coveting of that which
is our neighbour's, on the other hand, are not in this
lowest Buddhist code, but are, however, emphatically
enjoined upon all laymen as well as the members of
the Sangha, in many other passages.   Thus we
read :—

Whosoever, being rich, does not support mother or father
when old and past their youth, let one know him as an outcast.

---

[1] *Buddhaghosha's Parables*, chap. xxiii. p. 153.

[2] Matt. v. 28.   But Buddhism regards the wrong as not done to
the woman, but to her guardian.

[3] This is plain enough from the fact that our Lord's first miracle
consisted in the turning of water into wine at the marriage in Cana
(John ii.) ; from His appointment of wine, the fermented juice of the
grape, to be the symbol of His blood in the Holy Supper (Matt. xxvii.
29 ; cf. 1 Cor. xi. 21 *et seq*) ; and, finally, from Rom. xiv. 21, where
wine drinking and eating flesh are both reckoned indifferent.

Whosoever strikes or by words annoys mother or father, brother, sister, or mother-in-law, let one know him as an outcast.[1]

Freedom from covetousness is commended in the following :—

Whosoever has here overcome lust, . . . he does not covet.[2]

Such, then, is the first code of Buddhist ethics, that rule of life which, if not made compulsory, is earnestly commended by the Buddha to all who, though not prepared to enter the Noble Path to *Nirvàna* by joining the Order, yet desire, so far as is consistent with worldly occupations, to lead a right life. While we do not find even here perfect agreement with the law of Christian morals, yet all will freely admit that, despite the fact that a few things are enjoined which are not—according to the Christian standard—duties universally, if duties at all, yet we have a code which, carefully observed, would give a community more correct in life than any which perhaps actually exists anywhere in all the world.

For all that is of the truth in these precepts we can only be thankful, and gladly recognise the undoubted fact that in this *pachasìla* and its connected duties the Buddha evinced a clearness of moral perception as regards the duties due from man to man, and their necessity to religion, rarely, if ever, equalled by any teacher outside of the Christian Scriptures.

[1] *Sutta Nipàta; Vasala Sutta*, 9, 10 ; *S. B. E.*, vol. x. pp. 21, 22.
[2] *Sutta Nipàta ; Attadanda Sutta*, 14 ; *S. B. E.*, vol. x. p. 179.

It should be added that, although only the observance of these moral duties was enjoined by the
Buddha upon those who, without forsaking the world,
would yet become his disciples, yet it was recom-
mended that in addition to the vow to observe these
five commandments, the pious Buddhist layman should
add a vow to keep for a limited period, or for his
whole life, three precepts more—namely, "Not to eat
at prohibited seasons;" "Not to wear wreaths or use
perfumes;" "Not to sleep on a high, broad bed."

Thus to the enumeration of the five above-named
precepts in the *Dhammika Sutta*, as to the duties of
the Buddhist householder, it is added, "Let him not at
night eat untimely food, let him not wear wreaths nor
use perfumes, let him lie on a couch spread on the
earth." [1]

This is a summary of the duties required of the
Buddhist layman. But it is of great consequence to
notice that, according to the Buddha, the observance
of these precepts would not *of itself* conduct to that
salvation which he proclaimed. Though no man could
be saved who should neglect these eight precepts, yet
their observance alone would not bring the man to

---

[1] *Sutta Nipáta ; Dhammika Sutta*, 25, 26 ; *S. B. E.*, vol. x. p. 66.
In the *Mahásudassana Sutta* the Buddha is represented as giving to
the kings of the East six commandments, five of which are as above,
to which is added, "Ye shall eat as ye have eaten," which Mr. Davids
supposes to mean they should observe their own customs as to things
clean and unclean. See *Mahásudassana Sutta*, i. 15 ; *S. B. E.*, vol. xi.
p. 253. Observe, at the bottom of the page, note 1.

Nirvâna. For at the end of the *Dhammika Sutta* before cited, after the complete enumeration of the householder's duties, we read that "The householder who observes these strenuously goes to the gods by name *Sayampabhas.*" [1] And in the *Mahâparinibbâna Sutta* it is said that as one of five gains to the householder, "through his practice of rectitude, on the dissolution of the body he is reborn into some happy state in heaven." [2] But so long as the next life is in any one of the Buddhist heavens, even though it be in the highest of them, so long *Nirvâna* is not attained. Hence to "observe these precepts strenuously" is not enough. One may have done all this, according to the Buddha, and yet never have entered the Noble Path. This is only the lowest code of Buddhist ethics. For him who will really enter the path that conducts to *Nirvâna*, to the extinction of desire and completed victory over what the Buddhist regards as sin, there is prescribed a higher law. This is the second code of the Buddhist ethics, and is in substance as follows:—

For the command in the layman's or householder's code, not to commit adultery, is substituted the command to live a life of chaste celibacy; and then .to the five thus modified, are added the five following precepts—viz. (6) Not to eat at prohibited seasons; (7)

---

[1] *Sutta Nipâta; Dhammika Sutta,* 29 ; *S. B. E.,* vol. x. part 2, p. 66 ; *Mahàvagga,* i. 56.

[2] *Mahâparinibbâna Sutta,* i. 24 ; *S. B. E.,* vol. xi. p. 17.

Not to wear wreaths, or use dentrifices or perfumes; (8) Not to sleep on a high or broad bed; (9) To abstain from dancing, music, and stage plays; (10) To abstain from the use of gold or silver.[1]

He who will enter the Noble Path must take the vow to keep these ten.

These are the famous "Ten Commandments" of Buddhism, in which some, catching at the chance coincidence in number, have ventured to suggest a connection with the ten commandments of Moses. But the bare enumeration of the precepts of the Buddhist decalogue, as above given, is enough to dispel this fancy. The commands of the first table of the Mosaic decalogue are absent altogether. The division of the two tables does not correspond. Instead of four and six, as in the law of Moses, the Buddhist code is divided either into five and five, or eight and two. The commands of the first table of the Buddhist law are indeed similar in part to those of the second table of the Mosaic. But even here the differences are as important as the agreements. For the command "not to commit adultery," the Buddhist "decalogue" substitutes an absolute prohibition of the married life. The command "not to covet" is not in the Buddhist decalogue; the command "not to drink what can intoxicate" is not in the Mosaic. As for the last five of the Buddhist code, there is *nothing* corresponding to

---

[1] These will be found, *Mahâvagga*, i. 56; *S. B. E.*, vol. xiii. pp. 211, 212.

them either in the law of Moses, or anywhere else in the Christian Scriptures. Plainly those who are so zealous to make out, at all hazards, an essential agreement between Buddhism and Christianity, will be wise to have as little as possible to do with the two decalogues. But, as remarked above, even this decalogue does not include the whole of Buddhist ethics. He who will attain the ideal life set forth, and reach *Nirvâna*, must do much more than merely keep these ten commandments. For him there is yet a *third* series of injunctions, which, if he will gain his end, he must carefully observe. In comparison with this, the observance of the moral precepts of the first code, and that of the second code, is called "a mere trifle, only a lower thing."[1] And what is this third and highest law of life? To answer this fully would take us far beyond the limits allowable in this book. We must content ourselves with indicating the highest law in merest outline, with a brief exposition of the meaning of the most important and distinctive precepts. This, however, will fully serve our purpose; for it will furnish an adequate basis for a just comparison of the complete ethical system of Buddhism with that of Christianity.

Mr. Rhys Davids has summed up the highest Buddhist law as consisting of two classes of precepts, *positive* and *negative*.[2] The positive precepts consist in the

---

[1] *Brahmajâla Sutta*, i. 10; quoted by Mr. Rhys Davids; *Origin and Growth of Religion*, etc. (Hibbert Lectures, 1881), p. 205.

[2] *Origin and Growth of Religion*, etc. (Hibbert Lectures, 1881), p. 205.

observance of what the Buddhists call "the Seven Jewels of the Law ;" the negative, of the overcoming of "the Ten Fetters," or, as they are sometimes called, "the Ten Sins." The *Mahâparinibbâna Sutta,* which purports to be an account of the instructions given by the Buddha to his disciples just before his decease, enumerates the Seven Jewels of the Law as follows :—

Which, then, O brethren, are the truths which, when I had perceived, I made known to you, which, when you have mastered, it behoves you to practice, meditate upon and spread abroad, in order that pure religion may last long and be perpetuated, . . . out of pity for the world, to the good, and the gain, and the weal of gods and men ?

They are these :—

> The four earnest meditations ;
> The fourfold great struggle against sin ;
> The four roads to saintship ;
> The five moral powers ;
> The five organs of spiritual sense ;
> The seven kinds of wisdom ; and
> The noble eightfold path.[1]

But this enumeration gives one little insight into the meaning and nature of this law. We can only give a brief exposition, such as may enable one to form some conception as to the degree of agreement herein with the wisdom of the Christian Scriptures.

The four earnest meditations are explained as follows :—viz. (1) Meditation on the impurity of the body ; (2) On the sensations, the evil that pertains to them ; (3) On the impermanence of ideas ; (4) On

---

[1] *Mahâparinibbâna Sutta,* iii. 65 ; *S. B. E.,* vol. xi. pp. 60, 61.

reason and character.[1]   Not to go through these in
detail, the first may be illustrated by the following :—

This body which is put together with bones and sinews,
plastered with membrane and flesh, and covered with skin, is
not seen as it really is.   It is filled with the intestines, the
stomach, the lump of the liver, the abdomen, the heart, the
lungs, the kidneys, the spleen ; with mucus, saliva, perspiration,
lymph, blood, the fluid that lubricates the joints, bile, and fat.
Then in nine streams impurity always flows from it. . . . Then
its hollow head is filled with the brain.   A fool led by ignorance
thinks it a fine thing.[2]

The drift of the meditation which the pious Buddhist
should fix upon the sensations, is indicated in the following :—

Whatever pain there is, is all in consequence of the sensations, . . . but from the complete destruction of the sensations,
through absence of passion, there is no origin of pain.[3]

Not to dwell longer on the meditations, we have
next " the fourfold earnest struggle against sin."   This
sounds admirable, but what the ethical value of this
" Jewel of the Law " may be, and how far removed its
significance is from that " resisting unto blood, striving
against sin," which is the ideal of Christian life,[4] we
shall see below, when we come to the exposition of the
nature of the " Ten Fetters," or " Ten Sins," which the
pious Buddhist who would attain *Nirvâna* is directed
to overcome.

[1] *Sacred Books of the East*, vol. xi. p. 62, note 2.
[2] *Sutta Nipâta* ; *Vijaya Sutta*, 2-5, 7 ; *S. B. E.*, vol. x. p. 32.
[3] *Sutta Nipâta* ; *Dvayatànupassanà Sutta*, 14 ; *S. B. E.*, vol. x. pp.
136, 137.   [4] Heb. xii. 4.

The " Four Roads to Saintship " consist of the will, exertion, preparation of the heart, or thought, and investigation united to earnest meditation (of the kind above indicated), and the struggle against sin.[1]   What the " saintship," however, may be, which is to be thus sought and attained, it is hard to say with precision. Whether, as in the opinion of some, it is to be understood merely of the complete observance of the threefold law, especially as developed in the Noble Eightfold Path, or whether the Buddhist " saint " (Aràhat) was always conceived of as a man who had with his saintship acquired certain supernatural powers, is a matter still in debate among Buddhist scholars.   But it is not essential to our argument that this should be decided one way or the other.   It is enough for us to observe that, in any case, as will appear more clearly shortly, Buddhist " saintship " is very different from anything which could be so called according to any Christian standard.

The next two " Jewels of the Law " are called " the five moral powers," and " the five organs of spiritual sense."   The enumeration under each of these two heads is identical, and is as follows : " Faith, energy, thought, contemplation, wisdom.   Then next in order we have " the seven kinds of wisdom," in which, again, are repeated three of the foregoing list—viz. " energy, thought, and contemplation," while four particulars are added as follows : " investigation (of scripture), joy, re-

---

[1] See *Cetokhila Sutta*, 26 ; *S. B. E.*, vol. xi. p. 232.

pose, serenity." What may be the precise scope and content of each of these various terms, and the reason for so much repetition, is not altogether certain, and for our present purpose we may safely pass these by. Last and most important of these seven " Jewels of the Law," is " The Noble Eightfold Path." This, it will be remembered, is the fourth of the Four Noble Truths, and deserves special attention in any comparison of the moral system of Buddhism with that of Christianity. The Noble Path is thus set forth in words which are attributed to the Buddha himself :—

There are two extremes, O Bhikkhus, which the man who has given up the world ought not to follow—the habitual practice, on the one hand, of those things whose attraction depends upon the passions, and especially of sensuality, . . . and the habitual practice, on the other hand, of asceticism (or self-mortification), which is painful, unworthy, and unprofitable.

There is a middle path, O *Bhikkhus*, avoiding these two extremes, discovered by the *Tathâgata*—a path which opens the eyes and bestows understanding, which leads to peace of mind, to the higher wisdom, to full enlightenment, to *Nirvâna*. . . . Verily ! it is this noble eightfold path ; that is to say :

Right views ;
Right aspirations ;
Right speech ;
Right conduct ;
Right livelihood ;
Right effort ;
Right mindfulness ; and
Right contemplation.[1]

---

[1] *Dhammacakkappavattana Sutta*, 2-4 ; *S. B. E.*, vol. xi. pp. 146, 147. See also in *Mahâvagga*, i. 6, 17-20 ; *S. B. E.*, vol. xiii. pp. 94, 95.

There can be no doubt that all this sounds most excellent. *Rightness* in one's views, aims, speech, conduct, livelihood, exertions, state of mind, and meditations—surely the path which is thus marked should be a "noble path," and the man who walks in it a noble man. But while this is true, it seems to be often forgotten by those who extol the Noble Eightfold Path, that its moral excellence depends altogether upon the standard of "rightness" in all these things, which the Buddha had before his mind in laying down this law for his disciples. We must then at once ask, When, according to the Buddhist doctrine, are a man's views, for instance, "right"? What answer must be given, is not a matter of doubt. By "right views" are intended those views of life which are set forth in the Four Noble Truths, already so often repeated—viz. that all existence is sorrow; that all sorrow springs from desire; that the extinction of sorrow must therefore be sought in the extinction of desire; and lastly, that the extinction of desire is to be attained by walking in the eightfold path which we have before us. These "right views," which are so essential to the Buddhist system, prove thus to be according to the unanimous conviction of all Christians—of all men except a few pessimistic atheists—views utterly *wrong* and *mistaken*. They can only be *right*, if *atheism* be *true*, and *pessimism* the *only gospel* of mankind.

The "right aims" are explained as "such as are free from malice and cruelty, and such as tend to a

renouncing of the world."[1] Quite "right" are these, we
shall admit, as regards the first specification, but no
less certainly wrong as regards the second particular.
For by the renouncing of the world, it must be remembered, is not here intended a renunciation of the
world in the inward and *spiritual* sense, such as is
binding upon all Christians; it is instead the renouncing of the world in the *monastic* sense, such as is commended in the Romish Church, but with this important
difference—that even in the Romish sense this renunciation of the world is not by any means made
essential to salvation, whereas, according to the Buddhist authorities, salvation, *Nirvàna, practically* cannot
be attained outside of the monastic order.[2] The good
layman may go to heaven, though not to stay; but if
he wishes to attain in this life *Nirvàna,* he must forsake
wife and children, house and lands, and enter the
Order. By "right speech," "right conduct," and "right
livelihood," are intended essentially the observance of
such precepts as are included in the *ethical* portion of
the Buddhist decalogue. To these specifications no
Christian will make serious objection, excepting only
that rightness of livelihood, in accordance with the
Buddhist first commandment, includes the prohibition
of any mode of obtaining a livelihood which may in-
jure *any sentient being.* Thus, not only such callings as

[1] See *The One Religion,* by John Wordsworth, M.A. (Bampton
Lectures, 1881) ; Appendix i., by Professor Frankfurter, pp. 347, 348.

[2] We are told of only two exceptions. *Vid.* Rhys Davids, *Buddhism,*
p. 125.

may harm a fellow-man are hereby prohibited, but no less, for example, is that of a butcher, a hunter, or fisherman.[1]

Rightness of effort consists in such efforts and occupations as shall tend to destroy any evil state of mind, and prevent such states from arising. But here, again, well as this sounds, the Buddhist understands very different states of mind from those which we denominate as evil. The right efforts are to be aimed at the uprooting and prevention of desire of any sensuous enjoyment, of existence, here or hereafter, for a time or for ever, or even for non-existence.[2]

"Right-mindfulness" is expounded in a no less Buddhistic manner, and again denotes something wholly foreign to anything which the phrase would suggest to a Western mind. Professor Frankfurter tells us that this word denotes the "continual recollection of the natural weakness and impurity of the body, the evils of sensation, the evanescence of thought, and the conditions of existence" (always assumed as wholly evil). He explains the "right contemplation" as "those profound meditations by which the believer's mind is purged from all earthly emotions, but no thought of a higher being is ever suggested."[3]

Such, then, is the Noble Eightfold Path which has been so highly extolled; which the Buddhists themselves have thought to be that in their system which

[1] See *Buddhaghosha's Parables*, chap. xxvii. pp. 182, 183.
[2] See *Sutta Nipáta*, *Pabajja Sutta*, 20 ; *S. B. E.*, vol. x. p. 69.
[3] *The One Religion* (Bampton Lectures, 1881) ; Appendix i. p.348.

specially deserved the name of "noble." How far the Path merits this epithet, we may safely leave to the reader to judge. That great importance is assigned therein to "rightness" is clear, but how as to the nobleness of a "right" which, according to the judgment of the most of mankind, is wrong?

But we have as yet only set forth the positive side of the ethical law appointed for him who will attain *Nirvàna*. This alone is not enough; or rather, in order to fulfil this law, the would-be saint must overcome the "Ten Fetters," or, as they are often called, the "Ten Sins." To say that in order to perfection a man must overcome all sin sounds well; but we shall at once see that, according to the teachings of Buddhism, the sins which the saint needs to overcome are so different from what are recognised as sins in Christian ethics, that here again, as so often before, there is much more of contrast than of agreement between the two religions.

The Ten Sins which the saint has to overcome, according to Mr. Rhys Davids, are as follows: (1) The Delusion of self; (2) Doubt; (3) Dependence on rites; (4) Sensuality, or bodily passions; (5) Hatred; (6) Love of life on earth; (7) Desire for life in heaven; (8) Pride; (9) Self-righteousness; (10) Ignorance.

Comparing these now with the prohibitions of Christian ethics, it is evident at once that the two systems are at one in the prohibition of dependence upon rites for salvation, of hatred, pride, and self-

X

righteousness, as also in their prohibition of all sensuality.   It only needs to be remembered, as regards the last head, that the Buddhist understands much more by " sensuality " than unlawful or excessive indulgence in the pleasures of sense.   *All* such indulgence, however temperate, even in ways that the Bible regards as lawful, and not inconsistent with the deepest piety, is rigidly prohibited under the head of this fourth sin.

But along with these prohibitions, which are strictly moral in their character, we here find states and desires of the mind stigmatised as sinful, which, according to Christian ethics, not only are not to be so regarded, but are even of moral obligation.   For not only does Buddhism stamp hatred, pride, and lust as sins, but, no less, the belief in the existence of self, or soul; all "doubt" of the truth of the Buddhist doctrine, its atheism and all included ; and all desire for existence of any kind, here or elsewhere, on earth or in heaven. Neither is the "ignorance" which is named as the tenth sin, ignorance of anything that is true, and which one therefore ought to know, but the ignorance of the Four Noble Truths, which are not truths at all,— namely, that existence is inseparable from sorrow, and that sorrow is dependent upon desire, and so on.[1]   In a word, then, the Buddhist system of morals, in what

[1] "Not to know Suffering, not to know the Cause of Suffering, not to know the Path that leads to the cessation of Suffering, this is called Ignorance."—*Sammàditthi Suttanta,* quoted by Rhys Davids and Oldenberg in their *Notes* to the *Mahàvagga; S. B. E.,* vol. xiii. p. 75, note 2.

they regard as its highest expression and fullest exposition, forbids hatred, pride, self-righteousness, and other real sins, but no less with these the very desire of life which is natural to all men, desire for any and every enjoyment which arises from the senses, the belief in the existence of our own soul, and finally, all "doubt" that this amazing system of doctrine and of morals, is the final and absolute truth, according to which all men should regulate their lives !

To sum up the comparison,—it thus appears that not only does the ethical system of the Buddha leave out, as was inevitable, all those moral duties which have to do with man's relation to God, but it is also widely variant from the Christian system of morals, even as regards the duties of man to himself and others.

In the first place, in Buddhist ethics, that which is really right or wrong is constantly confounded with that which is morally indifferent. Prohibitions of eating at wrong times, or of sleeping in a high or broad bed, are classified together with the prohibition of lying and theft.[1] In a list of offences requiring confession and expiation, along with lying and slander, are enumerated digging the ground, or causing it to be dug; sprinkling on the ground water with living creatures in it; poking one another with the finger; and, with certain specified exceptions, bathing oftener

[1] *Sutta Nipàta ; Dhammika Sutta*, 19-29 ; *S. B. E.*, vol. x. part 2, pp. 65, 66.

than once in two weeks!¹ The confusion is the worse
that not only things indifferent, but even duties are
stigmatised as sins. The same law which some are
wont so to extol, the law which condemns pride and
self-righteousness, also, and no less sternly, forbids
belief in our own personality, and all desire for existence either here or hereafter. The philosophy of this
it is not hard to discover. It is evidently the natural
effect of the Buddhist denial of the existence of God.
Therewith Buddhism loses of necessity the one absolute
standard of right and wrong. Moral confusion is the
inevitable result.

This moral confusion is further illustrated by the
Buddhist conceptions even with regard to what are
really virtues. These, in many cases, are in Buddhism
so exaggerated, their necessary limitations so dis-
regarded, that the Buddhist illustrations of their
nature are nothing less than wild caricatures of the
reality. Thus, we are told, as an example of the
practice by the Buddha in a former existence of the
virtue of almsgiving, that upon a certain occasion "a
demon, hearing of the *Bodhisatta's* inclination to giving,
approached him in the guise of a Brahman and asked
him for his two children. The *Bodhisatta*, exclaiming,
'I give my children to the Brahman,' cheerfully gave
up both the children. The demon, while the *Bodhisatta*
looked on, devoured the children like a bunch of roots.

¹ *Pâtimokkha; Pâcittiyâ Dhamma*, 1, 3, 10, 20, 52, 57. See
S. B. E., vol. xiii. pp. 32-55 in full.

Not a particle of sorrow arose in the *Bodhisatta* as he looked on the demon, and saw his mouth as he opened it disgorging streams of blood like flames of fire, nay, a great joy and satisfaction welled within him as he thought, ' My gift was well given.' And he put up the prayer, ' By the merit of this deed may rays of light emanate from me.' " [1]   So, we are told again, in illustration of the high perfection which had been attained by the Buddha in a former life in this Perfection of Almsgiving, that " when the archangel Indra came to him in the disguise of a Brahman, and asked him for his eyes, then, as he took them out and gave them away, laughter arose within him." The Buddhist writer adds, " Hence we see that as regards almsgiving the *Bodhisatta* can have no satiety." [2]

So we read much of the virtue of Equanimity. Whatever happens, a man must remain unruffled and undisturbed. He must be free from passion. He must not be elated by adversity nor cast down by adversity, but must endure all with unvarying tranquillity. A very desirable state of mind this, and one which reminds us of the happy attainment of the Apostle Paul, who had learned in whatsoever state he was, therewith to be content.[3] But unfortunately Buddhism does not stop with this. As with the virtue of almsgiving, so here, it recklessly disallows all limits to this virtue, even such as morality would

---

[1] *Buddhist Birth Stories*, vol. i. p. 33.
[2] *Ibid.* pp. 36, 37.   [3] Phil. iv. 11.

impose. The virtue of equanimity in its perfection
requires, according to Buddhist ethics, not only that I
shall accept with unruffled mind alike the joys and the
sorrows of life, but that not even the contemplation of
virtue or of vice shall disturb the absolute tranquillity
of the mind. We are told that one cannot say that
the " purity " which is the Buddhist ideal exists " by
virtue and holy works ; nor by absence of virtue and
holy works either."   It is added, " Having abandoned
these without adopting anything else, let man, calm
and independent, not desire existence." [1]   Again, the
man is described who, " If he falls off from virtue and
(holy) works, he trembles, having missed (his) work ;
he prays for purity in this world, as one who has lost
his caravan, or wandered away from his house."   This
were an excellent state of mind, we should say.   But
not so the Buddha ; it is only described to be condemned, as a state of mind inconsistent with " tranquillity."   And so we read immediately :—

Having left virtue and (holy) works altogether, and both
wrong and blameless work, not praying for purity or impurity,
he wanders, abstaining (from both purity and impurity) without
having embraced peace.

And this remarkable language is emphasised by the
consideration that—

For him who wishes (for something, there are always) desires, and trembling in (the midst of his) plans.[2]

---

[1] *Sutta Nipáta ; Mágandiya Sutta*, 5 ; *S. B. E.*, vol. x. p. 160.

[2] *Sutta Nipáta ; Mahàviyúha Sutta*, 5, 6, 8 ; *S. B. E.*, vol. x. pp.
171, 172.

In accordance with these conceptions of ethical wisdom, we are told that the wise man will not allow even the reproaches of conscience to trouble him. These are to be resolutely stifled. They are inconsistent with "Equanimity." Hence it is written that the Muni (the wise man) " being wise, does not cling to the world, neither does he blame himself." [1] To the same effect in the *Dhammapada*, the true Brahman or saint is described as one " who in this world is above good and evil, above the bondage of both." [2] Professor Oldenberg, referring to this verse, clearly sums up the Buddhist teaching on this point thus : " To do good works is fitting to him who is striving after perfection ; (but) the perfected man himself has overcome both good and evil." [3]

Again, it is important to notice that while the most of the strictly moral portion of the Buddhist ethics is comprehended in the five commands, yet it is not on the keeping of the moral part of the law that Buddhism lays the most stress. The precepts of the second and third codes are explicitly put above the code of the five commands, with its several excellent injunctions. For we are plainly taught that the observance of these latter alone, will not suffice to bring a man to *Nirvàna;* if one will really enter on the Noble Path and reach that goal, he must undertake to keep the second and

[1] *Sutta Nipàta; Mahàviyùha Sutta,* 19 ; *S. B. E.,* vol. x. p. 174.
[2] *Dhammapada,* 412.
[3] *Buddha, sein Leben, seine Lehre, seine Gemeinde,* S. 311.

third codes also. But, as we have already clearly seen, these higher precepts, which alone can conduct by their observance to *Nirvàna*, differ from the law of the five commands,—*not* in requiring a more rigid morality,— but in adding to strictly moral requirements a multitude of other directions, which either enjoin what has in itself no moral character, or what is absolutely wrong. The higher law, in a word, is not the law which directs me not to steal or lie—though it includes these—but that which forbids me to use a broad bed, to use perfumes or tooth-powders, as also to believe in my own personality, or to desire to go to heaven!! Precepts such as these distinguish the higher from the lower law !   And so, after all, it proves not to be true which we are so often told, that Buddhism gives morality, as we understand the word, the *highest* place in its system of salvation ! [1]

And this leads to the remark that Buddhist ethics as contrasted with the Christian are in the last degree *ascetic.*   It is a singular fact that although Buddhism constantly denounces asceticism in the letter, yet, the highest law which it prescribes for the regulation of life, is in the last degree an ascetic law.   Herein the Buddhist ethics stands in contrast, not only with the Protestant ethical system, but also with the Romish, with which in many respects it has so manifest and

---

[1] "What we understand by morality is almost confined to the lowest of the three rules of life."—Rhys Davids, *The Origin and Growth of Religion,* etc. (Hibbert Lectures, 1881), p. 205.

striking analogy. For although, according to the Romish system, the life of celibacy and austerity is the *ideal* spiritual life, yet it is never reckoned as by any means essential to salvation. But according to the Buddhist teaching " the *Dhamma* (law) that destroys sin," or as in the same *Sutta* it is phrased a little farther on, " That *complete Bhikkhu-dhamma cannot* be carried out by one who is taken up by (worldly) occupations."[1] What this means is the plainer that, immediately after this, the Buddha is represented as setting forth a lower law—the *first* of the three codes above described—for the benefit of " the householder;" as the result of observing which, it is said—not that he shall obtain *Nirvâna*, but—what according to Buddhist notions is a much lower thing—he shall go to heaven, " to the gods by name Sayampabhas." [2] The ascetic life, in any case, if not absolutely indispensable to the attainment of *Nirvâna*, is so nearly and universally so, that we are told of only two exceptions.

As contrasted therefore with the ethical system of the New Testament, which is understood by Protestants generally as prohibiting the ascetic life, Buddhism, while in the letter it forbids asceticism, in reality exalts it to the highest place. The matter is of so much consequence in a comparison of Buddhist and Christian ethics that it may well be illustrated with some fulness.

It is to be observed, then, in the first place, that

[1] *Sutta Nipàta; Dhammika Sutta*, 18 ; *S. B. E.*, vol. x. part 2, p. 65.   [2] *Ibid.* p. 66.

everywhere and always, as contrasted with Christianity, Buddhism discourages the married life. All the most sacred and blessed relations of the family it declares to be hindrances to salvation. What the attitude of the New Testament is upon this subject is sufficiently clear. It is true that in a single chapter Paul tells the Corinthians that " it is good for a man not to touch a woman," and that while " he that giveth his own virgin daughter in marriage doeth well, he that giveth her not . . . doeth better;"[1] and the words, as every one knows, have been often used to prove that the Apostle regarded the married as inferior to the celibate life. That this was not his real intention, however, even in this place, should be plain from the express limitation which in that chapter he puts upon his words on this subject. For if we read, that it is better for the unmarried " so to abide," " that they may serve the Lord without distraction," we are as plainly told that what he says in regard to this subject in that place, was to be understood, not universally, but " for the present distress."[2] That is to say, in the times then present, so full of distress, by reason of persecution for the young Christian communities,—times when the married man or woman, under the pressure of such conditions, might be easily tempted to seek how the wife or the husband might be best pleased rather than the Lord, it were better not to marry. The counsels given are clearly and formally restricted in their appli-

[1] 1 Cor. vii. 1, 38.   [2] *Ibid.* vers. 26, 35.

cation to certain exceptional conditions of life. Even
under such conditions, however, he is careful to say,
" Art thou bound unto a wife ? seek not to be loosed."[1]
To forsake one's wife under the plea of religion, even
under circumstances which, were a man single, might
make it inexpedient for him as a Christian to marry,
is forbidden, as being contrary to religion.

As regards marriage in general, instead of stigma-
tising the married and family life as evil, it is in the
highest degree exalted, even by this same Paul.   He
teaches that the relation of marriage, apart from its
earthly significance and intention, has an exalted
spiritual meaning; that it is divinely intended to be
a perpetual image and eloquent symbol of that most
holy, blessed and ineffable union which, according to
the New Testament, subsists between the incarnate
Son of God, Christ Jesus, and His chosen and beloved
Church.   Not once or twice, but commonly and universally, in the Old and New Testament, is the marriage
relation used as the best earthly type of the most holy
and heavenly relation which it is possible for a human
soul to sustain.[2]

With such conceptions of the married and family
life — conceptions to the influence of which in our
homes we owe, it is not too much to say, all that
eminently distinguishes the family life of Christian

[1] 1 Cor. vii. 27.
[2] See Eph. v. 25-32 ; Rev. xix. 7, and the Old Testament prophets,
passim.

lands from that of others, may be contrasted such passages as the following from the Buddhist scriptures :—

The house-life is pain, the seat of impurity. . . . Leading an
ascetic life, he avoided with his body sinful deeds, and having
also abandoned sin in words, he cleansed his life.[1]

From acquaintanceship arises fear, from house-life arises defilement ; the houseless life, freedom from acquaintanceship, this
is indeed the view of a Muni (a wise man).[2]

A just life, a religious life, this they call the best gem, if
any one has gone forth from house-life to a houseless life.[3]

In him who has intercourse with others affections arise (and
then) the pain that follows affection ; considering the misery
that originates in affection, let one wander alone like a rhinoceros. Just as a large bamboo-tree (with its branches) entangled
(in each other, such is) the care one has with children and wife ;
(but) like the shoot of a bamboo not clinging (to anything) let
one wander alone like a rhinoceros.[4]

So long as the love of man toward women, even the smallest,
is not destroyed, so long is his mind in bondage, as the calf that
drinks milk is to its mother.[5]

Nor by such sayings is it merely intended to extol
the celibate as superior to the married state. Buddhism goes much further, and where Paul charges the
Christian who is married not to seek to be loosed from
his wife, even though she be not a Christian,[6] Buddhism teaches that the man who has faith in the

---

[1] *Sutta Nipàta ; Pabbajja Sutta*, 2, 3 ; *S. B. E.*, vol. x. part 2,
p. 67.

[2] *Ibid., Muni Sutta*, 1 ; *S. B. E.*, vol. x. part 2, p. 33.

[3] *Ibid., Kapila Sutta*, 1 ; *S. B. E.*, vol. x. part 2, p. 46.

[4] *Khaggavisàna Sutta*, 2, 4 ; *S. B. E.*, vol. x. part 2, p. 6.

[5] *Dhammapada*, 284.   [6] 1 Cor. vii. 12.

Buddha should leave his family, forsake wife and children to shift for themselves as best they may, as the Buddha did before them.   For it is written :—

A householder . . . on hearing the truth has faith in the Tathâgata, and when he has acquired that faith he considers with himself : Full of hindrances is household life, a path defiled by passion ; free as the air is the life of him who has renounced all worldly things. How difficult it is for the man who lives at home to live the higher life in all its fulness, in all its purity, in all its bright perfection ! . . . Let me then go forth from a household life into the homeless state !

Then, before long, forsaking his portion of wealth, be it great or be it small ; forsaking his circle of relatives, be they many or be they few, he cuts off his hair and beard, he clothes· himself in the orange-coloured robes, and he goes forth from the household life into the homeless state.[1]

We are told that just before the death of the Buddha, one of his disciples, *Ananda*, asked him :—

"How are we to conduct ourselves, lord, with regard to womankind ?"

" Do not see them, Ânanda."

" But if we should see them, what are we to do ?"

" Abstain from speech, Ânanda."

" But if they should speak to us, lord, what are we to do ?"

" Keep wide awake, Ânanda."[2]

But there is no need that we should further multiply citations. It is never to be forgotten, when we hear Buddhism so extolled as it is by some, that the home, with all its blessed influences and peculiar

---

[1] *Tevijja Sutta*, i. 47 ; *S. B. E.*, vol. xi. pp. 187, 188.

[2] *Mahâparinibbâna Sutta*, v. 23 ; *S. B. E.*, vol. xi. p. 91.

possibilities of blessing, the family state, which is represented in the Scriptures as instituted by God Himself, and that not as a curse but as a *blessing* for man, is everywhere and always in the Buddhist authorities stigmatised as evil, one of the chief sources of impurity and defilement.

The ascetic principle which is fundamental to the Buddhist scheme of practical life involves yet another contrast with Christian morals. The New Testament continually insists, in every way, that those who will follow the law of Christ shall not separate themselves from the active world, but shall remain in it, and that in order that they may bless and save others. Instead, therefore, of "wandering alone like a rhinoceros," they are to "let their light shine among men, that men seeing their good works may glorify their Father which is in heaven."[1] In order to this, the Christian is taught that instead of abandoning the world, or giving up any honourable calling in which he may be engaged when converted, he is to "abide in that same calling wherein he was called."[2] Instead of being directed to give up all secular employment that they may give themselves to a distinctively religious life, believers are charged to "maintain good works for necessary uses,"[3] "to labour with their hands that they may have to give to him that needeth."[4] Instead of a sanction to a life of idleness and unnecessary dependence on the alms of

[1] See Matt. v. 13-16.   [2] 1 Cor. vii. 20.
[3] Titus, iii. 14.   [4] Eph. iv. 28.

others, from the lips of the chief Apostle comes the ringing prohibition, " If any will not work, neither let him eat." [1]

What the precepts of the Buddha were on this matter we have already seen in part. Further illustration will bring his teaching more clearly before us. Thus the man who would attain moral perfection is directed to " wander alone like a rhinoceros." [2]   Each part of the " higher wisdom" is said to be " dependent on seclusion," [3] as the necessary condition of its acquisition. Once and again we are told that the Buddha, when approaching his death, assured his disciples that their welfare depended on this, that they should " delight themselves in a life of solitude," and that they should " not frequent or indulge in society." [4]   Again, the Buddha, when asked, as the story goes, to explain to one *Nàlaka* " the highest state," told him that the wise man,

" after going about for alms, should repair to the outskirts of the wood ; . . . then, when night is passing away, let him repair to the outskirts of the village ; let him not delight in being invited ; let him not, after going to the village, walk about to the houses in haste ; cutting off (all) talk while seeking food, let him not utter any coherent speech. . . . For the sake of a solitary life . . . let him learn, solitariness is called wisdom." [5]

---

[1] See 2 Thess. iii. 7-12.

[2] *Sutta Nipàta; Khaggavisàna Sutta*, throughout ; *S. B. E.*, vol. x. part 2, pp. 6-11.

[3] *Sabbàsava Sutta*, 36 ; *S. B. E.*, vol. xi. p. 306.

[4] *Mahàparinibbàna Sutta*, 6, 7 ; *S. B. E.*, vol. xi. pp. 6, 7.

[5] *Sutta Nipàta ; Nàlaka Sutta*, 30, 33, 40 ; *S. B. E.*, vol. x. part 2, pp. 129, 130.

To *Màgandiya*, again, the Buddha is represented as using similar language, saying that the wise man must leave his house, " wandering about houseless, not making acquaintances in the village." [1]   Again, he tells us that his disciple must "not be engaged in purchase and sale; . . . let him not from love of gain speak to people." [2]   And while ordinarily the member of the Fraternity is permitted to go at stated times, after the manner above enjoined, and beg for his daily pittance from the villagers, yet in the *Dhammapada* we are told that he is the true Brahman "who keeps aloof from both laymen and mendicants, who frequents no houses." [3]   More explicit still is the answer said to have been given by the Buddha to *Vàsettha* and *Bhàradvaja*, who inquired of him what were the characteristics of a true Brahman, the truly religious man.   They are expressly told, in language which stamps every occupation of trade, etc., as incompatible with the highest type of religious life, that it is

" the man who does not mix with householders nor with the houseless, who wanders about without a house, . . . who has no desire for this world or the next, . . . who, after leaving human attachment, has overcome divine attachment, and is liberated from all attachment,—he is indeed to be called a Brahman." [4]

---

[1] *Sutta Nipàta; Màgandiya Sutta*, 10 ; *S. B. E.*, vol. x. part 2, pp. 161, 162.

[2] *Ibid., Tuvataka Sutta*, 15 ; *S. B. E.*, vol. x. part 2, p. 176.

[3] *Dhammapada*, 404.

[4] *Sutta Nipàta; Vàsettha Sutta*, 35, 41, 48 ; *S. B. E.*, vol. x. part 2, pp. 114, 115.

But, on the contrary,

Whosoever amongst men lives by different mechanical arts,
. . . he is an artisan, not a Bràhmana.

Whoever amongst men lives by trade, . . . he is a merchant,
not a Bràhmana.

Whoever amongst men lives by serving others, . . . he is a
servant, not a Bràhmana.

Whoever amongst men possesses villages and countries, . . .
he is a king, not a Bràhmana.[1]

From such expressions as these it is plain that
poverty is by the Buddha made *indispensable* to the
highest saintship; the life of a saint *must* be the life
of a mendicant. Even more formal directions to this
effect may be cited from the Buddhist scriptures. Thus
in the *Tevijja Sutta*, in " The Short Paragraphs on
Conduct," which prescribe the course of life for him
who has entered on the Fourfold Path, we find that
the faithful disciple is not only described as one who
puts away theft, unchastity, lying, slander, bitterness of
speech, and foolish talk, eats only one meal a day,
and abstains from using garlands, and sleeping in a
high bed; but to all this is added the following :—

He abstains from the getting of silver or gold. He abstains
from the getting of grain uncooked. . . . He abstains from the
getting of bondmen or bondwomen. He abstains from the getting of sheep or goats. He abstains from the getting of fowls or
swine. He abstains from the getting of elephants, cattle, horses,
and mares. He abstains from the getting of fields or lands.[2]

---

[1] *Sutta Nipàta; Vàseṭṭha Sutta*, 20-22, 26 ; *S. B. E.*, vol. x. part
2, p. 112.

[2] *Tevijja Sutta*, ii. 9 ; *S. B. E.*, vol. xi. p. 191. In the *Pàtimokkha*,

We are told, indeed, now and then, that Jesus of Nazareth taught the same. Some have attempted to show that certain directions of His were intended to prohibit the possession of wealth. We are asked, Did Christ not tell a certain young ruler to sell all that he had, and give to the poor, and make that the condition of his salvation ?[1]   Did He not give similar directions to His disciples ?[2]   Do we not also read in the Epistle of James, " God hath chosen the poor of this world rich in faith, and heirs of the kingdom which he hath promised to them that love him ?"[3]

But a more careful study of the ethics of the New Testament and the entire scope of its teachings on this subject, will show that Jesus no more made poverty a condition of salvation and a test of discipleship than any other merely outward state. He did indeed teach, and the apostles after Him, that there was extreme *danger* to the soul in the possession or acquisition of wealth. He said, undoubtedly, that it was " easier for a camel to go through the eye of a needle, than for a rich man to enter into the kingdom of God."[4]   But that this was not intended to teach that the gaining or possession of riches was inconsistent with salvation, as some have urged, should be plain enough from the added fact that when His disciples put this interpreta-

---

Nissaggiyà Pàcittiyà Dhamma, 18, 19, are detailed penalties for the member of the Order who may violate these rules.—*S. B. E.*, vol. xiii. pp. 26, 27.   [1] Matt. xix. 21.   [2] Luke xii. 33.
[3] James ii. 5.   [4] Matt. xix. 24.

tion on His words, He immediately corrected them for
supposing that He meant that a rich man could not be
saved ; for He said, " With men this is impossible; but
with God all things are possible."[1]   The truth is that
the few direct commands to give up all one's posses-
sions were only intended to apply to the particular
persons addressed, and to others only in so far as their
cases might be similar.   For if the selling of all was
once or twice enjoined, and once even made a condition
of salvation, in other cases not a word was said of it
even to rich men.   Zaccheus, for example, was rich, but
the Lord did not command him to give up his wealth
if he would be His disciple; He only commended him for
his right use of his wealth in restitution of what he had
unjustly gained, whereby he showed that his repentance
was sincere, so that " salvation was come to his house."[2]

In a word, then, the New Testament, instead of
exalting poverty to the place that it holds in the
Buddhist religion, represents riches—as well as everything else which a man may have—as a sacred trust
from God, to be held and used according to His law,
and given up cheerfully at His bidding.   We are not
commanded, like the Buddhist saint, not to be rich or
to get money, but only that we get and use it as
God's stewards ;—not for personal and selfish ends, but
for the help of the needy and the interests of the kingdom of God.   To this effect is the parable of the unjust steward.[3]   To this end also Paul directed Timothy

[1] Matt. xix. 26.   [2] Luke xix. 9.   [3] Luke xvi. 1-13.

to charge the rich—not that they should give away all their property and reduce themselves to voluntary poverty, but—that "they have not their hope set on the uncertainty of riches, but on God who giveth us richly all things to enjoy ; that they do good, that they be rich in good works, that they be ready to distribute, willing to communicate" to others out of their own abundance.[1]

It is thus perfectly clear, despite the efforts of some to show the contrary, that in this respect also the precepts of Buddhism stand in the sharpest contrast with those of the moral law as taught by Christ. With the Buddha the renunciation of all riches and of all activities which might enable one to acquire money, is positively enjoined upon all who will enter the Noble Path which conducts to *Nirvàna*. With Christ, while indeed the poor are comforted with the thought that God has chosen them to be heirs of His kingdom,[2] these are not those who have made themselves poor in order to be saved. And while, again, the rich are solemnly warned that in the acquisition of wealth there is great danger, and that because of covetousness "the wrath of God cometh on the children of disobedience ;"[3] yet it is no less plainly taught that it is not the acquirement or possession of riches, but only the wrong use of riches and the love of money for money's sake, that will be found to exclude from the kingdom of God.

The stern asceticism of the Buddhist law is further

---

[1] 1 Tim. vi. 17, 18 (R.V.)   [2] James ii. 5.   [3] Col. iii. 6.

illustrated by the contrast between Buddhist and
Christian ethics, with respect to the light in which
they severally regard the body. That a system of
ethics like the Christian, based, as it is, upon the
doctrine of the resurrection of the body to everlasting
glory, should disparage and depreciate the body, were
impossible. Thus we find that in every way the
Christian Scriptures teach us to regard the embodiment of spirit in matter as not only not evil, but as
consistent with, if not even necessary to, the highest
perfection and most exalted activity. Those Scriptures
teach us, in the first place, that even the eternal Son
of God, He who was one with the Father, of His own
free will, out of love to man, became incarnate as a
man ; they teach us further that this incarnation of the
Divine Being, instead of being in its *essential* nature a
humiliation, and a temporary expedient for a merely
temporary purpose, is a fact which is everlasting. For
they emphatically teach that our Lord Jesus Christ has
put everlasting honour upon the body, in that through
resurrection having triumphed over death and corruption, He has glorified the body, and shown His power
thereby "to subdue all things," even this material
nature, to Himself,[1] so that the Supreme Creator of all
worlds of matter and spirit, now and for ever exists and
reigns in the highest heavens in a human form. " In
him dwelleth," both now and for ever, " all the fulness
of the Godhead bodily."[2]   On this stupendous fact is

[1] Phil. iii. 21.   [2] Col. ii. 9.

based the whole body of Christian doctrine and precept
concerning the body.   It is indeed true that the New
Testament describes with truth the body, in its *present
earthly condition*, as weak, corruptible, a body of humiliation and dishonour.[1]   But it everywhere teaches
that this is solely because of sin, through which only
death has entered,[2] and none the less insists that the
body, even as it is, should be regarded by the Christian
as a thing of high dignity and worth, and a most
sacred trust from God.   Thus while Christian law indeed commands us that we take heed to keep the body
under,[3] in due subordination to the spirit, yielding our
members " as servants to righteousness unto holiness,"[4]
it also ever reminds him that the body, no less than
the soul, has been purchased by the atoning blood of
Christ, and has become the temple of the Holy Spirit.
For we read, "Know ye not that your body is a temple
of the Holy Ghost which is in you, and ye are not
your own ?   For ye were bought with a price : glorify
God therefore in your body."[5]   Instead of teaching,
therefore, that the attainment of supreme good involves
the everlasting separation of the soul from the body,—
as if the body never were nor could be anything but a
hateful encumbrance to the free activity of the spirit,
—Christ and His apostles constantly insisted that the
resurrection of the body, in a form indeed different from
and vastly higher than the present, yet none the less

[1] 1 Cor. xv. 43 ; Phil. iii. 21 *et passim.*   [2] Rom. v. 12.
[3] 1 Cor. ix. 27.   [4] Rom. vi. 19.   [5] 1 Cor. vi. 19, 20 (R.V.)

material, was a doctrine absolutely fundamental in importance; and that the resurrection of the body was the most transcendent and momentous event to be expected in our future. Thus we read : " The whole creation groaneth and travaileth in pain together until now : and not only so, but we ourselves also, which have the first-fruits of the Spirit, . . . groan within ourselves, waiting for our adoption, to wit, the redemption of our body."[1] Hence this, the high destiny of the body, is made a powerful argument for personal bodily purity ; for we read again, " The body is not for fornication, but for the Lord; and the Lord for the body. And God both raised the Lord, and will raise up us through his power. Know ye not that your bodies are the members of Christ ? shall I then take away the members of Christ, and make them the members of a harlot ? God forbid."[2]

How profound the contrast between such exalted conceptions and representations as these and the uniform teachings of the Buddhist scriptures upon the same subject, as expressed in such passages as the following !—

Look at this dressed-up lump, covered with wounds, joined together, sickly, full of many thoughts, which has no strength, no hold !

This body is wasted, full of sickness, and frail ; this heap of corruption breaks to pieces, life indeed ends in death.

After a stronghold has been made of the bones, it is covered

---

[1] Rom. viii. 22, 23. [2] 1 Cor. vi. 14, 15 (R.V.)

with flesh and blood, and there dwell in it old age and death, pride and deceit.

Hunger is the worst of diseases, the body the worst of pains ; if one knows this truly, that is *Nirvâna*, the highest happiness.[1]

This (body) with two feet is cherished although impure, ill-smelling, filled with various kinds of stench, and trickling here and there.

He who with such a body thinks to exalt himself or to despise others—what else (is) this but blindness ![2]

As a man might with loathing shake off a corpse bound upon his shoulders ;

And depart, secure, independent, master of himself ; even so let me depart, regretting nothing, wanting nothing.

Leaving this perishable body, this collection of many foul vapours.

And as men deposit filth upon a dung-heap, and depart, regretting nothing, wanting nothing,

So will I depart, leaving this body filled with foul vapours.[3]

Hence, while we hear the Apostle Paul, under the pressure of bodily pain and weakness, yet saying that although, while in "the earthly house of this tabernacle," he "groaned, being burdened," it was "not that he might be unclothed, but clothed upon " with that other "house from heaven ;"[4] upon such a state of mind the Buddha, on the contrary, pronounces unsparing condemnation. For we read again :—

---

[1] *Dhammapada*, 147, 148, 150, 203.

[2] *Sutta Nipâta ; Vijaya Sutta*, 13, 14 ; also see the whole *Sutta, S. B. E.*, vol. x. part 2, p. 33.

[3] *Nidâna Kathâ*, 30-33 ; Fausböll's *Buddhist Birth Stories*, vol. i. p. 7.   [4] 2 Cor. v. 1-4.

By the noble the cessation of the existing body is regarded with pleasure :[1]

For, as it is written again :—

When a brother has not got rid of the passion after a body, has not got rid of the attraction to a body, has not got rid of the thirst for a body, has not got rid of the fever of a body, has not got rid of the craving after a body, his mind does not incline to zeal, exertion, perseverance, and struggle.[2]

Hence by logical and necessary consequence we find Buddhism attaching the greatest consequence to countless regulations designed to vex and humiliate the body and keep it under. The man who has entered the Path which conducts to *Nirvâna* is, for example, never to sway his head or his arms going or standing ;[3] he is not to bathe oftener than once in two weeks ;[4] when he receives in alms curry and rice in his bowl, he must not cover the curry with rice, " desiring to make it nicer," etc.[5]—" The Four Resources "—of a religious life are declared to be (1) morsels of food given in alms for food ; (2) for clothing, rags taken from a dust-heap ; (3) for shelter, he is to dwell at the foot of a tree ; (4) for medicine, " decomposing urine," or, elsewhere, " the four kinds of filth—dung,

[1] *Sutta Nipâta ; Dvayatânupassanâ Sutta*, 38 ; *S. B. E.* vol. x. part 2, p. 144.

[2] *Cetokhila Sutta*, 9 ; *S. B. E.*, vol. xi. p. 226.

[3] *Pâtimokkha ; Sekhiyâ Dhamma*, 15-20 ; *S. B. E.*, vol. xiii. pp. 60, 61.

[4] *Ibid., Pâcittiyâ Dhamma*, 57 ; *S. B. E.*, vol. xiii. p. 44.

[5] *Ibid., Sekhiyâ Dhamma*, 36 ; *S. B. E.*, vol. xiii. p. 63.

urine, ashes, and clay."[1]   In a word, in full conformity
with the sentiments above expressed with regard to
the body, it is to be counted as one's worst enemy
throughout, and treated accordingly.

Thus it is precisely that which in the ethics of the
New Testament is made one of the chief elements of
hope for the future in the prospect of death, which in
the Buddhist system is denounced as something even
to desire which is absolutely incompatible with the
attainment of salvation. Never, according to the Buddhist conception, was Paul further from the "right
views" which stand at the very beginning of the
Noble Eightfold Path than when to the Corinthians he
exalted the body as a sacred trust bought by the Lord
with His blood to be kept holy for the Lord, destined
by Him for glory everlasting;[2] never further from
"right views" than when writing to the Thessalonians,
he exhorted them to comfort one another with these
words : "them which sleep in Jesus, God will
bring with him: for the Lord shall descend from
heaven with a shout, and the dead in Christ shall
rise."[3]

We must not omit to remark one characteristic of

---

[1] *Mahàvagga*, i. 30, 4; *S. B. E.*, vol. xiii. pp. 73, 74; see also
Mahàvagga, v. 14, 6; *S. B. E.*, vol. xvii. p. 59. This may not be
pleasant reading, but in a day when men brought up in Christian
lands are for exalting Buddhism to a level with the Gospel as a system
of moral discipline, it cannot be amiss to show this beautiful system as
it stands in its own highest authorities.

[2] 1 Cor. vi. 13 *et seq.*   [3] 1 Thess. iv. 14, 16.

Buddhist ethics in which some as, for instance, Köppen, think that it should be admitted that it has even transcended Christianity. This is found in the attitude of Buddhism toward non-Buddhistic religions. Köppen rightly tells us that those who honour the Buddha do not make the " pretension to be in the exclusive possession of all religious truth." They do not make the rejection of the Buddhist religion by any means a hopelessly fatal thing. So far are they from this that, as he tells us, the Mongolian authorities even assign to " those who without having known of the Buddha and his doctrine have yet fulfilled the measure of virtue, and all their duties, to places in the thirteenth, fourteenth, and fifteenth of their twenty-six (temporary) heavens."[1]   To quote further the words of Köppen :—

As from the standpoint of Buddhism all men, nay, all beings, are brothers, children of one sin, sons of the same nonentity, thus all the religions of the globe appear to it as related, as sprung from one source, all pursuing the same end, and aiming at the same goal. The religious views, creeds, etc. . . . of all nations, churches, schools, sects, and parties, howsoever diverse they may seem, are hence, according to the conception of the believing Buddhist, not alien, but inwardly akin. They are merely peculiar forms, modifications, obscurations, degenerations, of the same truth, of one law, one faith, one redemption. For him there is only one Doctrine and one Way ; and all religions belong in one way or another to this Doctrine, and are all on that Way.[2]

---

[1] *Die Religion des Buddha*, i. Bd. S. 258, 463.
[2] *Ibid.*, S. 462.

Thus it comes to pass, according to Köppen, that,

even with the Buddhist who is most zealous for the faith, there remains at least the possibility of taking a candid view of the religious convictions of the professors of other religions,—a possibility which must be denied to the believing adherents of the only saving and alone orthodox Church.[1]

For the members of the Christian Church, in his opinion, by the very position which they hold, are incapable of candour and impartiality in their views of other religions. While, on the other hand, " the Buddhist is far beyond such an antagonism, and thus " (in contrast, be it observed, to Christianity) " at least approaches a rational conception of religion."[2]

That this spirit of tolerance, or, more precisely, of indifference toward other creeds and religions is characteristic of Buddhist morals, cannot be disputed. The story which Köppen tells us of the Singhalese Buddhist who sent his son to a Christian school, and allowed him to attend Christian worship, assuring the missionary that he cherished the same regard for the doctrines of Christianity as for those of Buddhism,[3] is quite in keeping with the usual attitude of the Buddhist mind. The story is no less in harmony with the doctrinal teaching of Buddhism as to religious truth. For *if* the atheism which is at the basis of Buddhism be granted, then all religions are human developments ; and if the doctrine of the Buddha as to the place of moral discipline in

---

[1] *Die Religion des Buddha*, i. Bd. S. 463.
[2] *Ibid.* S. 464.   [3] *Ibid.* S. 463, 2.

that self-subjugation which shall tend toward peace of
mind here and the final extinction of existence, be
granted, then, doubtless, any and every religion, in so
far as it prescribes such self-control, *is* "on the right
way;" and, as the Buddhist in the above story
assured the missionary, Christianity is "a very sure
support of Buddhism." On this atheistic assumption—
and on that only—can we truly say that Buddhism
excels Christianity in having "a more rational conception of religion."

But if, on the other hand, there is a God, then—
whether Christianity be true or not—the question
whether a system of doctrine or morals shall acknow-
ledge Him or not, cannot be a trifling one. Neither,
if there is a personal God, is it by any means certain or even probable, from the light of nature alone,
that all religions, even the most antagonistic in doctrine and morals, can be pleasing to God, and all
conduct their votaries to one blessed end. Thus, if we
grant the truth,—not of Christianity, but of theism
merely,—then this which in the judgment of Köppen
makes the ethics of Buddhism eminently rational, in
fact makes it most irrational. And again, still more,
if Christianity be true,—if the bare fact be granted
that Jesus of Nazareth, after that marvellous life and
death, really rose from the dead,—then it is, if possible,
more certain than ever that that indifference to all
religions which counts them all alike good, marks a
degree of irrationality which it is not easy to measure.

To call one's self a Christian, and affect such an attitude of mind, as is the fashion with so many, however rational from a Buddhist point of view, is in reality the consummation of folly. Thus, even assuming the truth of theism in any form, and much more if we assume the truth of Christianity, this attitude of indifference toward the claims of various religions, which Köppen and many others with him think should be set down to the praise of the Buddhist system of morals, is in reality one of its most pernicious and fatal defects.

4. *The Motives in the Two Systems.*

We come now, in the third place, to compare the two systems of morals with reference to that which they each regard as the supreme motive. The word "motive," it scarcely need be remarked, is used in two senses ; sometimes as denoting *the final cause* of action, the outward end which determines it ; sometimes, again, as denoting *the inward disposition* which prompts to the act. The phrase "motive," therefore, may denote either the highest end which a given system proposes as the aim of moral action, or the highest inward principle to which it appeals as the incentive to effort for that highest good. In the present comparison, we shall need to inquire as to the highest motive in each of these two senses.

Before entering on the comparison of the Buddhist and Christian ethics in these two respects, it may not be amiss to remind the reader of the pre-eminent importance of this question of *motive*, in determining the moral value either of any individual action, or of any system of ethics. We all know that, as a matter of constant experience, all men estimate, and that with abundant reason, the moral value of any action or course of life, above all things else, by the *motive* which determines the action. In fact, until the motive be known, we cannot in any given case determine the credit which is to be assigned to any act, however excellent it be in itself. We see, for example, a man giving to the poor. The action is good, without doubt. But how we shall estimate it we cannot tell till we know what is the end that the man has in view. If we learn that he is prompted merely by love to a suffering fellow creature,—if the circumstances are such as to preclude the idea that he had any selfish end to gain by the alms,—then, indeed, we justly deem the man worthy of high praise. But, on the other hand, if it should appear that by his largesses to the poor he hoped to win their goodwill and so attract customers to his mercantile establishment, or secure a larger vote in a coming election where he had large personal interests at stake, all men would agree that the moral quality of his almsgiving was, at the best, of a low order. The application of these considerations to the case of the present comparison is evident. Even though it could be shown that as to the letter of the precepts the ethical system of the Buddha and that of the Christ were absolutely identical, which no one has ever yet claimed, still that would by no means prove that therefore the one was equal to the other. We should still need, even in that case, to inquire what were the supreme motives, objective and subjective, which each system proposed to man for his action, and as these should appear to be, so would we estimate the systems.

What, then, we have to inquire in the first place, is the highest *objective* motive which Buddhist and Christian ethics each propose for human action ? In other words, what, according to each of the two systems, is regarded as the highest good ? In this question it is plain that the very phrase " the highest good " implies that an ethical system may and does recognise other " goods " of a lower order, which may lawfully be, in a subordinate way, motives to action. But it is not the mere recognition of certain things as good and as lawful aims of human action that will suffice to prove the two systems equal in excellence. That will plainly be determined by the question which of various recognised goods the two systems severally make the *supreme* good.

That in the system of morals taught in the New Testament *many* things are represented as good, in such sense that they are lawful ends of action, all will admit. Thus pain, for example, is undoubtedly regarded as evil, and happiness and enjoyment are regarded as good. Hence these are constantly made motives to the avoidance or pursuit of a certain mode of life. But when we inquire what is the *highest* good which Christian ethics sets before man, as that which should be the *supreme* end of all his efforts, there can be only one answer. It may best be given in the very words of the Lord, " Seek ye first the kingdom of God and his righteousness."[1] What this means will not be disputed. It means that the highest good is the complete and most absolute realisation of the will of the infinitely good, righteous, and holy God. The attainment of this end, as regards ourselves and the whole world, is thus made the *highest motive*, in the objective sense, to all action. And here we must observe that, in the very nature of the case, if there really is such a Being as the God whose existence Christian ethics assumes, then it follows that this conception of the highest good is necessarily correct. It will follow that this absolute and complete realisation of the will of such a Being in all creatures, not only must be, in a relative way, the highest good in *Christian* ethics, but the highest good absolutely. For it is self-evident that a greater good than the triumph over all righteousness, wisdom, and power of wills finite and erring, of a will whose righteousness, wisdom, and goodness is absolutely without limit, of perfection absolutely boundless, is not even thinkable. If there be a God, this not only *may* be, but of necessity *must* be the highest good ; and hence, whatever system of

[1] Matt. vi. 33.

Z

ethics makes anything else than this—however excellent
and desirable in itself—the highest good, and therefore
the supreme end of moral action, must be fatally
defective. It will not only be lower as a moral
system, but will be *infinitely* lower. For if, again,
there be such a Being as the Christian's God, then the
triumph of His will, the realisation in the individual
and the universe of the dominion or kingdom of God,
must not only be the highest good, but a good infinitely
transcending all other good whatever. Not only this,
but every good, so called, will be determined as *really*
or only *apparently* good, according as it does or does
not conduce to the realisation of this *supreme* and
infinite good. . Such, then, is the conception of the
highest good as we have it in the ethics of the Bible.
What is made the highest good in the ethics of the
Buddha ?

That it cannot be the kingdom of God and His
righteousness is plain before saying it, because of the
simple fact that Buddhism knows nothing of any such
Being as a God of any kind whatever. *Infinite* righteousness, *infinite* wisdom, *infinite* goodness, there is
none, only such righteousness, wisdom, and goodness
as is possible to man.[1]

Neither can it be virtue, in itself considered,
whether of the individual or of the whole race. It is
indeed true that single passages might be cited which, if

---

[1] In Buddhist opinion, however, the Buddha attained this infinity :
the man made himself, by his own unaided efforts, God !

taken by themselves, might seem to teach this. Thus
we read, in words of singular beauty, already referred
to in another connection,—

Waiting on mother and father, protecting child and wife, and
a quiet calling, this is the greatest blessing.

Giving alms, living religiously, protecting relatives, blameless
deeds, this is the greatest blessing.

Ceasing and abstaining from sin, refraining from intoxicating
drink, perseverance in the law, this is the highest blessing.

Reverence and humility, contentment and gratitude, the
hearing of the law at due seasons, this is the highest blessing.[1]

But such words as these cannot be taken by themselves. They must be read in the light of the fundamental principles of the Buddhist system. When we
recall these to our mind it is plain that virtue is
constantly represented, *not* as itself the supreme end,
but as a *means* to an end. That the end must be
greater than the means is self-evident. Were the
means in any case a higher good than the end proposed, then it is clear that one would *rest* in the means,
or rather would regard the means as itself the end.
Whatever be the end, therefore, to which virtue is
represented by the Buddha as the means, that end, and
not virtue itself, must be regarded as the higher good.
What that end may be is not hard to learn. It is
plainly taught in the Four Noble Truths which are
the summary of the whole Buddhist system.

The Buddhist conception of a virtuous life, as we

[1] *Sutta Nipâta; Mahâmangala Sutta*, 5-8 ; *S. B. E.*, vol. x. part 2,
p. 44.

have seen, is brought before us in the Noble Eightfold
Path, which is called the fourth of the Noble Truths.
But it is expressly set forth not as an end, but as a
means to an end.   It is called "the eightfold holy way
that *leads to the quieting of pain*."[1]   As, therefore, "the
eightfold holy way" is everywhere insisted on, not for
its own sake, but always as a means to the "quieting
of pain," we must say that not virtue, but the extinction of pain, is the higher good in the Buddhist system.
Thus, at the best, we cannot say more for the Buddhist
morals than this, that it makes the highest good to
consist in deliverance from pain.   Pain is the supreme
evil, and not sin; and freedom from pain is the
supreme good, and not holiness.

It will be said, no doubt, that Christian ethics also
makes deliverance from pain a motive to the practice
of virtue, while yet no one would say that Christianity
made happiness the supreme good.   But the objection
rests on a misapprehension.   That Christianity does use
the dread of pain and desire of happiness as a motive
to right living is quite true.   Again and again are
men urged to repent out of regard to the awful doom
of pain that must follow a life of sin.   But though
pain is thus recognised in the Christian system as an
evil and therefore freedom from pain as a good, it is
not true of Christianity, as of Buddhism, that it
recognises no greater good than freedom from pain.
Holiness and righteousness—that is, the triumph of

[1] *Dhammapada*, 191.

the Divine will in our own hearts and lives—are constantly presented as a greater good than freedom from pain. This is plain, because we are uniformly taught that whenever a man finds himself in a place where he has to choose between the two,—the freedom from suffering or the doing or enduring the will of God,—he is always to choose the suffering on the pain of losing his soul. But this is not the ethics of Buddhism. Our charge against it is not that it makes freedom from pain a good, but that it knows of no higher good.

In a word, then, we must say that as regards the conceptions which Christianity and Buddhism severally form of the highest good, and thus of the highest motive to all moral action, the former finds that end in God, and the latter in man. The highest end, according to Christian ethics, is the glory of the ever blessed and most righteous and merciful God; the highest end, according to Buddhist ethics, is the happiness of man. While, therefore, self-seeking as the highest end is excluded from Christian morals, it is of the essence of Buddhist morals.

It is true, indeed, that this is strenuously denied by many apologists for Buddhism. We are assured by them that, on the contrary, it is *Christian* ethics which never rises beyond the motive of self-advantage; for is not the Christian continually assured of a hereafter wherein he shall reap for all he does and all he suffers a thousandfold? On the other hand, we are reminded

that, according to orthodox Buddhism, whatever a man
does that is good, it is not he himself that shall reap
the fruit of it, but some one else. Here, surely, you
have disinterested virtue, which one cannot have in the
Christian system.

To this two things may be said in reply. In the
first place, it is a misrepresentation of Christian ethics
to say that because the Christian has a promise of
future reward, therefore he cannot do what is right
from disinterested motives. Will any one say that if
a boy knows that his father will reward him for
obedience, that makes it impossible for him to be
disinterested in his obedience ? In the second place,
it is no less a misrepresentation of Buddhist morals to
say that because they do not, according to the orthodox
interpretation, hold forth a promise of personal future
happiness, therefore, when the Buddhist is commanded
to do right, to be kind to all, etc., therefore he must be
disinterested, and can have nothing in mind but the
good action itself or the benefit that it may be to others.
This is contradicted by the fact that, as we have so
fully seen, all this goodness is not represented in the
Buddhist books as an *end* in itself, but always as a
means to an end, which end, the attaining of freedom
here from pain, in that state of mind which is *Nirvâna*,
is itself, in his mind, of the nature of a reward.
Further, it is of the greatest consequence to observe
that, coming down from airy theories to solid facts,
this beautiful theory of disinterested goodness which

the pious Buddhist is supposed to illustrate in such a signal manner as compared with the Christian, has no realisation in experience. It is the uniform testimony of those familiar with the Buddhists in their own lands, that it would be hard to find a people anywhere who are *less* disinterested in their goodness. *All* is for the acquirement of merit, which is supposed in some way or other to bring about their betterment. Here is the testimony of one who lived with the Buddhists for a quarter of a century, and whose works on Buddhism are reckoned among the highest authorities. The Rev. Mr. Hardy writes :—

From the absence of a superior motive to obedience, Buddhism becomes a system of selfishness. The principle set forth in the vicarious endurances of the Bodhisat is forgotten. It is a vast scheme of profits and losses, reduced to regular order. The acquirement of merit by the Buddhist is as mercenary an act as the toils of the merchant to secure the possession of wealth. Hence the custom of the Chinese is in entire consistence with the teachings of the *bàna*. They have a work called " Merits and Demerits Examined," in which a man is directed to keep a debtor and creditor account with himself of the acts of each day, and at the end of the year he winds it up. If the balance is in his favour, it is carried on to the amount of next year; but if against him, something must be done to make up the deficiency.[1]

To sum up, then, this part of the argument, we freely admit that in prescribing moral observances— charity and kindness to our fellow - creatures — as necessary to him who would attain that salvation which consists in the quieting of all pain, Sâkya Muni,

[1] *Manual of Buddhism*, p. 526.

the Buddha, rose in his conception far above the common Brahmanism, in the midst of which he worked out his system, which proposed to attain that end by ritual, and made very little of a moral life. In this, we cheerfully grant that the Buddha showed a degree of moral insight far beyond that which most heathen have attained, that he perceived that the root of pain lay in our *moral* nature, and that if freedom from pain be attained at all, it must be attained in some way by a *moral* transformation. But none the less is it true that the Buddha never rose above a system of morals purely selfish in its fundamental principle.

It is not then a fault of Buddhism that it tells us to do right and we shall be happy, but that it never gets beyond this—this is its fatal defect. It is not that it makes happiness an end of action—Christianity does this—but that it makes happiness, in the sense of freedom from pain, its *chief* end, that is the fatal error. *Nibbàna* is the highest good, because it is a mental state which brings "the quieting of pain." All other things are good according as they conduce more or less directly to this end. *Freedom from pain*—this is the one ever recurring argument, the one highest good which is ever made the supreme motive to right action. " In the body restraint is good, good is restraint in speech, in thought restraint is good, good is restraint in all things. A Bhikkhu, restrained in all things, is freed from all pain." [1]

[1] *Dhammapada*, 361.

By this one standard everything is judged, and, as the case may be, approved or condemned.[1]   As the natural consequence, not only do we find that what the common conscience of all men would regard as sin, is condemned, but also, as we have repeatedly seen, much also that is most right.   Only when we understand that this freedom from pain and trouble is the one end of Buddhist morals, shall we be able to see how it is that various desires and acts, sinful and not sinful, as we understand the word, are classified together as sins.   We are indeed told not to be covetous, unchaste, proud, envious, because these feelings cause pain.   But then, the love of the husband to his wife and family, the more intense it is, the more may become an occasion for pain, and so we read, " Let no man love anything ; loss of the beloved is evil." [2]   Even the desire of life hereafter, as we all know, may and does often become an occasional pain ; therefore, that also is reckoned among the " ten sins."   Indeed, according to the first of the Four Noble Truths, existence everywhere and always is inevitably connected with sorrow, therefore to desire existence anywhere again, judged by this same standard, must be reckoned a sin, so that we read that he is the true Brahman " who fosters no desires for this world or the next." [3]

In conclusion, we may see in the light of this principle how much truth there is in the statement often

[1] *Dhammapada,* 117 *et passim.*   [2] *Ibid.* 211.
[3] *Ibid.* 410.

made that annihilation is held up in Buddhism as the highest good. In a sense this is true. The absolute extinction of *parinibbàna* is undoubtedly held up as a supreme good in many passages of the Buddhist scriptures. " Who except the noble deserve the well understood state of *Nibbàna?* Having perfectly conceived this state, those free from passion are completely extinguished." [1]

Especially distinct is the famous passage, before quoted :—

> " How transient are all component things !
> Growth is their nature and decay ;
> They are produced, they are dissolved again ;
> And then is best, when they have sunk to rest !" [2]

But it would be a mistake, I think, to infer from this that annihilation was regarded as a supreme good, *in itself,* and without reference to the reason *why* it is best when anything has ceased to be. It is best when they have ceased to be, because, according to the First Noble Truth, to be is to suffer. The *ending of pain* is the supreme good, and it is because extinction of being, attained by the method prescribed in the Noble Eightfold Path, is the one and only means to the everlasting extinction of pain, that extinction of being is held up as an end to be supremely desired. " From the destruction of consciousness will arise the destruction of pain,

---

[1] *Sutta Nipàta ; Dvayatànupassanà Sutta,* 42 ; *S. B. E.,* vol. x. part 2, p. 145.

[2] To the same effect *Nidàna Kathà,* p. 5.

having understood this exactly, the wise, who have true views, . . . do not go to rebirth."[1]

This discussion of the highest good and the supreme *objective* motive has brought us now naturally to the comparison of the two systems of ethics as regards the highest *subjective* motive to which they appeal. As to what subjective principle the Scriptures make their highest motive to law-keeping, there will be no doubt. We are to do all from supreme love to God. We are to love others also, no doubt, and do good to all men as we have opportunity; but this is not the *highest* motive. Love to others is itself argued from the principle of love to God. "He that saith he loveth God and hateth his brother, abideth in darkness." "If God so loved us, we ought also to love one another."[2] . . . If ever the two loves seem to come in conflict, so that we cannot obey the promptings of both, then the love to God must take the first place and determine our action. Even the love of father or mother, wife or children, is to form no exception to this rule. Hence our Lord Jesus Christ said, in language of startling plainness, "If any man cometh to me, and hateth not his own father, and mother, and wife, and children, and brethren, and sisters, yea, and his own life also, he cannot be my disciple."[3]   In particular, appeal is made to the motive of gratitude as a

---

[1] *Sutta Nipáta; Dvayatánupassaná Sutta*, 9, 10 ; *S. B. E.*, vol. x. part 2, p. 135.   [2] 1 John iv. 11.

[3] Luke xiv. 26.

reason for pleasing God. The keeping of the moral law, in Christian ethics, is not presented as a means to salvation, but as the expression of gratitude for the great salvation wrought out for the believer by Christ. Self-seeking by law-keeping thus disappears. The spirit of the ethics of the gospel finds expression in such words as these, "We love, because he first loved us."[1] "Even as the Father hath loved me," said the Lord Jesus, "I also have loved you; abide ye in my love."[2] Paul states the case, not for himself only, but for all believers, "The love of Christ constraineth us."[3]

In Buddhism all is in sharpest contrast with this. As there is no God in the system, there can be no such motive as the love of an infinitely holy and glorious God. Instead of the keeping of the law, such as it is, being made the spontaneous expression of a heart grateful for a salvation already received, Buddhism makes all keeping of the law to be in order to our salvation, on the ground of personal merit acquired. Thus, if we ask what is the highest subjective principle to which the Buddhist ethics makes appeal, the answer must be, the love of self. As for gratitude to God, that is out of the question; for there is no God. When the apostle tells us, "Whether ye eat, or drink, or whatsoever ye do, do all to the glory of God," he suggested an end and motive of which the Buddha never had so much as a glimpse. As for gratitude to

[1] 1 John iv. 19 (R.V.)   [2] John xv. 9.   [3] 2 Cor. v. 14.

the Buddha, for his wondrous way of salvation (?)—
that too is nowhere suggested ; for the Buddha is long
ago dead and gone. "That in him by which he said, 'I
am,' has been utterly extinguished." Never, in a word,
in the appeals to kindness, beneficence, etc., which we
find in the Buddhist books, are we carried above the
level of mere personal expediency. No doubt we are
exhorted to do good, to feel sympathy with all living
things, and so on, but all is in order that one may
acquire merit, and thereby the painless peace of
Nirvàna, either here or in a future birth, when, as the
reward for acts of merit here acquired, a more favourable birth shall be obtained.

All this is the plainer that, although we are
directed—in the lower code of morals—to love and do
many things out of love to others, yet whenever the
two loves, the love to others and the love to self, come
in conflict, then, of the two, the love to others, even
our natural love to parents and children, wife and
friends, must give way. This appears from the numerous injunctions which are given to him who has
entered on the Noble Path, by walking in which he
shall attain *Nirvàna*, that he shall give up all those
affections which all men hold the most sacred. And
in so doing he will but imitate the Buddha, who in
order to attain the Buddhaship, and, according to the
legend, to discover a way of deliverance from pain for
man, deserted wife and child, and violated all the
most sacred relations and obligations of life.

It is true that in the lowest code of morals,—which, as we have seen, includes all that is made in any sense obligatory upon the Buddhist layman,—all the domestic duties are enjoined or implied. But if a man will really make the attainment of salvation the business of his life, then the Buddha speaks in a very different tone. Then we hear such words as these :—

> The complete Bhikkhu-dharmma (religion of the Buddhist Monk) cannot be carried out by one who is taken up by worldly occupations.[1]
>
> Let no man love anything, for loss of the beloved is evil.[2]
>
> From affection comes grief, from affection comes fear ; he who is free from affection, knows neither grief nor fear.[3]

Hence the Buddhist saint is described as one " to whom there are no affections whatsoever, and who will therefore wander rightly in the world." [4]   Hence while Christianity commands all who will follow Christ that they abide every man in the calling wherein he is called,[5] and seek therein to glorify God; while Christ tells us that true Christians are " the light of the world " and the " salt of " the world,[6] all which implies that they are to remain in the world ; Buddhism, on the contrary, commands him who would be perfect, that he give up home and friends, live separate from the

---

[1] *Sutta Nipāta ; Dhammika Sutta*, 18 ; *S. B. E.*, vol. x. part 2, p. 65.   [2] *Dhammapada*, 211.   [3] *Ibid.* 213.

[4] *Sutta Nipāta ; Sammāparibājaniya Sutta*, 11 ; *S. B. E.*, vol. x. part 2, p. 61.   [5] 1 Cor. vii. 20.   [6] Matt. v. 13, 14.

world, and "wander alone like a rhinoceros."[1]   It is true that love and good-will to all is commanded, even to the *Bhikkhu*, but not because, as in Christianity, this is the law of God, and again because God loves me, but because by hatred comes pain, and by love and good-will comes the diminishing of pain.

Professor Oldenberg has well expressed the state of the case when he says, "Buddhism demands not so much that we love our enemies, as that we do not hate them.   It awakens and cherishes the feeling of friendly kindness and compassion toward all beings, a feeling in which, not the unreasoning, mysterious self-devotion of love is the impelling force, but rather reflecting prudence,—the conviction that so it is best for all, and moreover, not least of all, the anticipation that the natural law of recompense will with such a course of action connect the richest reward."[2] . . . So with regard to the forgiveness of injuries, the thought which underlies this injunction is that "in the affairs of the world, forgiveness and reconciliation is the more advantageous policy."[3]   That this is a correct understanding of the Buddhist injunctions to love and freedom from passion, becomes the more clear when we observe that the love enjoined is a love

---

[1] *Sutta Nipâta ; Khaggavisâna Sutta, et passim.*

[2] *Buddha, sein Leben, seine Lehre, seine Gemeinde,* i. Bd. S. 298.

[3] *Ibid.* S. 302. See also the story of *Dîghâvu* and *Dîghîtî,* wherein the son of a murdered prince forgives and spares the life of the royal murderer, expressly on this ground.—*Mahâvagga,* x. 2-3-20 ; *S. B. E.,* vol. xvii. pp. 293-305.

wherein is no trace of moral discrimination.   If a
man is not to hate his enemies, neither is he to hate
anything ; if he is not to be angry and indignant when
he is himself the object of wrong, neither is he under
any other circumstances.   Of high moral wrath and
righteous indignation at the sight of sin, Buddhism
knows nothing and can know nothing.   The Buddhist
who has entered the Noble Path is to maintain the
same imperturbable attitude of mind alike toward the
best and the worst of men.   No cruelty or oppression,
no enormity of wickedness is to be allowed to ruffle the
serenity of his composure.   Of this thought it is easy
to give abundant illustration from the Buddhist
scriptures.   Thus we read :—

> I am the same alike to those who increase my pain and
> who give me joy.   Inclination and hatred I know not.   In joy
> and sorrow, in honour and dishonour, I remain unmoved.   That
> is the perfection of my equanimity.[1]

He is commended " who does not cling to virtue
and (holy) works, to what is good and what is evil." [2]
We may thus say truly with Professor Oldenberg that
the Buddhist love is not the same with that which
Christian ethics enjoins, that, in fact, for that grace
which is eulogised in 1 Cor. xiii., Buddhism has not
even a name.[3]

But to this it is often rejoined that in the legend

[1] *Cariyà Pitaka*, iii. 15 ; quoted by Oldenberg, *op. cit.*, S. 304, 305.
[2] *Sutta Nipàta ; Suddhatthaka Sutta*, 3 ; *S. B. E.*, vol. x. part 2, p.151.
[3] *Buddha, sein Leben, seine Lehre, seine Gemeinde*, S. 298.

of the Buddha, the Buddha himself is represented, in terms which singularly remind us of the teaching of the Gospel with regard to the coming of Christ, as having voluntarily deferred the attainment of that *Nirvàna* which was within his power, out of pure love to man, in order that he might become a Buddha and so declare to man the way of deliverance from pain. According to this story, the love of the Buddha, so far from being represented as having been a means for his attainment of *Nirvàna*, is set forth as a purely unselfish and most noble feeling. He was not willing, we are told, to go on and attain *Nirvàna*, when he might have done so and thus put an end to pain, but preferred to undergo the misery of repeated births and deaths that so he might do good to man.[1]

That this is true no one will dispute. But that the spirit expressed in the legend is not that which we find in the formal development of the Buddhist morals in the many works we have cited, seems abundantly clear. It is very possible that the original suggestion of this idea of the benevolence of the Buddha may have come from the kindly character of Gautama himself. Even supposing the doctrine which he taught to have been exactly that which has been so fully represented in the numerous extracts we have given from the oldest Buddhist authorities, it would not have been the first or the last time that a man has been happily inconsistent with his own speculative

[1] See above, chap. iii. pp. 66, 67.

2 A

beliefs.   But such a fact cannot be allowed in such cases to alter our judgment of a system, however it may heighten our estimate of the personal character of its author.[1]

But, again, as regards that conception of disinterested, self-sacrificing love which is so emphasised in the legend, it is quite possible that other influence than the remembered character of the Buddha may have worked, if not possibly in the origination, yet in the full development of the idea of the self-denying love of the Buddha.[2]   We have already seen that there are strong reasons for suspecting that the legend of the Buddha may have been more or less modified by the influence of early Christianity in Asia.[3]   And when we observe, what we believe to be the fact, that this feature of the legend cannot be traced back with any certainty nearly to the time of Christ, it at least becomes a very real possibility that the conception of the self-sacrificing love of the Buddha, so inconsistent with the dogmatic teachings of Buddhism as it appears in the oldest authorities, should be attributed to a faint reflection of Christian thought upon an ancient version

[1] "That strange figure of selfish unselfishness and austere gentleness."—*The One Religion* (Bampton Lectures, 1881), p. 82.

[2] The full development of this conception, which held out as an object "the attainment of Bodhisatship from a desire to save all living creatures in the ages that will come," belongs to the later Northern Buddhism, called that of the *Mahâyana*, or "Great Vehicle." See Rhys Davids, *The Origin and Growth of Religion* illustrated by Buddhism (Hibbert Lectures, 1884), pp. 112, 254, 255.

[3] See above, chap. iv. pp. 159-162.

of the story, in the early Christian centuries. Of the possibility of the introduction of such a conception from such a source, the analogous representations of the Hindoo *Puràna*,—confessedly of late origin,—give an instructive illustration. There also we read how the god Vishnu, for the love of man, again and again became incarnate to remove the burdens of the world, and to save his worshippers. The influence of Christian thought in the *Puràna*, has been often acknowledged. What happened in those cases may easily have happened in the case of the Buddha legend, which embodies exactly the same and most distinctive Christian thought. But in that case it would not be correct to credit Buddhist ethics with the conception thus expressed.

5. *Practical Working of the two Systems.*

Last of all, in our comparison of the Buddhist with the Christian ethics, must be considered the actual practical working and historical effects of the general reception by a people or community of one or the other religion. It may be admitted that in some respects Buddhism has exercised a humanising influence upon many races that have embraced it. It were indeed the natural consequence of its emphatic prohibition of the taking of life that the cruelty and bloodthirstiness of savage races under its influence should be diminished. Köppen, in particular, has

gathered together a number of testimonies from trav-
ellers and missionaries, which illustrate this fact.[1]
All will agree that Buddhism, in comparison with the
rude cults of Central Asia, which it supplanted, as
also with the profoundly immoral system of Brahmanism, which it held repressed for a time, must be
acknowledged to be a great improvement. But all
this is not to the point of the present argument.
We have to inquire as to the historical operation of
Buddhist *as compared with that of Christian ethics?*

That so-called Christian countries are far enough
from presenting an ideal moral picture is to be frankly
acknowledged. But it is to be remembered that a
large proportion—probably, in many miscalled Christian
lands, a majority—of the population do not profess
any faith whatever in the truth of the Christian religion. Of those again, who give an *intellectual* assent
to the divine character of Christianity, the great
majority do not, in any land, even profess to have in
such manner yielded themselves to the requirements
of Christ, as set forth in the New Testament, as to
test the moral and spiritual result of so doing. Even
in the United States of America, where perhaps the
proportion of this class is as large as in any other
nominally Christian country, the communicants in
Protestant churches are only one-fifth of the population.
In any comparison of the effects of the two religions,
these facts need to be kept in mind. It is by no

[1] *Die Religion des Buddha*, i. Bd. S. 456 *et seq.*

means true that all the population of the United States, for example, are to be reckoned Christian, according to the New Testament standard, in the same sense in which we may account the population of Siam or Burmah to be nearly all Buddhists. The sincere and hearty reception of Buddhism in those countries is certainly far more extensive than a similar reception of the Gospel in any of the so-called Christian lands. In strict fairness, therefore, if we will compare the working of the two systems, we should compare— not the whole population of Christian countries—but that part of it which professes to have honestly undertaken to carry out Christ's commands, with that portion of the population of Buddhist lands, who, having joined the *Sangha*,[1] and donned the yellow robe of the Buddhist monk, profess to have entered on the Noble Path which Buddha pointed out. Can there be any question with any intelligent person what the result of such comparison is ? Is it not the undoubted fact that, even if we accord to the Buddhist monks all that their most enthusiastic apologists have claimed for them, they present us with a type of character far inferior to that of the average of those who profess to have taken on themselves the yoke of Christ ?

Still, in judging the two systems, we may take a broader survey than this. The evangelical churches undoubtedly exercise an influence far beyond their own membership. In like manner, the influence of

[1] Community of Buddhist monks.

Buddhism in the countries where it prevails is felt
throughout the whole social and political body. How
stands the record of · the moral working of the two
systems in their general influence upon the communities where they each chiefly prevail ?   What
answer one must give cannot be doubted by any
person having any real acquaintance with the state of
society in Buddhist countries. In the first place, wherever the Christianity of the New Testament has gone
with its open Bible, there, as a matter of undeniable.
history, idolatry and superstition have disappeared.
But Buddhism, no less really than Christianity, according to its theory, stamps idolatry as folly. Man is his
own Saviour; there is no such being as a god to
whom man may pray ; so that, according to Buddhism,
idolatry, if not a sin, at least becomes an absurdity of
the first order. And yet, for all this, never in any
country has Buddhism been able to vanquish idolatry.
In all Buddhist countries the images of the Buddha
himself are venerated ; while in some places either the
Buddha himself, or, as in China and elsewhere, the
Maitreya Bodhisat of the future, is worshipped as a
God. The system, which began by refusing to worship
God, has everywhere ended by worshipping man. A
most significant fact is this ! It attests at once both
the moral weakness of Buddhism,—its utter powerlessness in the face of man's tendency to idolatry,—and
also that deep, never-to-be-silenced sense of need
which keeps men ever praying and worshipping some-

thing, though it be a Buddha dead and gone, or an imaginary Buddha yet to be, even while they profess all the time to be holding to a faith which stamps all this as utter folly.

Neither has Buddhism proved itself equal to grappling with polygamy and polyandria. It were certainly unjust to represent Buddhism, as it were, the responsible author of the polygamy and polyandria of countries where it prevails. It neither authorises nor approves them. Instead of this, as we have already seen, it declares the chaste celibate life as ordinarily essential to salvation. So neither does it sanction lying or theft, but denounces them in the most unsparing terms. But has it shown power to deal with and diminish these vices, at least among the respectable classes of the community? As for Southern Buddhism we may take, as an example, Ceylon, where Buddhism is at present found in its purest existing type. Of the state of things there Sir James Emerson Tennent says, with regard to the mass of the population, "In their daily intercourse morality and virtue, so far from being apparent in practice, are barely discernible as the exception."[1] As to the state of things in Japan, as representing the Northern Buddhism, Dr. Gordon, of Kiyoto, Japan, speaking of the low morality of the Japanese Buddhists, uses the following language: "It is unfair to hold any religion responsible for all that is done in its name, or to infer evil tendencies in a religion

[1] *Christianity in Ceylon*, p. 228.

because it has been believed by some very bad men.
Still *it is not unfair to judge a religion in the light of
the general conduct of the great body of its recognised
teachers.* . . . What, then, is the moral condition of the
Buddhist priesthood of Japan ?   Are they held in
repute for a high sense of honour, for an exalted love
of truth, for great purity of life ?   Does not such a
question seem almost ludicrous ?   Have they not a
reputation for exactly the opposite characteristics ?"
In illustration of this charge he refers to the systematic
lying and stealing, on the part of the priests, out of the
contributions for the building or repair of a temple, as
admitted by the priests themselves.   "The lying in
this case," he says, "is systematic and universal."   To
this he adds that, "as regards licentiousness the case
is even worse."   In proof of this he tells us that
when he " asked a priest, who had criticised Protestant
Christianity for not requiring celibacy on the part of
its teachers, what proportion of the Buddhist priests
are pure, his reply was, that hardly three in ten are
so !"[1]   Another gave a testimony still more damaging.
This testimony, as coming from the very class against
whom the charges of vice are made, should be held
deserving of credit.   It is confirmed, as Dr. Gordon
shows, by hospital statistics.[2]

[1] *Proceedings of the General Conference of the Protestant Missionaries
in Japan, held at Osaka, Japan, April,* 1883, p. 100, Yokohama,
1883.

[2] In the Okayama Hospital, for the year ending 30th June 1882, the
proportion of "immoral diseases" to all cases treated was, in the case

Dr. Edkins gives similar testimony with regard to Buddhist morality in China. He says, " What virtue the people have among them is due to the Confucian system. Buddhism has added to it only idolatry, and a false view of the future state, but has not contributed to make the people more virtuous. . . . The monks are subject constantly to the Confucianist criticism that they are not filial to parents, nor useful working members of the community." [1]

Similar are the facts in Burmah. Dr. Edkins cites Mr. Hordern, Director of Public Instruction in Burmah, as saying that "the poor (Burmese) heathen is guided in his daily life by precepts not less noble than the precepts of Christianity." [2]   But however excellent the precepts may be, others tell us a different story. Bishop Bigandet says, " If the Buddhist moral code in itself has the power to influence a people so far as to render them virtuous and devotional, independently of the element of intellectual superiority, we still lack the evidence of it." [3]   Buddhist ethics rightly denounces pride, and places it among the Ten Sins which must be rooted out by him who will attain *Nirvàna*. But it has had no power to do away with the pride it denounces. Bishop Bigandet tells us, again, with regard to the members of the Order in Burmah : "Their pride

of the general population, 1 in 3·846 ; in the case of the priests, 1 in 3·8. Where is the Protestant country from which like statistics could be produced ? *Proceedings*, etc., as above, p. 101.

[1] *Chinese Buddhism*, pp. 200, 201.   [2] *Ibid.*, p. 200.
[3] *Vie de Gaudama*, p. 412, quoted by Edkins, *op. cit.*, p. 202.

is such that they believe it to be derogatory to their dignity to return civility for civility, or thanks for the alms people bestow upon them."[1]   Stealing is denounced in Buddhist ethics in terms which leave nothing to be desired.   But acquaintances of the writer, who, after having lived in Hindustan, have resided in Burmah, have assured him afterward that the Hindoos, who are not too rigid in their notions of honesty, are an honest people as compared with the Burmese.

In respect to its practical working, then, as compared with Christianity, Buddhist ethics must be written as a failure.   No doubt, as in all lands, there are in Buddhist countries individuals to whom these strictures will not without qualification apply.   But that, as a whole, the members of the Buddhist Order, corresponding most closely to the membership of the Protestant churches with us, fall far below the latter in practical morality, cannot, upon the evidence, fairly be denied by any candid person.   There are no doubt some, who, professing to have some personal acquaintance with Buddhists in their own lands, will tell a different story, but we have observed that all these charitable gentlemen, when the time comes for the education of their children, are careful to get them away from these extolled influences of Buddhism into some Christian land.   Learned professors and others in Europe and America, studying theoretical Buddhism from a comfortable distance, and eulogising

[1] *The Legend of Gaudama*, vol. ii. p. 316.

that of which they have not had the slightest
practical experience, would do well to listen to the
words of the deservedly eminent Bishop Schereschew-
sky, the Episcopal missionary bishop of Shanghai,
China. He says, "For more than twenty years I
have been a student of Buddhism; I have thoroughly
studied the Buddhist books; I have talked with
hundreds of Buddhist priests and monks, Chinese,
Mongolian, and Thibetan; I have visited many Buddhist temples, I have even lived in such. Therefore,
laying aside all mock modesty, . . . I feel competent to
state that a more gigantic system of fraud, superstition,
and idolatry than Buddhism as it now is, has seldom
been inflicted by any false religion upon mankind."[1]

Nor has Buddhism ever promoted liberty. That
Bible Christianity, everywhere, with its emphasis on
the transcendent worth of even a single human
soul, and upon the responsibility of every individual
man for himself to God, has everywhere inspired the
people with the spirit of liberty, no candid person
will deny. It is the fact that whatever of liberty,
political and religious, there is in the world to-day,
is to be found in those lands alone where Christianity prevails. On the other hand, Buddhism, with
all that tolerance for which Professor Köppen so extols it, has never yet in a solitary nation awakened
the spirit of liberty. It has proved—not the enemy—
but the support of tyranny. And this indeed is only

[1] *New York Semi-Weekly Tribune*, 16th March 1883.

the inevitable consequence of those tenets to which
our attention has been directed. The absolute prohibition of all resistance to wickedness and falsehood,
the constant insistence that no degree of wrong shall
ever be allowed to disturb the equanimity of the saint,
the ever reiterated words as to the utter evil of existence, and the worthlessness of manhood, in this respect
have but borne their inevitable and necessary fruit.

Yet again, whereas Christianity has ever shown
itself the friend of all education and culture, not
spiritual only, but intellectual, and of whatever else
may help to make man a nobler and fitter instrument
for good to his fellows, and for the glory of his Lord
and Saviour, Buddhist ethics, wherever accepted, have
exactly the opposite influence. And how, indeed, could
it be otherwise ? For, as we have fully seen, Buddhism everywhere stigmatises this earthly existence as
everywhere and always evil. It tells us with regard
to all that exists, that "then is best when they have
sunk to rest." It tells us that every honest trade and
honourable occupation is but a snare, and a hindrance
to the attainment of *Nirvâna.* It describes the saint
as one who

" is no follower of philosophical views, *nor a friend of knowledge :* and having penetrated the opinions that have arisen
amongst people, he is *indifferent to learning,* while others
acquire it." [1]

----

[1] *Sutta Nipâta; Mahâviyûha Sutta,* 17; *S. B. E.,* vol. x. part 2,
p. 174.

With such an ideal of life held before a people, we
naturally look in vain in Buddhist lands for communities marked by a progressive scholarship ; in vain
for any advance in scientific knowledge ; in vain for
progress in any of the arts which help to enhance the
value and increase the happiness and comfort of life,
and make existence more easy and enjoyable.   It is
true that in Burmah and Siam, for example, the Buddhist monks do a good service by teaching schools,
where *boys only* are taught to read and write and
acquire the elements of arithmetic ; but we are told
that in these schools in Burmah they get " no information except that which comes from their religious books."[1]
What the character of the information contained in
these school-books is, a Siamese nobleman tells us
in the book which has been translated for us by Mr.
Alabaster.   He says, " The course (of study) which is
at present followed in the temples is unprofitable.
That course consists of the spelling-book, religious
formulæ, and tales, . . . jingling sound without sense."[2]
As to the results of such education, the facts are so
well known that to refer to them might seem superfluous.   Mr. Alabaster, of Siam, says, " When the
(Siamese) language is mastered, the literature it opens
to us is for the most part silly and unprofitable."[3]
So also the Siamese nobleman, whose work he in part

[1] Bigandet, *The Legend of Gaudama*, vol. ii. pp. 298, 299, 304.

[2] *The Wheel of the Law*, p. 4.

[3] *Ibid.*, It should be remembered that Mr. Alabaster is a strenuous
apologist for Buddhism.

translates, himself a Buddhist, uses even stronger language. He says, " Our Siamese literature is not only scanty but nonsensical ; . . . and even those works which profess to teach anything, generally teach it wrong, so that there is not the least profit, though one studies them from morning till night."[1]

Not to multiply, however, illustrations without need, it will suffice to ask any one to name any great literary work, any scientific discovery, any valuable invention, which has been of lasting historical importance, in the elevation of our race, which has been produced by a Buddhist ?

Finally, Buddhism, as already suggested, has proved a signal failure in that, as its own history clearly testifies, it has never been able to satisfy the deepest instincts of the human heart. For, after all, the weary, sinful, weak and erring soul of man cannot get along without God. And if there is an instructive lesson in history on this subject, it is that which is furnished by the history of the corruptions of Buddhism. We have called Buddhism atheistic, and so, judged by its own supreme authorities, it certainly is. But, notwithstanding this, the heart of the Buddhist has cried out for the living God, no less truly than the heart of others. And thus it has come to pass that from the atheistic doctrine of Sâkya Muni has developed in Thibet the doctrine of the *Âdi-Buddha*, or Primal

[1] *The Wheel of the Law*, pp. 4, 5.

Buddha,[1] held to be the Supreme Being, self-existent, omnipresent, and omniscient, out of whom all the Buddhas in succession emanate. Nay, the Thibetan Buddhists must even have a god incarnate, and so they regard the Grand Lama of Lhassa as a continual incarnation of *Avalokiteswara*, the Spirit of the Buddhas, and practically make him God. In like manner the Chinese have deified the imaginary Maitreya Buddha, the Buddha who is yet to come, supposed to be resident in heaven ; and so they devoutly venerate her image in the Buddhist temples.

In the face of such facts as these, to extol the ethical system of the Buddhists, as if it were the quintessence of wisdom, and as if for originating it the Buddha almost deserved to share with Christ Himself the title of the Light of the world, is nothing less than preposterous folly, for which ignorance of the facts can be the only apology. We thankfully re-cognise what is commendable in the Buddhist moral system, and especially this, that in theory, at least, morality, and the maintenance of good-will between man and man, has been held to be an essential element in religion. But, for all this, no one who will carefully

---

[1] Already in the *Saddharmapundarîka* (before 250 A.D.), although the Buddha is not called Âdi-Buddha, he is declared to be "the father of the world," self-born (*lokapitâ, svayambhah*), and claims to have "roused and brought to maturity the innumerable Bodhisattvas (and to be the one), who, although he announces final extinction, does not himself become extinct."—*Saddharmapundarîka*, chap. xiv. *passim ;* S. B. E., vol. xxi. pp. 310, 302, 309, 304. See also Professor Kern's remarks, *Ibid.*, Introduction, p. xxv.

and candidly study the subject in accessible Buddhist authorities will be able to avoid the conclusion that the Buddhist moral system, alike in the postulates on which it rests, in the law which it sets forth, in the ends and motives which it sets before us, is in all things far below, and in many most momentous matters in direct antagonism with, the moral system of the New Testament. No more for its ethics, then, than for its dogmatic system, can any man rightly call the religion of the Buddha the Light of Asia.

CHAPTER VII.

RETROSPECT AND CONCLUSION.

THE foregoing investigation and comparison has prepared us now to sum up the case between Buddhism
and Christianity. It is one of the distinguishing
marks of the Christian religion that in support of its
high claims it appeals to history. In this, which is
often forgotten, it stands alone among the religions of
mankind. For confirmation of the truth of its doctrines
and the authority of its precepts it appeals to certain
definite historical facts, the truth of which it asserts,
and stakes all upon their actual occurrence.[1]   The
asserted events are of such a kind that, at the time
when they are said to have taken place, it must have
been very easy to determine whether they really
occurred or not.   It is agreed by the orthodox and
the rationalist critics alike that the testimony upon

---

[1] Note, for example, the words of Paul : "If Christ hath not been
raised, then is our preaching vain, your faith also is vain, . . . ye are
yet in your sins. Then they also which are fallen asleep in Christ
have perished."—1 Cor. xv. 14, 17, 18.

2 B

which Christianity rests its claim to acceptance is contemporaneous with the alleged events; its date, as also the place where it was first delivered, we are able to fix with all necessary precision. The Christian religion thus challenges the closest investigation in the clear light of historical criticism, conscious that from such investigation it has nothing to fear. And the history of the past fifty years, especially, has shown that the result of such critical examination of the witnesses upon whom we depend, has been to settle the testimony to the stupendous facts upon which Christianity bases its claim to be received as a revelation from God, upon a more impregnable and immovable foundation than ever.

With Buddhism the case is the exact reverse. It appeals to no historical facts in support of any of its stupendous assertions. It asks that men believe all on the simple word of this Buddha. And yet what precisely his word may have been, beyond some few elements of doctrine, we are in great uncertainty. The Light of Asia rises above the historical horizon in a fog of obscurity so dense as to have caused many to doubt whether it ever rose at all; and even, at the best, the date of its appearance has never been exactly determined. Yet there was, no doubt, a Buddha, who became the founder—whether he intended it or not— of the religion which bears his name. And the one thing which is clearest is this, that he came to men in his own name; and yet, without a word of certainly contemporary evidence as to what his teachings really were, without a pretence of any established confirmation of his teachings, such as Christ, according to the Gospel testimony, gave for what He taught, men are asked to accept the extraordinary teachings of this *Sàkya Muni* as the true and final solution of the dark enigma of life. Those teachings of his contradict some of the most undoubted intuitions of the human mind, and belie and brand as evil many of the most deeply-rooted, persistent, and noble instincts of our nature. Yet men are asked to receive them as final truth on the bare uncertain word of the Buddha, and rapt admirers even in Christendom are found ready to fall down and adore him as the Light of Asia !

When, again, we compare the wonderful legend of the Buddha, about which of late in the Western world we have been hearing so much, we find again the most striking and suggestive contrasts with the story of the doings and the teachings of our Lord as we have it in the Gospels. Instead of being able to trace that legend back, as we can the Gospel, to the generation that saw Him of whom the story tells, this Buddha story cannot with certainty in any part be traced nearly to the century in which the Buddha lived, while it cannot well be doubted that large parts of it date many centuries later.

As to the substance of the legend, while we can catch glimpses through the dim confusion of a truly noble and earnest character,—one who, moreover, seems

to have 'exercised a wonderful fascination over those
who knew him,—yet he is not represented as having
been of a sinless nature more than other men.   He
appears in the legend as simply a lost and needy
sinner like the rest of us, who long groped after saving
light, and apparently at last thought that he had found
it.   As for the miracles which " consecrate " this record,
they stand in the sharpest contrast with those which
are recorded in the Gospel, and even outdo in their
purposeless folly those which the apocryphal gospels tell
of the Lord Jesus.   In the miracles of the Buddha legend
we have the wildly grotesque, the extravagant and
absurd ; in the miracles of the Gospel, dignity, majesty,
and simplicity.   In the former, we see no trace of a
power working for redemptive ends, but rather intent
on mere self-display ; in the latter, each new wonder
points with more or less distinctness to the advent of
a power mighty to save from sin and from the curse
which is its doom—worthy attestations always of a
revelation in itself most worthy of God.

Of the coincidences between certain features in the
Buddha legend and in the Gospel story we have seen
that a large part are imaginary, and disappear upon a
close examination of the facts in each case ; while of
the remainder we have shown that, for different reasons
in different cases, there is not a single feature of agreement which can be shown to cast a just doubt upon
the originality and thorough credibility of the Gospel
narrative.

As regards the doctrinal teachings of the two religions, instead of being at one in the most essential points, it is just at these points that they stand in the most absolute antagonism. Buddhism tells man that even the necessary judgments of his mind cannot be trusted; that his conviction of his own personality and of his possession of a soul is a delusion; that his noblest desires—especially that after everlasting life and .a blessed immortality beyond the grave—are doomed to an eternal disappointment! It teaches that there is no God, and no hope, either of final and conscious everlasting bliss and holiness for the individual, or of future redemption from sin and the curse for the world. It holds forth the most unmitigated system of pessimism the world has perhaps ever seen, as "Noble Truth," and exalts it into a religion. The best that man can reach is only what by his own unaided powers he may be able to make himself. His ability in this respect, indeed, it magnifies to the highest degree, though in so doing it sets the testimony of all history at defiance. Man, it teaches, has plenary ability to save himself with all the salvation he needs. There is no Saviour, and man needs none. It is with full justice that Buddhism has been described by a recent writer as "Pelagianism run mad."[1]   But

[1] "Buddhism, in one main aspect, is Pelagianism run mad, tempered with this proviso, that directly a man reflects on his own merit he entirely loses the benefit which it was earning for him."—John Wordsworth, A.M., in the *One Religion* (Bampton Lectures, 1881), p. 90.

to attain even the best that Buddhism offers—the apathy of *Nirvàna*, followed by "the extinction of consciousness"—it tells man that he must stifle all his holiest inborn affections and his natural longings for eternal love and immortality, destroy the home, and trample underfoot all the highest and most sacred obligations of life.

What a contrast here with the religion of Christ! It does indeed tell man that he is lost and helpless, but in the same breath tells him of an Almighty and Divine Saviour, who died and lives again that He may exalt all who will take Him as theirs, to heights of ever-lasting glory beyond anything that the Buddha ever imagined. More fully, it answers our longings after a boundless and immortal love to trust and an infinite wisdom and power on which to rest, by telling us that there is a living God, the Creator and Omnipresent Ruler of heaven and earth; that this living God is Love, and our Father; that He has so loved us as to send His only begotten Son to die for our salvation. It tells us that this God of love is also the God of truth; and that our nature which He has made is therefore not a lie, but truth; that we can therefore safely believe in what all men by the constitution of their nature are compelled to believe; and that the universal aspirations of the human heart for a personal life after death are not put in us to be mocked with an inevitable disappointment. It assures us that death will not end all; that the soul will live on, and that

in fulness of time the body also will be raised to live
again; and that if we honestly forsake all sin, and
trust for salvation solely in the merits and the mighty
power of the crucified, risen, and ascended Son of God,
then we shall in resurrection inherit a life of everlasting glory, honour, and immortality.   It tells us that
instead of our possibilities of blessedness being limited
by our own weak powers, it is the Almighty God, the
same that made the earth and the heavens, and raised up
Jesus our Lord from the dead, who has formed us for
this destiny of glory.   Finally, it tells us that this great
redemption will not stop with the individual, but will
at last include all the inhabitants of the world, that
the kingdom of God shall at last in very truth come,
and the will of God be done on earth as it is done in
heaven.   Truly there is *light* in this; and well indeed,
if this is true, did the Risen One who proclaimed all
this call Himself " the Light of the World."   But if
this is light, must we not then say that Buddhism is
very night and impenetrable darkness ?

The best in Buddhism is its system of morals.   To
this all agree.   Even in this, however, only to a very
limited degree can we find accordance with that which
is the law of the Christian life, and nothing at all of saving power.   Like Christianity, Buddhism recognises the
fact that ritual will not save man ; it sees that the
trouble which is the root of sorrow lies deep in man's
moral nature—though how deep the Buddha never
dreamed ; man's need of a regeneration from on high

such as Jesus taught—this he never saw. But he did
see, yet again, the inevitable nexus between sin and
retribution, and affirmed it with great power. Perceiving this, he insisted upon morality, humanity, kindness, charity, purity, and peace. Because of these
things we may conceive that Buddhism might become
a schoolmaster, according to its measure, to bring men
to Christ.

More than this, however, we cannot say. The *postulates* on which the moral system of the Buddha rests,
as we have seen, are false, and defiant even of the very
consciousness of man. Its *law* is without commanding
power, and is full of confusion. It ignores the highest
of all duties *in toto*. It confounds the good and obligatory with the evil and the indifferent; and continually blunders into calling good evil and evil good.
It stamps human nature as evil, not because it is sinful, but simply because it exists; for all existence
is evil. The body is evil and a curse; the relations
of life—husband and wife, parent and child—are evil;
he who will attain *Nirvàna* must cut loose from them
all. Even truths and virtues are by Buddhism exaggerated till they become falsehoods and vices. It
emphasises the dignity of manhood; but, not content
with that, it deifies him. It is tolerant of other creeds;
but it is the tolerance of that indifference to truth
which comes to him who has become convinced that
life itself is a falsehood and a mockery, with nothing
in it but pain and vanity, and nothing better beyond.

Finally, its motives, if not always evil, are always of
the earth—earthly. Its highest conception of unselfishness is to be unselfish for the selfish end of attaining a solitary *Nirvàna*, in which one shall desire neither
existence nor non-existence any longer, and so make
an end of pain. As for the practical results, tried by
this final test, it is found wanting. That it has done
some good where it has come in as a substitute for a
worse and savage cult, any candid man will admit;
but its results at the best have been sadly incomplete.
It has never yet raised a single type of character of
so high an order as many of the heroes of the Christian
Church; it has never yet advanced a nation higher
than China or Siam. Where is the unbeliever in
Christendom to-day, the most earnest and sincere
apologist for Buddhism, who would rather raise his children in Chinese, Siamese, Burmese, or Thibetan society,
than to bring them up in England or America?

Over against this moral system of the Buddha
we place that of the Gospel. Its postulates are in full
accordance with the necessary judgments of man, and
the dictates of his conscience. They assume the being
of a God, the Lawgiver; and of a free spirit in man,
the responsible subject. Because there is a God, and
He supreme perfection and moral beauty, therefore, in
the foremost place, Christian ethics places our obligation to love Him supremely, and serve Him loyally and
gladly. And this and all its precepts are grounded on
the authority of God, an authority at once most wise,

most holy, most kind, and almighty. Its law is
simplicity. It is summed up in this that we shall
love this God with all our heart, and our neighbour as
ourselves. Instead of traducing and defaming human
nature as it came from the hand of the Creator, it tells
us that man, apart from sin, in the essential constitution of his nature, is good; that both soul and body
are capable of a glorious immortality. Thus, not only
the spiritual, but also the earthly side of man's nature
is reached by the law of Christ, and that to sanctify
and ennoble it. The body is to be held in honour;
"marriage is honourable in all, and the bed undefiled;"
the relation of husband and wife, as also human fatherhood and motherhood, are glorified; for these are
represented as types and prophecies of yet higher
relations which are divine and everlasting. As for its
motives, Christian ethics certainly does not ignore the
lower motives or refrain from appeals to our hopes
and fears. This were indeed a style of government
which no one has ever yet thought of carrying out in
this sinful world, nor could do so with success, either
in family or state. But in Christian morals these
motives are kept in due subordination to the highest
motives that can possibly have place in a moral system.
For despite the sophistry of some who would persuade
us that gratitude is a sordid emotion, we must insist
that this is false, and in this we have the full consciousness that the judgment of humanity is with us. If a
God exists, a Being of infinite perfection, who crowns

our lives with loving kindness and tender mercies, then surely he is only deserving of condemnation who is so afraid of being moved by sordid motives that he will not be grateful, and be moved by that gratitude to loving obedience. And so Christ pleads with us on this ground: " As the Father hath loved me, so have I loved you : abide ye in my love." And not only this, but over and over, as especially in the Psalms, are we exhorted to serve and love God simply for what He is ; which is simply saying that devotion to the ends set before us by supreme wisdom, righteousness, and goodness, ought to determine our lives. Finally, as regards the results of the Christian system of morals, with the great Christian motives behind it, there can be no difference of opinion among candid and intelligent men. There is, no doubt, still enough of sin and wickedness in Christian lands. But that does not alter the fact, that just so far as the religion of Christ has been received and practically believed, it has wrought good and only good, and that in a degree which appears nowhere in any Buddhist land or anywhere else, in the history of mankind. It has elevated woman, it has ennobled man : it has developed the intellect and purified the affections. It has produced in rich abundance the noblest fruits of righteousness and peace and unselfish love, alike from the dry wastes of philosophical infidelity and the malarious marshes of materialism and sensuality. It has created that supreme earthly blessing, the Christian home ; in the state, it alone has given whatever of true liberty man has as yet attained. This is undeniable history, and, happily for us in Christian lands, a matter of happy experience. No instance can be shown where the Gospel has ever failed to produce these effects, just in proportion as by an individual or community it has been heartily believed and received, and its precepts taken as the law of life.

Again we may well pause to ask, Can any man doubt which of the two religions, Christianity or Buddhism, can be fitly called the Light of Asia or of the world?

From all this argument and these facts, two or three corollaries of the highest consequence immediately and of necessity follow. In the first place, the facts which have passed under our observation make it very clear that for any man to assert or suggest that both Buddhism and Christianity are from that God who is the Truth, is a folly so extreme as only to be excused on the ground of a most deplorable ignorance of the actual facts of the case. For that the two religions stand in the most open and unqualified contradiction to each other on those matters which are the most essential in religion, has been proved, we venture to claim, beyond all controversy. But that two contradictory systems should *both* be delivered to man for his belief by a God of Truth, is incredible and absurd. The assertion can only escape the charge of blasphemy on the plea of a total ignorance or mis-apprehension of the facts.

Again, notwithstanding the high authority in the scientific world which has ventured to assert the contrary, we insist that all the facts which have passed under review in the comparison of this book, demonstrate that the old-fashioned distinction between religions as "true" and "false," is not invalid and unscientific, but the most valid and important distinction possible. If Christianity present a true system of doctrine and morals, then it is certain that Buddhism presents one which is false, and is justly called a false religion. If one is "light," the other cannot but be darkness.

It follows from this, again, that it is impossible that both Buddhism and Christianity should become means of salvation to those who receive them and regulate their beliefs and conduct by their respective teachings. That systems so profoundly antagonistic should both lead a man to the same place and the same end, is a moral impossibility. If one leads to God, then it is perfectly certain that the other must lead away from Him. And since, if there be a God, it is certain that a man's life and eternal happiness must be in finding and knowing Him, and in realising His will, therefore it is certain that if a man follows the Buddha he will be lost. The lauded "*Light*" of Asia will prove, even as it is proving for all that trust in it, an *ignis fatuus*, leading men—not to their Father's home of light and life—but into the dark morasses of hopeless sin and fatal alienation from God.

Last of all, the facts which have been brought together in this book should be a most cogent argument for such a degree of Christian zeal to carry the Gospel to the Buddhist world as we never yet have seen. In their missionary spirit the early Buddhists may well put many Christians to shame. It was, as we have seen, but a very pitiful salvation that they had to proclaim, and one which ill deserved the name—a salvation without a Saviour, and that not everlasting. Yet their earnestness and devotion in the proclamation of what they supposed to be the truth, more than deserves the emulation of all Christians. Be it so that they were taught that they would thus acquire merit, make an end of what they deemed sin, and so at last reach the rest of *Nirvàna*, the extinction of existence and pain. All the more should we be fired with zeal and missionary enthusiasm, who have a message so much grander and more blessed,—one so eloquent with heavenly hope. All the more should we be inspired for this holy work, who for a motive have something so much higher, even a love which is infinite and everlasting; and who, as "the joy that is set before us," look forward,—not to a *Nirvàna* of apathy and final extinction,—but to the complete and everlasting triumph of righteousness and eternal life in Christ over sin and death, throughout this curse-burdened earth: a triumph which, while it comprehends the whole race in its scope, brings in for us also as individuals the attainment of a perfect manhood, transfigured with the glory of the incarnate Son of God, and a most holy, exalted, and never-ending fellowship with Him, who alone is the eternal Life and Light, not of Asia only, but also of the whole world.

INDEX OF TOPICS.

2 C

THE END.

Printed by R. & R. CLARK, *Edinburgh.*